NO PLACE for an ANGEL

ALSO BY ELIZABETH SPENCER

NOVELS

The Night Travellers

The Salt Line

The Snare

Knights and Dragons

The Light in the Piazza

The Voice at the Back Door

This Crooked Way

Fire in the Morning

STORY COLLECTIONS

Starting Over

The Southern Woman

On the Gulf

Jack of Diamonds and Other Stories

Marilee

Ship Island and Other Stories

MEMOIR

Landscapes of the Heart

Elizabeth Spencer

NO PLACE for an ANGEL

A NOVEL

LIVERIGHT PUBLISHING CORPORATION
A Division of W. W. Norton & Company
New York • London

First published as a Liveright paperback 2015

Printed in the United States of America

For information about permission to reproduce selections from this book,
write to Permissions, Liveright Publishing Corporation,
a division of W. W. Norton & Company, Inc.,
500 Fifth Avenue, New York, NY 10110

For information about special discounts for bulk purchases, please contact
W. W. Norton Special Sales at specialsales@wwnorton.com or 800-233-4830

Manufacturing by Courier Westford
Book design by Ellen Cipriano
Production manager: Lauren Abbate

Library of Congress Cataloging-in-Publication Data

Spencer, Elizabeth, 1921–
No place for an angel : a novel / Elizabeth Spencer.
pages cm
ISBN 978-1-63149-063-7 (pbk.)
1. Married people—Fiction. I. Title.
PS3537.P4454N64 2015
813'.54—dc23

2015009094

Liveright Publishing Corporation
500 Fifth Avenue, New York, N.Y. 10110
www.wwnorton.com

W. W. Norton & Company Ltd.
Castle House, 75/76 Wells Street, London W1T 3QT

1 2 3 4 5 6 7 8 9 0

To Tonny and Cynthia Vartan

Contents

BLOOD SPORTS *1*

DANGEROUS JOURNEYS *65*

ONE ◆ TWO ◆ THREE ◆ FOUR

WHERE PATHS DIVIDE *279*

THE GREY WORLD *303*

Blood Sports

"Why, Barry Day!"

He had just said something designed to shock her, but Irene only laughed instead, and a minute later could not remember it, for she was half-asleep. Lying on the warm summer grass, listening to the lively running of the stream, with her eyes closed, letting the sun brown her face and throat, she could almost sense the journey and impulse of the turning earth beneath her back.

The young man, whose fate it was to be always nervous and detached, sat a few feet away with elbows carelessly at rest across his knees. Now he picked up a small stick and broke it in two; now he threw rocks, doubtless left along the bank by the stream's spring overflow, into the water, skipping the flat ones with a snap of his wrist, the way he must have done countless times when a boy, frowning, even then.

"I started the angel yesterday," he said.

This was, Irene knew at once, an important disclosure. She did not answer or open her eyes. She was sensitive and critical, and she did not like discouraging him, but he got out of her anyway what she believed.

"Angels don't belong in America," she finally said. "You should have done it in Rome."

"There're a hell of a lot of them around on Christmas and Easter," he said.

"That's all commercial. Angels, I tell you, never crossed the Atlantic in their lives. God crossed, but He left the angels."

At that he hurled a rather large stone, and in the recurring silence must have thought her really asleep, for he reached her left hand which lay stretched out toward him on the grass and covered it with his own. She did not stir, though it did cross her mind that her husband had warned her some time ago, "Of course, he'll fall in love with you." "Then he'll just have to transfer it to somebody else," she had returned. "Anyway, artists are always falling in love. They don't mean it—I mean they only do it to stimulate their work. It's like politicians marrying somebody who will make a good hostess." This was one of her and Charles' Sunday morning breakfast talks, back in town. An ant, journeying uphill through the pleasant savannahs of her right forearm, lightly brushed with beige reeds of hair, stung her; she drew her hand away from Barry to destroy it.

"God," she said, sitting up, "I may have lain in an ant bed." But she hadn't. She glanced at him, wondering when her husband and the other couple who had come out with them, the Giffords, would return with the sandwiches. Barry looked straight in front of him, tensely forgetting rocks and sticks. "I don't blame you for being cross," she said, "but you must remember I don't know anything about art. Nor angels either. How should I be able to say?"

"It's just that I knew what you would say before you said it. And then I've built my own trap, you see. I think you must be always right. This makes me angry."

She found it easy to laugh, chuckle rather. She was a strongly built woman, who just, by some exercise of pride or taste, missed being too heavy, and she was at least five years older than Barry Day, who, at the close of a dissatisfied silence, turned to her and pulled her toward him. He was as strong as some thin wild animal, who has to scavenge and fight several times a day, a fox maybe. He held her by the shoulder; his mouth bumped clumsily against her own; their teeth cracked together.

Far from being startled, she kept on laughing. It was such a happy, perfect day; did she have to let him worry her? She really could not put her mind on him.

He pulled away from the moment's harsh tussle—he would do an angel if he wanted to, he inwardly vowed—and retrieved one battered loafer from the grass. Irene combed her hair. She was cross, and said nothing. He had told her once that the artist was always isolated—that must have been one winter evening. Well, if he has to act like a wild man, let him be isolated, she thought. It's not my problem. All around her, softly surrounding them, mildly falling away toward its own identity, the New England countryside slept in the Sunday sunlight. They were the only people within the frame. But a red barn trimmed in white showed just at the notch of two hills, and farther away still to the left, down where the road wound which had taken Charles and the Giffords away, some cows grazed uphill along a warm, green slope.

You know, I always meant to tell you, Barry Day is not my name."

They had known him well for three years now, she and Charles, had been acquainted with him since 1951 which was all of seven years ago, and they had discussed him quite often, the way they did, piecing together shrewd guesses; they were sharp and quick and nothing much got by them.

"Then what, pray, is your name?" The scene around her became unreal, as though she had sat down in the middle of a painting. Those cows had not moved an inch for an hour; surely the stream made no noise.

"Now don't laugh. It's Bernard Desportes."

"Why should I laugh?"

"It's too theatrical. I changed it after the war. It sounds, you see, too much like an artist. When you hear it you can almost see a whole damned gallery full of Desportes, all looking slightly like a cross between Matisse and early Van Gogh, with imitations of every other school cutting in for a flower here, a fish there."

"You're making this up," she said, doubtfully.

"No, not at all."

"You let me know you for three years as a friend, and never once told me this—oh, honestly!"

"I never told Charles either. I've never told anyone. What difference does it make? Anyway, I'm telling you now."

"I suppose you are."

Why, she wondered, was it so hard to tell exactly where one stood in anything? She felt disagreeable and realized she was hungry. "I think they're never coming back with those sandwiches."

But at that moment, in the curve of the road, Charles' black Mercury broke into view. Ruth Gifford sat on the front seat with a huge brown paper sack beside her, and when Clint Gifford got out of the back he carried cold drinks, dripping through their paper carton.

Charles was jubilant at his success and came down the path to them, shouting:

"I thought I remembered some little restaurant with a grocer in the back, it's been ages since we came here—remember, Irene, that other time? And sure enough, there it was, so we've got olives, we've got French mustard, we've anchovies, and pickles and homemade relish put up for the locals only, and we've got—yes, by God, I even remembered the can opener with the built-in bottle opener." He waved the nickel-colored object in the air with a gesture of triumph.

There was certain to be a long sweating slow-moving ill-tempered on the parkway, so returning to New York Charles made them all stop in a town off the highway and go to a movie. It didn't matter that no one agreed with him on this being a good idea. Headstrong and argumentative, he said he would far rather look at Betty Grable than at some child vomiting on the pavement at his front bumper.

"Betty Grable hasn't been in the movies in years," said Ruth Gifford. She did not try to eliminate the annoyance from her voice. She and Clint would have to ring up the apartment in New York to talk with the baby-sitter. This was the second time this week they had been delayed. But there was no stopping Charles; Barry saw that Irene was saying nothing, and knew she was not going to try. Of course, she didn't want to sit through a movie; she never went willingly to anything, even concerts. Charles read the map and drove with one hand on the wheel, one eye on the road. The Mercury went butting about the streets of an awkward, forsaken-looking Sunday town, Charles like a jeep-high Allied commander riding into a conquered village.

"Where's the movie, please!" he thundered out the window at a woman pushing a baby. She looked surprised and small. At times everyone looked small around Charles. He was big and bald, except for a blond fringe, with a strong, mobile mouth and pale grey eyes. When he played tennis, fished, or golfed, his shirttail was always pulled half out of his trousers; he had very little time for small people.

The woman pointed, directing him. "She's probably wrong," he said, carelessly loud enough to be heard. At the movie house he bought the tickets and drove the group ahead of him like so many children.

"See? What did I tell you? It's Betty Grable."

"It is not," said Irene, provably right, in the largest of letters, directly in front of their eyes. "It's Virginia Mayo."

"Same thing," said Charles, undismayed, and bought popcorn for everybody. "All in glorious Technicolor," he gloated. "All the color of a strawberry ice cream soda."

It was after nine before they were released from this plush nonsense. Barry, who had contrived to sit on the end, had slipped out after ten minutes and gone for a walk around the town. He was waiting in the smelly little lobby for them when they filed out. "It's raining," was all he said.

The parkway was fairly empty when they approached the city, and loose traffic skimmed in easily, rapidly, over the soaring bridges. "A good idea of mine," Charles boomed, driving as fast as possible.

"How lovely it was to see so much green," Ruth Gifford said.

Irene laughed. "Yes, that's what I'm remembering too." She rode on the front seat, beside Charles. The grey vertical landscape of the great city moved forward to enclose them. But the smell of rain on the green roadsides lingered and the picnic still lingered sunlit in their heads; their skin was still warm with it.

"Do you remember," Ruth Gifford went on, determined, it would seem, to put everyone in some sort of human mood, "how we used to long for green growth in Italy? Strong big heavy trees, shaggy roadsides . . . I used even to wish for weeds."

"Yes, I remember, too," her husband at last agreed.

"You could get all that," said Barry, after an even longer pause, "up in the Alban hills, up near Lago Albano. And then there was always the Aniene beyond Tivoli, and there was the countryside near Ostia Antica."

"I know what she means, though," said Irene. "One always felt that country to be used up in some way, as though the prime of it was over."

The city opened up to them, shifted with grey abstract angularity to close them in behind. It was a homecoming, like others. Details came back to them: was the delicatessen still open for milk? Would someone have stolen the Sunday *Times?* The sink was full of dishes.

Charles drew up on East 55th, beside a tiny tree. "We'd ask you in for a drink," Ruth Gifford said, "but the children—"

This was really too nice, Irene thought impatiently. Everybody knew, didn't they?, that all of them were browned off with Charles. Now she had to make appropriate purring noises. "No, no, of course not."

"I'll get out here," said Barry, when the Giffords had alighted on the sidewalk. He had put his tweed jacket on over his crumpled, tieless shirt. His khaki trousers looked like army pants. "I have to make a stop near here," he explained, looking bare to the elements, vulnerable to bad colds and fevers, a portrait of the artist dying young. Charles reached out, inexplicably, and took his hand to give it a shake. "Nice, nice," said Charles, as though Barry had given the picnic. Irene gave them all a smile and a wave, and so they parted.

What good was it ever, Irene thought, as they drove away, taking a rapid corner, what good did it ever do, to fight with Charles? She would only wind up saying things like he had spoiled the picnic, such a perfect day, as perhaps indeed he had for the Giffords and Barry, though not, she realized, for herself. She had loved it; the sun had warmed her heart; she was happy. She had, of course, herself ruined Barry's pleasure, saying what she had about angels. It was why he had left the movie, it was why he had got out of the car. But did it really displease her to think she had this power over him? It took more to displease Irene than it did to please her. And Charles, if he was not getting a tongue lashing for his miserable taste and overbearing manners, was at least being silently deprived of knowing what she now knew, that Barry Day was, for some reason, not Barry Day, nor had he ever been.

Charles liked to learn things like this, and sooner or later she was going to break down and discuss it with him. But she wasn't going to now, and when she did he was going to know that she had kept it from him for a time. Thus contemplative, her gaze had wandered to his reflection in the rear-view mirror, whence his eyes suddenly turned to hers, except for brows and bridge of nose so disembodied as to seem, out of the narrow rectangle of the glass, an apparition, a highly personal spirit.

"We should go to the movies more often," he said. "A damned good idea."

◆

When Irene did not hear either from Barry Day or the Giffords in the two weeks that followed, she was given to momentary anxiety. Charles had succeeded, again, in losing all their friends. No one, no human, would tolerate his arrogance. Then she got letters from members of both sides of the family: everyone was all right, getting better, looking forward to something, prosperous, reasonably pleasant. Irene became very happy, went shopping, had lunch at Schrafft's, had her hair done and came home. The letters still lay on the breakfast table, and the phone was ringing. It was Barry, calling from a drugstore below. The world was as perfect as it could be; the day was warm, burgeoning. She went down to meet him, at a corner table in the sun, and heard his troubles.

Barry always had troubles.

"So what's with him?" Charles wanted to know at dinner.

She had made lasagna and there was Chianti—they were, for a rarity, alone.

"Well, let's see: he said my new make-up was archaic."

"Great."

"That's what I said, but he explained that archaic was not an uncomplimentary term—it refers to Greek art before the age of Pericles. The faces look monolithic."

"Great," Charles repeated. He squinted at her. "You do look odd."

She giggled. "I feel glamorous as hell."

He poured himself more wine. "So what's with Barry?"

"He's having to change studios. Short of money again. Anyway, I seem to have offered to keep a few things here, as there isn't room at present in the new place. I do wish he could get a show."

"But he had one offered him."

"With other people he didn't care for."

"But why be so godawful exclusive?"

"I don't know . . . I understand how he feels."

She went to grate some cheese wearing a long robe of white crepe. "I assume," said Charles, "that you went and spent a fortune for that robe after Barry told you you looked archaic."

"It's three years old," she returned. "How unobservant can you get?"

"Has Day ever tried making love to you?"

"Of course not. Why?"

"Why? If I don't ask you, somebody else will."

"I mean why ask me now? All I did was have coffee with him downstairs in that drugstore that's like a cardboard box with picture windows."

"I had a feeling of something like that on that picnic a week or so back. There was something damn peculiar going on."

"Well," said Irene, "the peculiar thing was that he suddenly told me, while you were gone with the Giffords, that all this time he's been going under an assumed name. His name isn't Barry Day at all."

Charles gave a snort. "A likely tale. If it isn't Barry Day what is it?"

"Bernard Desportes."

Charles snorted again.

"Well, it might be," Irene said.

"So what difference does it make if it is or isn't?"

"I don't know," said Irene. And indeed, asked it that way, she was uncertain. "But why," she pursued, "don't you believe it? I mean if it doesn't make any difference, why should he make it up?"

"It makes him molto più interessante, especially to you."

"Oh, for heaven's sake, Charles. We've known Barry for years."

"But have we known this mysterious stranger, this Bernard Deschamps?"

"Desportes," Irene corrected. "Anyway," she continued, "as long as you're being like this, you needn't look my way for the woman in question . . . he's got somebody now. She looks existentialist and wears black stockings, low heels and a black wool top with powder specks and bits of hair stuck on it. He says she's extremely talented."

"What a character."

Irene always felt as if Charles was going to drop Barry, whom she knew to be touchy. If we really succeed in doing the wrong thing to him, he'll never come back once he's gone, she thought. She needed Barry's particular kind of sensitivity. It was fulfilling to her to have somebody like him to talk to. If they could raise the money anonymously, or use influence, perhaps do both. . . .

"But that would put him off worse than anything, if he found out."

"What would?"

"To help him get a show."

"That's true," said Charles. "It would." It was his admission, not at all begrudged, of Barry's true worth.

"I'll try to pick something out of his stuff that we can stand to live with. I know you don't like it."

"I'll not take this role of husband-who-knows-nothing-about-art, Irene. I just won't do it. I do know a hawk from a handsaw. Barry is not going to wring from my lips that a handsaw is aesthetically satisfying even if he sculpts one out of golden coathangers."

"He's started an angel now," Irene recalled, by way of reassurance.

"That's the best news I've heard about him." He passed the candle toward her, lighting her cigarette, and changed the subject.

◆

Bernard Desportes, alias Barry Day, was scared, but then he thought that perhaps everybody was. He could not be sure, that was all.

He sat in bars in the late evening listening to people talk. Sometimes they gave themselves away. They were scared, too, and admitted it. He felt relieved. It was the time of one of the worst bomb scares. The papers said it daily: the world hung on the brink of World War III. Every day he must at some point have crossed the very crux and center of the target, the biggest one in the free world. Daily, he felt a Russian pointer reach out and touch his spine.

"It will either happen or it won't happen," he said out loud at parties. Everyone agreed. "That's what I think," they all said. He grinned jauntily. His stomach turned upside-down. Am I really a coward? Was I, all this time? he wondered.

He sat in his favorite bar down near West 12th Street and watched television. "This will be a show about people," a voice said. "It will not tell any one story, for there is no story to tell. You will see what you see, hear what you hear. That is all." He was startled. The camera roved beautifully, over rooftops, lowered to a street where a woman at a distance walked thoughtfully. He had sat straight up really to pay attention. "Turn that off," somebody said. "Perry Mason is on six."

Barry, for one, could never get Perry Mason straight. There were people in the bar who did it easily, even after six beers. "Thought so," they muttered, nodding to one another when the murderer was pointed out or, seeing what was coming, broke down, or bolted. For himself, Barry thought he would never understand what had happened if he saw it four times through cold sober.

Somebody had left a loaded gun by a sleeping man and a

woman came in and thought the gun was empty and the man was dead and called the police; then somebody else came in and found the man awake and the gun handy and shot him, but was it that gun or one brought for the purpose and did they switch guns and why was the man asleep if he hadn't been doped and what was the woman doing there in the first place? Perry Mason always reconstructed the whole event, but Barry Day could never follow it. He got too busy watching the sleeping man, the alert lovely startled woman, the hand of the man hanging toward the floor, his shirt rumpled and head pillowed on his elbow, the tiny frown beginning between the woman's big velvet eyes, the sudden dawn of alarm, then terror. A car drew up to a rainy door. Then cabs, the police, the district attorney, Perry, Della Street, Paul, all came spilling out like face cards in a worn, familiar deck. He could never understand what they were saying or doing. Who can follow a story any more? What story is worth following? He didn't know.

Before taking up sculpture, he had been a painter. Surfaces drew him as if many magnets had been secretly installed in them, the way Russians installed tiny microphones any and everywhere. Door sills, the full firm limbs of girls, their knees, ankles, etc., babies' heels and eyebrows, the slippery hexagonal surface of a beer stein, the flat composed length of the bar, a man's shoulder beneath an unpressed coat . . . anything he clapped his eyes on he seemed to stick to. The only way to get rid of what he saw was to sketch it, paint it, mould it, farm it off onto something else. Out of this impulse he had started, quite young. And this, he now suddenly realized, was why he was scared of bombs. To see those surfaces break and crumble, tear, shatter, burst, dissolve, sink into rubble and carnage. Irreplaceable, every one of them, and irreplaceable, too, the eye of Bernard Desportes, alias Barry Day, who saw them as they were. He steadied himself on beer and television. What would the show have said, the one they turned off?

He worked all day, lunched on peanut butter, needed to find a girl.

"You from the South, ain't you?" the bartender asked him after three months.

"That's right," he said.

"What line you in?"

He said something, worked uptown crating dress goods, that would do. It was true he had done this for a while, when he got back to New York after a time in Rome. Once he had told somebody who asked him this that he was a jockey. Though far from home, having left himself wide open for getting run out of the South ten years ago, he still knew himself by what had been said about him in his childhood, and once when he was about twelve his uncle had taken him to the races in New Orleans and had said on the way home, guzzling beer from one roadhouse to the other, all the way back to the Gulf coast: "Boy, if you don't grow any more you going to make a good jockey." He had grown some more, but not much, and he would still make a good jockey, he often thought, could see himself sometimes in that Lautrec picture of the horse with the big satin behind galloping off on an inside track. But down in New Orleans, not the Champ de Mars.

Barry kept himself from calling Irene too much. He had a compulsion to call her from a not uncommon reason. She knew the woman he loved and wanted to marry; she had been in on it all. It wouldn't work and was never going to. It made him hurt to think about it, but around Irene he felt more at home with it. When alone, he could not think about it, nor could he think too much about what he saw around him since the bomb was about to land on it all. How not to love too much, not to suffer for, what is threatened and may be about to crumble utterly? When he really got going, trees on a corner caused him a stab of pain, just by standing there, as did cats sleeping precise in their habits on sunny windowsills, children playing in a poor street, a girl with a pony-tail flying out for milk or bread. The list was infinite, and he had to stop for it. He stopped it by thinking about the angel.

The angel was all his contemplation could bear. What we meditate on is the most important thing in our lives: he knew that much. It is the source of strength or the root of ruin. What sort of angel? He sat over his beer stein and watched it form, blotting out the TV screen, towering up in crumpled, wind-beaten clothes just above floor level, a great bird creature whose intelligence and innocence went far beyond the human potential, jet-powered, superb, and yet searching. Bright-eyed, self-careless, without fear, yet always looking for something. He had finally broken down and mentioned it to Irene and she had obliged him by banishing them all. You had to be careful whom you spoke to. It was a rule.

The next day he met a girl. Her name was Joanna—she was a mixture of English and Slav, and would wait for him on spring afternoons near the corner of Sheridan Square. She didn't mind meeting him on corners, something he would never have asked Irene to do, nor the woman from the South he was in love with. They would have felt there was something not quite good enough in this, and so did he. But Joanna had a real gift: she didn't think anything about it one way or the other. Thus he could look her over before getting to her and notice her broad feet in run-over shoes and how she never looked completely clean. However, he decided not to quarrel with blessing.

The warm spring afternoon brought them instantly into their best mood; they clasped hands and there was a lot to laugh about. They took the subway to the park and walked around. Some days they went to a movie or an art gallery, then took the bus back to his place and stayed there till after dark.

When he woke one afternoon he saw a long line of heads, torsos, arms, along with some small abstract structures, lying in a row across the floor. He remembered that he was moving in a day or so. Joanna was up eating peanut butter and bread. She was near the window, where late light stood between the slats of the blinds, but did not enter. She was assuming he was asleep. Should he mention marrying her?

It seemed a pleasant enough thought. He immediately began to recall the endless queue of Joannas there had already been in his life. He could not remember their names now, or just where he had met them, but once he had either dreamed or fancied that they were all of them on a train and the train was pulling out of some station, like Rome, perhaps, or Milan, for certainly it was a European train in a warm country. As far down the track as he could see, they were leaning out like a chorus line, out of all the windows, waving handkerchiefs and calling, "Goodbye, Barry, goodbye, Barry!" He looked and there went the last one, on the observation car, waving: it was Joanna.

"That bread is stale, isn't it?" he asked.

"Delicious!" she assured him, smiling through a density of peanut butter.

Because of Joanna, he put the angel aside, though it returned from time to time to nag him, like a sciatic nerve. Again, easing, it drew a misty elegiac horizon around the green edges of the park, hovered above the lake, back of flowering apple trees, or mingled in the shattering color of redbud; it had just left skyscrapers at dusk.

In his boyhood near New Orleans there had been a place for angels. His Catholic father had sometimes taken him to church and he had seen them as gilded wood, holding candles. And his Baptist mother had sung about them, how they trod on bright feet by some river or other; he saw in his mind a lot of barefoot blond high-school-looking figures with wings strung awkwardly down their backs wading around at a spring picnic. Over in the French Quarter after a certain hour of the night and the drinking, they came in a band for to carry the Negro musicians home, or so you could get them to say in a song if you asked for it.

The weather turned hot and humid; asphalt patching went gummy on the streets, and people had begun to creep out on doorsteps on the first evenings when dark did nothing but intensify the heat, just as neon stabbed it, and odors of buses, sweat, exhausts, coffee steam and cigarettes pressed down like silt, toward the stone sea floor, at last pervading and mastering, as evening came definitely on, the clangor of traffic.

Irene rang up. He couldn't afford a phone, but the boy in the bar below came up to tell him. He came down in his T-shirt and went into a phone booth which smelled of all humanity. The number was not hers. It was another phone booth, he supposed, that she was calling from. Was something wrong? It must be, and it was. Charles had lost his job. "Why? Did they give a reason?" He knew, of course, perfectly well why, but was surprised to hear Irene come right out with it, meaning that "they" had come right out with it, too.

"He can't seem to get on with people. We thought all these people in his division were our friends. They entertain us. We entertain them. God, when I think of the meals I've stuffed them with. They weren't worth a decent plate of spaghetti. The complaint was, verbatim: He can't take his army boots off. It seems now you have to apple-polish everybody. Then, the other thing was—this'll kill you—his department was too far ahead of the others! Too far ahead. We could understand behind, but not ahead. The big word is coordination."

"He'll land something in no time," said Barry.

There was a pause. She had been drinking, probably to keep Charles company, he supposed. She laughed. "We may have to move into your old studio."

"Nothing is going to happen. I bet he has a job in three days."

"Barry, do you remember Clint Gifford?"

"Yes, on the picnic that day."

"Well, he's got something incurable. I wondered why they

didn't ring up. I thought they were angry with Charles and me. Now we hear through the grapevine that— So you never can tell, can you?"

"I have the evil eye," said Barry. "Mal occhio."

There was a silence in which he knew he did not care profoundly about Irene and Charles. He had been interested in them, but it was more interesting to see them in action with their money, their energy, their taste and clever friends and good fortune, moving at full speed, cutting the blue surface of life. Their misfortunes did not affect him deeply. For one thing, he never had enough money himself, and it seemed only just that they should at least, once in a great while, feel that especial cold wind at their backs. But news of someone incurably ill. . . . "What is it? Cancer?"

"I think so."

"Can I call you?"

"Yes, but don't let on to Charles I called you."

"I get it. Irene? Coraggio."

"Oh, Barry, thank you, thank you."

◆

That was June.

In September, Barry was back in the Mercury with the Waddells, riding down to Florida. Charles, who still had not found a position that suited him, was determined to spend his last thousand in some memorable way. He had charged in one evening, so Irene related, saying:

"Florida! The Keys! That's the place!"

He had read or remembered reading about Hemingway in Florida, and envisioned in those coastal waters the beauties of September. The delicious repose of out-of-season places. Their mystery. The clear distant light. He had even thought of hurricanes. "The warnings are out days ahead now; we can easily pack up and leave before there's any danger."

What was said in the inner enclave when they decided to invite Barry, he would never know. They wanted to take along their two boys, twins, who had spent all summer in camp and were now visiting some of Irene's family in Maryland. If the boys had not been too old to need it, Barry would have thought they wanted him to baby-sit. He said he would go without inquiring too closely into the devious Waddell motives. He had worn thin with the heat, had had weekend invitations out on Long Island, but nothing better or farther away, was tired of the sound of the electric fan at night, could not afford air conditioning, was tired of the smell of little metal filings and gilt paint in his studio. Joanna had left him.

She had flounced out of a 23rd Street movie house when they were sitting in the air-conditioned foyer, waiting for the feature to be over. She had been telling him a long story and he must have said, "Yes, I know how it is," instead of, "Don't underrate yourself," because she had burst out, "You never listen to anything I say," and walked out. He went to the movie anyway, as it was something he had really wanted to see and had missed on the first go-round, and when he came home she had moved out of the studio, suitcase and all. He guessed she must have waited an hour for him to rush in and make up, had seen he wasn't going to (not, at least, until the movie was over), had cried up two Kleenexes, and then had made her big decision. He found a note: "Dear Barry, I *repeat*, in case you didn't hear me, you never listen to anything I say. See you around. J."

When Irene called up and started about Florida, he actually consented to go far too quickly for her. She had been prepared to talk a great deal more, persuading him. She loved making plans—but he said he would drop in one evening during the week to talk it over. Yet a shadow, even then, walked in his mind, and before he hung up, he said:

"This has nothing to do with Catherine, has it?"

"I don't even know where Catherine is," said Irene. "Why?"

"I was thinking about that other time. In Siracusa."

"But you hadn't met Catherine then."

"I know, but I—"

"You what?"

"I just wanted to clear it, capisci?"

"Six, caro. Ciao."

"Ciao."

But just the mention of Catherine to Irene would have tripped a switch. Now she was telling Charles, "You know what he asked me? The oddest thing—" The incident would be good for perhaps an hour's speculation, mainly on Irene's part, before the Waddells got back to their favorite subject—themselves. As for Barry, having had to speak of her because she had apparently by her own choice, wherever she was, popped into his head at that juncture, he had opened the door on entirely too much. He meant to be sensible about it and get it over with quickly, so bought a bottle of cheap whiskey and drank most of it up, giving himself an awful head the next day. The cure was worse than the disease, he decided, and in even being able to decide that, he realized that he had succeeded. He had stumbled on the verge of an old crisis, but had not fallen into it.

◆

Irene understood perfectly that Barry had invented a friend in Washington whom he had to see in order to keep from stopping in with her relatives in Maryland. She sat on beaches all along the Atlantic coast and knew this, without animosity; a friend, even a "best friend"—if such a thing existed—took no interest in one's family. She was aware, like all her generation, of having been created by the war. Family was a dream you sometimes had, awakening conscience; like an occasional religious phase, they passed quickly out of your mind again as soon as you actually did anything about them. Family having kept the boys, Tom and Will, and having now been visited, now could be set aside. The boys were back again, as they always would be, and all together, the four Waddells had picked up Barry Day off a particular Washington streetcorner at 2 P.M. on Sunday. Afterwards, driving South, all America, in late summer shaggy weight of green and silent cloud-filled skies, came forward to meet them, over and over, and so often seemed a friend. But a lot of it lay waste and was horrible.

They loved the coast and drove along it when they could. Tacitly, they agreed to indulge in a childlike companionship, and spoke only of which road to take, and where to spend the night, of the mileage, the car, and food. Every evening Charles drank a good deal of gin and Irene went out alone on the beach, while the boys wandered away like strangers.

Barry walked in whatever towns there were; once when there wasn't a town he came on Irene, sitting beside a wild clump of reeds near the sea.

"I wish he would get off the bottle," she said. "I wish he would discuss things.

"What makes it so awful now for me and Charles," she continued, "is all the past history, the great big thunderous, horrible, glorious times we went through. He was always in it, heart and soul; even before the war, he took it all in the soundest way. Then the war, Europe, us—all that glory. Well, you remember. Now, look. All of a sudden, his place in the world is gone; he feels he's a has-been and wonders who cares. Oh, Barry, I do thank you for coming. Do you think I can come right out and sympathize? Say all this to him? I can just remember how it all was, how great, and decide not to stir him up about it all. When men get up against it, they're always alone."

"What about you?" Barry asked.

She shrugged. "I've had my good times and bad. Don't tell me you've forgotten. Didn't I use them all up, right to the last notch?"

He was silent. It made him uncomfortable for Irene to need him, even more restless for her to admit it. What could he do? The Waddells would keep right on anyway toward whatever disaster or triumph their energy was leading them. He would as soon sit on an explosion as try to lend a helping hand; they would be the first to give him a hard time over stupid well-wishing. He could listen to her. He guessed that was the most that was indicated.

He could even see a long way into what she meant. Americans had flowed to Europe, for the war, the liberation and afterwards, and the times the Waddells had kept in step with had been touched with greatness. Now this seemed to have been snatched away, and Charles, who had been a big man, had made a wrong turn somewhere and was off in a motel on the North Carolina coast, drinking gin alone. Barry let this soak in on him. Not saying much, they listened to the sea.

"Look what a tan I'm getting. God knows this is better than sitting around the apartment. I thought I'd go mad."

"It's a fine apartment," Barry said, sincerely complimenting her taste.

"Well, but things begin to seem empty—all things are just things, you know, once the motion stops."

She bit her lip, feeling older in spite of all she could do. Mention of the apartment had brought to mind the dust on the African knickknacks, the tarnish on the silver cigarette boxes; all that and more and worse would silently wait their return. "It's getting used to a thing like this happening, that's what we can't seem to do. Charles feels like a machine has gone bad on him. He wants to kick hell out of it, hear it cough and turn over; and if it won't do that, he wants to ring up the manufacturer and tell them to send for it."

The sea rolled behind her phrases; it seemed to turn them, lift them, exalt them, and dump them, time after time.

"It's just that everything and everybody has to go p.r. now.

And Charles won't learn it, and he wasn't quite big enough to get away with not learning it. He thought he was, but he wasn't."

It seemed a reasonable explanation, and Barry believed she must be right.

"But there're other jobs," he said. "Millions of them. So everybody has been telling me all my life, wanting me to get one."

"He's at the stage where it all looks black," she said. "So he's sensibly drinking his way deeper in," she added bitterly.

"I doubt if he's drinking any more than usual," said Barry. "You could keep him company," he suggested.

"He doesn't want me around," she said. "He knows I know his weaknesses. It's his pride."

They went all the way down to Florida like this, and Irene would always remember walking at night by moonlight, the great full moon beating silently down on the great sea. She began to think of it all as a phase, the trouble they had got into.

They stopped for an extra day or so in Savannah where Charles took the boys fishing, and Barry plundered the town for art and antique shops and believed that he had found a Corot. It needed restoring, but he could get that done cheaply; and if Charles and Irene would put out the $500 (perhaps less) to have it, he thought they could get that back many times over in New York, even if it wasn't a real Corot, it was such a damn fine picture. But then he knew he wasn't going to interest them in anything like that now; they weren't keen any more; he would come nearer to interesting one of the twins, who were so bright they could probably make up the sum out of their piggy banks.

He went back to the motel in the Mercury (he had borrowed

it for the afternoon) and found Irene by the swimming pool, rather deep in a sleazy flirtation with the owner's son, who also served as the lifeguard. He had no idea how far this had gone and Irene never asked herself that any more than Barry did. She licked the corner of her mouth where some lipstick had crumbled, and reflected on things.

It had got really hot—a heat wave, the papers said. Once on the way again, they scarcely spoke to one another any more when outside of air conditioning. One place they stopped in to lunch had a pool with water too hot to swim in, and Barry began to get the twins mixed up, whereas before he had never had any trouble. "Well," said Irene, irritably, "it's what they get for buying identical blue sweatshirts." "If you'd let us get tattooed," said one of them, "then it would be more convenient." "I think that's revolting," said Irene. "I think tattoos are revolting. I could never stand anyone with skin trouble." "Warren was tattooed," said the other twin. "Who is Warren?" asked Charles. "The lifeguard back at Savannah," said the first twin. They all rode silently then for what seemed another week of hot sun and flashing overheated highway and sun-glazed plants and trees. Their dark glasses made red sweat-rims against their cheeks, and hot wind streamed constantly through the windows, dulling their skin to the numbness of leather. Irene's bright scarf ruffled and snapped in the air stream with an apparent variety which could not be thought about.

The twins had dark brown hair and grey eyes and were of a height, about as tall as Irene, slightly shorter than Barry, and not within shouting distance of Charles. Though only sixteen, they seemed nearly to have attained their full size. They had identical secret bland faces and could never be surprised or found without information. They always listened, were quiet and seemed entirely happy. After speaking, their mouths closed pleasantly, in exactly the same way, over white teeth, each with a slight overlap in the very front. Being happy alone would have made them seem twins, Barry supposed, even if they had not been born that way. He had never known any twins before. It was rather restful, as if by being two, one could escape areas of uncertainty and self-doubt. He wondered if there had been any psychoanalytical studies of twins, and reflected that no one was more likely to know and tell him cheerfully than themselves. But he said nothing.

They drove through Miami with their eyes shut, it was horrible, they all agreed, and in another hour or so reached the Keys, open on either side, swept by agreeable breezes, a landscape more to their notion. They looked for somewhere to spend the night.

◆

There were very few people in the motel they selected, only themselves and another couple from Indiana with (by coincidence) two boys, though not twins. Barry's money was running low; he thought he would have to leave and hitchhike back to New York any time now. But then the motel couple, who were exceedingly kind, and so attuned to human plight and error one could almost believe one had arrived in some sort of understated paradise—that is, a place where people came up to what one was always hoping they might do—this remarkable pair discerned that Barry might not like to rent a whole unit for himself and offered him for next to nothing a small room adjoining the office, where, during the crowded months, their assistant lived. Thus, he shook away temporarily from the Waddells, twins and all, and was in no time making himself useful around the boats and the beach, refilling the diving tanks and sweeping sand out of the laundry. The water lay halcyon, pale blue, tranquil; time dropped away; after one night's sleep it was no longer clear how long they had been there.

The motel couple lived in screened rooms above their office, the entire house being set apart a stone's throw from the units. Surrounding porches with ferns and tropical plants secluded them in a shadowy privacy that made them seem nearer to the palms and the water of the cove than to their business. Yet, the moment the units began to seem routine, with their air conditioning and efficiency kitchens and identical furnishing—that is, about twilight of the second day—down the long steps from her parents' house came a marvelous little girl with straight thick sunburnt hair and bangs, and asked the Waddells to have drinks with her mother and father. The couple from Indiana were invited as well and everyone had the same idea about the boys who were left to scrub in the showers. Even Barry had bathed and dressed and produced from somewhere (he had bought it down the road at Matecumbe) a clean white sport shirt. The women all wore their raw silk shorts with tropical shirts and the men in shorts and sandals sprawled in lean skeletal chairs, talking easily. Charles volunteered a good many lies on what he was doing in New York, but as all of it as information was exact (it was what he had done before he was let out), it seemed not to be a lie at all.

The Indiana couple were in light machinery, which ran to lawn equipment, mowers, hedge clippers, and this ran the conversation naturally into electronic imports such as Charles' company dealt in. Both Charles and the Indiana man were therefore mutually acquainted with certain types of steel gaskets perfected in West Germany, which Charles had got a contract for distributing to manufacturers along with a photographic device. Here the motel owner wanted to know about his own lawn mower, which Barry had coaxed into running that afternoon.

"Oh, God," said Charles, "don't ask me anything practical."

"No," said Irene, "He discusses these things in conference, but who repairs the electric blender? I do."

"She once blended a finger in with the daiquiris," said Charles.

Barry had heard variations of this routine, and lapped up more gin, while explaining what he had done to the lawn mower. The motel owner said that the repairman at the garage had charged him five dollars for doing the same thing but it hadn't worked, and his wife said they had a way of charging now simply for diagnosis, you had to ask them humbly, as if they were medical specialists, if they wished to go ahead and do the work. She had an example or two of that, which made everyone laugh. A breeze blew through the ferns and screens. The Indiana woman asked about mosquito preparations. One of her boys seemed to be allergic to the bites.

Her husband mentioned his war years in Italy and disclosed that he had been at Salerno, whereas Charles had been at Naples during the same period. That was going back a long way—Irene a young mother in the States, V-letters, rationed shoes, gas and sugar, a sense of the world waiting in the wings. Then the war finished and it started, made its entrance, that real thing she had waited for all her life, the moment she left to join Charles in Germany after the war. All the late '40's had been Paris, just as the early '50's was Italy, and the late '50's ought to be New York, if only Charles would—

"I was nursing babies all through the war," she said.

"It's an experience I missed," said Charles, "mixing midnight formulas. I was trying to keep the Neapolitans from trading us out of all our supplies."

"I thought the trading was mutual," said the Indiana man.

"It was. Lots of Italian G.I.'s, of course, but it went on in all quarters. A case of mutual rapport. The Italians never wanted, really, to fight a war. And Americans were never very angry at Italians. They sold everything they knew to us for a bar of Palmolive. For a tin of Nescafé or a package of Gillette blades they would describe the whereabouts of a whole gun emplacement. For cigarettes you could raise a regiment of spies."

"Sell their sisters," the Indiana man grinned.

"Oh, the sisters went early on. Hardly worth a Hershey bar."

Charles was at his best.

"I'll give you a problem none of you has," he said. "How to keep the top of one's head from sunburn, provided one's head is like my head."

"Get a sun hat," their hosts suggested.

"You mean I'm to look like somebody's old cullud yard man? The sun goes straight through that flimsy cap I bought."

"I can find you something here maybe," their host offered.

"Mine were war babies, too," the Indiana woman said. "Harold was already born but Davey was the result of home leave."

"Too much champagne," said the Indiana man. "Just before leaving for ETO. Jesus God, what a time that was, those few days! I was green: I'd made up my mind to die. Can you imagine? Now it seems crazy to get worked up to that degree. I was Hemingway, I was Robert Jordan, I was Gary Cooper and G.I. Joe."

"A lot of people did die," said Irene.

"Yes, but how safe we all are now. Really. Here we are a dozen years later, everybody making money. Everybody I know of is making money. No real problems." He laughed. "Not at least until they drop the big one."

"You think they'll do it?" the hostess said, in such a way that one felt on a foreign island, remote among warm winds, evening, sea and alcohol.

"Sure they will," said Charles. "Sure they will someday," he added.

"Well, I hope I'm right under it," said the Indiana man.

"That's crazy," said his wife. "You're always saying that."

"No messing around for me. No shelters, no Hiroshima scar tissue. No prolonged radiation death sentence. Just one big bang is all I ask, dear Lord."

"It's noiseless," said the motel owner's wife, unexpectedly.

"That's right," Charles nodded.

"And they say the colors are stupendous," Irene said with a tiny laugh.

"A super-colossal Cinerama show that only the Japanese

have so far been treated to," said Charles. "What makes them so special? I call it discrimination!"

"You're sounding sick," said Irene.

Barry ate a lot of hors d'oeuvres. He had long ago got in the habit of eating large quantities at other people's houses. He never had enough money to feed himself and had often gone hungry.

Charles had said, the first time after they had invited him to dinner in Rome, "What's eating him?" To which Irene in a collapse of laughter had replied, "You mean what's he eating? He's hungry, poor boy. I never saw any American come to a dinner party really wanting food."

So she was already interested in him. In so many ways, he seemed like something new.

◆

They went out on a hired boat the next day, the twins, Irene, Barry and Charles. A local "character" took them out, one who had cultivated his grizzly white beard, no doubt, though his knowledge of the area and its waters and fish seemed genuine. Charles wore the sun hat, as advised. Irene, slathered in oils she trusted, wound her head in the bright scarf. The twins got darker by the minute, and stood around not missing anything, but refused to fish. They leaned against the rail, looking into the water, conversing seriously.

"I think they're abnormal," Charles complained. "All boys love to fish."

"If they start getting fat I can't stand it," said Irene, doting on their straight backs and trim legs.

"I should love to catch a turtle weighing two hundred pounds," said Charles. "They have wise faces."

"I think they're horrible," said Irene. "Except for shells. And soup, of course. Those awful feet."

"Enchanting feet," said Charles. "Life's first blundering attempt at a foot. The most honest foot of all. What's pretty about the human foot? Why, turtles have beautiful feet."

"You can have them," said Irene.

It was Barry who caught a turtle, though a small one. The boat owner smashed its head in and said that he had killed it, though Irene believed that it died by degrees on deck beneath the sun, contorting beneath its plated shell, upside down and waving its feet in the air. She did not speak for several hours and refused lunch.

"Blood sports are cruel," she finally said. "I loved turtles more than I thought."

"This isn't a blood sport," Charles argued. "Fishing a blood sport?" He stamped about the deck with his big feet flattened out in canvas shoes. There was a thin wash of fish blood on the planking. He gulped cold beer from a can.

They came back in the early afternoon. "My darlings, my darlings," said Irene, drawing her two boys to her. "Don't have identical sunstrokes, please?" They laughed at her; their teeth flashed whiter than milk.

There had been a silken overcast during a good part of the afternoon, thin and sheer across the sun's fierce eye. Irene's nose was blistered. When she laughed with her two sons, the three of them had all looked fleetingly alike. So Barry observed.

The haze deepened; there was a sense of quiet, with no threat of wind or any sort of weather; the boat steadily cut the sheer blue surface, as true as a drawn line.

All such returns are like homecomings, and as though the motel were indeed a home, Barry sensed the instant they stepped onto the pier that something was wrong. There was a silence, a stillness more than silence, an especial meditative beauty beneath the palm shade, and the way the shadow of the thatched sun huts lay upon the tumbled sand stirred Barry's hand to itch for a brush to paint it in just that way.

"A terrible thing happened while you were gone," the motel owner's wife said.

She had come down to Barry's room about an hour after their return. He had showered and dressed and was wondering what to put on his blazing nose. But most of all he continued to sense the unnatural quiet which had had its moment of beauty and now had grown eerie, alive with its secret as though the surface flesh of the place were creeping. Then there had been the small knock at the door.

"Come in," he said, opening the door wider.

"I can't. I've too much to do." She smiled wanly. "Well, no matter what happens, I think you should know. My husband and I discussed it and thought we'd go ahead and tell you."

Briefly, she told him.

The elder son of the Indiana people had electrocuted himself on a generator owned by the motel neighbors, a Miami family who kept a little pure white Spanish-style villa just across the inlet. The event had been clearly visible from the motel couple's balcony and had been witnessed by the boy's mother and father. They had come upstairs to ask about renting a boat with scuba diving equipment the next day, and were standing at the balcony watching the boys swim. They saw when they crawled out on the opposite shore, where the steps of the little villa went down into the water. Though a huge sign in red letters spelled out the voltage in the generator and advised one to keep away, the boys went toward it anyway. Their mother called to them from the balcony, and was joined by their father, who called also. They were both within easy hearing distance, separated from the adults only by the height of the second story and the narrow inlet of water they had been swimming in. They stood with their hands on their narrow hips, squinting back across the distance and arguing with their mother. Their father stepped in and cupping his hands to his mouth demanded that they return to the motel. "I know what I'm doing," said the older boy, and walking to the generator, deliberately put his hand to the outlet. He was wet from swimming and fell at once. In the motel they were for an incredulous instant stricken silent, except for the boy's mother who cried aloud: "He knew I didn't love him!" Later, neither she nor anyone could imagine why she had said this. It wasn't true, she said. The words had simply sprung out of her. Whether some suppressed truth had come to light, or whether she was trying to remove her husband's possible sense of being to blame, or whether it was merely hysterical and meant nothing, the motel owner's wife couldn't say. She sat on Barry's bed with her hands linked tightly together, her face white, bleached out, and her eyes swollen. There had been a general rush, she said, from then on for two or three hours—they had done all the right things, including a dash to the hospital in Miami with the ambulance. And now it was all over. Doctors and undertakers and nurses with sedatives and people who arranged these things had been prompt to take charge. It all seemed like something swallowed up into past history before the white paving near the Spanish villa could dry in the sun from the boys' splashes where they had come up out of the water. "So it's hard to believe now," she said. "But we thought you'd see it in the paper. There was a reporter here—heaven knows where he came from; he seemed to spring out of a tree. So many people come and go and nothing out of the way happens, and then a thing like this—there was no doubt they were the very best sort of people, genuine and kind and honest . . . they were just what they seemed to be. And there was no doubt either that the boy did kill himself. It was straight suicide, there was no mistaking that." Her husband, she said, had taken their little daughter for a drive. The child was terribly upset in her own deep way; they knew that. "When he gets back, I hope he will take me for a drive. I need to be talked to as much as anyone."

"But to be told what?" asked Barry. He really wanted to know.

"If I knew, I'd tell you." And she gave it to him again: her wan, sweet smile.

They went on the next day, on to Key West. Irene decided that it had all happened the moment the turtle was killed; she was apt to think things were true just because she had thought of them. Afterwards, the little cove with the white Spanish villa just across the inlet, blazing pure in the sun, seemed more of a dream than ever; they left and drove on, down a length of bare highway over vistas sometimes swampy, sometimes craggy with shells, past commercial fishing harbors, and towns sandwiched narrowly out between the concrete and the water on either hand. Then the highway at last became an abstraction, a single line unreeling infinitely on above water, under sky.

At Key West they viewed the large white-painted house where the President used to come to get away from Washington. They stood on the point which was farthest South in the whole U.S.A. and saw that it said only ninety miles to Cuba. They considered the huge white clouds.

Charles deliberately turned his back to the sign about Cuba, which might have come to seem at that moment like the next stopping place. He turned his back on the Atlantic Ocean and the Caribbean Sea.

"What I'm going to have lies due north of here," he announced. "They needn't think they can push me off the edge."

"Who?" Barry asked. "Who's trying to?"

"Oh, get with it," said Charles. He was laughing.

◆

When Barry got down to $23 and something, he did not tell the Waddells, but left in the night. Key West had its true mystery all about its streets at 3 A.M. It became close kin to port towns in the Indies, Mexico, a distant relative of Spain. There was the dry stirring of a night wind in the palms and certain streets looked darker than anyone would care to think about. The bus station, in a hot nook of the city surrounded by warehouses and garages, burned a blue fluorescent light inside, so that bugs kept crashing against the windows. Barry stood in the shadows. He was alone there except for a Negro man sitting on a suitcase, immobile as an image. The bus appeared from around the corner and the driver sold them tickets. Before they left, a carload of sailors drove up and helped three of their number aboard. They reeked from drinking and fell asleep before the lights went out. When the bus stopped at Marathon, the air was fresh and cool. It smelled really good then and the lights of fishing boats looked in some way blessed, far out on the water. The highway unspoiled infinitely, leading north.

Barry left a note for Irene and Charles. They found it shoved under the door when they went out for breakfast. "It's clear I have mal occhio or nothing would have happened about the turtle or the child. See you back in New York. Ciao. B.D."

The Waddells breakfasted beside the pool. The twins were still asleep.

A waiter came and handed Charles a note, and for one moment Irene thought it would be a phone call from New York offering Charles a new position—Come at once and take over Such and Such company, etc. But the note said, "My wife and I have a question—can you always tell your boys apart?" Charles glanced up and a silly couple waved at him. He penciled out firmly: "We do not speak the English," and sent the note back.

"Where do we go from here?" Irene asked. She was just as aware as he was that they were down to the bottom of the barrel.

They had spent far more than they had foreseen; they could not even get back to New York.

"There are three alternatives," said Charles. "Drive north, stay here, or take a boat away."

"Every one of them costs money," said Irene.

"Perhaps I'll get a job here, then."

She gave him a dark glance. Was he joking? "Why not?" he asked.

Irene finished her coffee and stood up. "Anything you want," she said. "Anything you want to do."

She walked back to the motel cabin. She wore a pink cotton shirt with the sleeves rolled up, striped pink-and-white cotton shorts, and dark glasses. She looked exactly right and knew it. She let herself in and sat on the edge of the bed.

She acknowledged it now; the cold had got inside. I know this world that is now, she thought, know exactly what I want out of it and how to use it, and I can't afford to live in it. Wasn't it meant to be a good joke, so neatly worked out? You couldn't believe that it hadn't been done on purpose.

◆

Barry had some idea about going back to Savannah when he left the Keys, but what was drawing him there, he knew, was the fact that he thought he had seen someone who looked like Catherine, just when he went out of the art shop into the street. He had followed and satisfied himself that it was not Catherine, but still, like a scent, the resemblance drew him. He evaluated this, saw it as an empty fancy, and at Miami bought a ticket to Pensacola instead. From there he could decide whether to go home to the Gulf coast or head up toward North Carolina where he had an army friend he could call on for money. In Pensacola, he did exactly what Charles had predicted to Irene that he would do; he found a girl in the bus station and put up with her for a time. She even got him a job that kept him alive and fed. He would not have denied that it had been desire, pure and simple, that made him leave the Waddells; he had had a terrible attack of it since the child's death; he guessed that the Waddells had felt the same, but then they had each other. He explained all this to the girl and she said that it sounded to her as if any excuse was a good one. He disliked this reply and knew he would soon be leaving. . . .

"Barry had his mind on women," Charles said, when he joined Irene in the cabin. She was still sitting on the edge of the bed.

"Charles," she said, "we cannot live without money. It's a habit."

"I never suggested trying." There were two double beds in the lavish, shadowy unit where the air conditioner purred as gently as a kitten.

"You had only to throw a little weight around," Irene said. "With Mercer and Paul both in Europe, of course they picked that time to knife you. They did it because they wanted your spot."

"The sons of bitches." Charles pulled out his shirttail and scratched.

"Why didn't you give them a fight?" she demanded.

"But if I sort them out, there're only more behind them. The world is full of bastards. Phalanxes of bastards . . ."

"All in grey flannel suits," she said. "That's the oldest argument on earth."

"You've saved a lot of breath, all the way down the Eastern seaboard," he observed. "This must be Land's End."

She didn't answer. It occurred to her that if a child could commit suicide anyone could, and that a suicidal tendency could exist in anyone. Irene herself loved nothing so much as life and hung back from the names of things, especially the emotions, as if to say I love, I hate, involved one in a commitment; it was like giving a pledge or a charm away and could be produced at the worst possible moment, exhibiting one's own signature, perhaps in blood, demanding recognition.

"Do you remember Siracusa?" Charles asked.

She looked up, obliquely. "Of course."

"We were all three there. Only Mario is missing."

"And Catherine," said Irene.

"Catherine was not in Siracusa," said Charles.

"That's right, she wasn't. I can't think why I thought she was."

"Are you going to turn on me," Charles inquired, "with all your womanish contempt? Or are you going to say, I love you so much I'll live with you in a suburban development on $6,000 a year?"

"Neither one," said Irene.

"Then what are you going to do?" he asked.

"It's for you to do something, not me." She trailed away to thoughtfulness. "I'll get a job," she offered, like a diver coming up with he didn't yet know what in his hand. "I had one once."

"You weren't any good at it," Charles said. "You used all the office telephones for making social engagements."

"Everybody was doing that. And society was part of it, that was clear from the first."

"I won't have you working," said Charles. "Your life is too perfect. You worked it all out like a mathematical equation. I never saw anything add up so well."

"I thought you liked that," she said, after a silence.

"You didn't think anything. You followed your instincts. You always follow your nose."

"Next you'll be calling me a bitch."

"Is it just because I'm necessary to your life that you want me around? Is that all?"

"What a question! As if anybody could sort things like that out."

"Isn't it always something from outside that makes us necessary to each other? After the boy's death, for instance, you are urgent, you have to be with me. . . ."

"You too," she softly edged aside.

"But I think that always, almost every damn time it's more than habit, it's because something has stirred you. It's nothing to do with me."

"Oh, Charles, why are you sitting there tearing the two of us up like an old theatre program? I think I'll shriek."

"The cabin's soundproof, love, there's none to hear you."

She laughed, and getting up, ran a comb through her hair. I'm here in this little box, she thought, on this distant spit of land, a little black comma on the globe. There is the big blue sea and the big white clouds and the enormous sky.

"You have not only solved life like a mathematical theorem, you've turned it into a perpetual motion machine. There will never come a season when Irene is not interested in the new styles, the new buildings, the good restaurants, the new people, the good places to go."

"Oh, Charles!" She flung down the comb. "There're the boys, after all."

"Yes," he agreed. "There're the boys."

"And anyway," she argued, "if I have this gift you should be glad of it. It's all to benefit you," she was inspired to add.

"That isn't true *at* all," he said. "Not one little bit. Women can usually be trapped in some way by life. If they can't be trapped any other way, then children will trap them. But this was where you were cleverest. You had twins. Twin boys. Charming, intelligent, beautifully adjusted, liking nothing so much, so far, as each other's company."

"I'm going out now," she said coldly.

"Where to?" Charles asked.

"I don't know."

She was not really angry with him, she knew. In fact, his nagging her this way told her only that his malaise was about to end; it was running out just about the right time, just when the land ran out, and the money. He would swing into action any minute now, she assured herself, and at that point, approaching the pool, she looked up and saw the twins poised left and right at the pool's end on diving boards. They waved at her and she saw their lips say Watch, and then they shot down beautifully matched. The water leaped crystal in the sun.

The angels are all human here, thought Irene, remembering

her conversation with Barry. Smiling, she made a clapping gesture as their two brown heads sleekly broke the surface, eyes at once seeking her.

◆

But Charles did not return to New York with Irene. Barry found her alone in the apartment in November. He himself was looking fine; he had had adventures. He had stopped in with his army friend in North Carolina and been introduced to a man who was going to California and wanted some advice on modern art, which he intended to buy from a dealer in San Francisco. He seemed to roll in money and invited Barry, an old friend, and the old friend's wife to an enormous new house in a suburb of Charlotte, and also to dinners at the country club. There were ways in which one could not remember, after a couple of drinks, if one was at the country club or the house. The man's kindness exceeded everything. If he had wanted pictures in the first place to please his wife, he now wanted them all the more to do a favor to Barry. It would never be clear if he himself actually wanted anything to do with art or not, and Barry gave up completely trying to have an answer about this, one way or another. He decided to relax and enjoy the whole debauchery.

"So I went along with them," he said to Irene. "A first-class flight there and back. I will be entered as a deduction on next year's income tax. I was 'art adviser.'"

"What was his wife like?" Irene giggled.

"Blonde and plump. She was okay. It was a nice trip."

"So you didn't go to New Orleans?"

Barry did not really come from New Orleans. This was something he had tried several times to explain to Irene, and she always returned to saying he was from New Orleans. He came from a town near there, along the Gulf.

"I meant to go there from Pensacola, but there had been a storm, wires down on the roads, and the bus being all I could afford, I went up to North Carolina first, and then the fates took charge.

"So what's with Charles?" he asked.

"Oh, God," said Irene. "Oh, God!"

"Is he still in Key West?"

"He's doing some sort of real estate work in the Keys. He stayed in Key West till the tourists started coming. He wants me to come there and live with him."

"You won't do it?"

"I had to put the boys in school. Besides, I know Charles better than to think he's going to be satisfied there indefinitely. He'll want back in the swim and far better for him if I keep a foothold here. I took a job—dentist's receptionist, nine to five. I work crossword puzzles and answer the phone. I flew down once."

"Has Charles been here?" Barry inquired. It was not his business and Irene seemed not to hear him.

"After a while the Keys begin to smell like fish. All day long." She tucked her blouse in meditatively, a cigarette dangling from her mouth. "The thing is, he has to be first or nothing, and the humiliation of getting kicked out of that firm by a collusion of little guys in Brooks Brothers suits—that was what hit him."

"But he could have fought it," Barry prompted, recalling that she herself had said so too.

"But that would have been acknowledging they existed," she pointed out. "Now he's staring every day at the sun and the sky and the water and the girls in bikinis. At twilight three martinis explode in his head. And one day he'll know what makes it all run."

"You think he's nuts, I guess," said Barry.

"I don't think anything."

Is there somebody else? Barry wondered. For one or the other or both? There didn't seem to be anybody for Irene. She was dressed rather more strictly than not, and had let her hair go; it was dark and oily, streaked with grey. Her look was still direct and clear. It burned for a second across him, then strayed away.

"You're not going to get a divorce or anything?"

"Not that I know of."

As he went out, Irene told him at the door, still chain-smoking, "People here think he's in the Keys for his health. I think they've made it up that he has arthritis or TB or something. Well, I don't care. Let them make up anything they want to."

Barry went away, walking home. Buses seamed by in the late afternoon traffic, edging along the park. The air was sodden and gloomy, but the trees in the park had trapped some violet light among the cold branches.

He was more at peace than he could ever remember having been, and all things looked to him exactly as they were. The heavy war threat had shifted off for a time and even the skyscrapers looked the freer for it—when threatened they seemed to know it. There was a way of thinking that he had caught to himself the life that had flagged for Irene and Charles. But he did not want to admit even this as something he believed. He felt any idea was best left as another object one could look at.

◆

When Barry left, Irene locked herself in alone. She leaned out of the bedroom window, looking down an austere drop of opposite façade to a street lined by skimpy trees. She saw herself as a girl, standing in a doorway, saying, "But Mother, if you'd only tell me what it is . . . if you'd only say . . . please say. . . ." "No one has understood my life," said the voice out of the dark. "Not a single soul." "Would you be happy if I was pretty and had a lot of dates and friends and things, and a lot of people came to see me?" The voice inside was instantly defensive. "Well, that's not my fault. You needn't make me sound to blame." "But Mother, I didn't mean . . . I did not mean. . . . Listen, please, listen, if only I could go to another school . . . somewhere near, but not that one." "You know the problem . . . you know the financial problem very well. You want to hurt my pride by making it an issue. I try not to blame anyone, God knows how hard I try."

There was the old-fashioned street outside, the porch of the old white house with its red brick front yard, and the school across the way—that awful girls' school. Between entering the room where her mother lay in the dark and talked that way and crossing the street to go inside that school, there was no choice at all in Irene's mind. She was trapped like the pendulum in a clock.

Then there was Charles.

As she stood remembering, the phone rang from the empty foyer, and it was Catherine. She was in New York and wanted to see Irene.

This late! Irene thought. And with Barry just gone. But I can't, she thought. She felt afraid and her heart began to go fast. "I'm alone, you know, Catherine," she said. "Charles is—is away on business."

"But it's you I wanted to see," the voice continued.

It was the kind of voice used to speaking to doctors, to saying, "but can you please just tell me what . . ." If there was anything Irene kept herself away from, it was authority. Nobody knew. She had learned it long ago. But how to stay clear of someone who could not retreat from authority because of some inner weakness, exploited infinitely? Wasn't that what Catherine permitted? Or was it? The highway to Key West began to unreel in Irene's head by way of a nonsense answer. The road to Siracusa had led south also. But Catherine, innocent as a lamb, had been in neither of these places.

"Yes, certainly, Catherine. Why, yes, do come round."

What else could I say? she heard herself asking Charles. What else could I do? Can you tell me?

◆

There was no one like Catherine Sasser. A lot of men had said that, and Irene had always to agree: there was no one else like Catherine. She entered gently, not looking quite well, not entirely in good health, but in total command of such wonderful manners, asking if the boys were there, and saying how disappointing it was to miss them.

Irene took her coat. "You look wonderful," she lied, though in a way it was always true. To steady herself, she had bolted a vodka in the kitchen before the doorbell rang, and now got herself another and a whiskey for Catherine, who let it sit on the coffee table while the ice melted. What she was doing in New York was vague; Irene suspected doctors and did not press for an answer.

"So I wonder how Barry is?" she asked.

Something in Irene's head grew stubborn as flint. This is not my business, she thought. Why should I let them make it my business? "I think Barry may need his privacy these days," she said. "I assume this as I don't see much of him. Perhaps that's all he needs to turn out some really great work. This is what Charles thinks, what several critics we know were frank in saying *they* think."

She went on in this vein, knowing only too well how to package a thing in a New York way, to give it the sound of the latest, the different, the explosive, the final, soon-to-be-revealed, superlative word. She had been a little taken in herself by this quality in New York when she had first come there to live, but then her energy, stirred, had risen to meet and challenge it; she saw that it was only a game, and started, forthwith, to play it. "So I think the best we can do for him—"

Catherine, reading a match folder in her lap, did not seem to hear the end of the sentence. "I see. Well, I'm so glad, really so glad."

Irene laughed. "The last time I saw him, he said, It's happier not being in love; it's really great . . ."

"Oh, but I didn't mean . . . !"

"Oh, good heavens, he didn't mean you," Irene hastened to explain. "I think he had a fling with an odd-ball girl down in the Village. Charles called it his existentialist period—ten years too late. I never saw her but once and she looked slightly dirty. Those girls like that—I always want to say, Look, honey, what you need, first of all, is a good long bath."

"I see."

Once Catherine did think she saw, she would not embarrass anyone by continuing to pursue the matter. She would put herself in Irene's place; Irene was obviously doing her best to be kind. She brightly asked all about Charles. Charles was traveling a lot, Irene said; the company was expanding, it was having tiny replicas of its New York offices all over, one after another, like kittens. At present, he was in Miami.

Catherine accepted this. She never looked deeply into business matters of other people. The instant one said "company" she stopped listening.

"I'm going away in a few days," she told Irene.

There were distances in her voice which made a chill down Irene's spine. It was always in the realm of the possible that Catherine was being seen for the last time. And here was Irene keeping her from seeing Barry.

"Where are you going?"

Catherine stood up. "To South America. Chile, I think. They say it's rather beautiful. I've never been there."

"Look," said Irene, "I want you to take Barry's number. I'll give you the address. It's not for me to say whether or not—"

"Please, no," said Catherine. "To think of hurting any more people. It was through not having much of anything but his work that he got attached to me, and pretty soon, before I knew it, I was everything to him. But I didn't know it. You must understand that. I never guessed. I know it sounds ridiculous."

"Catherine," said Irene, "did you ever get a divorce from Jerry Sasser?"

She shook her head. "Perhaps I should do it yet. Some people said one thing, some another. To me it seemed an added strain. Once you start it, you have to go on with it—" she laughed—"like being drawn up in a vacuum cleaner." She could flash so lightly through saying such a thing, and it was in moments like this that Irene felt the tug of Catherine's whole history, and she felt, too, almost like a puzzle laid out to be put together, the strong lure of a challenge; namely, to solve the riddle of Catherine. And forty years later I would wind up, thought Irene (with her own kind of ironic humor closed beneath a smooth countenance), worn to emotional fragments, and Catherine, mad as ever, would be completely the same.

She walked to the desk and pulled out a note pad. "Here," she said, writing.

"What is it?"

"It's Barry's address and number. I think he may even have got in the phone book but he's moved since."

Catherine took the small leaf, torn out neatly along its perforation, and tucked it in her small leather bag. "I don't think I shall use it," she reassured Irene. "Not after what you told me." She pulled on her gloves and was gone soon after, had melted from view like an apparition.

◆

When Irene got Charles' long soul-searching letter from Florida announcing his decision to return, she skimmed it in one minute to get to the heart of the matter: back on Saturday.

She did not call the twins to tell them the news, though she had promised to. On the drive back from Florida, they had sweetly consoled her. "This happens to a lot of boys' parents," they had said, citing all the examples they knew. One boy's father had chased his mother around the house at 3 A.M. with a gun. Some things like this were made up and told for melodramatic effect, but the twins believed this to be true. "And then they come back, sometimes," said Will. "*Most* of the time," said Tom. "Do we know enough to make up a statistical sampling?" he asked. "I think it would not be representative," said Will. "As if a statistical average ever comforted anybody," said Irene, passing a Pepsi-Cola truck. "Why, of course, they comfort people," said Will. "Certainly," said Tom. "They run graphs in the newspaper about the Gross National Product every time there's a serious drop in the market." "I wish you weren't so damn bright," said Irene. They both laughed. "It will bring you nothing but trouble," she threatened darkly. "I need some new loafers," said Will. "These are just about gone."

All the way, Charles' head had loomed high and lonely in her mind, dominating Key West as it had Siracusa. The clouds passed high over it, drifting; the head was domed, bald, high, beak-nosed, blue-eyed, and thin-lipped. Who knew what Charles was better than the clouds did? If clouds knew him, he was, of course, imperial, and could desert her if he chose without explaining anything. Nature is acquainted with emperors. A car honked her aside. She gasped and set herself straight with the white line. There was no good having a wreck and killing the boys. The job in hand always kept Irene going; to get the boys in school as quickly as she could now led her on. They ate hamburgers and peanuts all the way, but were not sick. God knows, she thought, they couldn't be a more docile pair, they even have fool-proof digestive systems. "Darlings," she murmured, having left the president's office at a moderately well-known Virginia academy where she had fixed up the problem of expenses and tuition with no great loss of face "Angels." She put her arms around them, on the broad flight of entrance steps. This parting too she grouped in with all the rest of their latest phase: the waspish young men who had got Charles out, the turtle, the child's suicide, Barry's flight, her own desertion. The autumn sun was elegiac and warm. There was a distant view of gallant Virginia hills, a sense of the yellow leaf stoutly clinging till its full ripe moment was attained.

Only after Charles' letter came could she evaluate Catherine's visit. The city rushed with autumn rain, now white, now black. Soon the planet, tilting somberly like a lowering acquiescent head, would take its crown of chill stone with it, down into the long damp winter. She saw that Catherine had been able to seem important merely because she herself was alone. What difference did it make what I said or did? She thought of Catherine as a nice silk scarf which one folded and put away in a drawer. It slept there in the dark and kept the scent of something.

Late on the appointed day Charles appeared and dropped his suitcases, one from either hand. "There still isn't any job," he said, embracing her. "There still isn't any money."

"There're some letters waiting," she said.

There were indeed some letters. They were from people she and Charles had known in Paris, one from a man who dated back as far as Naples during the war, having been a major to Charles' captain.

"Your being let out," it ran, "merely affirms what we all know, that this new set of bright boys want all the cake and all the crumbs too; they want to be first at the punch bowl and when they leave there's nothing left but a weak lump of ice. They only confirm that by the time they give us these ever-loving tests and go Umm and Is that so? the only job we're going to be scientifically fit for is sweeping up after the party. Well, you and me, we ain't sitting around to take no tests. We ain't even coming to that particular blow-out. We're having our own—old style, best style, and the job is still going to get done. Which is to say, Come over to the office the minute you get back and we'll see what we can see."

"That's real friendship," said Charles, and his eyes filmed over. "I call that real friendship," he said to Irene. She had gone to get him a drink, but he put it aside and pulled her to him, enveloping her hungrily, tight and always closer, burying his face against her neck and shoulder. "If you weren't here I'd walk a hundred miles to find you. No, I wouldn't either, I'd run."

The rewards of famished love were now to be heaped upon her and their marriage reappeared like a triumphal procession with plumes and elephants, dancing girls and flowing wine, lions and tigers and captive queens and hordes of barbarian slaves. If either of them felt she had been badly treated, they never mentioned it. In the late hours while Charles slept, Irene, again at windows, saw life come streaming at her over every rooftop, past every TV antenna, a flood tide, welcome as rain after drought, giving every small tree along the street far below its true meaning, its very being. She had, all along, been conscious of more that was going on than she had realized. She knew, now that she thought of it, every new style trend, the set of a shoulder, the tilt of a heel, the play that was talked about most. There was a new make of china being brought out from West Germany, a new way of serving hot buffets without a lot of mess. For ages she had needed something done to the kitchen which would give her more space; for months she had been bored with the scent of her perfume. And in the spare moments one could consider the islands for future trips, for people were saying that Florida was overrun now and that everyone should have an island, one favorite little-known idyllic spot. She did not know how she knew people were talking this way since she had not seen anyone who would say anything like this since her return.

"Charles," she said at breakfast, "did you know we were quite wrong about Clint Gifford? He hasn't any more got cancer than I have. He got a promotion, that's all, about the time they decided to shove you out the door. They were embarrassed to call us."

"The son of a bitch," said Charles, absently, reading the

market pages. "If he's the kind they want," he presently came to the surface to remark, "I'm glad they let me out."

"It makes their bad taste uniform," said Irene. "Something to be counted on."

"Nice to know," said Charles. "Encouraging."

When he left she returned to the window, but now to see a world strong and sharp with cold sunlight. When she spread out her arms in her long robe and the sleeves slid back to her shoulders, the gesture was one of welcome to the return of absolutely everything.

◆

"But you must have seen Irene?" said Barry, for the third time. "How would you know where to find me?"

"Yes," Catherine admitted, "but she advised me not to see you. She said how well you were doing in your work. Perhaps I was wrong to come."

He had entered to find her just sitting there before him in the twilight which seemed to close down thirty minutes earlier each day. At first he thought he was seeing things, then she got up and kissed him. She said she had found the door unlocked, one of those statements that teeter from side to side for quite some while in the mind before toppling over into truth.

"It would be worse to be in New York and not see me, wouldn't it?"

"Not if you didn't know it." This was what he thought of as a Catherine-answer. They both smiled.

"I'd find it out from Irene, in case you saw her, or anybody she knew. It would be hard to avoid seeing at least one person Irene knew. I guess you have, though. I'll bet you've been here in town any number of times without letting us know." He paused. She did not answer. He switched on lamps and she noticed that his eyes looked red, as though from drinking, work, sleeplessness, strain. "Is there something special now? Something the matter? . . . Well, anyway, you're here. I used to have a fairly nice-looking place." He glanced around ruefully, aware for the first time in weeks of the odd smell of something gone bad in the kitchenette, of soot on the windowsill and the unlamented death of an ivy plant.

Catherine was folded silkenly in the only good chair. It did not make him suffer as much to see her in the flesh as it did to see her ghost. The thought that she had, after all, not forgotten him had blown his spirits sky-high for a moment. He had breathed the air of paradise. She herself had been shaky; wouldn't it turn out, after all, that Irene was right, and she shouldn't, for any number of reasons, do this? She had to be soothed with gin.

"I thought there would be someone here. Some girl—" She glanced around. "A friend perhaps."

He laughed. "There's no one hung up in the closet, if that's what you mean."

Catherine was too polite to ask him any more. If she had heard for certain that he had got married and divorced in the months since they had parted, she would have waited for him to tell her about it. Irene could ask him easily in two minutes what Catherine would never get around to in two years. She herself indulged in bursts of unrelated confidences.

"I told Irene I might go to Chile. I did think of it for a time.

You see, I had a strange dream which made such an impression I couldn't forget it. It was about the—now, don't laugh, please—about the Antarctic."

He laughed anyway. "Catherine, in a dream how on earth would you know the Arctic from the Antarctic?"

"It was *my* dream, and so I knew. Listen. All the ice and snow were gone; it was all green, a thin, fresh green, the kind you get in cold climates. There were a lot of rocks strewn on the ground where the glaciers had slid away and melted and then they made stone fences out of the rocks and a road went by along the wall."

Crazy or not, she could give him a strong vision. He could see it; she could draw him in. There was some madness, he supposed, in everyone. One advantage of it was that he didn't have to work around to subjects with Catherine; he could just tell her, for instance, that he still loved her. "I still love you," he said.

"I had to see you, Barry. Had to."

They would soon go out and eat somewhere, wander far afield, he would go back to wherever she was staying. He foresaw it all.

Thirty hours later he wandered alone through a dark empty city of damp stone. He could seriously, for moments together, entertain the idea that the signal had been given, the sirens had sounded and everybody had heard them but him and Catherine. Or had the secret weapon struck and dissolved all available flesh, scientifically, properly, carefully preserving the valuable stone, the great New York apparatus, all intact? Only the worrisome human weed exterminated. Then he passed a late bar or two and saw a bus snarl by: he gained then his own vision of himself as a grey heap of garbage; that stubborn glint of something battered, and perhaps useless, was his soul; that sawdust had poured out of the side of his head. The rest was not worth probing into, even with a stick. He was empty, exhausted, worthless, and at peace. She had, after all, not forgotten him—Rome where he had met her, the hills of Circe at the sea where he had taken her, the sand flats below Sperlonga, the moon beating on the sea. But she was not in love with him. She had had to see him. Why? To bring back those memories? Yes, and to get herself through something new, he guessed, something far nearer to the quick of her than he could ever get except to pinch-hit for—

Quick, he shut his mind to it. It was enough not to know. When the dead heap of peaceful garbage stirred to life, he would begin to ache again. Well, so what? he thought. He groped for his key and laughed, for he found the door unlocked just as she had found it. Within, two glasses sat on the dusty table. The cigarettes had been left to smoke themselves down to ash, with no harm, no damage done, insentient things being meticulous at such times, as though aware that humans have abandoned them perhaps to make a total mess of things.

◆

Charles' new job was with a printing firm which had one or two small contracts with national political committees. Irene saw at once that, in a national election year, this particular branch might burgeon. She came home one day with a mass of books.

"You've gone and got pink hair," said Barry Day, who was waiting for her downstairs.

"Don't you love it?" said Irene, fresh with some concentrate of winter sweetness, which doubtless cost thirty dollars an ounce. When they prospered they really laid it on, Barry thought. It almost made him sick.

He helped her with the books.

"I read all those at the office," said Charles, who was at home with a cold, "but never mind."

"Then I'll read them," said Irene, "we have to know everything now."

"Look," said Barry, "I may as well tell you that I saw Catherine anyway, in spite of your advice."

"Advice!" said Irene. "It was I who gave her your address."

"She was on her way back to Dallas."

"I thought she said Chile."

"She did, but that was a dream she had."

"Poor Catherine," said Irene. The books were glossy and decorative; their bold, modern designs and strongly colored lettering made a splashy array just as she dropped them on the broad coffee table; in short, to Barry, a canvas. Charles sat muffled to the ears in a yellow towel, a hot water bottle on his head, drinking a hot toddy.

"I think it's a dangerous journey," said Barry. "I guess all journeys are dangerous," he added, as Irene, who was busy getting out of her coat, gloves and hat, did not say anything.

"The park smells cold and absolutely dead," she said.

"I mean," he said, "I think America is murderous in some respects. I think it is murderous to Catherine."

"Yes," said Irene, "but she—"

"She what?" he nagged. "She what?" When Irene only

frowned without replying, Barry went on, flopping down in a huge comfortable chair. "We suffer more than any people on earth." But the truth was he was happy to see Charles and Irene now they had got their good times back.

"It isn't true," said Charles. "We're just brought up to play the happy-happy game, join the Optimist Club and the world smiles with you. Then we get unduly damaged when the facts of life emerge. We are unprepared. But that doesn't mean I wish to've been born a Sicilian peasant." He sneezed.

"What do you think of Catherine?" Barry asked him.

"Catherine? I've never gotten her attention," said Charles. "We were once marooned in Rome after a party and couldn't get a cab. She said she would walk home and was gone before I could offer to go with her. I must have had a few. After she left I was afraid something might have come out and eaten her."

"Exactly what I mean," said Barry.

"But then it doesn't happen," said Irene, sharply. "She's always perfectly all right. Why doesn't somebody worry that way about me?"

"My, my," said Charles. "We are arching our backs, aren't we?"

She was silent and thought of Mario, an Italian she had loved for a time, down in Siracusa when she thought Barry would die. At the window, it began, astonishingly, to snow.

Barry, with an awesome contraction in his heart, felt that Catherine was leaving them inexorably again, was by now no more than a speck disappearing at high speed into distant light.

"She will be gone for a long time," he murmured.

Charles looked up, but did not reply.

Dangerous Journeys

ONE

More than likely Catherine herself knew better than anyone else that she never had the slightest idea of going to Chile. This was the sort of blind, a delicately decorated screen, replete with incident, people, flora and fauna, which she knew well by now how to raise around herself.

From Barry she went on to see her son, Latham, at his school in Massachusetts, and straight from there, as she had known for a month now she would do, she flew to Washington where she met her husband, Jerry Sasser.

He used to be so handsome but in the two years since they had parted, some inner slackening off had come out clearly on his features. She wondered if this effect might not come from too much drinking and she wondered how well he was doing. He had a way of charging through doors and stopping suddenly to take note of the terrain before him; rather like a lion entering an unfamiliar stretch of jungle, he went to work at once looking for a victim or an enemy, striking an attitude which always had its effect on whatever room he entered. In this case it was the lobby of the Mayflower Hotel, and Catherine, watching from the depths of a green armchair, while the familiar scene unfolded, saw at least a dozen heads lift as though from grazing and slowly turn. He spotted her at last, almost, you might guess, when he chose to, a battered lion, possibly in a bad humor, showing it now and again by a twitch of his tail. She braced herself; for when he got near, within a dozen feet or so, she was going to see again the shadow of the boy, young man, husband, father, she had always loved. Would it never go away, that shadow? Why didn't it, like a light, simply burn out?

"Hello, Jerry."

"Hello, Catherine."

Back of every mad person there is a person who never would answer. Well, if he never would answer then at least he could and would sign, for the papers she brought were about money—a bond investment, held jointly, had matured—and though she could have let it drift into the estate until such time as he got an accounting done and found it, she knew he always needed money and so chose to bring it to him herself. Her family, if they knew of it, would have thought she was either in another crisis, or had gone back to him, or both. But even in the world's worst marriage there are moments of comfort, like the settling of an old quilt over tired limbs, when two people meet again. So they sat in green armchairs in the hotel lobby, a low table between them, discussing Latham, relatives, health and money.

Catherine had known Jerry Sasser all her life. If a table now sat between them every time they met, it was a table with an imaginary chess game laid out upon it. The chess game, she had come to see thus late on, had been going on for nearly forty years. At each meeting one or the other of them might reach down and make a move. Then again, they might not. The possibility was always present, but not always acted on. The game itself, she now saw clearly, would never end. They had grown together like two trees; they had sapped life from each other. There had always been a sense of mystery about him, first there to draw her, win her, possess her, and later to poison her. There was, later on, a specific point, never cleared up, but always present; something he wouldn't say.

"Who did try to kill you that time, Jerry?" She had asked him that at least a hundred times.

He always laughed. But this time, unexpectedly, he answered her. "You did." The move was made.

She started. "Don't be an idiot. If I ask you a serious question—"

"Sure it was you." He grinned, worrying out a match, and dropped it on the growing litter in the too-small ash tray before him. "Who else would?"

"You think I would?"

"You wanted to plenty of times."

"Jerry, I never—"

"The gate was locked."

"Those men—!"

"You think they would? Just when I was making over a fortune. You blanked out, that's all. Strain and crisis . . . same old trouble. I never blamed you."

She sat quietly, hands folded, allowing the recent memory of a young man's hoarse whisper in her ear to sustain her. Jerry would still wreck me if he could, she thought coldly.

He drove her back to her hotel.

"I suppose you see the Waddells," he said.

"I saw Irene in New York," she said. "Charles seems to travel a lot. It's some promotion or other, I gather. A company extension . . . that's it."

"She told you that, did she? Well, that's good, if true. The last I heard he was beachcombing in Florida, pretty definitely 'between jobs.'"

"I'm sure that isn't true. Irene seemed perfectly confident about things."

"She's that type."

"Jerry, they are my friends, not yours. Just because you happened into Charles on a business matter, you can't simply move in. . . ."

"There was a time when he could have put money in that company, but he preferred to think it was his brain power, background, or something vague like imagination they wanted, that that was the valuable part. Well, there's more than one with all that to spare, and of course it isn't even supremely valuable, not to excess."

"You mean they've let him out."

"I guess we must have heard different things. Maybe not."

He knew his way around Washington and drove well. They passed the White House.

"What do people say about politics?" Catherine asked.

"What a question," said Jerry. "Then there was that artist, Barry something."

Good old Jerry, good old Jerry, she thought. "I think he went South to work."

"You'd think he'd live in Italy."

"Why?"

"People like that should live abroad." He lost interest. "Catherine, why are you going home?"

"To keep them from tearing up the landscape, if I can. I can't, of course. It all has to do with the new highway, the new suburb, the new Gateway to the West museum, the new . . . oh, the new everything. It exhausts me to try to stop it, if not stop it, at least to save the old farm the way it was; but I shall try. Then, in a month, I'm visiting with. . . ."

She had friends everywhere. She let them take her up from time to time, never questioning their motives, which were perhaps genuine. Her money, her history, her influence, her contacts, her precarious health, her willingness to help and be helped—she did not care to go into it herself, let alone point it out to Jerry. It came to her when she got out of the car on the cold sidewalk and the wind instantly bit her, that she had exploited Barry to fortify herself for meeting Jerry. Jerry would certainly be living with some woman who had a career in Washington and two divorces behind her already, and something shady here and there to keep her brain sharpened razor-fine. (She had heard a part of this rumored and the rest flowed easily into place.) I guess I'm as big a bitch as the next one, Catherine thought, and huddled her frail shoulders against the cold, moving her delicate shoes from time to time on the pavement. As for landscapes, she thought, the only one I'm liable to end up with is Jerry's face. Those two craters are his eyes, and there's a dark crumple of hair, straight across the forehead, flat except for one cowlick that won't lie down no matter what. And there were the high, Indian-straight cheekbones, reaching back like twin ridges, one of which, just beneath the eye, after a certain number of drinks, blotched with a mound of red.

"Goodbye, then," he said, and noticing that she was shivering, leaned down to kiss her cheek. "Keep well," he said. She entered her hotel through turning glass doors, intractable with the dark opaque look of winter water.

◆

It was still cold and cloudy the morning after Catherine saw Jerry. The cab to the airport wound past the wealthy suburbs with their stone mansions which were possibly legation headquarters or senatorial residences, into the small-farm, fenced properties of one-story white houses, copses of leafless oak along the slopes and empty fields covered sparsely with sage and bone-white winter grass. A road project lay fallow along the highway, great dumb earth movers stood silent to the cold, machines very close to animals in their souls. The cab driver had a noisy heater, which roared.

"Where you going, lady?"

"Dallas."

The last time Catherine had made this trip was with Jerry, the time he said she tried to kill him. It was hot summer and she hadn't wanted to be there. All the way to the airport she had sustained herself by imagining herself back along the green walks beside the Potomac, watching from cool shade while the plane took off. To the watcher below it would have to be a lovely sight: the plane, a long-nosed magnificent jet, rising silver in the cloudless summer blue, would seem to drift level as a boat above the Capitol, almost to dream, then tilting deliberately upward, to hang for a further second in the mesh of a dream. But before a doubt could gather around it, it would lift surely, beautifully, accomplish new heights of air, and seem to quiver itself with what it communicated—the delight and pride of power.

Herself borne aloft by it that summer day, Catherine felt the take-off in these terms, and her sense of glory, tired as she was, roused golden in her senses, then sank to apathy. Such moments vanished quickly and defied meaning; her mind had leveled off for the flight. The roar died to a drone, a soft insulated drumming from without. The tension slid behind into the jet stream. She had groped toward seat adjustments and magazines.

"Coffee, tea, or milk?"

"Shhh!" Catherine put her finger to her lips and indicated her husband, who had fallen asleep before the take-off. The stewardess nodded, and bending down with a smile, picked up a shoe which was sitting half out in the corridor and placed it neatly, along with its mate, under the edge of the seat; then she picked up an arm which had fallen limp and weary out into the line of passage and laid it across his lap. She nodded to Catherine—a young, trim girl with a dark cropped head, smooth olive cheeks and admirable lipstick. "Coffee, tea, or milk?" she whispered. "Coffee," said Catherine.

Despite his wife's reminder as they walked up the incline that this was a commercial flight, Jerry Sasser, from the moment he had flopped into his seat, had insisted on acting just as he did on the Western Star, Senator Ogden's private DC-6 Constellation, shucking his coat, loosening his belt, tie and top shirt buttons, dropping his shoes, banging the seat back to the hilt—there was nobody behind, thank God. "You can lose a vote that way," Catherine remarked, but he had crashed already, into the sudden oblivion of sleep. Aloft, the air conditioning gained total saturation. Now he'll catch cold, Catherine thought, with all that Washington perspiration drying off. She was fumbling to close the ventilating system when the coffee came.

When Jerry Sasser wakened they were somewhere over Tennessee and it was nearly dinnertime—the early dinnertime of planes and trains and hospitals—perhaps of all waiting people. He had been sprawled there, silently, a long while, then the seat snapped up and the coat which she had spread over his chest fell down into his lap. "What's that?" he demanded, catching it by the sleeve. "Oh"—he shifted his grasp to the collar and lifted it up, at which point the article became not only recognizable but his own—"my coat."

"I was afraid you might catch cold."

"Cold," he echoed, absently. He drew down his turned-back cuffs and buttoned them, slid his tie into place and fastened his belt. Then he quitted her in a men's-room sort of way. When he got back he leaned over her to look down at the U.S.A.

"You want to swap?"

"No, just trying to see where we are. What's that down there? The Mississippi?"

"The Tennessee, I think."

"Oh, sure. It wiggles. Lots of lakes."

"Wouldn't that be the TVA? I've been wondering."

"Sure, sure. The TVA."

He had damped and combed his hair and his hands smelled clean.

"You look better," she said.

He gave her a rare, direct glance. "You too."

"I feel better." She paused. "After all, we are going home. Aren't we? After Dallas?"

"I promised, didn't I?"

Later, after dinner, they sat in the observation lounge; they had a corner to themselves. The stewardess joined them. She knew Jerry, as it turned out; had met Catherine as well some months before on one of Senator Ogden's pre-campaign flights to the Midwest. Through the window, Catherine could watch the northwest flange of the sunset, streaming pink, mauve, crimson, violet, sinking a cool liquid play of satin light into one back-flung silver wing. Lights were already picking out the forest-green, darkening texture of the land below. There a city flashed up: "Little Rock," said the stewardess without even looking. She was bringing Jerry out about politics. Oh, yes, even way up here, Catherine thought wryly. This entire summer, she thought, is nothing whatever that isn't politics.

She wondered if even people who were out of it could escape, people who worked in filling stations and ten-cent stores, and she rather thought not, for the air that summer had been doctored, the water chemically treated: a sense of power permeated an entire continent. When a locomotive bears down on you, even if you are standing safely twelve feet back on the platform you will still feel the surge, the tingle, the something very close to joy and very close to fear. The little stewardess now with her professional ease refusing a drink was sitting on the chair arm opposite, waggling her foot, and all up and down her charming young self the message was flashing out that here before her was Someone in the Know. She was careful not to overplay her knowledge; she skillfully included Catherine in everything she said.

"It must really seem very peculiar to you both to take a commercial flight. What I mean is, how did it ever happen?"

"Oh, well, Senator Ogden—" Catherine began.

"He had to fly out yesterday," Jerry filled in. "They left me behind to clean up one or two little jobs. I'm sort of a glorified errand boy, you know."

The little stewardess knew just how to smile at that and say without saying it that Jerry's picture had been on the cover of a national magazine in recent months, a prototype of a rising class of quick-witted, well-heeled and powerfully connected young men in Washington who knew where to go and whom to see and how to make things happen.

"TV was as close as I could get to the conventions. I was at a girl friend's apartment in Denver. We both knew a couple of reporters there. Glenn Forrester was one. You may know him."

"Sure. Sure, I know Glenn. He's a friend of yours?"

"No. I know him through Edie. She knows him very well."

"Very well, huh? I see. This your girl friend in Denver? I see."

Learning forward slightly in his dark tropical-wear summer suit, sipping bourbon and water and ticking the heel of one heavily stitched expensive black shoe against the edge of his lounge chair, no more mindful of the land beneath him, of the gloriously fading sunset than if it were unfolding on a color TV screen someone else was looking at halfway across a motel lobby, Jerry Sasser was turning over in his mind something more important to him than the conversation. His wife was pretty positive what the something else was, and that it was not yet decided, only that it was being given a chance to develop. A nudge one way or the other and he might possibly forget it entirely. Catherine knew that given a very few more years the little stewardess, who had been so careful to make her very youth "interesting," could have been her and Jerry's daughter. Age, to Catherine, seemed a simple enough fact, but far from wanting to accept his own, Jerry had once gone dark with anger after a political tea party during which she had felt moved to show a recent snapshot of their son. At the time he had simply removed the photo from her hands, said it wasn't a good one, and put it in his coat pocket. The minute the door had closed on the last guest, and perhaps needing a drink rather acutely after all that coffee, he had turned on her and, flushed with anger, had ripped the photo apart. Could he have? Well, he had; he had done it. How could she, then, after the quarrel, the anger, the tears, the hurt, the inevitable slackening off of the shock, put herself in Jerry's place? Was it the loss of youth that was getting at him, month by month, more and more? She could not understand.

No bad-looking woman herself, with a somewhat tall figure as slim as ever, wearing naturally and well the ageless kind of hair-do, long and drawn into a knot, that few women can get away with, she had been known, more than a few times, to look positively regal. "Cath'en, you jes' look so goddamn *nice!*" was how one of the party chairmen (Southern) had put it. But even men who got enthusiastic were not referring so much to sex.

With Jerry it was different; he was known as a "sexy guy," a phrase she was always overhearing. The marvel of it was to Catherine that the more deeply he got involved in working out the nation's politics, the higher he climbed among famous names, the sexier he seemed to become. It was like a top-level collusion, a psychic conspiracy in the dark world of power. Maybe he had hardly guessed himself that the two things could mesh so perfectly together. Until it happened. Then suddenly there he was, a fusion of nerves and looks, of leanness, strength, control and possible ruthlessness, with the ability, above all, of knowing how not to miss the moment, how to get a thing done and make it stick. Jerry sat and walked and stood with his head tilted slightly, eyes with lids slightly lowered, moving restlessly—they seldom stopped on anything. It seemed to Catherine that the approach of age to anybody as vivid with energy as that must be any number of years away, but she guessed he didn't think so. Tactful toward this tender subject, she never mentioned it, but far more reassurance than she could provide was in charge of the little airline stewardess, who went on talking and nodding, eyes drawn increasingly to Jerry Sasser, cheeks flushing a little, lips parting, forgetting that Catherine was there at all. Well. She looked down through the night air, down to a small forlorn diagram of lighted streets, the sparse glimmer of car lights along a highway. He would have it the way he wanted it as long as he could. She knew that now. She moved her head slowly, like a person afraid sudden motion may reawaken injury.

"*Vogue*, Mrs. Sasser?"

The girl—Radley was her name, she had told them: Jan Radley—had duties to see to. But had found, just for them, her V.I.P.'s, new magazines, not yet put in the leather binders. Catherine accepted, nodding her thanks, while Jerry said, "Gee, that's great," and began to leaf through two news magazines. "Jesus God!" he said.

This kind of language had still not gone over in a big way with surprisingly large segments of the American public, and Jerry seldom indulged himself in using it. Catherine turned to him. He was staring at a news item, and Catherine had time to reflect that even in a state of genuine alarm nowadays Jerry looked slick—a snap of the lens, a negative emerging from the wash, a caption, and here he would be: Senator's Bright Young Man Alarmed at News Story. "Son of a bitch," said Jerry. His finger jabbed into the page.

"What is it?"

"The very thing I stayed over to stop. This morning. But it was already in print. Could we both have got the days mixed up, him and me? Else how could we sit there and agree about not running something already running?"

She took the magazine from him and glanced at it. "It's just a little paragraph."

"A little paragraph predicting a big story about to break next week. You got to read between the lines a little, but not much. The point is, not only the big story but the little one too was supposed to be thrown out, killed completely."

She returned the magazine to him. "Oh, well, Jerry, they

print these things in five or six places. Maybe he didn't know how to stop it if it was already printed in Chicago."

"To hell with that. They're paid to think of that, these guys. They know. Me, I know too. We even discussed it. And, hell, this magazine must have been put on in Washington."

"We came down in Memphis," she reminded him.

He thought it over. "Some damn little Southern bureau, you mean? Didn't get the word?"

"Maybe there're just a few advance copies. Maybe it won't get around."

"Maybe, maybe. Maybe he's knifed me. Maybe the cards were stacked that way."

"You sound like a gangster," Catherine laughed.

But she could not put him off; in fact, she knew better than to try. His lean hand, dark-haired and tense, curled, then knotted around the magazine. He stabbed the end of the roll against the lounge table, snapping its center ridge. Ruined for other people, was the commonplace thing she didn't say. There would be no earthly use trying to communicate anything to him now, for until the plane landed it would be his cage and when it landed he would proceed as directly, as deviously, as cunningly as he felt impelled, to reach the point of release, of wising up, of knowing exactly how much damage it had done him to have openly and completely failed in a commission he had been specifically instructed by Senator Ogden himself to accomplish in Washington that morning. And then, my love, Catherine thought—as at that moment, the little stewardess returned, walking expertly as the plane pitched into a warmer level of air, moving solicitously from passenger to passenger but with, of course, the Sassers sky-written in large letters upon her—and then, my dear, if you're still around, your chance will come all right.

Politics, tension, women—if they soared to the moon or plowed away to the South Pole in an atomic-powered submarine, all three would come anyway, inevitably materialize, winging like pigeons out of the air, homing to nestle on Jerry Sasser's shoulders.

Jan Radley was sitting down on the chair arm again, her soft voice purring just adequately above the undertone of the plane. Yes, she did by chance have a lay-over in Dallas, and yes she would just love to come to the Longhorn Hotel for a party tonight, and if the Vice-President-to-be—oh, she had been for him from the first; why, she was one of the few who had said, Well, why don't they get him for Vice-President, and Edie had said, Now, Jan, that's the silliest thing, but she said, Well, I can't see why it's so silly, and sure enough it began to happen right on the TV set— "Well, now," said Jerry, "we're making a mistake raiding Harvard for a brain trust. What about some of these girls' schools, eh, Catherine?"

"Why, yes, I think so," said Catherine, and smiled her warm approval.

"You're going to have to brief me someday on just how you figured that. Is it a promise?" And he leaned over to light the cigarette of the trim blue-suited girl, who bent her cropped head forward over the flame.

Does it have to be this way? Catherine wondered. To think it did not have to be that way was like getting up on impulse out of a bed of high fever from snakebite maybe, and saying that nothing was the matter at all.

◆

Catherine Latham and Jerry Sasser had been brought up together in a little Texas town called Merrill, about a hundred miles north of Dallas. It was one of the last of those Deep South-looking, deeply shaded little towns before the big West begins with its dry immensities of mesquite, cactus, arroyos, foothills, tumbleweeds, jackrabbits, alkali, desert and dust. Therefore the shade seems sweeter in little towns like Merrill and the water seems clearer and cooler and tastes better than in towns to the east of there.

All her life Catherine was conscious of living on the edge of something; always, they had assumed it was the West, but when she was a child and they struck oil on her father's land it seemed too that they had lived for a long while without knowing it on the edge of wealth. The Lathams were rich then, in a home-made, prodigious way. Before that they had just been farmers; not poor-white, not even quite dirt farmers, but just farmers who like most other farmers in those days didn't ever make much money. In those precious pre-wealthy days, they had got along fine with all the countryside and even went to revival meetings to sing all about it: "Makes me love ev-er-rie bo-die," they sang. But the first oil Ben Latham got was off a neighbor's land; he had bought up Olive Hickman's oil rights back when Olive needed the money.

From then on there was bad blood: Olive Hickman said he ought to be allowed to buy back the rights for all parts, parcels and sections of land where the Lathams hadn't struck oil yet. Ben Latham said he would be crazy to sell them back; it was only a matter of time until the oil came in. He wouldn't let go of a single one. Olive threatened to go to court and sue, and Hickman children did not speak to Latham children. They beat hell out of them instead and threw brickbats at them. The Lathams left the farm and moved into Merrill. They bought the biggest house on the best street, a great big tall white Victorian house with lots of porches and a turret with a flagpole on it. Catherine's sister was a prissy little girl who told at school that the house was so big she couldn't walk around it in a whole day. Her brother Edward from across the room (it was during a hailstorm and all the pupils were congregated in groups up in the auditorium, being unable to go outside) said, "You hush that up. It's a lie."

Out at the old place, out at the farm, about a mile from Merrill, two old uncles were still living, Uncle Dick and Uncle Mark. They wouldn't leave no matter how much money there was. They wouldn't even buy one new thing for fear of having to part with something old. Catherine would go out to see them in the summertime. They would give her cold water from the spring and peel peaches for her with their little fine whetstone-sharpened knife blades, laying the peeled peach sections on pieces of newspaper for her to eat. They would tell her stories about Sandy Gulch.

Sandy Gulch was nothing but a great big sandbar along a little stream most people wouldn't even call a branch, let alone a creek. In Texas it was called a river. Sometimes it dried up completely. The cottonwood, the eucalyptus trees and willows grew all along the horizon of Sandy Gulch. The wind had swept and ridged the sand which lay in pure white corrugations or gathered into damp glistening metallic fans, almost black, like horsehair sofas. The importance of Sandy Gulch, besides being a good place to go walking or wading or have a picnic, was that in the old days, the wagon trains for the West had crossed here. Uncle Mark and Uncle Dick didn't exactly remember it, but they had heard tell of it all their days. The wagons had come creaking out of the east to lower with shouts into the road that angled down from the eastern bank of Sandy Gulch into the sand. There they would have to stop and unload, like as not, because it was hard enough in some seasons to take even a horse across Sandy Gulch, let alone a wagon load of furniture and provisions.

They always had trouble. People sometimes walked up to the Latham house, way back then, asking, "Ain't there some other way across all that sand?" "No other way," all the Lathams would say. "Won't you stay for dinner?"

"Then," Uncle Mark would say to nobody in particular, "there was that boy that broke his back." "Oh, tell about it!" Catherine would cry.

Why did it give her such a thrill, this tale of suffering? She did not know, but could securely feel that she was no different in this from everybody else. Negroes told about it, and Indians and white people, and the story went that on clear September nights you could still hear the boy crying, some said he was crying "Mother, mother!" but others said "Mercy, mercy!"

He had been trying to get a foundering wagon across the sand and as the wheels had strained up a series of willow logs, the logs had slipped and one wheel had come down upon him. They had lifted the wheel away, but his back was broken.

The whole countryside had come, rising up along the edge of the bluffs that rimmed Sandy Gulch. The boy lay in the center of silent human circles, which enlarged continually. No one could touch him for fear of further harm. Someone rode for a doctor. The doctor did all he could but the boy died, toward morning. He was buried in the Latham graveyard—they offered it, like offering dinner. Then the wagons pushed on.

"You know, Mark," said Uncle Dick, for there was always some new part of the story you got when it was retold, "when Papa went out West in nineteen-oh-two he looked those people up. They had a little dry-goods business by then. They said that boy was no blood child of theirs, but an orphan. He had come along with them from west Tennessee."

"Well, now," said Uncle Mark, "they sacrificed the orphan. Hee, hee. That's how come he was under that wagon doing all that risky work. Warn't none of their'ern. Hee, hee."

"They never felt that way," said Uncle Dick. "They mourned him like their own blood kin."

"It's all right to say," said Uncle Mark.

But Catherine sat silent, bare feet tucked beneath her skirts on the porch steps, lost in the terrible event.

"And then there was a wedding down in Sandy Gulch," said Uncle Dick, observing her.

"A *wedding!*" said Uncle Mark. "I never heard about that."

"Well, there was," said Uncle Dick. "You're hearing about it now."

"Oh, tell about it!" Catherine cried.

"There was a wedding," said Uncle Dick, and poked a walnut hull off the side of the porch with the end of his walking cane, "because a whole train of wagons got stuck in Sandy Gulch, and a boy from one family in the train had got right well acquainted with a girl from another family in the train, along the way, and since they had got so bad stuck and Saturday night was coming on and then Sunday—they were strict religious people and wouldn't travel Sundays anyway—it seemed like a good time for marriage. So they took out a team and rode for the preacher that very night. Built a big bonfire, you could see from right this spot, danced in the firelight, played the banjo, all barefoot and happy on the sand. Played a tambourine," he added, looking at Catherine.

"I've got a tambourine!" Catherine cried, as though Uncle Dick didn't know it.

"I never heard that story in my life," said Uncle Mark.

"Sister Bessie remembered it," said Uncle Dick. "She baked a cake and took it down next morning."

"If they's in that big a hurry to get married," said Uncle Mark, "there must a been a pretty dern good reason."

"Hush your mouth," said Uncle Dick. "This is my story, not yours." And he got up and walked off toward the scuppernong arbor, looking very straight and angry.

Uncle Dick was good and Uncle Mark was mean, but they both died, Uncle Dick slowly, in the hospital, with cancer, and Uncle Mark quickly: he got caught out in a rain on a fishing trip, took pneumonia in his left lung and was gone after three or four days of coughing and wheezing and swilling whiskey. When

Catherine was home on holiday from finishing school, she went to see Uncle Dick in the hospital. He seemed about half the size of the man she remembered and his color was very bad, but his expression was pure sweetness, his eyes terribly bright, gentle and mild, so that she felt struck through with them, as though with a glance from an angel.

"Well, upon my soul," he said when he saw Catherine, "she's a regular young lady, and pretty as a picture. Well, bless my soul." He never took any advantage in his life and didn't now, saying nothing the whole time they were there to make them feel bad about his dying.

"He's a lover of the Lord," said Catherine's mother after they left, and dissolved into tears.

Bad times came upon the Lathams after Uncle Dick died. The bad times started out like good times, for a new oil field came in, this time on Latham land which had been turned over to cattle, but the cattle were going to have to be inconvenienced for a time before they could return to former pastures and graze among the derricks. Catherine's mother remarked about this time that now the Lathams had their own oil they could have given the Hickmans those leases back after all. Since Mrs. Latham had been patiently echoing through the years everything Catherine's father said about how unreasonable, foolish, jealous, spiteful, sinful and downright ridiculous the Hickmans were, the note so casually sounded indicated wrong-thinking to a degree nobody could even contemplate. Catherine's father, who had been known to lose his temper over much slighter things, did not even go so far as to recognize that the remark had ever been made. Catherine herself could not believe her ears. Her sister Priscilla and her brother Edward were looking up from their plates and staring, but nobody spoke until Catherine said, "Why, Mother? Why give them back?" "Well," said her mother, "what do we need with all that money?" Catherine's father had never stopped eating, or even looked up. She might as well have been sick with high fever, talking out of her head. He presently got up to leave the table. "On Christmas?" the three children asked, and their mother said it, too. "Oh," he laughed and sat back down. "I forgot all about it being Christmas."

Soon after the New Year Edward left home. He vanished. Troubles were upon them.

Catherine always believed that the troubles started around the dinner table when her mother revealed she had never been heart and soul involved in hating the Hickmans. Christmas afternoon, which contained all the assorted boredoms and depressions of ten family Sunday afternoons in one, Catherine saw Edward out under the oak trees in the side yard, alone. She went out to him. He was a sullen boy who had possessed the turret from the first. The day they moved into that big house they had missed him, and by then he had it—a tower to himself. No one was allowed to enter there. Whenever Catherine thought of Edward it seemed to her that he had lived forever and had been frowning and disdainful while the pyramids were being built. He would work with cattle but didn't like oil. Nobody could get any reason out of him. Lately, of all things, he had made friends with Alice Hickman. She was so plain nobody went with her, but Edward called himself helping her pass some kind of entrance examination to business school. "Don't you know why she's doing that?

Don't you know what everybody will say?" Their mother could use any weapon to keep them away from common people, so she gave Alice a dark motive: family revenge. But all she ever had against the Hickmans, it now seemed, was simply that they were common. "Better watch out," their father warned her, behind Edward's back. "He'll marry her to spite you."

When Catherine came outside on Christmas afternoon, eating biscuit with strawberry jam, Edward threw an oak ball at an oak tree and said, standing on the damp ground (it was hard to get grass to grow in Texas) on the russet wet fallen oak leaves that spread evenly up the gentle slope of their yard, "I've got so I hate everything here."

That would be true anywhere, Catherine thought, for already she was getting to be a wise little girl and studied psychology 2B at finishing school and loved figuring people out.

"Why don't you go off to college, Edward?" she asked.

"I went for two years," he said. "What are you eating?"

"Biscuit and butter and strawberry jam," she said.

"Don't you ever get enough? God A'mighty. Fifteen different things for Christmas dinner. Is that a different dress?"

"Yes."

"God A'mighty. Fifteen hundred different dresses."

That was the last conversation she ever had with him. He left early in the New Year, had been, apparently, planning the move for some time, for when they broke into his turret rooms they found everything smoothly packed away, with accurate labels written on the outside tabling the contents. On each, in capitals, he printed: NO NEED TO LOOK INSIDE AS THIS LIST IS CORRECT.

His mother, weeping, as usual in time of trial, locked the door so that he would find everything just as he left it when he got back. A post card arrived the next month from St. Louis which said: "Am fine. Have job here. Do not try to find me." Others came from time to time.

Catherine and Priscilla, whispering, drew closer after this. Quivering with those ideals that mushroom in the hearts of little girls taught to mind their manners day by day in Victorian households, they solemnly decided to make up to their parents for the loss of Edward. "Poor Mamma and Daddy," they said. "But we won't hate Edward either." So they vowed.

It was about this time, in the summer, that Jerry Sasser started asking Catherine for dates.

Why had she married Jerry? There had been lots of other boys. And Jerry Sasser in those days was not even particularly good-looking; nobody mentioned him as being much of anything, and girls did not giggle pleasurably among themselves when they talked about him. He did not really belong in Merrill, his father having come there to teach economics at a small agricultural junior college somewhat contemptuously known as the "Aggie." Catherine married him because he understood how Edward had grieved her father and mother; she knew he understood because he said so. One by one, and altogether, he heard them out on this matter with serious sympathetic nods, and when they finished, he said, "I understand." But once she was alone with him on that same evening, when the family had confided in him, almost like a son, for the first time, Catherine went on to say, "I don't want you just to listen to them all the time. My feelings aren't just about family things. I want to live my own life, even if I do think I'll never get over what Edward did." And Jerry Sasser looked at her over the wheel of the car—they had driven out to look at Sandy Gulch in the moonlight, which after the picture show and the drugstore was the standard thing to do—and said, "I understand."

When they were not busy understanding all these grave issues about the Latham family, they were doing everything together in high school, joining the band, getting out the paper, and being in plays together. Jerry made the highest grades, Catherine the next highest—they leapfrogged each other, it was like a game. Poor Priscilla wasn't in it, she trailed way behind, but got to be a cheerleader for the basketball team and screamed her lungs out. Then it was over, speeches all made and dances done and Catherine off at finishing school where she kept right on, serious way down where it mattered, considering motives, her own and everybody else's, thinking that she would like to do the right thing; but among the deep drives of life she might as well have spent her time counting eggs or smoothing out quilt scraps. The result was the same whether she had spent even five minutes thinking or not. She quit school and she and Jerry got married in Merrill at the First Baptist Church, and went to live in Dallas for two years while Jerry studied law, a blissful bit of canoe-drifting toward the war.

The war changed everything.

There had been a reconciliation of sorts between Catherine's parents and Edward, who, after ten years, had finally revealed his address, along with photos of a wife, a shoe business, and two babies, grinning in sunbonnets. Visits were exchanged and babies hugged and checks signed. "I just never did like oil," said Edward, the only excuse he ever offered anybody for all the anguish he had caused. "I'd like to kill him with my bare hands," said Priscilla, who, if she didn't watch out, was going to be an old maid. She was terribly glamorous, kept an apartment in Dallas, had dozens of men on her mind, and went to New York every winter to see all the plays.

Just before Jerry was drafted, Catherine made sure she got pregnant. For six months, until the doctor made her stop it, she chased around the army camp circuit to be near Jerry, squeezed up in day coaches with people whom she found awful, interesting and funny by turns, went for days without a bath, slept in dingy rooming houses where roaches and spiders ran through at night. Catherine's mother got wind of what things were really like on these wild trips and bitterly complained. "I know we used to be poor," she said a dozen times a day, "but we were always clean. Suppose you had a miscarriage in one of those places, what could you do, who could you call on?" "It's as bad as the Hickmans," Catherine agreed. "It certainly is," said her mother. For years now, the girls had had their little jokes about the Hickmans.

When Jerry went overseas, the grey density of the war years came down over them in earnest. Catherine cried at night; she cried the baby into birth a month too soon, she thought; at least, it always seemed that way. Did it really rain so much during the war? In Catherine's memory she was always at the house in Merrill and it was always a winter afternoon, the big living room chill and empty (they lived on a side porch and only went to the front to get the Dallas paper from the door around dusk), the baby to be fed, and after that the war news on the radio. So one day during the war was as like another as the footprints of one man walking on smooth sand.

Catherine's father was in a plane crash. He wasn't killed, but shattered one leg which refused to knit. He had to use a brace and crutch and acquired the nickname "President Roosevelt." He would hobble up and down the one long business street in Merrill and say, "I got inter-rested in a knot of black Angus cattle down near a fence corner, and I forgot I was in the plane. I really forgot it. I thought I was in the Cadillac. Any fool knows you can't run a plane like you run a Cadillac. You *pilot* one and you *drive* the other. I just got my words mixed up and now I've got to pay for it for the rest of my life by answering when people say President Roosevelt. A fellow could preach a sermon on it, if he had half a mind to." A Mexican who was riding with him got killed in the crash along with a black Angus bull who wouldn't get out of the way. Mr. Latham went to some trouble and expense locating the Mexican's family and paying for the funeral, but beyond this thought scarcely more about him than he had about the bull, though both of them remained in the story, which he went on telling and telling—his something to match the war.

You got to know the war like a person, Catherine and Priscilla agreed. And found out more bad things about it all the time, they would add. Edward, a PFC who did not aspire to be a sergeant, got shipped off to Bahia, of all places. Here he cooled his heels for three years and complained about the officers and the food. Edward, Catherine thought, should always have kept a Gunnison County sunburnt face and a sun-squint to go with his scornful mouth; he should have stayed tall. Instead, ever since he had revealed himself in the shoe business in St. Louis, he had a shopman's pallor and he was short, or rather medium height, and all his complaining now sounded querulous and dense, as though he hadn't once, ever in his life, caught on to the main point.

◆

"He couldn't have shrunk," said Jerry Sasser, some minutes later.

He and Catherine were sitting on a balcony in a Delaware resort overlooking the Atlantic. It was five years after the war and now they lived in Washington, but had driven here to enjoy a weekend of fine June weather and now it was Sunday afternoon. Jerry lay in a deck chair, his legs stretched out long, his eyes blotted out with dark glasses, awake or dozing, none could tell, not even himself, for pleasantly encompassed with sun, sea smell and distant rush, he drowsed within the area of her voice, his mind as much in his body as in his head.

"He couldn't have shrunk. You grew."

Catherine laughed. "I guess so. But you've grown taller since the war. I know you have, Jerry."

She was leaning against the end of the balcony in a white open-backed sun suit, turning her back to the sun. She had roped a bright silk scarf around her tucked-up long blond hair. White became her; she was looking relaxed and attractive, and she knew it.

"I wish we had more time together," she said.

"Latham," he said, with a yawn. "Latham's polio worried us to death."

"But now that's over," she said. "I really feel that it is, Jerry. I'm convinced he's going to be perfectly all right."

"Provided he's careful," Jerry said.

"Yes. Thank God he's old enough to understand. And intelligent and sweet enough to cooperate. He'll be careful."

"I think so. I think he'd better be."

"Jerry," Catherine said, "do you realize that you're the only strong one left? Uncle Dirk and Uncle Mark are gone, Daddy was never the same after the plane crash, Edward ran away, Latham's had polio already, it looks like Priscilla is going to be an old maid—did you ever think about it, Jerry? That you're the only one?"

He sat up restlessly, suddenly tense, leaning forward on the footrest of his deck chair, one knee on either side of the low seat, and for a long moment he became very still. His wife, also, watching him, shielded behind her glasses, felt a growing stillness within her. She often experienced this now, when she observed him. He was handsome, excellent to a fine degree, matured and rendered solid, confident and aware by his officer's experience—wasn't all this a cause for delight? Why should the stillness he sometimes caused in her show an urge to grow mysteriously until it enveloped her in its own space, large as a canyon down whose emptiness she wandered, not even inches tall? Was it because he had his own stillnesses too, sometimes observed to be intense, but they never touched her own? When would it all change back again? He had walked out of the war like this—that was all Catherine knew. He gave her at last a long glance which seemed to increase the length of the balcony lying between them.

"Of course I think about it," he said. "Why do you think I have nightmares?"

"I didn't know you did, Jerry. You never told me."

"You haven't heard anything in months, you've been so worried about Latham."

"That's only natural," she said, after considering it. "You've been worried too."

"Maybe I'm sick too," he said with a laugh. "Maybe to be sick you don't have to be in bed with something they can name. It's the responsibility. Just being alive is a burden. I sometimes wish the name came with it—polio, plane crash, something handy."

Catherine was astonished. "You've never talked like this! Is it Washington, the world situation? What can you trace it to?"

"I wish I knew," he said. "Postwar let-down, I guess. Hell, I don't know. What you said just now about being the only man in the family—I've thought that myself, so you got me started. In the middle of the night I can wake up and feel it, it's like a pressure here"—he touched his chest—"like something hitting in time with my heart only not quite, sometimes there's just a shade of difference in the rhythm. Whatever it is, it's there all right. I don't think I'm special. I think a lot of people feel this way. There's too much *on* us now, Catherine. In Washington you get it strong, the full blast. For years and years it's going to be this way. There's no end in sight for us. I cannot see any more—this is the worst part—I really cannot see, even if there were an end, what the end would mean, what it would matter."

"If you came out the other side what would you find? Is that what you mean?"

"That's it. I have to keep running, keep going, keep thinking, working, moving, caring. But I don't know why. I can't see why."

Catherine longed to help. "I think it's Latham's illness that's depressed you. I felt so down myself, I—"

"Depressed? No, I'm not depressed. It's just that I live with this feeling, and so I can't care."

"Jerry, that's absurd. You cared when Latham was sick. You know you cared!"

Yet she did remember the first few dark days when Latham was so sick and they had crossed the street near the hospital to a drugstore, trying, as they had been advised, to eat and keep their strength up. She had essayed a milkshake and she would remember all her life what a struggle it was to force the rich mixture down her throat, through the denser element of her fear. Jerry had eaten a chicken salad sandwich which kept coming apart on his fingers—he would lick celery and mayonnaise off his hands. He was thin; there was a terrible thin deep line between his eyes. In the mirrored wall opposite they looked aging and tired, but felt as helpless as two lost children with a dollar between them to spend in the drugstore. Jerry said abruptly, as if to himself, "I don't see why our child should get well, more than another person's should. I just can't see it." "Stop," Catherine begged. "Don't say things like that. Please don't." He stopped, but she saw now that she had not made him stop thinking what he thought, nor could she.

The funny thing was that Jerry Sasser, back before the war, down in Dallas, Texas, used to teach a Sunday school class. That had pleased everybody but Catherine, but intent on being a good young wife, she had kept quiet about it, even encouraged him in his folly of earnestly believing that every lesson had some modern application, if one only could spare the time to think it over and see just what it was. Earnest was the word for Jerry Sasser in those days—earnest and sincere and kind. Just the finest boy, everyone told Catherine; just the sweetest boy, they all said. Jerry and Catherine used to lie on the rug together on Sunday evenings, drinking beer and telling stories about when they were children. Most of them were funny stories about Merrill, which they had never realized was such a crazy little place until they moved to Dallas.

Some were not so funny, such as the time Jerry recalled when his father had told him to go up to the history classroom in the Aggie and wait for him. It was a December afternoon and the building was on a high treeless hill, seamed with dry gullies, and a wind was blowing. There was nobody in the building. The history classroom was in the upstairs back corner of the building overlooking the steepest fall of the land. The ceilings were high and the walls white and bare and too much light was coming in through the high curtainless windows—too much light for the sort of day it was, dark and blowing outside but all the light collecting here. The blackboards had all been cleaned and all the maps rolled up but one, which was hanging unevenly and went knock, knock at the corner. Jerry sat at a desk on the back row and waited and waited. His father, who had forgotten him, came just at dusk, after three hours. "Why didn't you come on home, son?" he asked. The question was a sensible one but Jerry couldn't answer it. In the room he had felt himself to be abandoned in a timeless eternal blank dream, consigned there, with no will of his own. His father was a tall, thin, stooped man and Jerry had heard his patient, mild walk for a long time, first on the walk outside, then in the hall below, then on the stairs, the hall outside and at the door itself, and still he had not moved. "Why did I do such a thing?" he had asked Catherine. "Daddy never meant to punish me in any way, sending me there." Catherine had tears in her eyes from the story—poor little boy, such a nightmare! "Your father's too gentle to punish anybody anyway," she pointed out. They spent a good deal of time complimenting their in-laws, trying to "understand" when some little thing went wrong and someone behaved in a puzzling way. They soberly agreed that Latham and Sasser typified the finest qualities that Texas had to offer. Jerry's creed was: "Not cattle, not oil either, but *pee-pul* are the glory of Texas." Lord, thought Catherine, there are some things to be thankful for. If it hadn't been for the war Jerry would probably still be saying that, at every Rotary Club luncheon from Corpus Christi to El Paso. But no denying that in those days they had had lots of fun. They wore loafers identical except for size—it was fun to pretend you got mixed up. Catherine, who was still in skirts and sweaters, often wore a clean shirt of Jerry's for a blouse. He understood her liking to. "I understand," he said.

Had he really changed? Were the little boy alone and immobilized in the white high room on a winter's afternoon and the man who now heard something else in his breast beside his heart, one and the same? If this could be the case, it's up to me to do some understanding now, she thought.

"What are you smiling at?" he asked, smiling also.

"Just thinking. Just happy." She was always happy, more or less, to be with him.

Soon they ran down from their balcony and played with a beach ball on the sand. Jerry swam, but Catherine, who liked water the temperature of Texas swimming pools, sat in the sand and made a house, as she used to make at Sandy Gulch when Uncle Dick took her walking there. She thought of the little girl she had wished for but lost after the war, and now could hope for no others. "You'll have to be your own little girl," Jerry had told her, a remark she had clung to at the time for its tenderness, but which she now put aside without looking into it. As they were about to return to the hotel, they both looked up and saw a strange and shocking thing.

One of the balconies of the new postwar structure, some distance to the left of their own, had, just a moment or two before, loosened from the wall at one end and was hanging perilously, while bits of cement dropped singly from around the supports of exposed iron rods. A man, clinging to the wall, the windowsill, now the doorknob, was trying to brace himself for shoving a lady with an enormous behind through the door to safety. Even while the outcome was still in doubt the scene was ludicrous and Catherine and Jerry stood laughing helplessly: it seemed they could not stop laughing.

In the car going home, Catherine exclaimed, "We were awful to laugh. Those people might have been killed."

"It wouldn't have been any less funny if they had been killed," Jerry said, and they both, at this outrageous thought, fell to laughing again.

A thin rain had set in, enveloping the lush green flats of the country south of Wilmington. She shivered, the air was so damp.

She saw his profile, a regular, smooth outline, a handsome lightness against the night. On a long curve, the car skidded; a truck approaching, slipping slightly also, skimmed perilously near. Catherine straightened, rolled up the window and pulled a sweater out from the tumble on the back seat. We're into a new phase after Latham's illness, she thought. I have to learn new ways.

◆

Catherine's sister Priscilla took warmly, even urgently, and with a certain fury to the idea that Catherine herself had once advanced, namely that somebody else had decided during the war to impersonate Jerry Sasser, and that the true Jerry Sasser had been killed in a kamikazi attack during the war. Though she had had two martinis and though the years of pretending that nothing was wrong between her and Jerry now stood as separate as an island in the gigantic ocean of the obvious, Catherine still could make a pronouncement like this lightly, as though to wring humor out of anything could always clear the air.

"You knew he fell in love?" Catherine asked.

"No!"

"It was after he and Latham went up to Maine on that fishing trip. Latham had a glorious time; I've never seen him so enthused. They played; they made up games, fell in the water, discovered a deserted town in a cove. Latham went off to school simply walking on air. Two weeks later Jerry became strangely absorbed, schedule gone crazy, odd appointments at weird hours—breakfast dates—you'd think he was in college. It ended suddenly. You could almost clock it with a stop watch. I don't mean predict it, but see it end, like writing off the edge of a sheet of paper."

"What was she like? Did you see her?"

"I did, as a matter of fact. Accidentally. She was meeting Jerry on a streetcorner, heading for the Marine Room where they probably had a date—they saw each other at a little distance and walked toward each other. Two people you've never seen before can meet and you know right away if they're in love. As I watched them, I felt they were both strangers to me and that they carried this magic of their own meeting with them; it made the air between them melt away. It was like that. One could even almost think that moment was part of their destiny, that my happening to be there saved them from having to tell me. She was such a perfect-looking little girl—new grey fall suit and black suede pumps, very, very efficient Washington white-collar girl, but pretty too. And you've got to admit, anybody has got to admit, even if they despise him, that Jerry is as attractive as hell. So put the two of them together that day, the beautiful fall afternoon, just so glorious and alive, why, the two of them meeting, being in love—it seemed to sweep everything before it, to be the simplest most profound natural force in the universe. My heart went straight down, I confess. I had to duck in a drugstore for an excuse to sit down. But almost immediately I began to think: Well, it's really over now. I began to see my life ahead alone. I'd build a house in Merrill to spend part of every year near Mamma and Daddy. I'd go to Europe every year, pick a favorite country, learn the language. I'd see Latham in the summers, mainly to talk things over, no major move without consulting him, taking care not to depend on him, or make him sorry for me. Oh, I saw it all. And I remember I sat there thinking that the drugstore was so much like the one near the clinic where Jerry and I used to try to get milkshakes down when Latham had polio, and I was having just about as hard a time with the coffee. I thought, nobody but me will ever know how much I really had been in love with Jerry Sasser before the war and how I thought it was really him that came back and I went on living with the impostor for ages, not knowing the difference, and then I saw the real answer: that Jerry Sasser got killed in the war."

"Oh!" cried Priscilla. "It might even be true."

"Don't be a goose," said Catherine. "Of course it isn't true. But sometimes there's a false explanation that answers everything and if you can only persuade yourself to believe in it, then everything falls into place—"

"But you know we really could investigate," said Priscilla. She had learned by experience that if appropriate sums were released toward a certain end, the end was generally accomplished. Anything on earth, anything, to get rid of Jerry Sasser, whom she despised. Something else suspicious came to her that she had always wondered about. How did anybody who started out as an army draftee wind up as a naval officer? But she had had this explained to her several times, something about transferring from one service to another. She guessed that it had made sense, she just could not remember it.

"So what happened?" Priscilla asked, and as Catherine wouldn't have another drink, poured one for herself.

"About what?"

"This girl Jerry was chasing around after?"

"You mean the one he was in love with? Oh, just as I told you. Three weeks later he could not—honestly could not—remember her name. I asked him: Wasn't she awfully hurt? She's so young. He said that they'd had a long talk together and that she said she understood. He has a talent, you know, for getting people to feel the way he wants them to feel. Not just say they feel that way, but really feel that way."

"He's never made me feel any way he wanted," Priscilla bridled.

"He's never wanted to," Catherine said carelessly, and went off to see her mother, up the street in Merrill from Priscilla's house, fanning the air before her mouth to get the gin smell out.

"I do wish you girls wouldn't *drink!*" her mother was going to say.

◆

Four years after this conversation, Catherine's sister Priscilla stood in the entrance to the patio brushing her hair. She had sprinkled on it a new product, a dry shampoo. So clever was this powder, which she had bought at Neiman-Marcus, that it perfumed, imparted sheen, and dry-cleaned the hair of oil, and whatever part of it fell on the carpet would not do any damage whatsoever. As if anyone would brush their hair over the living-room carpet, Priscilla thought, but here she was brushing hers in the patio because she had something to tell her husband.

For she had a husband now; had him safe and sound. His

name was Millard Warner, and he was lying in a deck chair near the swimming pool, reading. He was not an inspiring sight to many people. He was flat-chested and thin with surprisingly strong, wiry arms and legs. His hair was thinning, he wore glasses and a heavy mustache, which was seldom trimmed. In motion he was full of nervous energy and staccato phrases, uttered more or less to himself, beginning, "Now where the hell is . . . ?" and "Wouldn't it really be best to . . . ?" Most of the time he was not in motion at all, but lay immobile with a book braced between his hands and his diaphragm. He read heavy intellectual things—Kierkegaard, Sartre, Camus—and daily, with a baggy seersucker coat pulled over his knit, open-throated jersey, walked with long strides to the post office, whence he would return, sooner than you would have thought possible, usually carrying a package of books. One wing of his and Priscilla's house was his study, and additional bookshelves were now being contemplated on designs in the office of a Dallas architect. He looked like a science professor in a Midwestern university, was Jerry Sasser's judgment of him. Priscilla was wild about him. Up to the time she had met him she had been terribly unhappy and restless. She had got herself engaged during the war to a 4-F who taught music and wanted to be a concert pianist. There had been deep and soulful love between him and Priscilla, but something had gone wrong. Jerry, when he heard about it, was not prone to sympathize. When Millard Warner came along Jerry thought him suspect. He would not, for one thing, take much interest in Jerry's carefully culled and skillfully updated collection of dirty stories. "Ummm," he would say and smile, rather more politely than otherwise, as though he had been told that somebody in Merrill had to go to the hospital. "I see," he would say. There is nothing worse than being left with an off-color story, well told, hanging in the air unreceived. It is like meeting in a bar to talk business with someone who doesn't drink. Jerry good-humoredly got rid of his bad feelings behind Millard's back. "He and Priscilla are going to make love right in the living room in front of the guests some night. One can only hope they go about it in the standard, grade-A, nationally authorized way." "I'm so glad she's happy now," Catherine said. "He never talks to her," Jerry pointed out. "I wonder if they've ever had a conversation. A flat-chested intellectual with his head in a book." "He looks nice when he's dressed," said Catherine. "In a dinner jacket he can even look distinguished. And he's good to Mamma and Daddy," she added. "That Indian," Jerry pursued.

There had been, in truth, some story, circulated before Priscilla married Millard, about his being an Indian. He had come from Oklahoma, after all, people who believed the story always concluded, as if this in itself were enough to clinch it. At a woman's church group meeting in Dallas, a week before Priscilla's wedding, Catherine and Priscilla's mother had encountered an old friend from Fort Worth who knew everything. "He's got Indian blood," the friend pronounced, "and don't you let her do it, now." Mrs. Latham worried and worried. "Well, Mamma," Catherine said, "what if he has? Some of *us* probably have Indian blood." "I never heard of it," said Mrs. Latham. "Well, what's wrong with it?" Catherine asked. "Wrong with it! We just don't want it, that's all."

But no one, considering Priscilla's sensitivities and her infatuation and confronting Millard's air of detachment, had the courage to broach the subject.

So they got married, and (too late now) had two little girls with their veins just full of whatever blood there was—they were constantly over at their grandparents' house where Mrs. Latham was always, in the back of her mind, watching fearfully for some manifestation of a blood strain different from the pure Anglo-Saxon stream of the Lathams. "Well, he could have been a Jew," Ben Latham consoled her. "Or a pauper. Any number of things."

Neither Jew nor pauper, nor (so far as had been actually proved) an Indian, Millard Warner attended to his interests in Oklahoma by flying up there once or twice a month. He chose, of course, as any civilized man would choose, to live near Dallas.

Priscilla, to get his head out of his book, and force his total attention to turn to Jerry Sasser, came and sat on his chair arm, and kept on talking. He did not look up, but took her hand, fingered the plump flesh of her arm, grunted at appropriate pauses in her talk, and went on reading.

"Catherine says Jerry is a changeling, an impostor. Catherine says Jerry really got killed in the war. Do you think so, Millard? Do you think it might be true?"

Millard looked up, blinking in the sun. He had really heard her, for the voice was there and the words, and presently, in a minute, he would have total recall—there! His answer:

"No!"

He laid aside the book, stretched, and as she had already made a place beside him on the edge of the beach chair, pulled her down toward him. She sank gratefully, nesting her warm full breasts into the hollow concave of his chest.

"But what do you think of Jerry Sasser? What do you really think?"

This was still Priscilla and she was still after Millard. They had had each other, a Mozart symphony on the hi-fi, and a couple of bourbons, in that order, and were now having barbecued chicken on the patio. They wore napkins tucked under their chins and their faces were smeared with barbecue sauce and grease. Millard, his attention somewhat easier to engage at present, bit a succulent globule of dark flesh from a thigh joint and said:

"He doesn't have enough backing. Nothing solid behind him."

Priscilla laughed. "Are you trying to say the Lathams aren't *solid?*"

"The Lathams are but the Sassers aren't. Jerry doesn't have anything of his own but a junior partnership in a Washington law office and the best set of political connections in the entire country. Connections." He dropped the last gnawed bone on the big ceramic platter. His greasy finger indicated the tangle. "This chicken, also, was once well connected. In truth, it was an act of God. And look at it now. Why didn't Jerry go into politics? He had an excellent start. Right out of the war with a sunburst of fruit salad on his gleaming white navy uniform, he got appointed to fill a representative's unexpired term. Jerry Sasser represented Tremont, Smith and Gunnison counties in the halls of Congress. He did very well, too. Why didn't he keep it up?"

"Whether he did so well or not is another matter. But Catherine always said he didn't keep it up because—"

"Oh, Catherine, Catherine! She's a good wife. She said what Jerry told her to say. No sir, Jerry Sasser had rather stay in Washington and mingle with big names than have to come back to Tremont, Smith and Gunnison counties every two years and win an election. He hates the grass roots. Among the grass roots, anything named Sasser is a small, particularly revolting, dedicated, serious, peripatetic bug. Puny educational institutions on the bony hillsides, odd earnest religious sects, no fixed dwelling, door-to-door canvassing for fanatic causes. In Washington, with his $250 suits and his $50 shoes, button-down shirts—"

"Oh, now," said Priscilla, "if you keep on I'm going to be on his side. I can't stand Jerry Sasser, but I don't see anything wrong with spending money on clothes."

"Provided you don't think they do such an awful lot for you," said Millard, and wiped his greasy mustache. "We really need finger bowls with this, Priscilla."

"But still you say you *like* him?"

"Of course I like him, as much as I like anybody. He interests me, if you want to call that the same as liking. He does not inspire me with brotherly love. I believe, you understand, that we are all imprisoned. But his particular type of prison is unique in my experience, and his reactions to his imprisonment are interesting."

"I think that's awful," said Priscilla. "You got that out of all those old books you read."

"You're always wanting me to talk to you more and once I get started you think I'm just awful. Don't go so righteous and

Latham and First Baptist Church on me. You love everything bad I can think of about Jerry Sasser. What's your gentle mother's kind and Christian expression toward people she disapproves of? 'I'd like to wring his neck.'"

"But they love Jerry. They don't know a thing—I'm wild for them to find out—well, not everything; nobody knows what that is—but some little piece of gossip to let them in on it that the idol may have one clay foot."

Millard sighed. "They like his masculinity. Gossip wouldn't discourage them much. They think in the long run his heart belongs to their own gentle Catherine. Can't you see how Victorian they are? He makes them shudder with delight."

Here Priscilla could really grow furious. "I think it's the most ridiculous thing to think for one instant that Jerry Sasser is so damn masculine and attractive. Why, I just know you're twice as good in bed as he is. All this build-up is the most suspect thing in the world! These swaggering types who have to lead every woman they see straight to the couch—"

"Oh, stop it," said Millard, who could not stand frenzies. He poured himself some more Frascati and reached for a teakwood salad bowl as big as a tub.

Priscilla had to clamp her jaws shut to stop herself and even then she sat with a frown between her brows so deep it seemed to have been cut there with a hatchet. After her engagement to the 4-F musician had broken off, Jerry Sasser had made a trip on business, quite by coincidence, to that very little insignificant town, about a million miles away, in the middle of nowhere, west of the Pecos. What did he do it for? By inquiry she found the business was genuine, all right, and this made her angrier still. Could he be there and not poke around into what should remain her affair alone?

"I'll make you angrier yet if I tell you that I often envy our brother-in-law," Millard said. "What feelings do you think I get when I see those little high school girls prancing by with their short pleated skirts, twirling their little batons at the football game and flicking their little tails? You think I don't wonder if there isn't some way to implement the glorious sensations they arouse? Don't you realize, Priscilla, that I, like most men, simply can't think of any way to go about it? At a certain period girls showed up for me, they were there, I was willing, things happened. Now—well, damn it all, how *does* Sasser get with 'em? I'm going to swallow my pride and get him to brief me when next we meet. So much for your faithful husband, my love."

All of a sudden, Priscilla dropped the whole discussion, and giggled. She sank down into her own complaisant, deeper nature. The things Millard had discovered about her—they were always there for her, and she sank sighing into the mass of them, memories of childbirth and nursing babies as well, all told, the biggest, most Texas-size feather bed in the world.

Only one last thought lingered, and with it a slight frown. "But what about Catherine?" she asked, half to herself. She wiped what conservatively must have been an entire tube of lipstick mingled with half a bottle of barbecue sauce off her face and rising, with a clank of wooden sandals and a chink of gold bracelets, went in to get the finger bowls. The maid was always off on Sundays.

◆

Catherine herself often wondered: But what about me?

She had a couple of admirers. One was an ensign who also had been attached to the same admiral's staff that Jerry had lucked his way into during the war. He never liked Jerry; even then, he thought, Jerry was watching for the main chance. The idea during many long hours of close contact at sea had had a chance to take root firmly. But it was only after he had seen Catherine's picture that he had begun really to despise Jerry Sasser.

After the war he returned to his hometown in Virginia where he took over an Office Supply Company from his uncle; but he came to Washington from time to time and eventually he looked up Jerry Sasser who asked him home to dinner. So he finally saw that photograph in the bright flesh, and the damage was really done. Now, occasionally, every month or so, he would happen to be in Washington on business. Occasionally, Catherine would consent to meet him for dinner or a drink. He was five or six years younger than she.

"You better get married," she counseled him. "Relieve the mind of all those Lynchburg girls."

"I may someday," he said, "just not right away. Are you going to stay married to that guy, Catherine?"

"Well, you see, Jerry and I—" Catherine began.

"You're both from Texas. You grew up together. You're

from the same town. You married young. That doesn't answer my question."

Catherine became cross with him. He was looking at her in a reflective, worried way, through plumes of cigarette smoke, one knee propped up at the corner booth in a smart, dark little restaurant where your heels sank an inch into the carpets, small red lights glowed on the tables and abstract paintings lined the walls. What does he take me for, she wondered, a child? He was just like Priscilla—people who fell in love late, they always felt they knew it all. They were invariably authoritative, boring, and wrong. "You may as well know," she said, "that I don't love you, Frank. You may as well know that I never will."

"I was cross with him," she told Jerry. "I'm afraid I've hurt him."

Jerry had just had a bath and was nearly dressed. He was stamping into his shoes, late, as usual; gleaming, warm and hurried, he looked up from tying his shoe. "He took you to a smart, dark restaurant with squshy carpets, little table lamps and modern art on the walls. Corner table. Lots of cigarettes. Long sad face."

She burst out laughing. He had once confided in her long after the affair with the little Washington secretary that she had always wanted to converse like people did in Hemingway or worse still in a Humphrey Bogart movie. "It isn't all tea and roses," he had said, "this having pretty little girls fling themselves at you."

Catherine's other admirer was a widower, a lawyer like Jerry. He was what is always known as a "fine man," and in his case the term was a true one. He was grey, getting bald, with a strong-featured face, like a Caesar, a man of some delicacy, and much finesse. He and Catherine dined once or twice when Jerry was away on business. Though he never said anything in so many words, Catherine felt the shift of the wind. She mentioned casually to Jerry that she had seen him. "Umm," said Jerry, "dinner in a Victorian residence in Georgetown—you'd never think from the outside that it was a restaurant. Up a lovely old-fashioned staircase, discreet small high-ceiled dining room, moldings, crystal chandelier, no menu. But where the hell is the ladies' room?" This time she became angry with him. "You wouldn't understand anybody like him." "I know when I'm bored," he said, "and so do you." Then he was running out with a briefcase. She supposed that Guy Owen was a little bit boring.

My mistake is telling Jerry, she told herself. I ought to wait until I get really attached to somebody, then he wouldn't be able to do anything. Wait till it gets to the point when I can talk about Jerry with *them*. But oh, she thought, taking her coffee into the living room and drawing the curtains open on the clear morning light, that's just the trouble. I can never stand to hear anything against Jerry, much less say anything. She put down her coffee cup and sank down at a table, thinking, her head turned toward the street below. It was morning and her long hair had not yet been properly put up. Anyone coming in might at first glance, seeing her hair's slight disorder, her long robe and averted thoughtful face, have judged her the perfect recipient for a man's lifetime pledge of aid and courtesy, if that was what she wanted. Anyone seeing her, knowing Jerry Sasser halfway well, might have asked, as Priscilla did, "What about Catherine?"

But the feelings she aroused in others could not win her true attention. At this moment she was experiencing everywhere the recent pressure her husband had incised upon the rooms she stood in. The sound of his departing footsteps in the corridor and on the stair lingered in her hearing; his scent collected for a moment in one pocket of air, gravid as mercury. I'm married to a myth already; he is known everywhere and so he's turned into an image. Anything he does or says is the same as anything else he does or says. There isn't any good or bad he can do, even to tearing up his own son's picture. The name is Jerry Sasser: that's all there is to know.

◆

The commercial airlines flight bearing Mr. and Mrs. Jerry Sasser with airline hostess Miss Jan Radley landed at the Dallas airport about nine on Saturday night. By then it was all arranged. Miss Radley would go to the hotel, shower and change, and come up to Senator Ogden's suite on the twenty-fourth floor. Jerry and Catherine would be there by then, or if not she only had to mention that she was a friend of theirs. Catherine was cordiality itself. At the exit from the plane, along with the other passengers, she and Jerry received from the little stewardess their professional goodbyes. The girl was looking extremely pretty, her cheeks slightly flushed already with an evening's excitement at a really important big-name gathering in prospect—could hardly wait to tell Edie all about it probably, when next their paths crossed—but she stood her ground expertly at the door (one of a whole nation of amazing little girls, thought Catherine), and did not give any inkling of the game away. Maybe they'll all outsmart Jerry some day, Catherine thought. She put nothing beyond these small professional creatures. She envied their constant command. She had even once had breakfast with one, who, she was positive, had crawled out of Jerry's bed not thirty minutes before. That was in New York; she had flown up from Washington in the early morning, bringing his dinner jacket, as they had to appear at a U.N. function. The girl had passed herself off as a typist and stenographer, and her typewriter was there all right, along with her neat overnight case. They had all had breakfast together at the Beekman Towers, at a table overlooking the East River.

In the Dallas airport Jerry went straight to the newsstand to buy a copy of the magazine which had disturbed him on the plane. The regular concessionaire was off duty; a substitute suggested that perhaps the issue had already sold out. At any rate, there weren't any. Jerry started to go back to the plane for the one he had read there. "There'll be plenty at the hotel," Catherine said. Besides, looking back through the glass walls out to the runway, one could see that the plane had already been closed and was now being taxied away for servicing. The stewardess was nowhere in sight. "At the hotel," Catherine repeated. Jerry agreed.

But the hotel had none either. "Not till Monday, sir," they said. Jerry left the bags and Catherine with the bellboy and went out to a news shop. "What did they say?" Catherine asked when he returned. He was puzzled, worried. "They said not till Monday, too. Come to think of it, they're right. That magazine never gets to the stands before Monday."

"Well," said Catherine, "you know that story Senator Ogden tells about his mother. She was clearing out a closet and found a four-year-old newspaper. She thought the world was going right down the drain. She thought it was that day's paper."

"You mean I got an old one. Look, maybe the strain has been terrific, but it's not that bad. Christ." He had somehow managed already, by doing nothing more than stand in the middle of the floor and think, to inspire a collapse in the room's original order. The ashtrays were already full of cellophane, and twisted empty match folders. There was a blob of ash on the rug, and the bedspread looked to have been stirred with a spoon. Now he crouched by the telephone, his coat thrown off in a heap beside him. Twice his hand hovered toward the phone. The stewardess upstairs? Washington? The magazine's local bureau? No need to appear anxious. His hand dropped back.

"You'd better get dressed," he said to Catherine.

She stood by the window, looking out. "I'm getting very tired, Jerry. You remember what happened in Chicago. Well, Jerry, just this once, I'm asking you please to leave that one alone. Not that she's any different from the rest, not that she'll mean any more or any less, but just this once, please, pass it up."

He sat wriggling his toes in his sock feet. As always, his energy surmounted her. "She hasn't offered me anything," he pointed out. "You're thinking of going home to Merrill," he went on. "You've got all the symptoms. 'Oh, save me God from this weary corrupt political life and let me get back to the real thing and find my peace of soul!'"

She smiled. He was, in a way—given about a thousand-point handicap—good for her. The more she dodged the more she ran straight into him. But now, chain-smoking, with cuffs turned back on his wrists, he was back with the big worry. "That damned article."

"Ogden will understand," she said.

"It isn't a question of understanding," said Jerry. "It's not a question of anybody's feelings or loyalties or friendship or any human emotion. If I pull the necessary wires to keep Ogden balancing on the tightrope, riding a bicycle with a kitchen chair on his head and a monkey on top of that holding a pink umbrella, to stay in the clear on both sides of the civil rights question in order to keep the Texas vote in the fold, then nobody ought to know how the wires were pulled. But if there's a slip and everybody catches on, and if it further turns out that Jerry Sasser had any part in it, then Ogden is going to have to say I'm a half-witted friend of the family he got to lick stamps for him on weekends. He'll understand, sure. We'll all understand. We'll be the best of friends, before, during and after. It's just a question of who's going to still be around on Election Day Plus One. I'd like to be there," he concluded in an offhand way, looking at her reflectively, as though she were somebody he had just met the other day. "What dress are you wearing? Tell Jerry. Tell Jerry what dress."

"Jerry," said Catherine, "if it hadn't been for Daddy you never would have been dreamed of in a thousand years when they needed somebody for an unexpired term in Congress. You know that, don't you? You do realize it?"

"Catherine, dear—" He had been bending over to open the suitcase, ready to pull out for her, as he had often done before, the dress he chose for her to appear in. She was to provide background music and her dress was important. Now he rose and stood with his feet apart, his eyes closed, his hands halfway toward clenching. "Catherine, dear, we simply don't have the time to embark on one of our super-special quarrels. We'll do it tomorrow. At 10 A.M., after breakfast, before leaving for Merrill. Appointment for quarrel with Catherine."

"I only mean to state," she said, "in a very brief way that takes no time at all—one thing. I could leave you, Jerry."

"My only darling, you've said it to me time and time again. The last time we thrashed through it stroke by bloody stroke, we agreed to postpone our decision until after the election. You remember? In San Francisco, Mark Hopkins, weekend in August."

"I remember. You needn't talk to me as if I had gone permanently out of my mind."

"You agreed to try your level best, remember?"

"I do remember."

"Well, are you? Honestly, now, are you? Is this your level best? Catherine Latham's level best?"

The phone rang. He was on it like a panther, poised, waiting the second ring, no need to sound too eager. "Hello . . . oh, hello. Mrs. Sasser? Why, just a minute. Catherine?" He handed her the phone. It was Jan Radley. "Why, anything you have will be okay, I'm sure," Catherine said. "I'm wearing, now let's see. . . ." Jerry had already lifted it. "A black and white cotton sheer, off-the-shoulder. Does that help?"

"She didn't call about a dress," Catherine said, hanging up.

"She knows perfectly well what to wear. She called to hear the sound of my voice, to know which way the wind was blowing. I'm getting too good at this."

Jerry gave her an alarmed glance. Was she going into what he called one of her "truth serum" phases? Once she had circulated around an entire room telling everyone in great confidence and sincerity, something that went like this:

"Oh, well, you see, I'm here along with the wives of other important people just to present an image which ordinary people enjoy. It makes them feel safe when men on the inside are nicely paired off with attractive women who wear pretty clothes and look nice and smile like this. This dress is no accident, though I'm glad you like it. It's necessary, you see, to present an image. One thing to remember."

It was Senator Ogden who had heard the greater part of this and gleamed from under his eyebrows, summoning Jerry. Jerry had fended his way, talking, through the room, to Catherine's side and, smiling affectionately, with an arm around her shoulders all the way through the door, he had got the hell out of there with her. They walked down the corridor to their room together. Inside, he was terribly gentle. "Did you get too much to drink, darling?"

She put her hand to her brow. "I couldn't think of anything else to talk about. It seemed a relief just to let go and tell the truth, and a pretty good joke too. Anyway I was only quoting you. That night after the evening in San Francisco when you tore Latham's picture you said the same words—"

"Catherine, listen." He crouched down before her and took

her hands firmly in his own. "I've told you many times that I didn't tear Latham's picture. It got torn that night, but *I did not do it.*"

"I don't believe that," she said. "I never believed it. Who else would have done it, if you didn't?"

"Tell me this. Did you see me do it? Did you?"

She drew her hands back from his grasp, struggling to get free. He released her. "I think I saw you."

"But you aren't sure?"

"Yes, yes, yes! I'm sure. I know, I know it. I know you did it."

He would not recoil. His face before her, below and before her, did not draw away. He was steady and courageous, and how could she strike, how could she reject, a really steady and courageous man?

"Do you really hate me, Catherine? Do you really hate me so much as all that?"

She broke into a stifled cry, burying her long fingers in her hair. "You were angry when they all left. You were angry. You can't deny that. You were holding the torn picture and you were saying, 'Catherine, don't show pictures like this any more.' You said, 'It is necessary to present an image.' You know you said it. You know you did!"

"I'm sorry. I see how you took it and I'm sorry I said that. I've told you over and over how sorry I am. The thing you never wanted to understand was that with that particular group we had to appear young, we had to detail a program of youth, young marrieds, and what they want for the country. So when we get right in there with the babies and the nurseries, pablum, croup, and God alone knows whatever else can happen between midnight and four o'clock, here you whip out a set of photographs of a student at a boy's school in Massachusetts, and say, Here's our son!"

"Oh, it's so funny when you tell it! Oh, it's so awfully funny."

"Do you really hate me so much, Catherine?" Now he took her hands down out of her hair and held them again, this time in only one hand, while the other went up to smooth back her hair.

"No, I don't hate you. I wish I could hate you. I've tried and I can't, but I wish I could."

Now with her hands strongly secured, her hair smoothed attentively, she would hear, "If you can't hate me, then maybe you can love me a little?" The face would be there, courageous and strong.

She would think, fighting back the melting point, trying to freeze back the tears: Wait, wait! He doesn't mean it. I know from experience he doesn't mean it. I know better than he does he doesn't mean it. He hasn't got it in him any more to mean anything. Jerry Sasser lost whatever it is that it takes to mean anything during the war. It's been gone ever since and I know it is, I know it is. Still I have to give him my love because it is my love and it belongs to him and if I can't give it I might as well be dead.

So then she would start to cry and then it was as good as over in the strong sure tangle of his closer contact, when the black thoughts shivered away and disappeared as lightly as a dress, and could not, ever, have been true of her and Jerry. Then she would be lying in the dark, released, but with his warmth all within and about her still in the pitch dark, the hot dangerous electric snarl that had been, so shortly before, herself, all smoothed out, and her mind emptied of all but its own tranquility listening to the air conditioner purr away and to Jerry's muted breath and to her own occasional sigh on the pillow still slightly damp—this dampness, these small sighs being all that was left, it would seem, of their crisis.

Just the same, the sort of thing that had happened at that gathering in Ogden's hearing, could not, naturally, be risked. There was just no telling whether she wouldn't get going again some day and what would she say then? For while there were naturally a good many things she missed completely, there were also a good many things she heard and grasped and could articulate. She would of course know better than to say the speeches always threatening to break through. But sometimes she grew possessed and what was the cause? Anger? Or a sense of being—perhaps by Jerry, but more likely she would have preferred to say by whatever had taken up headquarters in Jerry's spirit—deliberately goaded and enraged.

Jerry spent a good many quiet hours with her. His physical energy stood him in magnificent stead: another man might have gone down under the strain. He took her to a psychiatrist, or rather to a whole clinic of them.

This was in Denver. Catherine feverishly inquired of a number of authorities that now seemed assembled to assist her what on earth was the matter with her that she should be here in the first place. In conversation, of course, all roads led to Jerry, and everyone very soon saw that without Jerry there (he had gone back to Washington with Senator Ogden's entourage) nothing could really be accomplished. Catherine herself realized that whereas with Jerry there rare and splendid six-syllable names might be attached to her by way of diagnosis, without Jerry she had to be labeled a victim of nervous exhaustion.

Jerry wired that he simply did not have time to be psychoanalyzed, but that he would be able to spend a weekend with her doctors and perhaps, given enough money, they might consent to thrash out the whole problem in a couple of long-running sessions. Catherine tried her best to persuade the doctors on this point. She said that they had no idea what Jerry was capable of once he began to work at anything. His powers of concentration and retention, his capacity for long hours of discussion, his strange, driving energy . . . she had to stop.

Expressions crossed their faces which she could not interpret—they were "making" all kinds of things out of this, she realized. But it was true; what she was saying was true. She took heart from the presence of truth and pushed on.

"We went up to Maine to visit our son last summer. Our son is not terribly strong. I think I told you—he had polio when he was eight years old. But he has a wonderful spirit, fine and thorough in everything he does, though not remarkably quick like his father. For a long time now he's wanted to be a naturalist. He studies the habits of creatures—fish, birds, deer, wild life of every kind. He got the idea at camp and now he goes every summer to some area in New England—oh, lots of them with the same idea correspond and there are magazines too—they know which areas to study in and what to look for. So my husband—Jerry—and I took him there, to his area, and saw him fixed up in quarters, and then Jerry, just all of a sudden, out of the blue, took an interest in Latham's work. He began to question him before dinner and all during dinner—we had an early dinner and Jerry wouldn't even take a drink, not even a cigarette—all his habits seemed to drop away and change in this great demand for knowing about Latham. I couldn't have got in a word if I'd wanted to, because Latham had brightened—oh, he was so happy, I've never seen anyone so happy. There was still an hour or so of light, so he took Jerry into the woods with him and showed him everything—how to watch for things, how to get pictures, habits of wild creatures—and then they came back, walking so eagerly in the dark across the meadow and upstairs they went past without a word to me—not that I cared, it seemed a grand thing to see them so absorbed. I thought it would be that way for good now. Latham brought out all his gear and explained the use of everything, showed all he'd done before and all he planned to do. They were up very late, and in the morning I drove Jerry to get the train and went back for a day or so with Latham before driving home. Oh, if I could make you see! That was all there was for Latham—he gave Jerry everything, so willingly, completely, all his treasure, and then what? Why, then nothing. Daddy is gone away, he finally said. And I saw he knew that Jerry had really gone away. He had already forgotten, until it may be useful to him someday to know about pheasants. He had forgotten Latham, too. You know when this happens, when you are forgotten. It was hard, because at the moment he had really entered into Latham's world, every inch. An experience is his when it happens, it's totally his own. He drains it dry perhaps, but he understands—most people leave with an impression, something here"—she touched her heart—"but when Jerry leaves, why, he has it all like something wrapped up to carry off. Maybe this is what separates us. Oh, I don't know!"

The men were silent. There were three of them and they had called her in to speak informally, it seemed, but something had got her started talking exhaustively and they let this continue. She felt that this, too, may have been intentional, for by inclination and training they must have been among the most devious people in creation. Their eyes were kind, concerned and quiet. They regarded her from behind desks.

"Perhaps I'm simply not on his level," she went on, collecting herself. "It's only normal for a man to be attracted to pretty girls and for a man like Jerry they would of course be constantly around him. I asked him to leave me and go with one of them, but he says he loves me and doesn't want anybody else. I think around girls Jerry may be the same as he is around Latham with his leaves and snails and microscopic film: he can't leave till he has everything, until he's taken all there is to take; then he can forget it. He has to understand and that's the only way. Is it so bad? I read somewhere once the only way to understand an oyster is to eat it, and then you've changed it slightly, haven't you?" She thought this rather funny, but the men did not smile.

"What do you think drives him?" one of them asked her.

She had begun to enjoy herself. Her words were coming easily and freely and the captive audience was hers as long as the bills were met, along with the quietly carpeted corridors, the flower-filled salons and sun decks with their views of the snow-topped Rockies and the grand distant cascading green of the lower forests. The thin air seemed Olympian and one began to get glimpses of what one might achieve—a rhapsodic mastery of life. Now they had stopped her.

"Drives him?" she repeated.

"What about his parents, his family? Are his mother and father living?"

"His mother's dead. His father—is a professor in a small college. He teaches economics."

When she said it like that, the way she always said it, a picture would form, of course, in the listener's mind and that picture would be all right. They would see Jerry growing up, a boy in a modest, but comfortable professor's house, dark living room with a Victorian oil or two, leather-bound sets behind glass shelves, the smell of a study, ink and paper mingling with familiar bathroom and tobacco odors, see him mowing a small lawn in the summer, perhaps, with his father, eating off some really good English china his mother had left, in a dining room—sunniest room in the house—where a bay window overlooked a bed of petunias. But thinking this herself as she had always done in the past as a means of impressing just that image upon a listener, she realized that here and now was not the time to create a false impression, and that made her, like one of Latham's small wild animals going about its usual business in the deep and dappled forest, pause. She saw that she had created the false impression of Jerry's father and of their house and life together not only to help Jerry—though it had at first been mainly that—but also to help herself not to think of the real thing, the true picture, which was not a pretty one.

The truth was that old Professor Sasser was a smelly old man, either from some ailment or from lack of bathing enough, and his house was a dusty little bungalow affair with all the paint worn off, set in a sunken space down below the level of the chipped and broken sidewalk, where the cows had wandered before the cement was dry, the same sidewalk that climbed up the long windy hill to the Aggie. There was a little entrance porch to the house, and two overgrown althea bushes on either side kept you from getting even a glimpse into the two front windows.

Jerry had taken Catherine there first one Sunday afternoon to call on his father. It was a week after they had got engaged and she had yet to darken the door. There were no rugs in the house. It was dingy and smelled like Professor Sasser. The board floors had been swept and there were some wicker chairs in the living room and some silly silhouettes hanging on the walls such as a woman of no taste might have put there—girls in flounced Southern-belle costumes flirting with gentlemen in tailcoats, girls of the 'twenties with long cigarette holders, leaning over wrought-iron balconies in the moonlight. The bookstands were full of books that did not look like books that other people had. They were thick with dark blue and dark green bindings. Catherine supposed they were textbooks. Jerry, who had grown silent and shaky, brought three glasses of iced tea on a red lacquered tray and they all sat there trying to think of something to say and feeling awkward and hot.

"I hear," said Professor Sasser, "that's you're to be Jerry's wife."

She nodded. She was trying to fight off thinking of what her mother was certainly going to point out, that being poor was one thing but being clean was another.

"You know, I suppose," Professor Sasser said, smiling at her, as superior, she thought afterwards, as a cannibal prince, "the one true way to live?"

"I've already told Catherine all about it," Jerry said quickly, "She's going to read the books."

"I have put them aside for her," said Professor Sasser. "I have many students at the agricultural college whose lives have been deeply affected by these precepts." He reached out a long hand and tapped his strong, yellowed nails upon the covers of a group of books set out on a table nearby. "If you want to understand my son and be a good wife to him, then you must read all of these books. There are many more, but I myself have selected these, out of all available."

Economics books, she thought, trying to steady herself into some orbit of reason, for even when the eyes of the smiling fanatic are gleaming into our own we still continue to trust that the world is, after all, a sane place, and that the little monsters that are now skipping across the twilight grass to meet us will only turn out to be toadfrogs or rabbits.

Professor Sasser continued to smile. "The mission of Jesus Christ in the world has been widely misunderstood from the very first century onwards," he said. "This, as Jerry must have long since explained to you, is the first thing to understand."

"Daddy," Jerry put in, "I think we both talked it over, don't you remember? We both said it would be better for Catherine just to take the books, and she will take the books, won't you, Catherine?"

"Oh, yes," said Catherine. "I'll take the books." She felt Jerry's terrible embarrassment. It was writhing all over the room.

"It goes back," Professor Sasser continued, smiling, "to the precise, original Hebrew meaning of the word *blood*, in contrast, you would understand if you had studied the original language, to the Greek meaning of the same word. Now, in the Greek—"

"I didn't know you taught Greek!" Catherine exclaimed. She was young then and the solution was born of desperation, but her voice was innocent and soft, her eyes wide, and somehow, somehow, it was going to work.

"Well, no, I don't teach Greek, but does that prevent me from studying, learning? No more than it prevents you—"

"I thought you taught economics, and here I learn that you teach Greek, too. That's marvelous!"

"No, I don't reach Greek, but I—"

"But Jerry told me you were a teacher, a professor out at the Aggie."

"He was entirely right."

"He teaches economics," Jerry said. He was looking down at his hands; it seemed he was going to cry.

"What's Greek got to do with economics?" she asked.

When they walked back home together, down the long hill, through the Merrill business section, all shut up for Sunday except the drugstore—it was Easter Sunday, which was why she was home from school—they did not say a word to each other. Reaching, at the opposite end of town, the concrete posts and iron gate before the Latham property, Jerry Sasser spoke at last. "I guess you're finished with me, Catherine."

She had been so stricken with disappointment on the way home she hadn't even noticed when they passed the drugstore. I knew he was old and he was poor and probably not very presentable—that's all okay—and I even realized he might be dirty, but I never dreamed he was crazy. She kept thinking this, every step of the way. She was terribly disheartened. "I don't know," she said to Jerry Sasser. "I'll have to think it over."

He looked down at the books he had been carrying for her. "If I take these back home," he said sadly, "Daddy will say I—he'll say I—It's just this crazy religion!" he burst out. "When he's not on that, he's not so bad. Really and truly, he's not!"

"Okay," she said finally. "I'll take the books." She watched him go away up the long familiar sidewalk. What an awful place to go back to, she thought. I couldn't stand it for even one afternoon; if I had to spend the night there I'd just die—I wouldn't sleep a wink. But he's lived there for years and years. Years and years.

She didn't know what she thought. She watched him all the way up the street until some dust blew across the road and her eye lost him. Then she went disconsolately into the Latham house—the big comfortable white house with the turret. It was there she first recognized that the impression of horror had caught firm hold of her.

Before she went back to school, Catherine hid the books in the attic. She thought of them sometimes in the night, sitting up near the ceiling, behind an old trunk, as a huge spider might sit dormant, hairy and full of blood. She had stolen a glance at the titles: *True Origin of the Blood Union of Messiah's Brotherhood. The One Revelation: Blood Union of Messiah's Brotherhood.* But she never opened them at all.

That summer, after she had not seen or heard from him in three months, Jerry Sasser suddenly reappeared. They saw each other daily at the new swimming pool. In a town as small as Merrill, there was no way not to see one another.

◆

When Priscilla heard that Catherine was in the hospital, she flew up to Denver to see her. Who told her was never clear. She heard in the same way she knew about Jerry's vast infidelities—she was a person who heard things. She called Jerry in Washington. "Sure, Catherine's out there," said Jerry cheerfully. "Why don't you go out and see her? Tell her I can't get away till next weekend. I was going to call her tonight."

Priscilla foresaw Catherine wandering about in a snake pit full of women in grey cotton dresses, X-rayed twice daily for suicidal weapons. Instead she found her smartly dressed, reading a novel in a room which looked out on Pikes Peak. The room was full of flowers. Catherine was glad to see Priscilla and had arranged that they were to go into town for lunch together. It was all so very pleasant. "Nervous exhaustion," Catherine said. "Really. You want to read the chart? I sneaked and saw it myself, one day in the office. Not a word about anything crazy. None of those sixty-four-dollar words. It's just that Jerry has too much energy for me. We have to keep going day and night right on through the election. He just never gets tired."

"Why do you have to go with him at all?" Priscilla demanded. She had asked too many questions already. Nobody ought to have to put up with so many questions as Priscilla could ask.

Nobody would but Catherine. Priscilla regarded Catherine as a sort of saint, or angel.

"Well, he says that I help to make a good impression, 'to present an image,' is the way they put it. I think that's rather sweet, don't you?"

Priscilla did not think that anything about Jerry Sasser was sweet. About Jerry she felt at bay in the entire family. Her mother and father, she felt, had every reason on earth to see through him; yet her mother never called him common and her father could not see that he was an opportunist. Jerry had always refused, technically, to touch a penny of Latham money, thus endearing himself to Latham hearts. But something more, something more than this was afoot, something that pierced below reason had linked them to Jerry Sasser. He was the son that Edward had failed to be. There was no explanation that Priscilla could discover for this peculiar idea. Her parents and Catherine had decided upon it without once referring any part of it to her. She could only be aware of it, and it enraged her.

Now, in Denver, in a pleasant Scandinavian restaurant with another picture post card view out the broad windows, on a bright chilly spring day, Priscilla felt thwarted again. Catherine looked well, they chatted on and on, the food was good, and with life so pleasant, so American, so secure, what on earth was there to worry about? Priscilla went home feeling foolish. She would take it out on Millard probably. Catherine realized all this, but did nothing about it. With a kiss and a bright smile, she waved her sister off. The thread of vision parted, and she turned back into the hospital with a dark heart.

She entered the pleasant room with all the flowers and closed the door. Every day they are getting closer and closer to it, she thought. Sooner or later, I will have to tell them and they will have to know. I can't keep it from them forever. Jerry must know I have to get it out some way, or he wouldn't have left me here. As she stood and thought of it, she felt it coming back again, starting to flash and race through her nerves as though she were wired for a certain current and once the circuit met a whole network jarred to life to tear at her. At such times she could look at any wall and it would begin to quiver.

It had happened in a city—oh, which one?—they had been in so many. Oh, in Kansas City, of course. Where Ethel lived, the old classmate whose acquaintance now had dwindled to a yearly note on a Christmas card. Ethel had got herself married to the owner and publisher of a string of corn-belt newspapers and every last one of them now supported what Jerry Sasser was committed to regarding as the wrong party, the one the country did not need. Ethel was terribly happy, her husband was rich and respected, she had two fine boys, and did not know how antiquated, not to say wrong, not to say even dangerous, the politics of her entire situation in life had become. It was the part of friends in such a case to warn her, especially since her husband was so influential. However, it must be done tactfully—so, at any rate, Jerry and Senator Ogden agreed after running through a sampling of Ethel's husband's editorials over the past eight years. Catherine was commissioned to call Ethel for a luncheon date. At lunch, if things went well, she was to try and get Ethel and her husband to come up to Senator Ogden's hotel suite for cocktails and even, if things went very well, for dinner. The lure was "to meet Jerry," who couldn't get away for lunch.

All this strategy proved entirely unnecessary. Ethel's husband, though in editorials he weekly slaughtered and supped on members of Senator Ogden's party, proved to be the kindest and most approachable of men, who invited himself along to lunch, just to meet Catherine, whom he had heard so much about. Ethel was getting too fat and looked expensively dowdy, but her husband was even fatter. He was careful with himself; indeed, they both gave the impression of being very careful about life; one could suppose that they still made out household budgets together and that the items did not include liquor. He held the floor, talking to the two women as though they were little girls; his glance dropped goodness and blessings upon them. One felt after fifteen minutes that he owned Kansas City. The state also was his domain; he played tunes upon it, benevolently hymning its prosperity and common sense. It was he who insisted that they should not wait for the appointed invitation (which they would be glad to accept), but should run up to Senator Ogden's suite right away— "Right away?" Catherine asked. "Well, just let me call." "You can call from the lobby," Ethel's husband boomed, and waved for the check. Everything was swept ahead of her, and the tide was all cordiality, hospitality, and the genial conviction of goodness, of doing the right thing, of pressing warmly the opponent's hand, he who was the guest in the plentiful strong household.

Ethel's husband was the sort of man who wore brown suits to which his own male odor was indissolubly attached, and said, "Excuse me," as he went forging ahead across a hotel lobby.

"You must let me call," said Catherine. "Honey," said Ethel, "Catherine feels she better call." "Right, right," he agreed.

Catherine rang twice but the line was engaged each time. She did not know what to do. Stopping Ethel's husband once was a problem; stopping him twice was an impossibility. They soon found themselves lined up together in the elevator where Ethel's husband removed his hat, a tan straw with a polka-dotted band. "Just let me go first," said Catherine, as she put her key in the lock.

She felt distinctly that it had been a mistake for them to entrust her with any political maneuvering; that she was not clever enough, nor quick enough, that she had nothing to trade with but sincerity and good will and that since these were genuine she could not turn them off and on at will. They were obviously of no use at all when it came to stopping 260-pound newspaper publishers from going wherever they wanted to go. She was already feeling resentment toward Jerry and Senator Ogden, whom she fully expected to find with their sock feet on the coffee table, drinking beer and scribbling notes and skipping about the country by telephone. Instead the room was empty; it was even in good order. There was a crumpled hankerchief lying on the couch along with a pair of short white gloves, and the telephone was lying off the hook.

Catherine had advanced to the center of the room before these things came together in her mind along with the sounds which were coming through the wall from the bedroom. She went cold all over. It was straight to the depths of her own most secret self that every heightening gasp and murmur from behind that wall went to find its double, magnifying itself unmistakably, and like the single sound reverberating from struck crystal, it overflowed her hearing until she did not know if anyone else could hear or not.

She removed her hat carefully and laid it on the dresser. "There doesn't seem to be anyone here," she said. "Just have a seat." Then she went through the bathroom and knocked on the bedroom door. "Is that you, Marianne?" she called. "Marianne, are you there?" With a loud rattle of the knob she opened the door, waited a moment before the dark slit without trying to see inside, then closed it. The sound had shut off like a phonograph.

"I declare," she said to Ethel and her husband, as she came out smiling, "it's Marianne Ogden, the Senator's daughter. She says that Jerry and Senator Ogden left about fifteen minutes ago. They had an appointment at some club—"

"That would be the Rook Club," said Ethel's husband, nodding. God, thought Catherine when recalling the scene much later, could anybody's mind get *that* full of Kansas City? She could only suppose that it had. "Marianne," she went on, "just flew in to see her mother and daddy. She's in school out from Chicago, you know. She's supposed to be catching up on her sleep—there was some dance or other last night—but how she could do it with those Dixieland records going in there I don't know. Or maybe it was the radio. I think she's not wide awake or dressed or she'd come out and meet you."

So they sat about, chatting for a time and Ethel went to powder her nose, and beyond the wall, the bedroom was as silent as the tomb. As they got ready to leave, Catherine returned to the bedroom door. "We're going now, Marianne," she called out. "You can sprawl around to your heart's content without dressing."

When they had gone, Catherine went downstairs and at the desk arranged for a room of her own. She said there was too much telephoning going on in hers and Jerry's quarters and she needed some rest. After she had tipped the bellboy and locked the door, she sat down in the air-conditioned room and the hand of ice that had both paralyzed her normal reactions and shocked her into a strange new pattern of utterly convincing deceit relaxed slowly, melted away. She raised the blinds and opened the curtains to let in some light, took off her shoes, her dress, which she hung up in the closet, and as she could not quit perspiring and shaking, she draped a large bath towel around her shoulders, and sat with her feet propped on the end of the bed, looking out and smoking.

I think I succeeded, she thought. I think I even brought it off. He'll have that to thank me for anyway, for the rest of his life. If he remembers anything at all. If he remembers anything, which I doubt. If you remember anything—anything small and human and unimportant, not powerful—then you are responsible for it; and so he just forgets.

But if I succeeded, she told herself, I succeeded because Ethel and her husband are good. Their politics may be screwy and they aren't very much fun and their ideas get S for stupid; but they are good. They did not suspect that my husband was laying the hat check girl or whoever it was, in the bedroom. They must have known somebody was laying somebody, but they wouldn't embarrass me by noticing and they won't even say out loud to each other that it might have been Jerry. So there is still just as much chance as there ever was that if Jerry can talk to them and Senator Ogden can talk to them they may see the light about their stupid politics, they may get wise to the world and know who is laying who and be as miserable as I am now.

Catherine called down to the lobby for a package of cigarettes and on second thought ordered also a bottle of whiskey. When Jerry found her she was quite drunk.

That was problem enough without starting any quarrel. Jerry barely got her sobered up in time to see Ethel and Ethel's husband again that evening. Ethel insisted on asking all about Marianne, much to Senator Ogden's delight; he could turn to mush when talking of his daughter. And whether it ever came out clearly that Marianne was nowhere within a thousand miles of Kansas City, Catherine did not know or really care. Everybody was getting drunk except Ethel's husband, who began to worry about Ethel. She had got entirely too genial since Catherine and the entourage had showed up in town. She was now longing fuzzily to reminisce. And pictures would soon come tumbling out, photos of children at all ages. "Oh, yes; oh, yes," said Ethel. "Just a tiny one," she said. "Ethel," said Ethel's husband sternly. "Remember where you are!" "Well, now, tell me, Senator Ogden," said Ethel, "really and truly. Who's going to be the next President of this great country?" Ethel's husband was terribly embarrassed when they finally left. His principles, his city, his state, his politics, his party, his religion—everything seemed to have shaken a bit for him, as though far underfoot the earth had stirred in its sleep. He courteously reminded his wife that her hat was crooked. Yes, a brick or two had shaken loose here and there, and life was going to need looking into a bit.

Catherine, now coolly sober after having been held under a cold shower by Jerry, who had also choked strong salt water down her until she vomited and finished her off with prairie oysters and dry crackers, allowed herself to be tugged to Ethel's warm bosom. She and Jerry were smiling at Ethel with indulgent affection and Ethel's husband, regarding them, felt them admirable. Hadn't they understood his wife's getting too much to drink? His handclasp showed his gratitude. There was some mention of a further meeting and when the door closed an impression of the Sassers lingered warmly in his mind as he prepared himself for that long talk he was going to have to have with Ethel. . . .

Jerry's story to Catherine was that he had not been the person she had heard at all. She knew this kind of response as a strategy and even saw the good sense to be made of it: as long as you do not say a person has a certain disease you don't have to talk about it. As for herself, she had never been more collected. She sat calmly at the most distant booth in the inevitable drugstore where all their crises had a way of flowering, and whether it was a blessing or a curse that over the length and breadth of a great country you could not tell one of these establishments from another, they had no way of knowing. She had ordered a fountain Coke which she did not particularly want and sat toying with the straw while he dumped milk in his coffee and stirred a vigorous whirlpool. Catherine let him light her cigarette.

"I don't want to argue about it," she said. "I know what I know. I'm going to leave you after the election, Jerry. I'll drag around with you until November, if that's what you want, but on Election Day Plus One it's got to be goodbye."

She had thought she would have to steel herself for saying this, but instead it came out naturally, easily, proving to her that it was the right thing. Her very soul felt suddenly clean and clear. Come the Revolution, she thought, come the Liberation. . . .

"I can't see what a great difference it will make to you, once you get used to the idea," she went on amiably. "You've got what it takes to please a whole nationwide assembly line of little college graduate career girls—"

"Stop it, Catherine. You must be crazy." He was toying with a match folder, hunched over his coffee which had ceased to swirl but which he had not touched. His eyes were moving restlessly; his voice sounded strained. The thing he had said about craziness bounced away without sticking.

"And you can still fish rabbits out of the hat for Senator Ogden. You aren't ever going to be dumb," she added, with a touch of pride.

"Catherine," said Jerry, "we have to consider Latham."

"He's under no illusions that we're happy," she told him. "I know that's true. And not because I told him."

Jerry nodded. "I believe you."

"After all," she went on, "he is intelligent."

"Does he still want to be a naturalist?" Jerry asked cautiously. He seemed aware that he might possibly be walking out on the air. Catherine was always receiving letters from Latham which she passed on to Jerry, though if he read them, he forgot what was in them, and sometimes he lost them. The letters now, for some weeks, had been full of plans for going North as soon as school was out. He would be picking up his wild life program just at the mating season. Why on earth, she wondered, would any man not be interested in a son like Latham? She felt her vision darkening as though with sunstroke. She felt she would faint. She felt as she had when the gasps and soft cries came through the wall, matching her own through the years, like the two halves of one big red Valentine heart, ripped in two.

What is the matter with you, Jerry? she wanted to cry. What in the world is wrong? But they had had that argument, so many many times before. "It isn't me, Catherine," he used to deny. "It isn't." "Then what is it?" "It's the world." "Oh, my God . . ." No, that quarrel was out. And don't get led off into the Latham quarrel either, she counseled herself.

"Want to be a naturalist?" she repeated. "I don't know."

Jerry seemed to accept that. No recollection of the many letters came to him to contradict it. His eyes flickered from there to here, to the door (he sat facing it), to his coffee (he remembered it and drank some), to her face. Suddenly, he raised his hand in a gesture of greeting and nodded, smiling.

"Who is it?" Catherine asked. But whoever it was was coming to them, a strange Italian gentleman with a large-toothed smile was being so glad to meet her. "Your husband," he was saying, "he tella me how to vote."

"Mr. Angelino is the headwaiter at the Rook Club," Jerry explained, "where I had lunch yesterday," he added.

"You husband sit, talka to me a long time," said Mr. Angelino. "Senator Ogden go, the customer all go, so we sit and we take the little brandy and we decide how to vote. Maybe you think he is gone with the pretty girl, eh?"

Laughing genially, he departed.

"You see, Catherine," said Jerry dolefully, "I told you I was there."

The next time they sat in a drugstore and got to converse any, they fell to wondering who it could have been in Senator Ogden's hotel suite. "Maybe it was Marianne," said Jerry. "Maybe she did fly in from school, found the bellboy—a likely youth—emptying ashtrays. Or the laundryman. Or the plumber. Or maybe the maid was there and the bellboy came in."

"Or the laundryman," said Catherine.

"Or the plumber."

"Come to think of it," Catherine said, "where did Senator Ogden go after lunch at the Rook Club?"

"Why, he said he went to see this guy—"

"About a horse?"

"Well, what do you know? So old Ogden met the maid—" He laughed. "Or the bellboy, or the laundryman—"

"It would have to be a very soprano bellboy," said Catherine.

"There are such things," said Jerry. "I kid you not."

"Where," Catherine inquired, "was Mrs. O.?"

Jerry was thunderstruck. "His wife! Well, the old devil!"

"They're bound to get together sometimes, I guess," said Catherine. They both fell to laughing.

"Catherine," said Jerry, "just out of curiosity, what record did you say was playing?"

"I said she liked Dixieland jazz . . . oh, I can't remember what."

"Dixieland jazz!" Jerry thought that was downright rare. He laughed till he hurt. While he was laughing it came over Catherine that Jerry Sasser would be capable of not only carrying on the conversation if he actually had been back of the wall but of savoring it even more than if he had not. And how could she, out of all the world, mistake any intimate echo of him for anyone else, out of all the world? Crazy? she thought. I would certainly have to be. Oh, God, she thought, suddenly breaking off with a long exhausted sigh.

"What's the matter?" Jerry asked, cutting off too.

"I can't take back anything," said Catherine, "no matter how we sit here and laugh. If it wasn't you this time, it could have been. Else what would there be to argue about at all? After the election, I'm still going, Jerry."

Jerry Sasser became very still. "We'll see about that," he said.

◆

When she was in Denver in the hospital, another person showed up to see her who wasn't Jerry either. It was Guy Owen, he of the broad Caesar's brow and old-fashioned tastes. He had had business, he explained, in Denver, and having heard she was there—

Catherine went out to dinner with him. "The rules are certainly very relaxed," he observed.

"That's because there's really nothing the matter with me," Catherine said. "I'm just tired. It's all this campaigning."

"Catherine," said Guy Owen, "I think your husband is—well, a smart guy—but for you—"

"For me, all wrong," she supplied.

"Well, a lot of my business, of course. You can always tell me to go to hell."

"Oh, I don't feel that way!" She looked at him across the small table, across the candlelight.

"Just then," he said, "the way you looked at me, you seemed to be appealing to me. Were you, Catherine?"

She knew how she had looked, saw how she had made him feel. Had it been genuine, her look? Did she want to make him feel this way? "I've been alone a lot," she evaded him, "since coming here."

He smiled his sad gentleman's smile. "And I've had too much wine."

"It's good of you—" she began, but he waved his hand.

"We won't have that," he advised.

She was still turning Guy Owen over in her mind after he had flown back to Washington, when the door opened and there stood Jerry, all full of fire and glory. "I came to spring you, baby," he said.

Oh, it was grand! They went dancing and drank champagne. They talked about days before the war, all their many army camp rendezvous, laughed about Priscilla and Millard, and back at the hotel, the night two-thirds gone, crawled up out of a sea of love to sleep like two young people on warm sand. Next morning the doctors insisted on interviews and pronounced grave warnings, all the while Jerry was writing out the check, and he and Catherine returned to Washington in the afternoon.

"There's somebody we have to give a dinner party for tomorrow night," he told her while opening the blinds and turning up the thermostat in the apartment. "I've arranged most of it on the telephone. Even typed out all the vital statistics for you. Didn't want to tire you. Look, you'll see. I got a caterer to write out the menu, spell it out—even a country boy like me can understand."

So in that instant, while getting her toothbrush out of the night case, while looking for her toothpaste, it all came back over her, grew out of his words and dragged her down, the claw of weariness and dread, the mind's awful immersion. Except now, she thought, reclining on the chaise longue and feeling physically unable to lift her arm for the necessary exertion of brushing her teeth, except now, I can always call up Guy Owen.

And she did.

"You know," said Jerry pleasantly, a few weeks later, "if this were England, old girl, and anybody mentioned divorce, the one of us with practically conclusive evidence would be me. Shall we race to see who gets there first?"

"You mean Guy," she said, "and there's nothing in it so far but conversation."

A few weeks later, Guy Owen's law firm was involved in a price-fixing scandal which got into all the Washington papers and failed by a thread to make the national press. Catherine for the first time in her life went to a detective agency. The agent, who was rather cautious with her—Catherine was now alert for people perhaps thinking she might be mad—reported that he could find no evidence whatever to point to Jerry Sasser. It seemed that Guy Owen also was equally guiltless. There had just been a slip-up somewhere, somebody had goofed. Now Guy, though as honorable and old-fashioned as ever, was bankrupt, and furthermore he looked old. Catherine, to her sorrow, noticed this immediately. His manners now seemed merely bitter. "I even have to thank your husband," he told her. "He managed singlehanded to keep it from blowing up into a front-page scandal. He knows how to derail these things, no doubt about it." Catherine put her hand to her brow, an attitude which she found helpful for reading the handwriting on the wall. "Owen's taking it too seriously," Jerry said. "He's got a lot of old leftover precepts to muddy up the waters. They could easily reorganize the firm and go right on." "I think," said Catherine, "that all the money's gone." "You've got a lot of old leftover precepts, too," said Jerry. "And one of them is that money means something. I've told you and told you—it doesn't mean anything." "We seem to spend an awful lot of it," said Catherine, "just the same."

"Well, what I want to know is," Priscilla said, "what exactly does Jerry do?" Among her own leftover precepts was the idea that there was an answer to a question like that.

"Do?" said Catherine. "I don't really know what he doesn't do."

"Well," said Priscilla, who was already getting exasperated, "can you name one or two things?"

"He's a lawyer," said Catherine. "All of Senator Ogden's legal affairs in Washington are in his hands. When Jerry was in the House, so was Ogden. They served on one or two committees together. They used to sit around after hours discussing the machinery of all the various decisions. Ogden told me once they made a good team: when anything came up, he wondered what it was and Jerry wondered how it worked. Then he shook hands with me. He always shakes your hand. He must shake his wife's hand every morning after breakfast. You see, Priscilla, the government—"

"Yes?" said Priscilla encouragingly.

"Well, it's all like a great big machine. You don't think at any one time whether any one small thing is all important or right or wrong, it's just whether all the smaller things are working together or not. If you try to get some direction toward broad goals, then a lot of people may get hurt or pushed aside, but others are necessary to come along with you and straighten up the details. If they can see the goals and agree with them, so much the better. Sometimes they're along for the glory, or just for the ride, or for some advantage to themselves. What Jerry is the world's wonder at, is sorting the people out. He has a magnificent memory for names and connections, ties between people, motives for why they might do this whereas they would never do that. To some people everybody looks just the same, like so many rats in a cage—to Jerry they never do. He can look at them and understand—he knows their weakness right away with very few clues. That's probably why he's so good with women," she went on, and Priscilla knew, settling back, that she had tripped the switch. The trouble with Catherine now was that whereas before she had kept things dutifully to herself, now she couldn't stop talking, and any odd suggestion might burst the dikes, and all roads led to Jerry. "He was in a wreck with a baby-sitter," Catherine said. "At the outside, she might have been a nurse; she'd come to see about Ogden's secretary's children one weekend. Eighteen years old anyway, and blonde. Slipping, I said. Of course, he denied it. He said he was running her home as a favor. I didn't inquire."

"Why not?"

"If I inquire it's always true," said Catherine. "Why do you think he's so valuable? Better people than I have tried to catch him. Ogden's got him stitched into a hundred fake payrolls."

"So that makes Ogden dishonest, too, doesn't it?" Priscilla asked.

Catherine smiled. "They don't call it that," she said.

"If you don't get a divorce, Catherine," said Priscilla, "why don't you get a hobby? Go back to your music."

"Hobby," said Catherine. "That's one of those words that makes me want to throw up on the floor."

Lottie Ogden, the Senator's wife, talked to Catherine. "You need to get inter-rested in business, honey," she said. "Look at So-and-so, look at So-and-so. The good times come and go in marriage. Oggie and I are just lucky we've always been so compatible. Oggie just worries about you. He really does."

There were always two ways to look at anything, Catherine thought. If Oggie worried about her, it was partly because of what he was afraid she might say right out in public during some fine luncheon. She almost said, right then, "Lottie, was it you and Oggie I heard through the hotel room wall in Kansas City? I've wondered for years, it was such a mystery." Some day, I know, she thought, I'm going to come right out with that. Then they'll pack me off to Denver again and all the doctors will say, This syndrome was foreseen two years ago. Why was the patient withdrawn? But let me get in the part about Dixieland jazz before somebody shuts me up.

"How did it all turn out this way?" Priscilla burst out.

"I don't know," said Catherine. "I just woke up and found it there."

◆

"The times, the times!" cried Jerry Sasser. He had his black intervals of sincere despair.

"It isn't the times, it's you," Catherine told him, good-humoredly. "You've got to be in on everything. You work yourself silly."

"It's better to work than worry," he said. "Even so I feel that it's all getting too much for me. It's going outside of anything I can imagine or control. I don't have the education, the degrees, the big-shot backing. I haven't written any books; I'm an expert on nothing."

His picture had just come out on a national magazine cover. Every newsstand they passed, there he was by the dozen. In hotel lobbies, airports, along the streets, the bright dark intense face—an artist's job on a candid photograph—unreeled freshly imprinted before their eyes.

"You were going to write a book about that Japanese island after the war. What happened to that?"

"I never had time to finish it." He stopped, pushing his heel in the sand (they were in Florida, on the beach) and thinking. "Maybe I could yet." For a moment he actually considered it, then he kissed her suddenly, jumped up and ran into the surf.

"Jerry," she said, when he returned, "why can't we just let the times go on without us, let them just roll over us? They're going to do what they want to anyway. It's only going to get bigger and bigger, more and more powerful. Why not let them just go, and be ourselves?"

He was dripping and the breeze was blowing. The salt drops clung to him whitely like a sort of fleece. A trim brunette nearby was reading the magazine; she nudged her husband from under her beach umbrella, pointed at the cover and then at Jerry. The water was a startling blue and the white gulls rode the breeze. Now the palm fronds along the shore drive stirred and the flags near the big square hotels fluttered and lifted. Steadily glittering, cars went past, past, past, along the shore drive. There were people everywhere, everywhere. Beautiful brown people, nourished to perfection, a constant kaleidoscopic glory of the flesh, sporting, Olympian and free, enjoying money, sex, sunlight, food, health, liquor, abandoned in the glad release of having stopped trying to make any sense out of anything. One sidelong glance at all this and her voice with its small argument simply disappeared. He rescued it. "Be ourselves?" he echoed, and rubbed his shoulders with a great fleecy towel.

Jerry went water skiing in the afternoon. Catherine tried her best to join him, but wearied early, was no good anyway. It was always like that. She was never strong enough to keep up. Jerry soaked up a sport as innocently as skin soaked up the sunlight. He hated Coney Island where they had gone once, just out of curiosity. People were so ugly there, like sea spawn, sprawling about like crabs. No one would have been surprised to see them all start copulating with the first available body—if only you found the right whistle and blew it, they would doubtless have gone at it instantly. He was depressed for hours, wrung in the fastidious recesses of his soul where he loved freshly starched shirts that fitted over brown firm skin. Oh, the glory.

◆

Latham Sasser, in the great charity of soul that had come to him since he had been studying animals, kept a journal in which he wrote down the doings of his father and mother, for parents, he told himself, were a curious species—one had only to listen to any of the boys talk; one had only to observe one's own.

Many things had been kept from him, and yet it was amazing how much he knew. One day, to relieve himself from wonder and dismay at himself (how he grew and what strong feelings awoke to contend within him, crosswinds, dark torrents, a buried rushing stream), he wrote down—It is known to me that Daddy and Mother are not happy. He finds whoever he can get away with.

He sat back, looking down at the page on which the words had appeared, in the chill-warm woodland silence, thick with the myriad consciousness of leaves. A bitter taste like brass came up in his mouth. Was the flaw himself? He drew his one slightly shrunken leg compulsively beneath him. He rubbed the back of his hand across his face several times, and shivered. He bit the side of his hand. How to strike out the words, to pretend that he had not put them down? Then slowly, unwillingly, with the firm gentleness with which he might lift some captive creature, his grip rendering helpless tooth, claw and wing, he saw the full shape of the words and what they did: they said what the trouble was and in so doing confined it. So he did not strike through or destroy the writing. Instead, deliberately, freeing the leg beneath him which had begun to cramp from being thrust awkwardly back, he wrote down: It is not my fault.

The words, as soon as he put them down, seemed even stronger than the others; they stood upon the page like an axe blow, severing his own inner life from theirs. He wavered for a moment like a child trying to stand alone, or like himself the day he gave up the crutch and began slowly to walk again. Then he steadied. He turned the page, away from parents, back to his notes on bird- and deer-watching. Sickness, before he was five, had taught him a certain grace, a way of not taking too much of a part in things. Yet he remembered, with whatever there was in it of pain and wonder, the man who had come to him one late afternoon, quick bright eyes drinking up all his words and a voice filling in. He remembered walking into the woods with this presence and returning and talking again, late into the night. Then the man left and never came back. It seemed now like the visit of a god, for when he saw his father again and expected it all to resume, his father had not recalled even what had happened. The creature had merely seemed to be his father, but in reality was feathered or richly furred, a person too radiant to regard. If a trick, it had been a trick played not especially to deceive him, Latham Sasser, but just for the joy of playing. He must talk it over some day with his mother. He did not know her intelligence, whether to value it or not, but he counted on her. He pictured her as always sitting somewhere reading a magazine and waiting, patient, exactly where he had thought she would be, even down to the particular chair. Possibly this was because she had so often literally done this in hospitals whence so many of his earliest memories stemmed. If he walked into this constant room where she sat reading and asked her anything she would tell him the truth. But suppose she didn't know the truth? Was some trick being played on her as well? Then her image dimmed, defacing. He saw the image of the radiant creature he had taken for his father dim also, for the telephone had sprung up, an urgent rage between them, and the man had dropped everything to answer it. Had that man really understood so much? How could it seem so if it wasn't true? It had been far more than anyone else understood, Latham determined, and looked quietly up into the eyes of a young deer with velvet horns.

◆

Catherine and Jerry Sasser finally came late on Sunday morning from Dallas to Merrill. Their minds were more harried by things that had not happened than by anything that had. Jerry had never been able to get in touch with anyone remotely connected with the magazine article he had read, to his dismay, on the day before. Nothing whatever had developed between him and the little airline hostess, who, at the Longhorn, had run into a boy she not only knew but also used to go out with fairly often in Seattle. This young man, obviously a good ten years younger than Jerry, resembled him in some hard-to-define way: he had the look of so many men in public or semi-public life. It was more a question of posture than anything else—they stood slightly forward, head tilted for listening, a drink held a few inches away from the chest with the left hand, while the right was free to shake hands, light cigarettes, smoke or move people gently aside by the shoulders while fending a path toward another quarter of a crowded room. The style had become as rigid as a coat of frozen armor. Talking to Jerry with Jan Radley between, the young man might have been speaking to an older brother.

Older, older, Catherine thought. Does Jerry notice that? He must have, everything was making him nervous. For one thing there was no chance to talk with Ogden alone, for the Vice-Presidential candidate was present and Oggie had a few nervous matters of his own to get straight. For another, when he learned that Catherine and Jerry would be going up to Merrill the next morning, he did not offer his plane. "Cutting expenses," he said, winking at Jerry. "No breath of scandal shall attach to us in these final, all-important weeks." That brought back the article. "I saw Turner in Washington," Jerry said. "I explained the situation to him and he said he understood." "So it won't come out," Ogden said. "Turner gave me his word on it," Jerry shrugged. "Good boy!" Ogden clasped his hand.

"How could you tell him that?" Catherine asked him. They were waiting at the airport, having engaged a private plane to take them out to Merrill. Jerry paced back and forth on the pavement outside the terminal. He walked to the edge of the shade, just entered the sun and returned. The glare was so intense he seemed to turn into a negative of himself each time he entered it.

"I don't know." He walked away and returned. He hated waiting. "What else could I do? Bluff it out. If advance copies got run off and released by mistake, then maybe Turner really will stop the article in the later press. Anyway, it's not that paragraph or two that matter but the wheels they'll set in motion about Ogden in general, Jerry Sasser in particular—" He frowned, bit the underside of his cheek, halted, then walked again. "Hell to pay."

On a distant runway, she now noticed that a small private plane had emerged; looking new, freshly painted in contrasting tones of white and red, and young, somehow—it would be theirs, she felt, even before they were called. "Did you ask that stewardess, that Miss Radley, about the magazine?"

"She didn't know anything. I should have taken it off the plane with me."

"What good would that have done?"

"Why, nothing. It might prove to me I wasn't seeing things."

Then they were shaking hands with the pilot.

The airport at Merrill was not a commercial one, but was only a hot flat space of ground, leveled, paved and striped with white and yellow lines, about five miles from town, in the desert. Though there was no road through, it was not so very far from Sandy Gulch and the old home place of the Lathams where Catherine used to visit Uncle Dick and Uncle Mark. They flew above and she could see down below the white expanse of sand, and even, from the air, what no one could any longer see on the ground, the ghost of the old road that had angled down into the sand and how it emerged on the other side, wandering off toward the West, California and the Great Dream.

She saw the old Latham house and the green line of eucalyptus, silkily blowing, poplar, mimosa, and cottonwood. Oh, to get there! That day or so of rest. She saw the image clearly, saw it, so far, as inaccessible, as if she had seen it on a movie screen, and then the land tilted up and blotted out all but the scrubby, dusty reaches of a poor field bristling with oil wells. They were coming down.

Nobody had spent any money to make the Merrill airport "nice." There was a big hangar of bright, corrugated iron sheets which thumped under the steady hammer of the sun as though somebody were hurling brickbats at it, and there was a large quonset hut, war surplus, set up as a shelter for waiting in. During the week a boy from Merrill kept it open as a small concession—there were cold drinks to be had and ice cream, candy and peanuts—but now his counter was concealed by a roll-down screen which was secured at the bottom by a heavy lock. A Coca-Cola machine was purring in the silence and Catherine, who had been moving all summer in the thickening heat from one air-conditioned oasis to another, sank down on a bench, convinced that she would smother. Jerry handed her a frosted bottle from the machine and went to telephone to see if the taxi he had rung up from Dallas to order was on the way. But now before he could dial, they heard it, just outside. Was it air-conditioned? It was.

"Aren't you Mr. Jerry Sasser?" the driver wanted to know, casting a glance behind him. "And Miss Catherine?"

"We don't want anybody to know we're here," Jerry said. "My wife needs a rest; we're just going out to the farm to be quiet for a day or so. There'll be an extra ten in it for you if you'll just not say anything about our being here."

They drove on in silence, mounting into the foothills. The scrubby trees were dropping back and the sandy soil; here was a clump of green, hanging limply in the heat, and there was the house with the cow-pool on one side of a two-acre lawn and a swimming pool on the other. The road curved toward Merrill.

"When you pass through," Jerry went on, "don't think it's peculiar if your passengers lean down so nobody can see us. We strictly mean it about wanting a day or so to ourselves. This election—"

The boy still did not answer. He drove steadily, into the green hills. The road tilted. Catherine began to feel a strange relief. No telephone, Jerry had promised. Normal hours, regular meals. Silence. Two days of this. Two whole days.

"Okay?" Jerry asked.

The boy turned his head. "I guess you didn't get the news, Mr. Sasser."

"What news?"

"Ain't Professor Sasser out at the Aggie your daddy?"

"Why, yes, he is."

"Well—Mr. Sasser, I hate to be the one to have to tell you this, but he died. Yesterday, I think it was, or maybe it was Friday. Friday night. They couldn't find you. I knew because my sister works at the exchange. They tried Washington all night long, trying for you and Senator Ogden, or anybody could tell you. So now they've decided to go on and have the funeral today. It's the only day the church presiders can come up from Dallas."

Jerry's shoulders collapsed forward. It all seemed so final, so dull and true. He rubbed his hands against his forehead. "Oh, God," he said finally. "Oh my God."

"You'll be just in time for the funeral," the driver encouraged him. "I can take you straight there."

Catherine had reached out at once to take his hand. "Poor

Jerry. Darling, darling, darling." She so seldom got to say that any more. Her tears fell on his hand. "Don't worry about anything. I'll go to Priscilla's. Very quietly. We'll stop there. She won't tell Mamma and Daddy we're here. We'll make her understand."

"Do you remember the day—he tried to give you those books, God help him."

"I took them. I did take them, darling."

"Thank you, Catherine. Thank God you did."

They clung together with wet cheeks and as the town thickened around them, they, its most famous couple whom all would have been proud to say they even waved to in passing, drew themselves forward and down until no head showed in the windows. They crouched there until the cab stopped in the Warners' back yard and the opening door let its oven-square of heat.

◆

"Edward's here," said Priscilla. "Did you know that?"

The sisters were sitting in the living room, where thin layers of sheer draperies kept out the sun.

"Look up the street," she said, "you can see him."

Catherine went to the window, cracked the curtains and peeped out. The big white house with the turret was only a few blocks away, across the one long street that was Merrill. Sure enough, there was Edward, walking around in the yard. "If you get close to him," said Priscilla, "you notice how he's aged. He's got practically no hair left, just a few fringes, and no color at all in his face. I told Mamma he might have something, but she said it had to do with shoe salesmen, that they never have any color. She said his general health was good. He's got another wife."

"I knew that, of course."

"I wonder how on earth Maureen kept all that drinking a secret all these years. Edward swears he didn't know it himself until a year before the divorce."

"There had to be an official story," said Catherine. "Anyway I'm glad Jerry put me off at the back. Edward would have seen us, otherwise."

"If you can get by with this in the middle of Merrill, it's a miracle. Remember when we used to think we had to lower every shade in the house to have a drink? It got so people used to watch our shades and then say, Drunk again, when they saw them down. The glass in this house cost me $2,000. It's the kind you can see out of but not into."

"Hello, Catherine," said Millard. He handed her a Bloody Mary. "You need a pick-up, I imagine. You going to get out without being seen?"

"I only thought we might because nobody we know belongs to that church Professor Sasser went to. Nobody but members of that church ever knew anything about Professor Sasser. Jerry asked the taxi driver to drive him to the church. It's one way to keep him from telling, to let him in on things."

"I thought it was all a secret," said Priscilla, "like lodges."

"He can sit outside." Her hand shook with the glass. "I just wanted to get out to the farm and rest. The strain—you've no idea."

"You can go in the pool around about a quarter of an hour from now. We'll have shade at one end, anyway."

"I've got a better idea," said Priscilla. "Go in the guest room and lie down for an hour. Do, do that, sweetie. We *want* to see you, but it's just plain brutal to make you sit up and talk."

Catherine put down her glass. "I'll do it. Please forgive me. When I've had a good rest, you'll both come out to the farm, Mamma and Daddy and Edward and the girls. Has Edward brought the family?"

Then she was inside the cool dark room with the bed so heavenly soft. Did Edward bring the family and what was the answer to that and what did she care? The only thing he had ever done was run away. Suppose he married forty times, eighteen alcoholics, sixteen prostitutes, and how many did that leave—six whats? What caused divorce? What did it matter? He had never done anything but run away that once. Now he was back, grey and bald with his head full of figures, talking with Daddy about how he saved on taxes this way or that way. Oh, why do I hate? she wondered. Why hate Edward, why hate anyone? We come to a handful of grey dust. Then she fell asleep.

She woke up in ten minutes with a jerk and thought for a minute that she was on an airplane and that it had lurched into another layer of air. Then she knew everything, and got up and dressed, combed her hair and put on her hat. She had to get to Jerry. How could she have left him?

Priscilla was in the kitchen. "I have to go to the funeral," Catherine said.

"Somebody will see you," Priscilla said.

"Not if I sneak out the back. The church isn't on the main street, it's down that road by the Negro section. It's my duty, Priscilla. I do know that."

She walked out the back, by the swimming pool. The hat was black with a large sheltering brim and everyone was shut up in air-conditioned houses from the summer heat, nobody would be out and maybe nobody would look out a back window because people looked out the front windows all the time or talked on the telephone. So maybe if anybody saw her they would take her for Priscilla, though she knew she must weigh twenty pounds less than Priscilla at least after all this strain and running around and quarreling with Jerry. Now just where was that little old brown church hot as a hotbox, covered with some kind of cheap asphalt siding made to look like brick and making itself purposely into a sort of spectacle by being poor and lonely-looking on an old muddy side road, trying to make you feel bad about everything, guilty, as though the only place God would deign to sit down would be on an old muddy side road in a tiny hotbox with orange and purple windowpanes like a cheap movie or even a whorehouse except for the steeple, a place you wouldn't be caught dead in. (Professor Sasser was being caught dead in it right now.) It was going to smell exactly like Professor Sasser. She paused with her hand to her face. The heat prickled into her and out of her. I can't, she thought, I just can't. She thought she would be sick or faint. The name came back to her, the lettered print on the books she never opened because there were spiders pressed inside. *Blood Union of Messiah's Brotherhood.* She could never get Jerry to talk about it. Now surely, she thought, taking heart and finding sudden strength, straightening and walking the path with sure firm steps, surely they can't turn me out. Being Jerry's wife and all, and them pretending to be Christians. Or maybe they even are.

The door had a white knob but was painted brown. She turned the knob and pushed. She entered the vestibule and there already she could smell the books, Jerry's old house, his father, the lacquered tray with the iced tea which did not taste like the iced tea at the Lathams'. If it had been cancer, like Mamma said (though she and Daddy thought everybody had it, being so scared of it themselves), then it took him twenty years to die of it. Or maybe it is the smell of his religion. It got in everywhere, like dust.

From inside, beyond a pair of swinging doors screened in green baize she could hear a swollen murmur of sound. What were they doing? What did they do? Could she find a place near Jerry? Would he be touched and pleased that she had come? Then a man came out. "Are you a member here?" he asked. "No," she whispered, "but I'm Professor Sasser's son's wife." "You have to wait outside." He stepped back inside, as though a fish had come up, spoken, and reentered the water. The air in the vestibule was close and breathless. Catherine put her hand to a slit in the green baize door and leaned to look through it.

The small church was full of people, some seated and some standing up, waiting their time to file by the coffin which was prominently displayed at the front of a rostrum where a long table stood, covered with books. The people who were marching by the coffin each stopped to look inside, then they said something, a sentence or two, some in low tones and some in shrill ones. Then they picked up a pitcher standing on a small table and drank out of the side of it. It was a cracked kitchen pitcher and it came to Catherine in the density of the hot air that there was blood in it. What else could there be? For certainly if sweetly bored Methodist congregations as patient as cows, and slightly more fervid Baptists with intent eyes, could claim to be indulging in something that represented flesh and blood, though it never spoiled their appetite for Sunday dinner, nothing Professor Sasser organized and belonged to was going to stop at representing only; it was much more likely—not even wanting to risk depending on a miracle—the real thing.

She glimpsed Jerry standing in the line and then she felt sick and sank down in the corner behind the green door, her eyes half-closed, her heart hammering, her face and hands like ice. I'm always outside, she thought.

Now there was singing, a weird raised key without music, then the tramp of feet. The door flew open, she was hidden behind it so that no one saw her. The coffin came past, now the outer doors swung open and new air rushed in, somewhat reviving her. "Jerry, Jerry," she whispered as he came by. She struggled to her feet. Astounded, he saw her. "Catherine!" "I came to be with you," she faltered. He swung her straight, holding her steady. "Straighten your hat," he said. She thought she would fall again, but didn't.

Priscilla was at the back picture window overlooking the patio when she saw the two of them together, Catherine and Jerry, coming up the lane. She had watched them all her life, first with little-girl curiosity, then with wonder, envy, admiration, more lately with rage and despair, which still was avid and charged. She kept watching while they opened the door to her and Millard's Cadillac, which was standing in the shade, and sat in it, talking. She saw Jerry lean forward and strike Catherine twice, the blows landing on the side of her cheek and neck near her ear. Catherine crumpled at once below the window level of the car, then she straightened, and leaning forward, put her face in her hands. Priscilla had often thought that she was going to see something like this happen some day but how to act when seeing it through two layers of glass from within a sealed air conditioned room was another matter. She saw Catherine get out of the car and come toward the house which she entered by the opposite wing, returning to the guest room. Jerry meantime left, a dark-suited rapid figure, returning down the lane to the church. He was going to be late to the cemetery.

Priscilla ran out of the front door to meet Millard, who was just now returning from the post office. "He struck her, he struck her! I saw it, Millard."

"Well, now," said Millard. "Men have a right to beat their wives."

"Not like this. Oh, you don't know! You just don't know!"

"There now," said Millard, "what if your Mother sees you out on the street in chartreuse pedal-pushers?"

When Jerry returned from the funeral, Catherine had not yet come out of her room. Sleeping or crying, who knew which? Priscilla shook back her hair at him. She simply could not help going slightly mad when Jerry Sasser was around.

"I saw what happened in the car, Jerry. You needn't think I didn't. If she weren't my sister you'd never get in this house. You needn't think I don't see through you."

"I don't know what you mean," said Jerry Sasser. "What happened in the car?"

"I saw you strike her."

"There was a bee after Catherine in the car. It stung her. We stopped there to talk because she was feeling tired. She shouldn't have tried to come to the funeral. I told her that."

"Ever so sweet, aren't you? And then you sweetly killed the bee."

"I tried to, yes. How sweet I was about it is another thing."

"Oh, you're smart. Oh, you're bright."

Millard came in. "I'm sorry to hear about your father, Jerry. Professor Sasser was a fine old fellow. I only wish we'd been more thoughtful, gone down to see him more often. One doesn't realize—" The two shook hands.

"We should have gone," said Priscilla. "To the funeral, I mean." She grudged out the words. "I only thought we wouldn't be allowed in your church, not being members."

"That's right," said Jerry. "You're exactly right." His tone cut completely, smoothly as the nasty blue jet of acetylene, underneath the "nice" thing she had brought herself to utter, and now she just said, "God!" and turned away.

"Well, Millard," said Jerry. "It's obvious I'm not too welcome, so I think we—"

"Not welcome?" Catherine had left the bedroom in the wing, moved across the patio near the swimming pool and now had opened the door and stepped inside. She had a light silk scarf tied around her neck, which was red below the ear.

"What's wrong with your neck?" Priscilla asked.

"A bee stung me, out in the car," said Catherine. . . .

"Oh, I hate him!" Priscilla said, writhing in her deck chair after Jerry and Catherine had gone.

"Now, dear. Now, baby. A rest at the farm may be all they need."

"Millard, you know that's not true."

"You want me to kill him? Lynch him? Castrate him? Liquidate him?" A new magazine had come, a Paris quarterly, but over the top of it when he turned the page, he could clearly make out that what she was extracting from the pocket of her chartreuse pedal-pushers, though the fashionably pulled-out shirttail of her handprinted Italian shirt may have concealed its outline, was a .44 revolver.

"I might even have done it," she said, and checked the safety catch and laid the gun on the table with its muzzle facing into the wall as a person trained to handle guns is taught to do. "I may some day."

Millard swallowed stiffly. "It's going to make you even madder to know this, but there really was a dead bee on the car seat. I noticed it when I went out to see them in the car. But now, for God's sake, don't shoot me."

"All right," said Priscilla balefully. "All right. Nobody will take me seriously, not even you. But he did strike her. I saw it and I know. If the bee was conveniently there to give him an excuse, that's his luck, isn't it? Don't you think I know when something looks vicious, it is vicious? In other words, don't you think I know Jerry Sasser? You've let them go off out there together, trying to be so reasonable, trying not to take anybody's side, and who's to guarantee what he'll do? Who's to guarantee it?"

"The female of the species," Millard quoted, "especially in Texas. Who's to protect Jerry if they let you out there? I never have liked him, but all he's managed to do so far is go to his father's funeral, like a dutiful son, and kill a bee that was stinging his wife."

Priscilla was really angry now. Her hair, shaken down, coiled about her face as though possessed of a life of its own. "Oh, you make me so mad! Why do you act so spineless? Nobody—*nobody*—understands Jerry Sasser but me!"

◆

So after the funeral they rode off together in Millard's second car, Catherine bending down low and Jerry, his hat pulled down to the rim of his dark glasses, edging the Cadillac through Merrill's one back lane, out to the highway.

"What's on your mouth, Jerry?" Catherine asked. She was crouched on the floor of the front seat, looking up at him.

He bobbed up toward the rear view mirror, at the same time wiping the back of his hand across his lips. "Millard gave me a Bloody Mary back at the house. I had to steady myself after Priscilla's attack. She hates my guts, that woman. I wonder why."

"She saw you hit me. She saw it, so she knows now. It was way too hard a slap for just a bee." She laughed. "I thought in the church that I saw everybody drinking blood out of a pitcher. Did I, Jerry?"

"Catherine, you came there to spy. We had agreed you weren't to come. You had promised not to come. Now you expect me to give you information you tried to get and couldn't. You want to have your cake and eat it too, you Lathams. Priscilla wants to go get a gun and shoot me because I don't believe she's a sweet little girl. Well, sweet little girls don't go get guns and shoot their brothers-in-law."

He was talking on and on the way he talked when he was tired and wound up and couldn't stop. It was nerves and anxiety. There was still the article. They had not seen a paper or heard a news report since morning. To catch Ogden, or Jerry Sasser maneuvering for Ogden, on the tender point of his civil rights fence-sitting, was enough to make headlines if the newspapers caught the hint from one leak. Jerry's head hummed like a defective TV set, sputtering out bars and cross patterns in black and grey, trying to produce a picture. Had he actually gone through his father's funeral thinking about the Presidential race? It not only seemed possible, Catherine believed it. It is one thing to sense the nation's power as a protective force, fatherly, somewhat absent-minded, but capable of powerful action, when aroused; it is another to feel the power grow nervous because of power itself, to see it pace the floor, prowl from window to window. It was what made him handsome, Catherine thought, looking at the rich muted blue-green carpeting of the Cadillac. Wall-to-wall. It was what made him have to have women and women have to have him. A case of mutual need. "When it really gets bad," he had told her once, "it's like being an alcoholic about everything—cigarettes, whiskey, women, talk—in other words, everything. It's the feeling that nothing can touch me, nothing can stop me, I can go anywhere, do anything, remake the world and throw it in the garbage." Another time he had said, doubtfully, weary and knowing it, "I think I may not be around much longer. There are lots of new men coming in. They've got degrees, they're talking smart in a new way. I've depended so much on Ogden and Ogden depends on a hundred other people. Nobody can control what happens to any one of us, least of all Oggie himself. Maybe they'll all gang up to show me up as a two-bit con man. I'm getting tired, Catherine."

But he wasn't tired now. He was on his toes and longing to know the score, but couldn't get a glimpse of the scoreboard. He was thinking about the election. His body was thinking it, it ran along his veins and played like green voltage in the delicate webbed nerves of his brain. He was aware that Priscilla had got out the gun, and this had in some way only brought him to a deeper focus. His father's death which he had not seemed really to think about might have been too like the final dropping off of a scaffolding. Hadn't he turned the feeling of it over to Catherine in the taxi coming in?

Am I afraid to go out there with him? Catherine wondered. It would not even have occurred to her except that Priscilla had been afraid for her to go. Much better to be with him somewhere in silence and alone than anywhere out in the world, asking questions that never get answered, hearing his lovemaking through a wall, observing his father's funeral through a slit of green baize. I'm so happy to go, she thought; happy and willing. She wondered how to tell Priscilla this and thought of writing the message on bits of paper and scattering it out the window along their path. Of course, once out at the farm she could always telephone. But she did not really want to do that, and Jerry for once anticipated her thought, when they arrived at the farmhouse, by unplugging all the phones.

"I promised you a rest, so you're going to get it," he said. "I won't have Priscilla ringing up here every five minutes."

"She's going to think you're trying to kill me," Catherine said. "She's going to think it because she thinks you've driven me crazy as it is." She laughed. The laugh rose through the country quiet they weren't used to yet.

Outside, the evening wind was drawing out toward the desert, pulling the silken green of the cottonwood trees. When you stood under them they made a sound like water or like lots of children's hands clapping at a distance. By now, Jerry had already switched on the air conditioning, so they could not hear anything but that. The old farmhouse had been all fixed up since the days of the two old uncles. The front porch was gone, had been incorporated into a great big living room full of rugs, couches, deep armchairs. There was a fireplace and a gun rack and several deer heads mounted on the wall.

"If Priscilla was here, she'd shoot you with one of those guns," said Catherine. She snuggled down in an armchair, and though she was a tallish woman she could look small in a big chair.

"I think all of life is some kind of contest, some sort of war," said Catherine. "It's either us and the Germans or us and the Japanese or us and the Russians. When it isn't war we have to get all excited over football, who's going to win what, or the World Series, who's going to win that, or the Democrats and Republicans. That's all people want to know, who's going to win. It's always us against somebody else. And when everything else runs out, there's always you and me."

"Oh, Catherine!"

"Listen, Jerry, did you ever think about the Japanese? They worshipped the sun, did you know that? They were children of the sun, and then at Hiroshima, look at what the sun did to them, because that's all the atom bomb is, isn't it? It's just the sun burning you up to a cinder. Did you ever think about that, Jerry? Listen, Jerry, you know Lottie Ogden? She's always telling me to get interested in something. Business, she said for a long time. Then she said, Honey, you've got to start reading American history. It's glorious, she said. So I thought, Well, I really will. So I took a long stack of books with me up to Maine the last time I drove Latham up there and I started reading. It was what you might call advanced history, and I remembered a lot of it from school but somehow in school it had lacked reality. I never knew any people in government then and so it couldn't get through to me. I thought, for instance, that we were good—on the good side. Whoever gives us the idea that we're so good? I read and I read and all it seemed like was people shooting down buffalo on an empty plain as far as you could see until the plain was covered with skinned carcasses of buffalo, left to rot because the hides were so valuable, and they had all been there so beautiful, so stupid and dignified, wandering in the sage grass and letting little birds live on their backs. I think about them whenever we get up from one of those long banquet tables where we've had fruit cup, chicken à la king in pastry shells, peas, mashed potatoes, salad with french dressing and ice cream with macaroons—I think about the buffalo or all those poor Japanese—"

He handed her a lighted cigarette. She used often to go on about one thing or another in her light pleasant voice, so that he could move about the room, draw open the curtains, adjust others against the sun, think with increasing ease. She did not ask to be listened to, and if the topics had changed since the old days, had imperceptibly drawn toward what might have been described as symptomatic, still she did not demand listening to.

"I guess we're better than the Germans," she went on. "They killed Jews instead of buffalo."

"That's good, Catherine," said Jerry. "That's great." He kissed her, lifting her half up out of the chair, then releasing her. "Is brain unwinding?" he asked. He picked up the suitcases, which were standing inside the door, and ran upstairs with them. She could hear him barging about. Presently he reappeared wearing shorts and the kind of sweatshirt that Millard Warner was always wearing. He must have borrowed Millard's. He looked about a thousand times better in anything than Millard Warner. Now he was opening the liquor closet. I wish that he loved me, Catherine thought. If he loved me I would not have nightmares about Hiroshima, I would not think so much about the buffalo or the Japanese. I wouldn't believe that Jerry drank blood out of a pitcher and it would never occur to me to object if I heard him making love through a wall, for I would know some girl got him there.

She closed her eyes. Her lids were warm. Now he was going into the kitchen with a drink in his hand, opening the deep freeze. She should get up and select something to thaw for dinner. "Is a steak all right?" Jerry called. She said that a steak would be all right.

In the armchair she fell asleep and dreamed. The dreams—there were a number of them—were full of warmth and love. She saw Uncle Dick again; they went walking in Sandy Gulch and built a sand house and while she waded he sat on the bank in the sun with his straw hat low over his eyes and his walking cane across his knees. He sat beside her sandals. On the way back to the house they passed a lot of people coming out of the fields, some riding on wagons and some walking. They said, Where are you going, and the people said, Haven't you heard? There's a boy who fell under a wheel and hurt himself. Don't you hear him crying? Then Uncle Dick took her hand and walked fast and faster, printing his cane in the dust. He said, That's just what they're saying, they're really going to a wedding. Didn't you see all the tambourines? Who would take a tambourine to see a boy die in the sand? They're going to dance on the sand. But she knew that wasn't true. She could hear the boy crying Mother, Mother! or was it Mercy, mercy! And it made her wild to go and find him and she couldn't eat the peaches Uncle Dick peeled for her and then Uncle Mark came up the hill and said He's dead, hee, hee, they killed the orphan. So his grave was on their hill and now she could eat and sleep because no matter what Uncle Mark said this was a place of love and graves even were loved because Grandfather went all the way to California to see the people who had lost the boy who died, maybe to let them know that the grave was tended to, was loved, to let them know something he never did say, never could say, that no one could say . . . to let them know. . . . Grandfather leaving in the stagecoach from Dallas looking at his gold watch, said, I will bring you back what you want most in the world, what is it? A tambourine? All right, I will bring you back a tambourine from Neiman-Marcus. Don't cry. Then the stagecoach door closed like in the movies. Grandfather sat on a velvet seat with his carpetbag beneath his feet and his little brass-bound trunk up above on the luggage rack, strapped on. There was a lady in full taffeta skirts inside and a drummer and a cowboy and grandfather. Grandfather took his hat off and said, How do you do, ma'am. Then they drove off through the plains where all the buffalo looked lonely and sad because they were about to die.

She awoke and the room was empty, quiet and cool. No one was there but herself. She went in the kitchen and saw that the steak was out thawing on the table. The sack of groceries, fresh butter, rolls, lettuce and watercress for a salad, all brought from Priscilla's, was sitting on the table. She put the things away in the refrigerator. "Jerry?" she said. "Jerry?" There was no answer. She went upstairs and found him asleep. He had kicked off his loafers, but otherwise had fallen just as he was across the spread. A pillow had been dragged free and stuffed beneath his head. How dark he is! Catherine observed. Against the white pillowcase his face looked swart, his hair, lashes and brows so dark they startled her. His head was thrown back and the attitude revealed long lines slanting down his cheeks. He isn't young any more, thought Catherine. God knows I'm not. She stepped out of her shoes and crossed the floor and went to look in the mirror. Her face was lightly and permanently freckled and scarcely ever showed an absence of make-up. She slipped off her blouse and skirt and unpinned her hair. Still hot from the outer day, it fell about her shoulders. Did something flicker in the mirror's depths? The room was shadowy, for the curtains had not been drawn open. She smiled to remember some story of vampires which had intrigued her as a girl—how they cannot be seen in mirrors. She turned, but there was only Jerry, sound asleep on the bed exactly as before.

I'm alone out here with him, she thought, and it came to her from seeing him stir just how long he would sleep and that he would want her when he waked. The thought was like rising out of chill dank water into sunlight and, happening to glimpse the mirror again, she saw the years drop away.

◆

"She's out there alone with him!" Priscilla cried. She put down the telephone for the thirtieth time and circled the room, madly smoking with one hand and tugging at locks of hair with the other. "Out there alone and do you know, do you realize, she's just about crazy as it is. What she says makes no sense at all sometimes."

"It's just the election," said Millard. "It could drive anybody nuts, and they're too near the nerve center not to get the full charge."

"You wouldn't believe it if you saw her snap right in front of your eyes."

"I'd have to know why."

"Why! You know Jerry Sasser as well as I do. You just won't admit it. It makes me furious."

"I think," said Millard Warner, "that you should spend more

time with the children, Priscilla. I ordered some children's books last week. All they are going to remember of life with us is Picasso paintings and what they find in the Post Toasties." He rubbed his face. "In spite of all I can do, life keeps turning into a vacuum. And you keep raging in it like a windy banshee. What do you want me to do about Catherine? It's obvious that your anger with Jerry Sasser is purely sexual."

With that Priscilla gave a shriek and went back to the phone.

After two days of this, still hearing nothing of Catherine, and still unable to reach her by phone, she harassed Millard until he drove out with her to the gates of the farm. But the gates were locked and silent, could be opened only from within. At a distance the house looked closed and quiet. Priscilla blew the horn, but as Millard pointed out, the house was too far away from them for the sound to reach it, and besides there was the air conditioning. On the second day, Priscilla made Millard get out the plane and fly over the farm. She wanted to fly so low over the house, trying to look down and see something, that they almost had a crash.

"It's not going to help Catherine one bit if we all get killed," she said, to which Millard heartily agreed.

On the third day, a long black car with Dallas license plates, chauffeur-driven, carrying strange men inside, eased through Merrill and departed out the road to the farm.

◆

Catherine had gone out for a walk, so she did not see anybody come. She had walked down to Sandy Gulch where the wagons used to cross, going West in the old days. It was where the frontier started and the sand was still there, though some fencing had been built across it to keep the cattle off it. The bluff made a tough semicircle around the north and east, but to the west there was the flatness stretching out toward one last sweet grove of eucalyptus before the West broke wide and dry and infinite. It was a funny place to have been born in and the boy who had died, she wondered if he hadn't thought it was a funny place to die. She was down by the creek bank by now, walking carefully, as Uncle Dick had taught her to be wary of snakes and quicksand or whatever stung, bit, damaged. There was a sense out in the country, in a hot land, that almost anything could turn into what would destroy you. She sat down near the thin, rusty, half-dried-up, half-stagnant stream, and looked back turning, and saw on top of the bluff the outline of an old man against the sky. She knew it was Uncle Dick. Of course, it wasn't really him—he was dead—and yet it was him more than if it had been. He wore what he had always worn, blue work trousers, an old tan linen coat, and an old panama with a crumpled, shapeless crown, pulled down as low as his ears. She got up at once and began to walk toward him. She wanted to tell him about Jerry. He was the only person she could tell. As she walked he raised his hand and waved to her, the way he always had done. She waved back and kept on walking. At the foot of the bluffs the path wound up. It had been worn so deep by cattle back in the old days—and they had used the old road the wagons had made—that the sides of the path rose like walls, taller than herself, and blotted out all but the steep ascent directly in front of her eyes. When she gained the top there was no one there and she sat down, catching her breath. The sense of his presence was everywhere; she even saw a compassionate expression in a cloud, which, as she watched, wheeled about upon itself, dispersed, changed and moved away. This was goodness—she had always understood; it had nothing to do with ambition, with power, with blood. She had her moment's paradise and knew the streets of heaven to be plain and shady, where the horses stood quietly and dogs lay waiting for their masters, who were greeting old friends and understood each other.

There was nobody she could tell.

She got to her feet at last and walked back toward the house, white in its softly blowing grove.

Halfway there she heard a shot.

She began to run. "Jerry, Jerry!" she came in calling. The living room was a mess. Plaster had fallen down in great hunks from the ceiling, an elk head had got loose from the wall and was hanging by one peg, the glass face of the old wooden clock was shattered. Jerry was nowhere to be seen, nor was anyone else. There was the sound of talking from the dining room and she ran in there. "It was just a crazy thing," said Jerry, who was sitting indestructibly at the end of the dining table with papers all around him and five men pulled up to the table. One of the men got up.

"I'm terribly sorry, Catherine. I was looking at the fine old gun collection out here—one of the best I've seen—and one of the early shotguns just went off in my hands. I have a collection of my own, as you know. Of course, some of us get mad enough to shoot each other, or so we say, but it hasn't happened yet. I guess you were terrified, just hearing a shot like that."

"Yes, yes, I was."

But it was not till late afternoon that she actually left. She had dressed again by then, and had overheard enough to know what was going on. "But it's Daddy's money," she thought. "That's the one thing we've never done."

◆

"But it's Daddy's money," said Priscilla, later on, to Millard, for they had at last been summoned out to the farm and the electric switch, controlled only from inside the house, had tripped the lock on the distant steel gates, and all the telephones were connected. Jerry had said that Catherine was all right, but it was certain that she wasn't there.

"Where is she?" Priscilla demanded of Millard. "He says she's gone out to be alone and may go to Dallas for a rest, but how do we know? Before all those millions get turned over to him, we certainly have a right to know where our sister is."

"It isn't millions," said Millard. "As I understand it, Daddy Latham is buying the magazine in order to sell it right back at a hundred-thousand-dollar loss and that way Jerry gets his publicity wish, Ogden stays out of hot water and the magazine gets to pay its debts and have another year or so to try at being solvent. Then Jerry pays back—"

"How?"

"Well, baby, there are ways and ways."

It was night and they were standing out near the barbecue pit. Once when Jerry had had a party there for Senator Ogden, they had roasted five steers and as the night was overcast, the light from the barbecue stained the sky far and wide, and Catherine and Priscilla had worn spangled Spanish costumes and looked, everyone said, perfectly marvelous. It was back when Catherine was still having fun.

Now they walked inside and Daddy Latham was sitting there with his foot in the brace stretched out and his cane beside him. He was sitting straighter than usual and his face looked strained; if you touched his money it was like an alteration, a surgery on his soul. Mama Latham sat still, like a lady in a family portrait. She grieved over it all, that it had all had to happen . . . she felt the pity of money, how much turned on it. No matter how much or how little was at stake, it could queer everything. And Jerry had never done anything like this before; it was the crack of doom with him and the Lathams. Was Priscilla glad? She could hardly wait to steer Millard down into the game room. Even a President had been there and had shot a game of pool.

"Listen, listen, now you're the one. You're the one." She said this to Millard, in her pride.

And he said, "Have you forgotten Edward?"

"Oh, they don't want him," said Priscilla. "They never have."

"But why? But why?"

"I don't know . . . he was created to sell shoes."

Millard sat on the edge of the billiard table and threw a red ball in the air. He looked ironic, somewhat sad, somewhat amused. There was an unmistakable footstep at the top of the stairs that led down into the billiard room.

"And if you are thinking anything," Jerry Sasser said, mainly down to the two of them, but also to everyone in general, "about Catherine leaving me, you may as well know the truth. She's at home here and she goes for walks here and yonder, but she always comes back. That's the way it could be anywhere, and I'm the one who knows. Catherine is never going to leave me. She can't leave me. She loves me. She's my wife."

"Then where is she?" Priscilla asked, sulkily, over her shoulder.

Millard got up lazily. Catherine's ghost seemed everywhere. Jerry came halfway down the steps and stopped; he was wearing slacks and a sport shirt and carrying a drink in his hand.

"You should have asked me for the money," Millard said quietly.

The truth of this came to Jerry Sasser instantly; you could almost, looking at him, see what color truth was. "By God, you're right."

"For," said Millard, spinning the ball on the green baize with long pale strong fingers, "I not only have it but I could provide it instantly, I could have kept quiet about it, and I could have understood why it was necessary. I even go so far as to share with you some conviction that it was important for this country that such a low and compromising thing be done."

Jerry leaned against the wall. Priscilla watched him fiercely, covertly. Had she watched him that way, all her born days?

"You're right, Millard. You're right," said Jerry Sasser. His sigh seemed to come from the very core of his strange, indecipherable earth; he had always been another country, another planet.

"I've made my mistake," he said quietly. He sat down, halfway down the stair. "Not but one was ever allowed to me," he said.

From up above, above the sunken playroom, above the ground

floor, too, they could hear the children. They were playing a jumping game, though not directly above the living room where the plaster had been knocked down when the gun went off—they had been warned, those two little Texas girls, against that. Did they want to knock the whole house down? "No, ma'am," they said.

Priscilla, having looked all her life at Jerry Sasser, suddenly did not want to look any more. She turned to Millard, to her husband, and fell in love with him. She more than fell in love: she loved him. I love you so, she wanted to say. It was like a stroke, from outside or inside, lightning or heart: it all but killed her. In her mind, in her heart, the country westered, stretching west, and her white bones would lie quiet someday beneath ground that the white clean cow skull lay above, and the grass would blow quiet and easy, and Priscilla, in all faith, would know nothing and everything at once, for when time is done there is forever, there is always.

Where is Catherine? she wondered. Where is my sister?

When Catherine knew what would happen she walked out of the house and kept on walking. Just as luck would have it, the five men who had been there got into their car and drove out; they passed her when she was almost to the gate. And they assumed that she knew where she was going and why and that it was okay. They assumed as she lived here and always had and her people owned it all, that she knew her way. So they asked her to ride in a joking way and then they all got out and spoke to her. From within the house Jerry had tripped the switch of the gate for them, else she never would have got out, but how could they know that? They must have imagined she could walk out any time she wanted to. (Thus it was Jerry Sasser who inadvertently let her go.) She said "No, thank you," and "Yes, how are you?" and "I didn't know you were going so soon," and "Do come back," and "See you in Los Angeles." She said all the right things, just as she had always (except for certain lapses) been so good at doing.

Then she said she was just going out to the highway for the mail, out for a walk. "In this heat," they said. "These Texas girls," they said. "They can take anything."

So she left under the dust of their wheels, she slipped through, or else Jerry wasn't looking maybe. She started walking; she probably had not walked anywhere in years and years and distances are long when you are out West. She seemed to herself like setting out on a journey to an ocean she wasn't even sure was there. But the dust, the dryness, the hidden snakes, and the nag of the constant wind, the bare deceptive unconscious landscape, the heat haze—one was sure of those things.

Jerry was the boy beneath the wagons, she thought. That has been true all the time.

At this everything came clear, as it usually does in the moment in which it closes off from us, from our living continuousness with it, and disappears into history.

How long she stood there beside a country road, alone in Texas, she did not know, but at some point a man stopped and asked her if she wanted a ride to Merrill. He was going there, he said. She got in. The car, though somewhat dusty, somewhat hot, and untidy, was commodious and expensive and this became a real surprise to her when she learned that the man's name was Hickman, because the Hickmans were supposed to be poor white trash and that was why the Lathams built a strong steel mesh fence with a gate electrically controlled from the inside when anyone was out there because the Hickmans were supposed to be anxious to get in and wreck things or set the house on fire out of revenge. But here this man Hickman was as nice as you please and talked and talked about how business was or wasn't—Catherine had reached the point where all business sounded alike.

From Merrill she went on into Dallas. Jerry has a mother, she was thinking, and he never knew it. Professor Sasser told me after the wedding. He said he never wanted to see her, but she lived in Dallas. And I never told Jerry. I didn't want to meet her, hear of her, have to put up with her. I didn't want to. He was ours, Jerry was; he was to be a Latham more than anything else, but now I can call at least and try to find out at least if any of the Sassers in the phone book could possibly be his mother, for even she has a right to know that her husband is dead and you would think that somehow that would have got looked into and attended to by one of the Blood Union of Messiah's Brotherhood, but you never know. The thing you think is surely, surely true is the one thing you might be wrong about. So she went to a phone booth in a cafe in Dallas and telephoned all the Sassers in the book—there were five of them—with five dimes in a little stack on the curved ledge in the phone booth and the smell of other people's expelled breath and spit and worry closed in all around her. Three were at home and were not Jerry's mother and one had moved away and the fifth did not answer, so she would have that to keep her going for a time.

And after that, she thought, and after that? She felt herself to be like the little light in the center of the TV screen that fades interminably and somehow carries your consciousness with it, as long as you care to watch it, and you have to watch it. You have to. It is you.

What's to keep me alive and going after I have called the fifth Sasser in the Dallas phone book and after I have made my weekly call to Latham and found out that he is all right, encompassed in the great care of nature, among those gentle New England woods? What is to keep me from going black?

There was the bee sting. It had not gone away. It had hurt like hell and had swollen and it was still a point of soreness.

And then, she thought, just before that fades, I know what is going to happen. I am going to see Jerry. I am going to look up on a street like this one and he is going to be there. He loves me. I belong to him.

◆

Priscilla and Millard had not heard the two little girls for some time and, wondering where they were, they went upstairs looking for them. It was just Edward and his second wife and the children who had arrived. They had driven up to the door and were getting out and now everybody had to face being nice to them though no one was especially proud to do so, and Priscilla in particular would have given anything to have got out of it.

"I'd give anything not to have to spend any time with those people at all," she said to Millard, climbing the steps. "They're my own flesh and blood, so I guess that's awful of me."

"I guess it is," said Millard, climbing the steps, "but don't let that stop you."

Suddenly, they kissed.

In the far upstairs bedroom, the one that looked out over the old well, they found the two little girls playing with an old deck of cards they had found. They had counted through them conscientiously; stacking them carefully according to suits: a ten, a four and a jack were missing, they said.

They looked up, laughing over nothing, and their faces, to Priscilla, looked like angels'.

TWO

When Catherine opened her eyes in Rome one spring afternoon she did not at first know where she was, or when it was, or why a young man was standing there. She had become one of those people—numerous in the world we have now—who have lived in so many different points on the globe that they have to think when they wake up, not just what room is this, or what house is this, or what hotel, motel, pension or resort is this, but what city is this in what country and what am I doing in it? Texas, a long shelf of dream over which white clouds passed in stately wind-drawn procession, sailing west, was an ocean away and inland far. She had walked away a year ago. Jerry Sasser's debacle over the magazine had got into the press anyway—a cog had failed to mesh, and not even he (though to have thought of the scheme at all had been audacious, like a final test of the power he had almost but not quite had) could bring it off. Almost, but not quite: it is a bitter phrase. For Senator Ogden, exposed on his civil rights nerve, a most sensitive one, though everybody knew how it was anyway, laid about himself with a staff-cutting "economy drive," in which heads rolled and were stuck on pikes to ornament the bridges over the Potomac. Jerry's handsome head, so recently on a magazine cover, had been among them. He first got the scalp of the newsman who had double-crossed him, but he still owed his wife's family $100,000. He still owed his wife a divorce which she had said she was unable to face going through at the point when it was mentioned. The doctors all agreed with her and the subject got postponed or mislaid.

The city now was Rome, the time was midafternoon, and the young man who was smiling at her did not look anything like Jerry Sasser.

He was an obviously poor young man, hardly taller than herself, spare and almost awkward, with concerned eyes. It is odd to have been watched while sleeping. It implies that we must absolutely trust or absolutely reject, before we can think or stop or help it, the person whose eyes we meet. When Catherine smiled at Barry Day, it meant that she instinctively trusted him.

"I promised to come," he said.

Then she remembered that, too. It was at a party yesterday. Now it all came back. The beautiful interior garden with twin baroque staircases lowering into flagstone walks past fountains, small eroded statues, beds of ivy, urns of verbena, trees of oleander. The shelter and rest of vine-covered walls. She was admiring everything when a startling thing happened: she heard her own name spoken behind her and turned and saw no one she knew.

"It's Catherine," a woman was saying. "It must be Catherine Latham."

The woman was, in the first place, beautifully dressed. Her dress, a cherry-colored rough silk tunic over a lighter silk mottled in various shades, was unmistakably Roman, as was the style of her smoothly mounted hair. Her voice was confident. If it should turn out that she was utterly mistaken and was addressing someone whose name in Rome one should never mistake for another's, she would not have disturbed herself about it. But she was not mistaken. Catherine supposed that she seldom was.

"I'm sorry," said Catherine. "I just arrived in Rome. You have to tell me who you are."

"Everything's a puzzle when you first come. You haven't changed a bit. I have! We were at a school in Baltimore together. I used to come across the street every morning and we went to music classes in that upstairs room where the radiator went hissss."

"I remember the school," said Catherine. "I was only there a year, I think."

"You were from Texas," the woman continued, "and I wanted to be from there. I wanted to be from anywhere but from right across the street from that school. I was fat and messy and always wiping ink off." Then she said her name, Irene something, her maiden name, since changed to Waddell.

"Oh, yes, yes, now I remember," Catherine lied.

"So now you're Mrs. . . . ?"

"Sasser."

"I can tell you're new in Rome, I can always tell."

"My husband isn't here," said Catherine. "I'm alone."

"You'll have to meet Charles. He isn't here either. You played the piano. I remember."

"Oh, dear," said Catherine. "But not in years." She could not help drawing back a little at this, like a bough the wind had idled aside.

It was right after that that Barry Day had appeared, straying toward the two women out of a babble of voices. . . .

"I remember," Catherine said to him next day, half sitting up on the couch in her sitting room where she had fallen asleep. "At the party, with that woman I was in school with. . . ."

"Mrs. Waddell," he said. "Listen, I'm sorry to barge in. I knocked twice and thought I heard you say, 'Come in.'"

"It's all right. Waddell. Now I remember."

He was still looking at her, attending to her closely. If you are always saying, "I remember," the chances are you are not quite sure of memory at all.

"I promised to help you move," he carefully recalled to her. "I found a place you'll like."

She glanced around. "My sister and her husband knew these people here and wrote them. They raved about this place." She grimaced. "It's supposed to be a palace, and look at it."

"It is a palace," Barry assured her.

"Bare walls, hard beds, no heat . . . I don't care what they call it." She leaned back. "I don't like Rome," she said. "Everybody is poor," she added. "It's a very poor city."

Barry was delighted. It took somebody from Texas to sit in an apartment like this on the Aventine with seventeenth-century gold-leaf Venetian furniture and frescoes dating back to the early Renaissance and a view from the windows clear over all of Rome to the Vatican and say, with no self-consciousness whatever, that she didn't like it.

"We'll try to do better," he said. "Now where are your things?"

◆

Irene had chattered too much at that party, and knew it, and couldn't stop. She blamed it on the martinis, but really she knew too that anyone out of her school past, her days of advance punishment for all the fun she could ever have afterwards, caused her to experience a mysterious self-revulsion. An automatic fracturing of her ego always occurred. Could that miserable-looking creature sitting in those rooms, walking those walks, allowing, in all ignorance, itself to be rawly exhibited in the school annual, possibly be Irene Waddell? It was the threat of being by some sleight-of-hand of fate—midnight striking, coaches changed to pumpkins—whisked back into that purgatory that made Irene nervous. She felt compelled to go up to whatever old schoolmate she saw, recall herself carefully to them, and then stone by stone build up with all the solidity and staying power at the Coliseum, that grand new image that was the real thing.

When Barry joined them, she kept right on going and so out-generaled herself, for, she was not long in seeing, given Barry's susceptibilities and Catherine Sasser's delicate helplessness and her own power to create an occasion, given spring and Rome and gin and that particular baroque garden, things were apt to take a turn before anybody knew it. She hauled up short. It was enough for her to do, simply to launch Barry and Catherine into conversation. She then branched off, circled the garden three times meeting old friends, let herself be led inside by her host, an oil company executive from California, to admire his new De Chirico, and returned to find the garden all but emptied in the twilight, Catherine Sasser hastening off without seeing her and Barry sitting on a stone bench with two empty glasses in his hands.

"You wanted to go with her," Irene noted, having said her goodbyes. Barry himself had suggested accompanying Irene to the party, as Charles was out of town, and taking her afterwards to eat a pizza.

"Oh, I asked her to come with us," said Barry. "She had to be somewhere else."

"She's a Texan. That means she's at the Hassler."

"No, she has some rooms on the Aventine. She hates it and wants to move."

"You've somebody else to help, is that it?" In the restaurant Irene read through the list of forty kinds of pizza. Barry was always running errands for people, or handing out free advice. He made half his friends this way. It was all he could do, he always protested. His knowledge of Rome, earned the hard way, from the ground up, was all he had to hand out. The friends usually had a good many more resources than he.

"There was this awful thing," Irene told him. "She got into this awful thing about her husband. He was in politics right after the war and then he got to working with one of those big Western senators, Ogden, I think, and things went from little to big. You saw his picture everywhere . . . I think Charles met him once or twice in Washington; oh, he knew absolutely everybody. I'm not sure what happened. They went back to Texas during the elections last year and there was something about bribing a magazine to keep a story out. Her whole family got involved in it—they had the money and he had to have it. It got out that she tried to kill him. Anyway, they broke up. There was a lot of gossip about him. I guess he was one too many. She had to go to psychiatrists. . . . Oh, you've no idea."

"Psychiatrists," said Barry, making it sound like a word out of fiction or slick movies, and indeed in Italy it did have this connotation. He had once met an Italian psychiatrist, who had told him sadly that all Italians needed his services but none of them thought they did. Barry supposed he was meant to be taking a warning from everything that Irene was going on about, but something in him was not only resisting her, but putting the whole story in a light favorable to the quiet face that had so recently been in soft focus before him. When Irene said psychiatry, he—with an artist's ruthlessness—threw the word out altogether. He gazed out across the pizzeria and thought of Washington, Texas, home cities in the rain. Irene thought she should let things alone. Why couldn't she?

"Barry, listen. She really is one I'd stay away from. Charles will tell you," she asserted confidently, though if this were to be true somebody would have to get to Charles, refresh his memory on the whole story and reason him into the proper attitude. He was out in the Middle East, figuring out the best uses for American aid to uncommitted nations, and the last person on his mind was Jerry Sasser.

"I can't think that doing a favor for her is going to make the sky fall on me," said Barry. "Anyway, what are you worried about?"

"Well, I don't know." She supposed she had overdone it. "Too bitchy for anything, am I?" What did she care? She held onto Barry, lightly, but seriously. A year ago she had saved his life and there were things he was privy to about her. If a woman came who was going to pull him into any strong orbit, Irene herself felt stirred to restless anxiety, wondered about a lover, longed to change something. Barry, not even deliberately, by going on to see Catherine Sasser against her advice, might be setting Irene's claim on him aside. Then again, she thought—amiably inclined—he might not.

"It just so happens the Farlands' apartment is up for grabs and they asked me just yesterday to see who I could get," he explained. "Then there she was. A perfect set-up. It's warm, it's modern, it's central, it's furnished, the elevator works, they've an honest maid who is a good cook and speaks English. What more could she want to fall into?"

"Okay. Can't you just do that for her and let it be your good deed?"

He steadily ate pizza and there was nothing she could do with him. She drank wine and her private thoughts mushroomed, giant-size. They always turned to Mario. Given one vacant instant in that beguiling air he would emerge, whole and expectant, out of the broad mouth of the Chianti measure on the table before her. When she shopped alone, every street-corner seemed about to yield him up to face her. Every bus stop appeared to disgorge him among a clutch of other shoulders, to scatter with them along the ceaseless rush of the streets. "Oh there you are! Figurati! Just imagine," she wanted to cry. "Oh, Mario, it's me! I just happened to see you. What a coincidence!" she could hear herself say. But it didn't happen. She had to seek him on purpose, or he her. Trying to disentangle themselves from each other, the whole winter through, they wrapped themselves in an endless tangle.

"Non mangia, signora?" asked the waiter. He was right; she hadn't eaten anything. Barry, who at least enjoyed a state of decision, in addition to the happy prospect of helping out an attractive new woman, was skillfully wiping up sauce. Decision was a good thing, Irene thought, and with that she made one herself. Suffering was not a good thing, she further recognized, and this obvious fact reinforced her. Okay, I'm going to find him. She almost said it aloud.

She began to eat again.

I had to come, she would say. I had to.

◆

"I had to come," she said. "I had to."

He had just passed an ice cream shop where she had been waiting. She had sat at a marble-topped table, inside the shop which was down in a poor quarter on the far side of the Tiber, smoking and waiting. When he went past she hastened out.

They would all know, the young men in the shop, whom she had come to find; they had probably guessed it the instant she alighted from the cab in her Via Condotti costume, her fine shoes passing spilled milk and straw on the rough cobbles, her own rich body's consciousness, vegetating tropically along the way, now grown towering. It would have struck them like a sharp reverberating sound. The men as good as said so. They stopped cleaning floors in the freshly emptied shop and she saw acknowledgment of herself spring up in their eyes. When she asked to sit down for a while, they did not ask if she wanted anything, but nodded without a word. She tucked up a strand of damp hair.

Coming out of the pizzeria with Barry from whom she had parted with scarcely a nod, her mind was filled with Mario. She had noticed, on a sidewalk table with a round dime-colored top, a handful of field poppies left to wilt. The color leaped up and bled at her vision. Crossing the Tiber, she saw light strike through the clouds, just before the dark, and rain fell. Her nerves and senses mingled in the wet spray. The silk of her dress pressed on her like an enclosure of ferns. At the table she felt herself to have been placed suffocatingly beneath a great glass bell showered with spray which kept jetting and spilling, dazzling with fresh hothouse variance down the convex sides. She sat in silk and thought of flower flesh, which bled or wept if broken. Then there he was. The bell lifted; the bird flew.

"Mario! Mario, it's me."

He had spun around when she spoke like something held already on a very tight string. It was really all she needed to know, just seeing that. She paused as they each steadied themselves.

"I had to come. I had to."

The words came out differently from anything she had imagined, low, almost meek, in a minor key, her face serious, her wings close-folded and dumb.

"Hai fatto bene," he replied, after what seemed to her long meditation. "You did well." He never denied her, never denied that what she was bringing him was first of all his own joy.

Irene had got herself involved with Mario Marcadante the year before on a trip to Siracusa, in Sicily. The journey had not been taken for pleasure; it was strictly emergency, unforeseen, and the reason for it was none other than Barry Day. In a way, it had all been Barry's fault. How tangled life was! Irene thought. Were we all involved in a continuous dance? she wondered. The pattern weaves, we touch, join hands, do steps as best we may, change partners, return and cling and change again. Or is it outside ourselves, like a mosaic, all there all the time? Water splashes over the pattern, over the stones, and they seem to shift and alter; then the water runs off and there it all is, cunningly worked out, just the way it has been all the time. Which was to say that both Mario and Barry had been there all the time, though Mario had so far only been a friend of her husband's, and Barry had so far never been dying before, not that she knew about.

She was absolutely certain he was dying then; in fact, she could never convince herself afterwards, not entirely, that he hadn't, in some sort of way, died.

She had got the message in Rome. "Terribly ill in Siracusa can you get me back to Rome." It had been addressed to Charles, who was away in Cairo with the American Economic Aid commission he had worked in so long and faithfully.

She stood in her shadowy early summer apartment and knew at once that though Barry had sent the wire to Charles he had meant it for her. It was she whom he meant to come there. Where did I get this mother thing about Barry? she wondered. It must have happened from the first and she hadn't known it, from seeing right away that he was hungry, that he accepted invitations, theirs, anybody's, out of necessity. And surely she must have known when she passed him back in the winter, in her chauffeur-driven car coming up the Via Nazionale in the late afternoon winter mist, almost rain, and saw him standing in a poor tan German duffle coat, waiting for the lights to shift, she must have recognized when she lifted her hand to him out of the warm car, a signal through the cold wet glimmer of the neon, that his coldness had gone to her heart in a very personal way which caused the pang of it to linger with her. But she had shoved the feeling aside. She was far too busy, she knew too many people, he was on her list and she did what she could for him and that had to be enough. But now that he was ill and had appealed to her, she knew she had to go. This feeling for him had been there all the time; there was no denying it, not in the quiet apartment alone, with Charles away.

How on earth had he got to Siracusa?

She finally learned this: he was too helpless not to tell her everything.

◆

Had Barry seen her that evening, deep in furs, warm in the sleek car's depth, her hand out to him whose thin trousers the wind pierced easily? If not that evening, then plenty of others, going here and there, her narrow Italian heels twinkling for a moment over rain-swept stone while he hustled along with a parcel or two of bread, cheese and mortadella, back to Piazza Navona and the two filaments in the electric stove which were all he had to meet the winter with. He had to be tough and he got tough. He got tougher and tougher. He could appreciate and not wish for the savor of Irene Waddell and people like her, and the doors that opened richly to let them in. It was the way Rome had always been, he reflected; there had to be people like him in order for luxury to be defined at all. In his studio near the Esedra, the wind whistled in through the window cracks, but the light was splendid and he forgot the wind for whole chunks of hours together, casting moulds and sanding away at stone surfaces. He wore an old beige sweater with a turtle neck and it filled up gradually with the uniform smell of stone dust. He went out for coffee and wondered if he should go in with somebody more cheaply on the Margutta. He hated loneliness until he could actually lose it; then it became a precious thing and was called privacy. The bars smelled of sawdust which was scattered on their stone floors to drink up the damp.

Then warm weather came, promising an early summer, and he was happy again. He had finished two nearly life-size works, and when the back of his neck got hot he felt rewarded by sunlight, by the universe itself, a nod of approval, and could afford by reason of an encouraging sale to some friends of Charles Waddell's to sit on the Via Veneto in front of Doney's, a swanky cafe, with a Swedish girl whose hair was yellow, whose cheeks were rosy and whose English was very good. Irene chanced to pass and waved at them. "Who was she?" Irene wanted to know when they next met. "She was the loveliest thing I ever saw." "She's with the Scandinavian Airlines." "Then her name is Inge. They're all named Inge." "Helga," he said (it wasn't). "Will that do?"

Then one day his wife showed up. He had been allowed ten days of sheer delight, which is a lot, he thought, sitting on the bunk in his studio with the letter in his hand wondering whether to stand or flee.

Her name was Linell McIntosh before she married him, one hasty weekend in New York where she had pursued him full of tears and that everlasting love which he had, at one time, not only believed in, but had himself introduced her to. She was from Arkansas and if he had never loved her it would not have been so bad. But he had loved her. He had crashed into love like falling through the roof of a greenhouse and there he was before he knew it within those numb transparent walls, moving among heavy odors, through heated air debilitating as paradise.

Irene was to learn all this in Siracusa as ravings from a bed of fever in a little pensione on the second floor of a building which overlooked the Ionian Sea.

◆

Irene had known from the first that Mario was in Sicily; he had been working for Charles and for others in the American bureaucracy abroad for some years. He and Charles had met during the war. He had done all the right things, had worked in the underground, been captured, escaped, gone over to the Allies at a time when it was worth your life to say so. Charles had been drawn to a group of such people, for whom his admiration was always great. ("They were the true heroes," he would say. "They were what the war was all about.") Mario, as his English was excellent, was easier to keep up with than some of the others. He continued to be satisfying. He appeared in Paris during the Waddells' time of residence there, and studied for a year at the Sorbonne. So he came often to their apartment. He was known to be working on some book or other, and not only working on it; Irene took note, after a year or so, that he had finished it and it was published! Irene cultivated artistic people, but often grew discouraged with them. Why talk so well about things and not do them? She was pleased with Mario and boasted of him and thought of whom he should meet: then he vanished back into Italy. "He has to get work," Charles explained to her. "Of course he does. He has a good family but isn't rich by any means. They work very hard there," he added. "It's a false reputation, this dolce far niente." He was angry at the French at the time, so that all Italians seemed like marvelous people.

Mario could have passed for anything, French or German, English or American. He had a face that openly presented his essence to the world—quick, sensitive, intelligent, withholding only for a while, until he smiled, an exceptional sense of humor: he liked absurdities; that was what you gratefully realized. So he was always changing from the serious young European political thinker, dour and frowning, to a performer's mimicry, his pliant mouth shooting up at the corners, his grey-blue eyes sharp and wild in a nest of wrinkles. For measure and timing he was accurate as a cat. "An aristocratic clown," Charles called him once. The Waddells loved discovering their superiors.

He's going to think I'm crazy, thought Irene, who alighted from the Rome-Catania plane, a bit wobbly in the knees, pale and dizzy. It was hot and the tarmac was like black paste. She telephoned to the Catania University for Mario and was directed to him at once by one of those surprising efficiencies that have to occur sometimes in Italy, as though to prove the system had really broken down.

"Irena!" he said, surprised, and offered to come out for her, but she, instead, got a cab in to him.

He came out of the university offices and met her on the street as she was alighting from the cab. "Signora," he said, ready to laugh. It was half a question. It meant what was she doing there and where was Charles and that the plane had obviously shaken her up and maybe even scared her.

"Oh, Mario," said Irene, "I'm in a crisis. Can you go to Siracusa with me? I have to rent a car. There's a bus but I think I'll need a car. We've a sick friend there, for all I know he's dying. I tried to telephone from Rome but no luck. You must remember him. Barry Day? An artist from the States. Molto magro."

"Si . . . Day . . . quello che aveva lo studio in Via Nazionale. Si, lo conosco."

"Charles would appreciate it more than you know. Traveling alone in Sicily . . . well, for a woman, I don't think it's a good idea."

"But they are courteous." He was still smiling. She felt more than ever that this was the right step and that with a little urging he would not only go but would also organize, take over a bit; yet he held back. "No one would harm you."

"I know, but I— What if he's terribly ill? What if there

should be a real emergency? First, I must call again from here to try and reach him or somebody there. Help me call, at least. The language is different. I feel I don't know enough."

"You are upset," said Mario. He hesitated.

"I sent a wire off to Charles. He's due in this weekend."

"Then perhaps he will come also."

"I hope so. I don't know."

Suddenly, she really did feel desperate. She thought of Barry in the sense of one of the twins who was lying ill and alone without her. "I have to get to him," she said to Mario. "I can get Charles to straighten it out with people here that you have to leave. Say it's my brother and he has—oh, something awful—scarlet fever. Peritonitis."

"You scare me too," said Mario. Then he consented. He said the work was all but done there and he had planned to return the next day.

In the rented car, Mario driving, they spoke sometimes Italian and sometimes English, and sometimes a little of both. How grand to have found him, thought Irene. She was astounded by her unparalleled luck. And though the mistress of the pensione in Siracusa had been half hysterical about the sick Americano, Mario had managed to get out of her that Barry was still alive. "She doesn't want anyone dying there," Mario concluded, hanging up the phone. "Sicilians are another race." He dismissed them all.

"But you said how courteous—" Irene protested.

"Well, they are old-fashioned. They pride themselves on being cavalieri. But here for years before the war they let themselves be Mafia-ridden, bandit-ridden, and now eleven years after the war where are they? The same as before. I think they will never throw it off. The American programs here are nothing; they come to the lectures one after another, week on top of week, and have no idea of English, or what is going on. They could perhaps do a polite conversation but scarcely more than that. How can they continue? Cultures have overflowed them, one after another, and still there is no mainstream here. No, no. The good ones will go to Rome, or get out entirely, and the others will simply sink back into family interest or form some little circle where they talk and dress well and please each other. It will go on like that. And oh my God, in the villages! There is this Guiliano worship. He was against the Mafia. The Mafia had him killed."

"Oh, I thought he was one of them."

"They used him for a time, but then he became inconvenient. There is no loyalty. Only what they want to call loyalty. It is all too complicated, and who can really know who did what? They say that his best friend was hired by the Mafia to kill him, but the police story is quite another. He became a problem to the state. So there is yet another story for the state. He was a handsome outlaw. That is all. The women dipped scarves in his blood. Half of their husbands had been murdered by the Mafia. What is there to do? Niente. Niente da fare. . . ." He glanced at her in the mirror. "Don't be worried, Signora. Your friend will live."

"How lucky I am to have found you," said Irene. She had said that a dozen times already.

"You would have made it all right," he said, and his eye flashed at her, again out of the mirror, as though out of the sky, an encouraging gleam. "American women always make it all right."

She saw that Mario was happy. He was happy to be with her, doing this very thing. When he spoke of Sicily, it had a different ring from when an American criticized something abroad because no matter how scathing he became he was still concerned. Italy drove him crazy but the country was always his own. She began to watch Etna; the cool snowy cone relieved the dense heat. "How fast you drive!" she remarked. "Fa presto."

"I like driving. Once in the war I escaped only by driving well. I passed just ahead of a train and cut off the military police. In the night, sometimes I dream, the train is still breathing in my face like a bull, I am little like a mouse, and I am not going to make it. But I did. There should have been a movie."

"This was when you left Rome?"

"The Germans were retreating by then. Rome was a chaos. They had been suspicious of me already. I had got through twice to report to the Allies on the defenses of Rome. When the advance pressed closer, suspicion of anyone was excuse enough to shoot. There was nothing more I could do. So I stole a jeep and left for Siena, to my aunt's villa in the country. Three checkpoints I passed okay and at the last, somebody there recognized me. Shouts and shots. It was night, about one o'clock. Very dark evening. I drove with my head down, hugging the floor. Then just at Santa Margherita—the train. I shall never forget it. . . . Your friend now"—he broke off, glancing at her again—"You are good to do this. I do not know if I would do it. I think so often, Americans are really very kind. For my brother perhaps, or someone in the family."

"Or Francesca," she smiled. She had met his fidanzata, that

quiet, pale, lovely girl. The odd thing was that she had never seen them together. She had once wanted to ask the girl to a dinner party, but Charles had advised her not to. "These things are pretty much family matters," he said. "But Mario is so modern," she insisted. She took his advice and let it drop.

"You think Francesca would be alone in Siracusa? Oh, Signora, first, at the very news, the family all falls to the floor. Spaventati. Tutti morti."

"When will you marry?" Irene asked him.

"I don't really know yet, for a while I wanted to go to the States, but just now it seems impossible. Even if I had the money, there would be this damned visa."

The reason Mario had had visa trouble was that after the war he had found himself with a good many Communist friends, some of long standing, some who had recently joined the Party, and others who argued about it all the time. He continued these friendships and even enjoyed them. Sometimes they even amused him. Nobody could think any more that Communists could be funny. Though Charles Waddell had got him several jobs, his visa had been turned down. Charles himself could not put up too much pressure in this direction, for there were ways of discovering that he himself was not as one-hundred-percent American as other one-hundred-percent Americans might contrive to think he should be. The times were nothing if not delicate. Delicate and brutal, thought Irene.

They drove through orange groves, past tiny stations cooking, burnishing, shrunken, drying desert-dry in the sun. Even one person could look so lonely and hopeless, walking, working a vineyard, leading a donkey, or just standing near a railroad station. You could think that life was hopeless for millions and millions of people on earth you didn't know; but maybe it only seems terrible to me, thought Irene, because I would have to leave what I am and know and turn into something I cannot begin to imagine—a Sicilian peasant woman in a worn black dress and drawn-back hair and knobby hands and big flat crusty feet in broken shoes, looking sixty at thirty and eighty at forty and never knowing anything but passionate love and passionate hate, motherhood, and some mumble about the Virgin or a saint. At the moment when her life seemed so superior to all the possible lives that birth might have cast her into, and her present moment certainly a fine one—a mission of rescue, of sheer humanity—it must have been about then that she ceased to think of herself in any way at all, for she began simply not to think at all. She began to talk to Mario and he to her: they talked up several hours without knowing it. Mario went on beautifully driving, his driving—really expert, she later thought—almost interpreting the swing of the curves, the cool rush of the orange groves, the blank stretches of nothing but sun. She thought later, too, a long time later, that if it had been a horse, a span of horses, that he drove that day, perhaps the way she felt might have been intenser yet; or even had they ridden together, galloping. But then she gave it up—that was too much; they both belonged to the mechanical age, to wheels, accelerators, brakes and carburetors. The road mounted curving through the orange groves and the long downward grade opened, leaning toward the sea, the salt flats and the white cliffs surrounding Siracusa shouldered distantly up against the translucent blue of greater distances yet, Africa was out there somewhere; it was impossible to think of horses. She would have been unable to talk at all, for one thing, jerked in the harsh rhythm of animals, worried at times about the poor things in the heat, her head would have hurt and her shoulders got tired. As it was she sat calmly, confident of the shifting wheel beside her, her voice carrying to him perfectly. It was a little like dancing, she thought, leaning to the motion; she lifted a strand of hair blown from under her scarf with one finger and tucked it underneath.

"I think perhaps, as regards America," said Mario, "that whatever it is about you, you must have been able to bring here to us as good as we could find it there. My ambition to go there fell away, was no longer primary to me the day I realized this. Now I also can see this idealism freeing itself, even from you, perhaps, going out to the world. What is it? Enthusiasm, a desire to excel, to perfect, and also to act with joy, to lose nothing in the action. There are many mistakes, of course—you fall short, as everyone does. Yet in thinking this for a time I lost my Italianism, my cinismo . . . then in the normal course, it returns. We do not go too far into one direction or another. For us, we miss our true natures in this way, we feel ourselves to be fools. But still I can see it—the splendid test, this quality of life like some sport, to achieve—not happiness, perhaps; a peasant may be happier than you; but if not happiness, then what? I would call it glory!" He turned his head to take her swiftly into his regard. "You are like that."

He broke off, coloring, and Irene, for the first time in miles, suddenly paused to reconsider. She had been getting on with him too well, she saw that. A road construction project caused them to slow down, and cut into the moment. Lavoro di stato. A long paragraph of explanation stood out in black letters on a white sign. It could be read while the car jounced, breaking the eyes' focus painfully, hurling the vision at times face to face with some Sicilian workman's face. The eyes looked straight at her without hesitancy or apology and without giving up anything to her; yet she gained for an instant a sense of both herself and the workman being uncomfortably involved in the trouble with the road, and that was a fleeting equality, wasn't it?, which she could take to herself. Yet his stare withheld everything of his own truth. Perhaps he even hated her—in her approach, while their eyes met, after she was gone. Who knew? One workman, swart, with a red bandanna wrapped pirate-fashion around his head, knotted at the side, and a gold earring in one ear, sweat pouring down his neck, flashed her a theatrical smile. He dressed like that just to do that, to wait for somebody like me to pass, she thought; either did it on purpose, or was glad it happened that way. Now his day is a little bit different. She remarked his sly folk-pride. But her mind returned to the blank and arrogant starer as being in some way the victor. My friend is italiano, she wanted to say. And he understands americani and he thinks we're glorious. He just said so.

Mario had scarcely noticed the workmen at all. Picking up the road again he had retired, she noted, into his quieter nature, and the brief attraction to him that had pulsed for a moment along her veins had vanished easily. As the road straightened, flattening out once more, they saw clearly now on the horizon ahead the high plain and the city which held her friend, helpless, sick and alone.

◆

Through a corner of the window he could see a corner of the sea. He could always hear it. The fever beat in his head, and his vision and hearing blurred the outlines of what was distant and what was near; his own body sometimes flowed out and was the sea; at others the sea came in and curled over him, washing and streaming, making a final slap against his ear as though on a stone. The Ionian Sea, he thought. The Ionian Sea.

He had run away from Rome to get to Sicily to get away from his estranged wife who scared hell out of him. Her name was Linell and she had been a pretty—meltingly pretty—little girl from Arkansas. She was still a meltingly pretty girl from Arkansas who had come to Rome to find him, the Lord alone knew why. It was because of her that he had stolen $2,000 from her father and uncle's company safe and had fled to New York seeking freedom, though this motive was not recognized by the law enforcement officers in Hoskins County, Arkansas, nor by Linell's family.

For they did not decide to "hush it up," "keep it in the family," make him "feel better about it," help him "live it down," "smooth things over," and think in terms of a "fresh start," the way they would have done for anyone not an artist who had got engaged to their daughter and niece. They said that because he was an artist they should never have given their consent to the marriage or believed anything he said, let alone thought that he could be trusted with the combination to the safe or the keys to the office. They had his background investigated and discovered that he was only calling himself Bernie Porter instead of Bernard Desportes, a suspicious name in itself. (Barry had changed it, just as he did the second time, for aesthetic reasons, but try telling them that.)

Looking back, he saw what a fool he had been. He saw, too, that he had had motives both good and pure, whole-souled and even passionate. For this had been his Americana phase, though at the time he had thought it was always and forever, a total commitment. It was his postwar-vibrant-new-life phase; his rediscovery-of-the-grass-roots-with-all-of-life-ahead-while-he-was-still-so-young-and-vigorous phase. He was going to be not only a Great Artist but a Good Guy; he was going to be One of the People; he was going to set loose a new kind of realization, binding art to life and both to the soil.

There was never anyone better fitted for carrying this off than Bernie Porter, who dreamed of settling down with some pretty, average girl and living among ordinary people, pursuing his art and doing whatever else was necessary to keep alive. He got a job in an Arkansas vocational school, once he got out of the army. He did not even have his period, as so many artists, writers, and others did, of living on his rocking-chair money, which was what they called the government allotment to veterans to bridge them over into civilian life.

Bernie Porter was to teach gym and coach basketball, in this town near the Ozarks, teach French—about which he knew very little—supervise study hall, and offer a class in drawing and painting. Could anything be more perfect than that? (He refused to take a Sunday school class.)

The children were brought to school in yellow buses which congregated in the broad, flat, nondescript schoolyard each afternoon waiting for the final bell. It was just after that final bell, one day, after the study hall was empty and nothing was left there of the children except their smell and the echoes of hurrying feet, a wrangle of voices, a whoop from the lower hall, the heavy clump of big boys' shoes. He looked out of the window toward the buses and saw the drivers, who sat on the steps of the school to smoke or talk, walk out to get inside. The tide of children overtook them, rushed around and ahead, submerging them. They dropped their cigarettes, exchanging so-longs, but more often saying nothing at all. They were apt to run to silence back up in the Ozark foothills, after the run and the whoop of the school years was done. Then the last footstep died from the resounding wood-floored hallway and scarped from the concrete steps. The tide went out. Here came one, a straggler in a hurry, running, her brown hair bouncing about her shoulders, back arched and feet flying. She had some books and a sweater she must have worn when she started out from home in the cool of the morning, looped between her arm and the books, the thin elbow of her free arm came to a point, pumping and running. This was Linell McIntosh, but he did not know it yet. He just felt a sudden affinity: she was the one.

It was purely Olympian—an Olympian moment.

He had been pleased with himself for weeks. Everything he had scarcely dared to hope for was working out. Simple children from the country could love art, after all. This was what he had wondered when he first—chewing his nails day after day in a cryptographer's hut in Wales during the war with constant rain aslant against the cramped windows and himself unable to draw even the profiles of the men he saw every day, all day long—thought of it, that whole glorious scheme. He had lived on it, fed on it, months on end. Now, step at a time, it was working. But this particular basic question—could ordinary children like art, be taught it and learn, if not to practice it, to make it a part of their lives—had been an uncertainty. And it was crucial, perhaps the most crucial part of the plan. Now it was happening. He already had a lively class of drawing going, and though some of the girls giggled at the young veteran, new at teaching, and one or two wrote him anonymous notes, more and more of them were getting interested in the work. He even had a fair scattering of boys. So he saw it stretching out before him, that for which he had longed, since his moment of resolution across the sea, to give his life to—the beautiful pastoral dream. It had been there all along—a possibility. It could be reached, attained, like anything else if you worked hard enough and understood what you were doing. If he could do it, then other people could and would. Perhaps they were at it also, here and there, across the great beloved land, at that moment. False images—the wartime images—God Bless America—all that crap—a course like this deliberately cast out. Furthermore, his basketball team was shaping up. Soon the buses would start rolling back in the evening for the night games in the gym, which would echo shouts and the slap and wham of the ball, all clear as hounds belling in the frosty night. But now the sun—hot, harsh, but bringing the faintest suggestion of dry, dusty, golden light—lay aslant; fall light, harsh against every windowpane, entered everywhere. It lay on the distant surrounding farms the children were going back to; the small farms that had reached that sad moment of the season's pause, the harvest, in some sense, never being the equal (he meditated) of the human effort and beauty that had been extracted to create it, though neither the earth nor the people could help themselves; it was the old timeless struggle with the earth. He was swept by love and understanding of it—of it all—and the girl with brown hair and slender arched back and narrow elbow went running, running on forever. She gained the school bus, the awkward, steep, rough steps, and climbed, her arm stretched out, grasping the rod near the door. Her face profiled, and it was the right face, the one he had had in mind. What was it they said about steering clear of students? Well, there would be ways of handling that one, too, he thought. Nothing was beyond Bernie Porter, who in addition was going to be a Great Artist.

In retrospect, lying sick and feverish in Siracusa where he had fled to get away from Linell McIntosh, it seemed remarkable not that he had failed in his golden quest, but that he had come so near succeeding.

Or did I, or did I? he wondered.

The sea turned back but came again; it rushed throbbing against the rock and his temples throbbed. His eyes throbbed also, and he closed them, and when even the tender veiling of the lids failed to shut out the pain, he opened them and there standing in the door was a cool vision: Irene.

Because his illness had slowly debauched the sense of life throughout his limbs, making him seem scattered and crushed below the bright and hardy surface of existence, Irene Waddell appeared to him as preternaturally lovely, her skin luminous and transparently radiant, her hair, brownish with red lights, curling crisply and naturally back from her broad cheeks where the convex planes were breaking and reforming, rearranging around the blasphemous idea she clearly had in her head—that all this was a little bit funny; that he was beyond a doubt going to live. But she was glad to see him, was nothing if not affectionate, and he couldn't quarrel with that, he just had to take it and be content with it. A crust is sustenance, after all; after all, she *had* come. But Charles—? It was Charles he had got word to, Charles, really, whom he wanted. A woman's presence embarrassed him. The padrona of the pensione had frightened him into a deeper despair, a well of fever, by telling him after Irene's call, only: "Qualcuna viene." "Una donna?" "Si." "Suo nome?" "Non so." He was afraid it was Linell. Linell McIntosh. Oh God, what a name to conjure with! Had she spoken Italian? he pursued. She had a friend, un signore; he was speaking well. That couldn't be Irene, whose Italian was excellent. Unless she was with Charles. But Charles was not good at languages. None of it made sense. When nothing made sense he always thought of Linell. It must be Linell. She had hired somebody to come with her. He almost panicked.

At first he tried to rise, dress, get out at all costs. But he could not walk. The infection in his knee had spread in a red stain up his thigh. The sight made him shudder. He could not bend his knee. And even if I dressed, he thought . . . if I got up, got into something, staggered out feverish into the sun, groped through street after street, where would I end, if I did not die before I got there, but at the sea? This is Land's End. Linell McIntosh has driven me to the ends of the earth, and I am dying.

One thing is certain. If she walks through that door, I shall either go out the window, or I shall throw her out of it.

He pulled the sheet up to his cheek, seeking coolness, and having resolved upon this course, closed his eyes.

But it was Irene who entered. A goddess, with a goddess' risky carelessness over human affairs—she didn't *have* to be interested—she was nonetheless there. Thank God, he was thinking, all the while he was getting angry with her for not being serious enough about him. "Where's Charles?" he asked, rejoicing in her cool touch across his forehead. She thinks I'm one of the twins, he thought, resenting it. But he was aware of her love. It became a medium in the day, like air and light, an element in his fever, a conductor through which the pain shot and throbbed. Oh, Irene, he thought, or whispered.

"Poor Barry," she said. "Poor Barry."

Charles was not with her. "He'll come if he can," she said. "If he gets the message he'll come." She touched his hand and head, her flesh like splashes of water. "We've got to see your doctor; where is he? Oh, I'm not alone. I found Mario in Catania—Mario Marcadante. He'll talk to the doctor, talk to everybody. Do sleep if you can. I brought some American aspirin."

"Aspirin! It's worse than that, Irene. Worse than that!" He gripped the sheets. Did he have to perish in front of her to make her understand?

"I know that, Barry. It's just that aspirin is all I have."

He closed his eyes. "It's hot . . . hot," he murmured. "It must be July."

"Just about," Irene confirmed.

She got him water, coaxed the aspirin down him, turned his pillow and wrung out a cloth for his head.

"It was in July the other thing happened," he rambled. "That day in Arkansas. I was marrying her in a week and lying under the jeep in her father's back yard and I heard them, and they never intended any of it. Oh, to marry her, sure, that was fine, but none of it about the art school. It was all a lie and they were going to get me out of it, as soon as we had got married, and the worse of it was that she knew, she knew it! She was lying too, and had been and would. She had heard the whole plan and the money for the art school was going to be mine and she went to drawing class day after day, talked and walked and lived it, all I dreamed about. It was a lie. I was flat out under her father's jeep to repair it, with oil dripping in my face and I heard it all. They were going to get me over that foolishness. They had never considered doing anything else. It was not till then I stole the money. I would never have thought of taking money otherwise."

Irene nodded. "Of course not, darling," she said.

"She followed me to New York. Sorry about everything. We'd have a new start. We got married. It was a lie, just a lie. A scheme to get me back to Arkansas. A hold on me forever. She never saw she had done anything wrong. She never saw she had done anything at all, except what was right. She thinks she's holy; she loves me forever; she's pretty and rich and sexy as hell.

I could beat her to a pulp and she'd never know the truth. She ruined me, destroyed me. Now she's pursuing. She'll follow me forever. She'll never let go."

"I won't let her in," Irene promised.

"You don't take me seriously."

"Would I be here at all if I didn't? Now, Barry, it's just the fever. You're going to be okay."

"I hope you aren't too sure," he said. "Irene, please be a little bit worried."

"I keep telling you that I am."

But if so, why laugh? he almost said, but had no strength to continue the argument. She had laughed; he knew it. He had heard it tinkle like ice in a glass, the kind of ice you chipped with an ice pick off a whole blue cold square, tightly crystalline at the core, the jagged lumps losing their sharp edges on the moment of entering the clear water. "Remember ice?" he almost said. (She would have thought he was raving again.)

She thinks I'm one of the twins, thought Barry. She knows too many strong people; she is too strong herself, and so she isn't careful. How can I live again, how can she know enough to let me? He did not know, but he had to trust her anyway.

◆

Irene and Mario sat in the doctor's office, and though the white streets were baked dry and hot, the interior was cool and shuttered, faintly damp, smelling of ether and antiseptics, and Irene, in her sleeveless dress, almost shivered. The doctor was scrubbed, immaculate, rather handsome. His face was dark and florid, his jacket flawlessly starched and white. There was no sign of his profession anywhere; no diploma was hung up, no nurse to be seen. Irene got the fleeting feeling that anyone might have come in off the street and put that jacket on. She did not trust Italian medicine and while still in Rome had telephoned to an American doctor, a friend from Charles' army days who had liked Italy and decided to come back to start a practice. He could not go with her, he said, but promised to give what advice he could on the phone and, if she really got desperate, to fly there.

Mario talked with the Sicilian doctor. Irene could not follow his accent; perhaps she was frightened, as he seemed to speak a correct, businessman's Italian. The gist of it was that Barry's injury to his knee, which had resulted from a motor-scooter accident he had on some rocks by a roadside near Agrigento, was three days old before the doctor had had a chance to look at it. Now he could only hope to have arrested the infection. This fever, these aches, quite possibly came largely from grippe. It was only a coincidence that the grippe—

Out in the street Irene blurted out her fears. "I don't believe it, I don't believe a word of it. Italian medicine is the closest thing to witchcraft." She stopped trying to be tactful. "It's clear he's aching because the poison is everywhere. I'm going to call Dr. Archer. . . ."

"Stop it," said Mario, and backed her out of the sun, into an empty doorway. He snapped her bag shut; she had been fumbling in it for gettoni to initiate a call. "Call him if you have to, but not in this mood. You're trembling."

"But what can I do? I can't sit around here and watch him die. He's an artist," she added, rather lamely.

"Maybe he's not dying. Maybe the doctor is right. It's only a summer fever."

"It's all connected. If he has to have a leg amputated in this godforsaken. . . ."

"The doctor is not that bad," said Mario.

"How would you know?"

"Okay, I'm just a stupid wop. Why did you want me to come? To chauffeur you?"

"I'm sorry, I'm sorry . . ." She fell silent and walked at his side to a bar. He sat her down and ordered her something.

"One always feels at the mercy of doctors. That is the trouble," Mario said. "For myself I have always watched animals closely. They cure themselves when sick. It was after I escaped from Rome I stayed at my aunt's villa near Siena. She had so many animals, a little goat used to run in the house and play. He had black hooves, very small and sharp. When sick he would not eat, or graze—even a goat. A goat will eat anything, but when sick? No, he looked out for a special herb."

It all seemed like more talk to Irene. She felt the total responsibility of Barry narrow down to her. How could anyone sit making charming conversations about goats while Rome burned? If the doctor had been there, he would have joined in with Mario. *He* would have known about a goat, too. That was the part that made her wild. But in one way Mario was right; she had to calm down.

"Now let me get it straight," she said. "Everything he told you." And from thenceforth launched herself, wholehearted and, at least in her view, singlehanded, into the struggle. I'm going to do everything I can, was her resolve.

Hardly sleeping at all, she sat up for two nights with Barry. She sneaked off to the first-class tourist hotel, Albergo degli Stranieri, and called Dr. Archer. She had by then as much information as a hospital might have been able to gather. She had not seen Charles through a long Mayo clinic checkup for nothing, or nursed the boys through duplicate attacks of mumps and flu.

His Yankee growl floating deviously down from Rome reassured her. How many units of penicillin . . . ? And were there red streaks . . . ? And could she tell if . . . ? And was the fever constant or did it rise and fall?

She brought a thermometer and got ice from the neighborhood bar. She kept Coca-Cola in a plastic bucket, to the marvel of the landlady, who must have heard something of the sort about Americans. She watched the sea break on the sun-heated rocks. The Ionian Sea, she said to herself. A sense of reality in that place easily took part of her to itself.

She forgot about Mario, whom she passed once in the street without recognizing until he was gone. Once she wondered if he had left for Catania or Rome; again she was grateful to remember that he showed up daily. Where was he staying? She didn't know.

On the evening of the second day, the doctor in Siracusa told her that the wound had to be reopened and drained. "But surely," she protested, "you will give an anesthetic." The doctor smiled in a faint professional way.

"If he wishes, but you will have to help me."

"Isn't there a hospital?"

"Why, yes, certainly. But it is scarcely necessary. And also to move him at such a time."

Yes, thought Irene with a sigh, and they would be sure to drop him on the way downstairs. She had no faith at all.

According to the doctor's instructions, she held a sponge soaked in ether above a cloth and slowly dripped the ether from the sponge onto a cloth which was under Barry's nose. The cloth, though clean, was rust-stained. A local anesthetic would have been far preferable, she pointed out, but then could not make out entirely from the argument why it was impossible to give one. Knees were more complicated than she thought, apparently.

Barry, as soon as he began to go out, began also to fight for consciousness; he fought against being knocked out in this dizzily frigid suffocation like one fighting against death, or himself fighting for freedom not to have to see Linell McIntosh again. He flung the reeking cloth aside and would have fallen out of bed if the doctor had not been holding him. They had to start all over again. The doctor borrowed a rope from the padrona and tied him down. The padrona was in terror of everything connected with medicine—she was worse than Irene—yet she had always pleaded for them to stay until the young man recovered. Irene concluded that nothing so interesting had ever befallen her. She would never be induced to come into the room, nor could she be persuaded to now. She feared the sight of blood, she said; it made her sick. Her liver, she supposed, was at the bottom of her weakness. She would be sick for days.

The doctor and Irene secured the rope and started again. She had been unable to find Mario and the doctor had to go out on another call, he told her. Thus they were into it again before she had known how to stop. Yet now that she had got this far, to show fear and back out would be the worst thing to do. She almost knocked herself out with the ether. "Breathe," she kept saying, "try to lie still. Breathe, try to lie still." He said afterward that it seemed her voice was coming to him out of the stratosphere. He saw planets race and was swept along by scarlet comets; all voices faded shrill away on that horizon which had been common once to all of life: the Ionian Sea. It was ordinary, grim, painful to look at, yet when it fled from his vision into black distance he felt a loss, a great loss. He saw a cart pass on a distant road and thought there was a box like a small coffin inside, a child's coffin, he decided, or it could be. He was trying to raise his arm to cross himself, but Irene had tied it down and he couldn't get it up because of her.

Irene was with him when he came around. He must have been sick already about fifty times. "It's all right," she kept saying, holding his head. She reminded him that mothers had to go through this so much they didn't think anything of it. Then he looked hurt to be thought a child, but couldn't help taking anything she said. And so, with wounded pride as well as everything else, he fell asleep, toward night.

The day had been overcast and grey with a heavy chill wind and low-running clouds toward evening. Mario appeared, bringing her some minestrone from the restaurant, but she was too tired to eat it.

"It was like an operation," she said, sighing. "Home style, the worst kind."

"You'd be twice as worried about him in the hospital,"

said Mario. "I went there to see. You can hear groaning and screaming—"

"Oh, my God," she shuddered, and could not eat another bite.

"You are doing your best," said Mario. "I'll stay with him. Go out and walk."

The town was white and ghostly. The young Sicilians, slim and cheaply dressed, walked in clusters past windows, faded into bars and came out again. She passed a Greek ruin and went as far as the good hotel where at the foot of a wall there was a spring, mysterious and commonplace at once, surrounded by iron railings, flowing out among papyrus reeds. This was where a nymph had plunged in and buried herself, or so one could read on the explanatory sign. Her name had been Arethusa and she was running away from the lustful river god who was going to have her whether she wanted him or not. She was a nymph and could run like the wind, Irene guessed; running was evidently the very thing she was good at. But he was catching her anyway and down she went, into the fountain. Like all legendary things, to stand there and look at it was different from reading about it elsewhere, because on the spot it seemed it actually might have happened, like something that happened in a pasture on the outskirts of some little American town a century or so before—Indian chasing local maiden who jumped in the creek. That spring had understood Arethusa and never cared for her pursuer, and so had snatched her in and shut him out, but how did a maiden, Irene wondered, come to dislike any man as much as that? What was his name again? She read it from the tablet near the spring, once more, circling, looking down at the water which tangled darkly among the narrow stems of the plants. Two men were circling with her, not speaking; she looked up and saw them and began to move away, not turning when they spoke, and so dropped them behind.

Not only Arethusa, but Barry Day had fled here, she smiled to reflect, pursued not by a river god but by a little girl from Arkansas. She had lied, she had cheated, she was two-faced and unscrupulous and she had got him to marry her and she thought he belonged to her forever and no one could ever convince her she had done anything wrong. She was even willing to forgive him for stealing $2,000 from her father's safe if only he would come home to Arkansas. Poor Barry Day, thought Irene, but why run so hard? There should have been some way of dodging her instead. She would never meet this charming creature, Irene somehow knew. Linell McIntosh was as mythical, as little a part of the universe Irene amply moved through, as nymphs named Arethusa. "So pretty and innocent," Barry had told her, unable to stop babbling. "So trusting and sweet. She even had talent. She could have painted anything she wanted to. It meant nothing to her, nothing. She got together with her family and smashed every dream I ever had."

As Irene walked back to the hotel, a boy followed her. He was small and leathery-looking, perhaps far older than his size indicated; a triumph perhaps of malnutrition. She was still unafraid and walked on. The streets grew narrower; few people were in evidence. She had been reassured by Mario that only toward each other were Sicilians apt to be violent, that any woman present as a stranger would be completely safe. Still, the footsteps behind her persisted block after block, then suddenly they stopped. She had about reached the pensione door, and as she opened it, she turned. The boy was stopped still, regarding her fixedly, and just lighting a cigarette, the match cupped in his hands at that precise moment flaring up to strongly illuminate his face. He meant that to happen, Irene realized; he wanted me to see. She remembered the road worker, the flash of that one gold earring. She opened the door and climbed the stair, feeling refreshed but weary.

"He wants you," said Mario, "but I will stay. I will sleep in the hall."

The fever, however, being somewhat lower, she told Mario that he could leave. "There's a boy hanging around," she said. "I don't know what he wants. *M'ha seguita.* He followed me."

"*Naturale*," said Mario.

"He wants admiration, I believe," she said.

"*Davvero?*" said Mario. He smiled at her.

◆

The next day Barry slept for hours on end. Irene went out with Mario to see something of the surroundings. She turned her attention to Siracusa and learned that it had once been a Greek city, much larger in those days than at present. It now sat shrunken on the empty plain it had once dominated. The remains of a great wall built by the tyrant Dionysus to keep out the invading Athenians could be seen, if one wanted to rent a carriage and guide. Dionysus had built it in a single night, Irene read with astonishment. Mario was not much interested. He said the Athenians had been enormously civilized but were always wearing themselves out in wars with barbaric people who finally weakened them until their glory faded.

"The same thing will happen to you," he told Irene. "In Europe you have had it easy; there is enough human decency to know what is barbaric. Everyone knew the Nazis, what they were. But when you go East, then what? And to Africa, what then? And you will go. Look at you now; here you arc." He laughed, teasing her. "Nothing can stop you; you will go on and on. And finally, like the Greeks, worn out, a discard."

"We shouldn't have let the car go," said Irene. "I knew it." He went on talking on the bus. The Sicilians were so barbaric that when they captured the Greek fleet they threw all the soldiers and sailors into slave pits and left them there to die. You could hear them crying for miles, pleading for food, for human answers, for anything but abandonment. "Abandonment is the worst," he said lightly; "I have never compared, but it must be worse than starving to death." He said he had never thought anything about Siracusa and had never known any of this before, but had been reading for the last two days: nothing else to do.

"I was afraid you were going to leave me here alone," said Irene.

They got off the bus that led out to the ruins and walked together down an empty white road. The rain had cooled things off the day before, but now the heat was returning tranquilly into its own.

They poked around from one mass of rubble to another and except for the Greek theatre, which Irene found remarkable, agreed there was nothing to get excited over. They took refuge from the sun beneath olive trees and in the shadow of ruined enclosures. Irene said that perhaps Rome had spoiled her for other places. Mario remarked that he had never liked ruins at all. "I think history must all be pretty awful," Irene said. "Killing people, one slaughter after another, always a different kind."

Mario's white American-style shirt had got inside her vision; it encountered her nerves with its discriminating absence of starch; she might have been enclosed in it herself by the time they stopped to get cold coffee at a dry, sun-desiccated collection of bare wooden tables and chairs under a rusty vine. There was a wooden bar and behind that a low windowless shack like a dark hole, a lair. A girl came out of it in tight-fitting black skirt and blouse, the kind of nondescript material so many of the peasant women wore; it had worn, rusted, past the stage of being an article which had been chosen, but seemed more like something which grew where it was. The skirt fitted tightly around the girl's hips, which were broad and strong, like an animal's. The blouse had a low V neck, and her breasts pressed up beneath the cloth, small and tight, acornlike. One could suppose she was young. "Sissignori." She took the order.

"They've no tourists," said Irene. "Nobody." She took off her straw sun hat and fanned herself in the self-amused way her cousins used to do, out on their Maryland farms, just in from gardening or standing by the steps of farmhouses. Her face was flushed, she knew, and her hair damp.

"So few," said Mario. "None at all. Have you seen a single one?"

"Oh, yes," she said, "the Golden Arrow bus still runs every day or so by the best hotel. I saw it twice."

"Ha ragione. I saw but I forgot. It is like these people do not exist—they are not tourists, but birds. They are never in the towns. They come to a first-class hotel, they eat, they compare the food to the last first-class hotel, they leave. Two serious scholars a year perhaps."

The girl brought the coffee; it was poured out of a milk bottle kept chill in an old iron iced-drink container. The sugar came in thin paper bags which said ZUCCHERO FINE in red letters. I will never forget what I am doing, seeing now, Irene thought.

"I think they still give performances in that theatre," she offered.

"Yes, but this is for nothing. It is of no interest. What do they think? That someone today really speaks ancient Greek? And even if they speak it, do they have a Greek heart? Tell me, do they?"

"I suppose not," she agreed.

"Well, then?" he demanded.

"I don't know," she returned. The coffee tasted bitter and cool. "Are we supposed to be quarreling?" she asked.

He broke off, his fair face coloring slightly, and shook his head. "Ancora niente di Charles?"

"I think he must still be away or he would have gotten the messages I left. I also sent a wire to the embassy. But things are always uncertain in Italy, aren't they?"

"Someday the light of America will strike us all. We will all be efficient then."

"Oh, really, Mario!"

His eyes passed hers; then he looked away into the distance.

"Your husband has been good to me," he said at last.

"I know that."

She thoughtfully bit her lower lip. She ached still from the trials of yesterday, but she also found them, now the worse was past, a fulfillment. She had been right to come and she really had done something, for Barry was sleeping a sound way back to health. He lay nested and at peace on the far horizon of her consciousness. She had awakened to the thought of Mario, and seeing a fair morning, her spirit had spread itself out like wings. When he nagged her she felt unduly stung and her eyes, astonishing herself as much as him, had filled up with tears. Was it this that made him blunder into what he had said about Charles? She did not ask, but sensed that in apparently ignoring her, contemplating his surroundings, he was righting himself.

Siracusa lay a good distance away; the bus had long since gone away from the white road that had brought them there. She supposed that another would come. Beyond Mario's shoulders, the plain, covered with a dry difficult rubble of white stones, stretched out toward the sea. Yet the sea was hidden from them by distance and the height of the plain.

"What are you thinking, Irena?"

Her strong body had settled already into a deep acquiescence which had not been a matter of decision. A singling out and choosing had been going on about Mario Marcadante, about various others as well, for who knew how long a time, for months maybe; now the wheels and circles and ciphers all had matched and linked, the small hasty dots of light had stopped threading a maze and now had halted, pair by pair in nicely drawn-up ranks, and from somewhere far below the level of hearing the tiniest possible click had unmistakably sounded.

"Whatever it is," she told him, "it's good."

They had only left to see the slave pit where all the Athenians had died. The path down to it led back of the café. The girl in black looked after them until the path dipped severely downward. Whatever Irene had expected to see, it was nothing so deep and wild as this. A breath of dense, fragrant air came up to meet them, and there far below, surrounded by towering brown earthen walls, lay a sunken garden, crossed with walks, filled with every sort of tree, plant and vine, deep green, damp and cool by reason, she supposed, of the ragged mouth of a cave that stood elephant-high and shadowy, a stream trickling out of it. She entered the terrible mystery of the place without hesitation, at once concluding that this rich growth must have got its start out of the breasts, fingers, shoulders, skulls and entrails of the men who had died there. She stopped in the pathway. One by one those unlucky men had dropped off into silence and all this of lime trees and great red flowers, cactus, vines and dense broad leaves speckled over with filtering sunlight had grown up out of them. The place kept their final silence yet. For it the last one had just closed his eyes. She had just yesterday herself been tussling close with something that had resembled death and corruption, had had to wash her hair three times to get the ether out, attend to bruises and scratches where in his frantic struggle Barry had tried to strike her loose from him.

She went down slowly with Mario and stood at the cave's mouth. There was no one down there except themselves. The guardian had confirmed this, evidently knowing on sight everything that was shaping up between them. "Non c'è nessuno dentro," he had said and climbed back up the path and disappeared. Irene smelled the dark earth from the cave. Gnats formed round her breathing; they danced around Mario's head. She longed to be taken exactly where she was, but had instead to accept in silence the regard he occasionally let fall directly upon her; its content of near anger, or wariness and latent resentment would have to burn out on his own nature: she would not deal with it: this was her decision from the first. An endless chain of lovers must have come here; now one more link was forming. She looked at the lofty walls, their crests at points scarcely visible. She followed him to a sheltered spot, and watched him spread his coat for her. "Many Athenians, now me," he said, his voice blurring out into the stark desire that had all but joined them already. He pulled her down beside him.

When he kissed her she rested and he kissed her for quite some time. When they moved momentarily apart the gnats rushed in to dance between their faces; she drew up from lying on her elbow. Mario lay beside her like a young tree. He brushed several times at the gnats and she smelled again the breath of the cave. It was cool with the special dark coolness of the earth itself; the earth that let tombs and secret passages be made of it. She could be at home with those too. The vegetation clung together, twined and rooted in whatever lived or rotted; they had entered a sunken island of jungle. It was his hand's motion against her thigh that brought the dead their peace.

Mario had sat up and was smoking. "It's for the insects," he said. "They do not like smoke."

"Nor do I," said Irene. She laid her wrist across his shoulder, the back of her hand brushed against his cheek. "Your mouth will taste like smoke."

"I know that. The choice was difficult."

As she watched, the light from high aloft shifted, falling steadily through layers of foliage like a rain of gold. "I feel," she whispered, "that we have come to the end of the world."

He glanced at her. "Then it is not so bad." Snuffing out the cigarette, he moved to bring her closer to him, as she wanted him to.

◆

In this way Irene in Siracusa turned from Barry to Mario and her full attention was his own. He could not miss the strength of it—that was what she knew. She scarcely spoke to him at all; she listened, watched, curved her vision to every chance motion of his hand, turn of his head, shift of his stance at a window—like a jungle plant, she devoured him silently within her soul. She did not tell him the one thought outside himself that obsessed her: that there wasn't enough time. She instead went wild with care to wall out the fact, to lock it up in the closet, having hit it on the head, and in its knocked-out state, she turned resolutely from it, pretended it wasn't even there, giving herself to him slowly with discrimination and deliberate quiet grace which said they had landed on an island nobody knew about and would never be found by anyone but each other.

Sometimes she lay silent, her limbs turned to beaten gold. What she thought was that it had happened now, the literal joining of herself to Italy. Maybe it was Charles who had unconsciously picked out Mario for her; his praise of Mario had let her know that here was someone to admire; "the finest sort you'll find in Italy," he had said. She would not have wanted less, or taken less, to quench herself with. The months before had been all waiting. She was only just now seeing it. Someone would arrive, she must have felt over and over; someone was coming. Who? And there he was, and not a stranger. Someone long known had quivered like the surface of water, muted and transformed into the figure of a lover. His fine almost transparent lids had lowered slightly, his cool quick eyes had grown hot, his humor, like the snapping off of a spectrum which had limned him publicly, had vanished utterly. So she meditated, and moved his sleeping hand and head to shift herself. She never hurried. As devoted as when she waited hand and foot on Barry, the modulation in her also seemed of the slightest nature that could be imagined, her pleasure itself hushed within her until the walls trembled and melted down before her eyes, and she died away with all those Athenians that she would never forget now and could practically, she assured herself, call by their first names.

"Perché ridi?" he asked her, waking up. "Why do you smile?"

"I don't know."

She recalled Catania, the way he had hesitated before consenting to come with her. "Did you know then, or guess?"

"I thought perhaps, but then I thought this several times before with you and nothing resolved itself. Several times in Paris, I had this impression of you, that someday me or somebody like me would take you, in a quiet place."

"And you never tried?"

"There were no quiet places."

"But from the time I appeared, you foresaw—"

"Well, not quite. I thought maybe the artist—but then if he had been your lover you would not have wanted anyone with you. Don't tell me you are helpless, Irena."

"What a little past we have to talk about."

"How is that? I have known you as long as anyone in Italy."

"As a wife, hostess."

"But you are good, no? I could admire you, dissolve the clothes from you while taking soup."

"If I remember all that, I have to remember getting your coat, seeing you leave the house without me."

"I extend the past for you and you don't want it."

"Only since Catania."

"Many little rules." He shook his head. "No, you knew what you were about. You brought me here. I foresaw . . . well, not for sure, but something. And now your rules will be no good. I haven't wished this for you. You will see change. I cannot spare you this—it has scared me for you."

"I never tried stopping anything. Don't you change either?"

"Call it the same for both of us." They fell into a long gravity of feeling and gave themselves to one change after another and each had to get a name and recognition and each fall away like a milestone behind while another took them on. It could not, Irene decided, continue. She felt dazed and crazy.

Gravely, after two days she offered to have a child for him. He shook his head, eyes brightening with tears. He could hardly lift his hand to touch her coarse hair. And she would have done it; he knew it and she knew it. The deep link forged, herself eclipsed, she slept the profoundest of all sleeps short of death, here at the mysterious dead center, the stillness of her life.

◆

Barry Day now had nothing to do but try to shift to a cooler spot in the bed in his lonely pensione room, to turn his pillow, portion out his cigarettes, to make himself stop reading the magazines, books and newspapers Irene had brought because they were giving him a blinding headache and he would soon know them off by heart. He hobbled around the room a few more turns each day, leaned out the window on elbows that almost turned to stone, watched the whitewashed buildings in the sun, the dusking over of the port, the scarflike unfurling of the waves, came alive out of himself slowly but unmistakably to the distantly perceived rhythm of Irene and Mario, somewhere together.

When they appeared, usually with a few minutes of each other, their skin luminous with each other's presence and pressure, almost impalpable with the chiaroscuro of love, their lines merging into every surface, a throb of life passed out to him. Had he, all along, been just an excuse? He was a little bitter, a little doubtful; but who is going really to question life too closely, as long as life is what it unmistakably is? Certainly not Barry, who had just come too close to losing it. He took what came, from them as he would have from anybody, except Linell McIntosh. He never criticized. They had a fine abundance he would not like to be caught quarreling with; by having him as an excuse they just missed the awful expertness they might have had if it had all been done on purpose. They owe it all to me, damn them, he thought. He reminded Irene when she appeared that she had forgotten his cigarettes, and off went Mario to get them. (Does somebody have to think of Charles? Does it have to be me?) He heard Irene, just outside, telling the padrona what to ask the restaurant to send him. He tried to think exclusively of food, for he was hungry now almost hourly and it should have been easy to do nothing but dream up menus, but instead his mind drifted to the two of them, their love glowing and flaring about the streets of this unlikely city. Where did it begin? Out among the ruins, he guessed. A classic place. Had Mario just said something about Greek poetry, had Irene turned her ankle on some broken steps, had she gone to sleep in the sun, been chased by a goat, frightened by a gypsy? More likely nothing had seemed helpless about her at all; she had probably just seduced him, or maybe they had turned, kissed and liked it. But why bring Mario down there at all if she hadn't realized—? Here Barrry refused to go further.

He stopped and began to draw sketches in his mind, for the sensuous delight of imagining Irene deep in her rapture, alone with Mario on the brink of a pool way off in a silent wood, might have driven Rubens crazy, or so it amused Barry to reflect. Golden light dripped through the painting. Mario's back and thigh were a white relief, contrasting with the dark of the foliage. Barry had been too sick when he arrived to notice if there was a wood or a garden within fifty miles of Siracusa, but he counted on Irene to inform herself and find it, if it existed. She was a perpetual tourist, he thought, and by God she was going to have it all, to the last drop.

She came back in and turned his pillow for him. She had moved into the good hotel, she told him, because now that he was better she was not needed here and it was cooler over there. "But don't tell Charles," she warned him. "He might wonder about Mario or something crazy like that." She was smoothing her hair at the mirror. Her radiance cross-stitched to him out of the reflection.

"Okay," he said. "You chose to stay with whoever had ten stitches in his knee."

She drew on lipstick, hardly listening. He guessed she would have admitted everything outright if he had asked her.

"Maybe we'll never leave," said Barry lazily, even his thoughts going in time to the idle flap of the oyster-colored curtain in the port breeze, his vision permanently snared in the slow unscrolling of waves on the shore. "Had you thought of that?"

She fitted the lipstick together. "I don't think at all. About anything."

Some weeks before, panicky, alone, half-dead with infection, his head flaming, he had closed hot eyes from hanging up the phone to Rome, where nobody had answered it, dizzily counted out lire for the gettoni to a clerk whose hands did not wish to touch them, and who turned away from him and whatever might be the matter with him, leaving him to stumble, blunder out into the street, clutching at every wall, jerky with fever—and had come to the very end of Italy. He had had the irony, in this extremity, to think: Will it vanish, too? He aimed twice at the pensione bell and missed it, finally hearing the jangle inside and the footsteps, like a last human hope. (She had threatened twice to throw him out on the street, fever and all.) He had also wondered, waiting for the door to open and quite possibly slam in his face, Will I ever leave here, ever?

Now a real change had come about: to Barry it was more profound than the inevitable fact that Irene and Mario had become lovers. It had happened to all of them, the three of them, and he was as much a part of it as they. It had happened while the two of them made love and while he lay mending, watching their faces when he could and when he couldn't watching the curtains, the sun, the shore and the sea. Siracusa. It was a refuge, the place that Linell McIntosh never got to. It felt like home.

Their love, if it had any chance to be more profound than a hit-and-miss encounter some place, any place, some time, any time, had far more to do with him than they knew. It had come out of the black blood, the curdled corruption that had poured from his wound, had sprung out fresh-fleshed and sensual as a bold flower. He believed that it lived on in his presence; even though they might be thinking (even saying) they wished he was at the bottom of the sea, he thought he had to do with the strength of its blooming, the whole day through. And the whole night, too, God knows, he thought, with a long exhausted sigh. He slept, sinking in upon his soul.

◆

Then Charles came, to take them home.

Irene saw him first, and was thunderstruck. She was trailing back to the hotel after breakfast in a café. She was alone, not hastening, keeping to the rhythm she had chosen from the first, though Mario had just said what he had had to: "We can't stay here forever; nobody can do that." She had not replied, but had carried it off alone, out of the hotel, to eat by herself and let his words soak in. Now she was returning along the esplanade and there was Charles, as though he had heard it too.

He was sitting on a bench, turned sideways to the water of the small harbor, facing directly toward her, though he had not yet seen her. He seemed taller than it was possible for anybody to be—Mario was scarcely taller than she. His long neck was stiff and high, his lip harshly straight, his bald brow creased with dissatisfaction and sun-glare. By some trick of perspective his contentious head cleared even the masts of the freighters anchored out in the harbor. She wondered if it might have been sighted in Africa. Her thought flashed to Mario, but there she was, with a river's width of bare distance between her and any point of escaping unseen. Irene herself was no small object, and when she moved the direction was usually forward. She advanced on numb feet and saw in the corner of her eye, just a short distance away, coming from the opposite direction, a quick urgent figure hastening down the steps that dropped down toward the esplanade. She knew it was Mario, but she could not look, warn, advise.

"Charles! It's you! I couldn't believe it!"

The garments of wifedom had already dropped over her, in spite of all she could do. The next step she made, she moved in them. She greeted him, exchanging a kiss.

As it turned out, Charles was impatient with everything. He had been in town for hours, had flown in on a charter plane from

Rome practically with the dawn, had gone all over Siracusa trying to find out where Barry was. Not in the hospital, where he went first, not in any hotel. He began to think he had died. As for Irene, nobody at all seemed ever to have heard of her or to know that an American lady was in town. He had strode about the streets for an hour or more, long-legged and angry and hot, demanding things. "You've made a vast impression," he crossly told her, mopping the back of his neck. "Nobody in the whole burg knows you're here." He leaped up. "Mario! Irene said you might stay. Just great of you." He snatched up Mario's hand to wring it and again Irene saw that whitening face—a shock in full sunlight.

The first Barry knew, the padrona of the pensione was upon him. She leaped through the door without warning. "É arrivato!" "Chi é arrivato?" "Il marito della signora. Chi altro?"

Oh Christ, thought Barry. He could see it all. Well, let them thrash it out, he thought. The padrona went on and on. Everyone in town had known immediately. They had all gone chasing here and there. No one could find the signora americana. No one could find her amico. They had come back to the padrona. She had to tell the sick americano.

"I can't walk anywhere," said Barry. "Non posso stare in piedi."

She was getting his walking stick out from behind the door. She knew he had been walking up and down the halls, all around his room. She was terribly excited.

"They won't kill each other," he reassured her. "It doesn't happen in America."

"Signore," she urged him. "Deve andar'. Vado io auitar'. Tranquillo. Man' mano. Facciamo tutto."

So he went hobbling slowly through the sun, uncertain out of doors, helped along to the esplanade by the padrona. But it was more than his room he was leaving, in this urgent recognition of Charles' arrival. With every slow step the framework, the home sense they had set up among them was receding. Why don't we hide from him; why didn't we get together like a city somebody is invading and decide what to do? Wall him out; throw him in the slave pit. Send him word that I died and Irene buried me and now she is gone back to Rome and that is all that is known. Bribe the doctor to draw up a certificate to say that I am dead. Bribe the padrona of the pensione as well. Any ransom was not too much for the continuation of happiness. Yet he could not help but move, step after step, slow, uncertain, occasionally painful. I am doing it, he thought, incredulous. I am destroying what life is all about and what people look the world over to find. And I cannot stop. If we could not defend the city we should have fled. From Charles Waddell, who is a good man come from Cairo where he has been doing good for the world. And there is Irene, there is Mario, sitting docilely before him, fixed by his pale blue eye. And here am I about to join them. The padrona, having launched him onto the esplanade, left him to go on alone. Greeting done, he sank into a chair, forming the total circle. Charles' eye swept over them like a searchlight.

"You all look terrible," he said.

◆

"Barry nearly died," said Irene, turning her dark glasses in her hand. "If it hadn't been for Mario to bring me here he would have,

I guess. Imagine driving here alone. You don't realize, Charles, what we've all been through. You just can't know."

Charles' gaze passed her face and strayed out to sea, lighting upon the distant freighter. No one looked at Mario, who felt himself plunged suddenly into an alien element in which no human thing could breathe and all lovers died.

"I've been up against it myself," said Charles. "Do you know what took so long in Cairo? You remember the bridge program, Mario? Well, they stole the plans."

In a moment he was deep into it. It may have been the Egyptian government which had supplied the American aid plans to the Communists, who had immediately agreed to carry them out without any discussion whatever. If the government had not been responsible for stealing the plans why had they kept on insisting that these were not the American plans, but merely by coincidence very like them. The Russians had fallen far behind in their own proposals for aid and development loans—their research had not been nearly so thorough as that of the American team. It was therefore possible that the Russians themselves had stolen the plans, but the greater opportunity had lain with the government. Mario thought perhaps one theory might be that the Russians had suggested that the government get hold of the American plans, and Charles said that he had also thought of that. He said that no one would ever know, quite likely. He also thought that in the long run the Russians too would be checkmated in that country, for the government was getting more Moslem nationalist by the minute. "They may have intended to pull the rug out from under both of us. Having sucked in the

Russians, they're trying to funnel larger commitments out of us toward a really major expenditure—a dam project in the whole Aswan basin. It's all a chess game, and good God, the filth. This is civilization, paradise, America itself. This morning I expected to find laundromats and the A&P around every streetcorner."

◆

"He came in a little silver plane," said Irene to Barry, later on. Barry had fainted in the sun, right after Charles mentioned the A&P, delaying them for another day. The three of them had had to carry him back to the pensione in a taxi. The padrona had decided that one of them had killed the other.

"He flew down out of the sky. First a speck, then something the size of a dime, then big as a toy, then a car, a truck, a bus."

"Maybe not that big," Barry encouraged her.

"Is this all?" It was a duffle bag of blue canvas laden mainly with books she had brought him to read. He nodded. She pushed back her hair. Her eyes looked smudged with ink. "It was just Charles," she said. "I'm always glad to see him. That's always true."

"And Mario?"

"He left last night. I saw him just for a minute. He said he just couldn't stand it any more. He kissed me and walked away. I couldn't stand it, either."

"I saw you through the restaurant window, after he had gone, I guess. It was raining and you were walking with Charles. You had on a black raincoat, didn't you?"

"Black, yes."

"I guess it was the perfect thing." He had thought that at the time, watching the slow, downcast propriety of her walk, the elegant rhythm. Where had she got it? The perfect thing.

She turned her broad wet face aside and tried to laugh. "You mean I was in mourning?" She leaned hard against the edge of the dresser. "Nobody's dead, not even you. We'll all be back in Rome. You were supposed to die."

"Sorry," said Barry.

"So nothing's really so bad, is it? I don't know why I'm crying. It's the strain, thinking Charles would guess, make scenes. For me he's still in Egypt. In Cairo a monkey jumped out of nowhere and sat on his head. He was terrified." She began laughing in earnest. Her tears kept sliding down her face. Barry could see them in the mirror.

"It's the time that's died, you know that," he relentlessly said.

Eleven o'clock and they faced about, straight as possible, ready as they could ever be. The car horn piped below. Charles had rented a car to drive them back to Rome. They left the room for the corridor and then left both forever. The padrona wept in the hallway. She embraced Barry like a son. The hot street sprang up at them. Their feet moved on.

◆

All that winter in Rome, Charles Waddell kept his own silence. He never mentioned that he noticed his wife was in love, much less gave any indication that he knew it was Mario. He was one of those people who do not believe in romantic love and he could thus maintain a steady pressure among charged and capricious emotions. He did not think she was really going anywhere. He counted on her absolute materialism to conquer all. Yet he suffered. He did not think it would lessen his suffering to talk about it.

Gossip was a danger to him personally because it might become an added threat to his position, and nobody more than he knew how weak that was from day to day. He never said the truth he suspected about the disaster in Egypt. When he told Mario and Irene his news, he was dress-rehearsing for the story he was going, not so much to tell, for even that would have to sound like top-secret, but to force himself to think even he believed, once he got back to Rome. What he knew was that somebody had goofed, trusted too much, got carried away, and let out the American program before any firm preliminary commitment had been agreed to. He even had a fair idea of who it was. His own position was clear; let someone else discover it. He firmly, deliberately, tenaciously, passed the winter, being called a failure in Cairo and a cuckold in Rome. He did his work only perfunctorily, and yet he did do it. A quiet visit he had been meant to make to Bulgaria was quietly canceled. He said nothing. In London for a week of talks on U.S. foreign aid programs, he could feel without needing confirmation that he was being carefully checked over. He lay dormant; never very popular, he had been sought after far and wide because he was important, because his wife entertained well, because together they made an exciting couple. His record, beginning with the Office of War Information, on through army liaison, the Nuremberg trials, European reconstruction programs and now foreign aid in the

Middle East, was solid rather than brilliant; he had not shot up rapidly nor had he ever had the rug pulled out from under him.

Now, in quietude, coiled and watchful, he lay cold on people's consciousness, and often on sunny days sat out on his large terrace in the Savoia quarter, having dragged huge pots of roses out with him to take the air. Like many men in whom realism outweighs everything, he got very serious about flowers. Sprayed, pruned, labeled with small rectangular wooden tabs, occasionally even in winter coaxed into bloom, the tub-size pots squatted about him in mysterious council. He did not seem to notice them. His head loomed imperially above them; his eyes read. All winter he called his wife "darling." "Thank you, darling. . . . Yes, darling. . . . Coming, darling." She knew that she knew what he knew and would not discuss. It was his peculiar triumph to keep her imagining that the subject was only Mario and not also Egypt.

"But why not bring it up?" she wailed to Barry. "Why not get it out in the open? I think I am honestly mad at him for not helping me with it. And yet I can't start it, I can't."

Sometimes she rocked with bitter laughter, at others she sank down among the iron filings, chunks of broken plaster, scrapings of pitch from the moulds, all the rubbish of his work, groveling tearfully around like any Sicilian maiden seduced and abandoned (though Mario had done neither of these things). It was a disturbance to Barry that he was the only person she could talk to, and talk she must. He was angry to be indebted to her for saving his life. His work satisfied him less than ever, and so he began to resent her. Siracusa with its firm simplicities of isolation stood solid in his experience like a monument, but Rome was subtle and complex; it was no good pretending after they returned to it that any of them were the same. He tried to tell Irene this.

"Things always move," he told her. "Even love moves."

"But where?" she said. "But where?" He felt sorry for her again. She was honest, anyway, and would have liked an answer.

He pressed the hard heel of his hand into wet clay, creating a shoulder. He esteemed Mario and whatever suffering he endured, far more than Irene. He did not tell her this. He could still see Mario's strained, disbelieving face the day Charles had arrived. Plopped down from the sky to sit with them by the spring of Arethusa and talk all about Egypt. There where the papyrus grew—an Egyptian plant in Siracusa, though no one but Barry would have noticed—and the little ducks paddled in among the stalks. He had seen Mario accept everything, like someone taking a crazy blow from a friend. What had happened had happened. What was, was. This Barry respected.

"You're fighting yourself," he told Irene. "Not Charles or Mario. Probably they both love you, in their own ways. What do you want to happen?"

"Everything." she said, and presently added. "Nothing."

"Great," said Barry. "Do you want a divorce, want to marry him?"

"But the Church—"

"Skip the Church. Mario isn't interested in the Church. Jump it like a mud puddle. Take him to the States. Civil marriage, job, house, children . . . set for life."

"You think I can pull him around like a puppet. You honestly consider him to be that sort of man!"

"You see, you are fighting yourself. I told you."

If he made her angry enough she would go. The trouble was, she wore him out. He had got it through the water, as Romans said when they meant the grapevine, that Mario's family had determined to say nothing whatever about the matter of the americana, but that his fiancee's family had gone crazy. Francesca herself, determined to be noble, had got ill, turned religious, decided on giving her life to Santa Chiara. Her family's anger, now that she had made a traditional step, partially abated. Barry decided from all he could hear that it was the family more than Mario who were making her suffer. He saw her once near the post office alone and decided that beneath that strained, pointed face there lived a center of calm which was not of Santa Chiara.

Mario moved into an apartment in a poor quarter across the Tiber. He gave up his embassy work and his lecturing, did translations to stay alive, and with a worn scarf muffled high around his throat like a disguise, ate in poor restaurants where the sauce and the wine were thin and the meat doubtless came from horses.

Charles genially one evening brought Irene what news he had learned of Mario, whose behavior he said that he found puzzling. "When I thought of the postwar European generation," said Charles, who was apt to turn sweeping, "I always thought of him. You remember the first time we heard him lecture. You said he looked like Camus. Now where is he? Holed up in Trastevere and poor as a stray dog. I thought he might have turned Communist, but that's not it either." He insisted that Irene call and ask him to dinner to see if they could help him. She got through the assignment somehow. Mario declined. "I think it must be some family problem," she said to Charles. "Something about Francesca going in the Church." "I'd even go to see his family, but he never introduced us. Very aristocratic Sienese. Probably we didn't rate."

Floundering about in her grand passion, Irene was getting fat. Barry sat on the Spanish Steps with his chin in his hands, called out by a morning's thin sunlight in a season of February rain. If she just got fat enough, everything would be over. And that too, he saw, would come not from Mario, but from her.

Long years afterwards, alone with Barry at a pool side near Charleston on their way to Key West, Charles closed up with the air conditioning drinking gin, Irene suddenly said, "You know, Barry, the best thing in Italy was Mario." "I thought that, too," he at once agreed. "He didn't even know he was good," she said. "He just was. More than anybody I ever knew. When he felt something it was all of him that felt it. He was complete. He suffered a lot," she reflectively added. "Does he still?" asked Barry. "I don't know. Do you think he does?" "Which way do you want it?" Barry asked. He felt she had never let him go.

Do people ever, he wondered, let go? Creatures of memory and truth, how can they, without destroying their own souls? But this was the angel who thought this for him. For himself he didn't know. He had certainly let go of Linell McIntosh because his soul had demanded it. Yet he never forgot her. Pretty-faced, gentle-hearted, soft-spoken, loving and faithful and good, for indefinable disaster, she sure took the cake. Quick as anything, he slammed that book shut and flung it aside.

When Irene broke off with Mario he went into automobile

racing, the mille miglia. He had always been a good driver and had a passion for cars. The idea of driving to Siracusa in a new rented mille centro had been a factor of some weight. He needed money now; the Francesca situation could not be touched even if he wanted to; his heart was sore and could not be thought of; his intellectual curiosity on the shelf along with his weary spirit. He could not work for the Americans any more and keep any pride at all; too much had depended on Charles. In addition, he had seen about all anyone could of America.

When she heard about the mille miglia, Irene concluded he was determined to kill himself and of course came flying to Barry, who hooted her out. "He needs money," he said, "and he's probably sick of emotions. It's time you got sick of them too." "I love him so," she said.

The twins had come out for Easter and she had gone on a strict diet. Charles was taking them to the Dolomites for spring skiing. There had been a recent shake-up in the ranks of bureaucracy abroad which she was very late getting straight and even then was not too certain about. Charles had a new title, a new office, and had decided the problem of keeping physically fit in Rome was a serious one which deserved his attention. "He won't go into the ins and outs of how this job came about," Irene complained. "You haven't been paying enough attention," said Barry. "I actually think he wanted to steer me off onto Mario to give himself a clear field. Do you know, this has crossed my mind more than once. He used to sit out with those damn roses or hole up with three electric stoves and write reports. We haven't had a conversation all winter. Until recently. Now he's got it made.

Line forms to the right. Off we go." "You're mad because you can't run them—either one of them." "I'm mad because some way, somehow, Charles Waddell has used me—he even used my feeling for Mario."

She was lingering in his studio, frowning and preoccupied, somewhat restless, and then he knew why. It was probably the last of the many conversations they were to have about Mario. Or if they talked of him again, the conversation would be of a different sort, a different quality. There would be a certain distance.

She said one more thing. "I offered to have a child for Mario."

Barry almost dropped a piece of yellow Sienese marble which weighed five kilos and had cost him 20,000 lire. The statement with its peculiar force of truth cast a strong backward light on them all from the moment he had stood in this particular spot and held the telegram from Linell McIntosh in his hand in place of marble, and thought, I've got to get away, I've got to get out of here.

So it was finally Irene and his thought of her which would never be quite the same. For she would have done it, gone through with it—he knew that.

◆

All spring and summer Mario Marcadante roared through Italian towns and villages from the Swiss border to Naples in his white racing Alfa-Romeo. His name got in the papers, he killed nothing but a stupid sheep on a hillside near Perugia, he did not even kill himself. He made a lot of money and grew empty of thought and ambition. In time he wrote Francesca in the convent where she was a novitiate and she came out and married him. In time she grew sophisticated in her own quiet, reserved, dark way, with an air of past suffering which faded, ripening into life. She had astonishing taste in clothes. Mario ran a rather select tourist agency on the Via Bissolati. It was said that Charles Waddell had something to do with getting him started. He became a great favorite in Rome and went up quickly in social circles, his old family name having come of itself to the fore, precisely when needed. In time Irene was to see pictures of this man and his lovely wife in an international fashion magazine. It was a full spread, showing their villa at Fregene, their three children, their graceful little boat, and the signora herself in several of the latest Roman fashions created for women like herself. She pored over this for some time, trying to find between the lines or upside down some thread, some phrase to link her with what she saw. But she could not. "Forever, forever," he had said to her. "You will be with me forever. Affinché la memoria non viene piú." He was never a light person; that she knew. Now, limpid to the transparency of absolute identity with his own life, his own people, he stood before her in a photograph, and did not think of her at all. If her mark was there it was totally invisible. Was it all nothing? she wondered. For if it wasn't, what was it? Barry was not with her and she had no one to ask. She imagined his saying that he didn't know. Suddenly, surprising herself, she yawned.

Soon after she had known she would give up Mario, she had looked up in a Roman garden and there was Catherine.

THREE

All that summer long in Rome, Catherine and Barry went to the beach together. They discovered Sperlonga, of later date so popular, a white village on a mountain above the sea, no streets, no motors, only precipitous steps and winding passages. Below, the beach was firm and good. Barry dug up shells and dived for shells; he stripped them of whatever life was in them and piled them in sculptural shapes. This was what he wanted now. Catherine made him able to work again. She sat in the sun in white shorts and a white shirt and dark glasses, sometimes reading, sometimes doing nothing at all. She watched him, brown and wiry in his longish, old-fashioned American-style trunks, diving and hauling, boating and beaching his boat. Sometimes she cooked for him in a white beach hut they had rented, sometimes when it was still and too hot for the beach, they went up to the village and ate in a trattoria. Once, driving back to Rome in the late afternoon, a white Alfa-Romeo passed them going like a bomb. The driver wore huge yellow goggles. His silk scarf blew in the wind. Barry believed it to have been Mario.

They did not see much of Irene, who was busy all that summer with Charles and the boys and what she called the barbarian invasion, which was apt to take almost any form. Even the nurse who had delivered her twins in Maryland, fourteen years before, while the doctor was trying to get there in time, showed up from nowhere, rang her, and had to be asked to dinner. As for Barry, Irene at once jumped to the conclusion that he would live on Catherine's money. He would not feel any compunction about doing so. A money morality had never got into his head. He took things the same way he took shells out of the sea. He could have picked any number of women with an unhappy past to feel sorry for; instead he chose a wealthy one. But had he just done it by instinct, without scheming, hence forever evading any guilt? This could make her impatient to think about. Irene expected something of Barry, of artists generally, which she thought of as "honest success." "You had better watch out," she told Barry. "She is very precarious. She may suddenly jump off a rock; she may just walk out into the night; you may wind up in a divorce suit. Texas people are all crazy to start with, and Catherine—" "You are not going to ruin a happy period," he said, and shook the dust of her elegant apartment off his feet.

Catherine let herself be led into a simple, peasantlike life, reminding her of her days way back at Sandy Gulch, and more recently, of her visits with Latham, in the New England schools and camps he had taken for home, though his surroundings were always slightly institutional. In some ways Latham was like Barry. They could absorb themselves in nature. They could open its door better while she was watching, and in this way she could see inside a little herself, as she could never have done alone.

Up and down the cliffs they came and went, in whites and sandals, straw hats from the local market, cheese, wine, meat and bread in shopping nets. And all to find seashells! The villagers thought they were both crazy. How they talked and how they didn't talk. Nobody thought they were in love, and this was true. It was only later Barry believed himself to have been in love with Catherine. He missed her after she was gone. He thought it might all have been different. He believed that one day they had both seen a dolphin.

But then events did move in on them and take them over in the most nonsensical way. One could only suppose the two of them had been, for all their supposed seclusion, like sitting ducks to be picked off whenever the wilfulness of things chanced to spot them.

It started in the slightest possible way, Barry thought later, as though the snap of one twig in a wilderness presaged the materializing of ten thousand Indians from behind every rock and tree. Soon after they began to go to Sperlonga, he had bought a car for $200 from a man at the Australian consulate. The car had British license plates and consequently had to be run up to the French border every six months to have the documents renewed. Barry felt rather devilish about this transaction. For one thing, he never owned anything but one good suit to go to Irene's parties. Corduroys, an old jacket, and fleece-lined suede boots got him through the winter. He was still, in summer, wearing the kind of seersucker suit that went out in the 'forties. He knew in his bones that Irene thought he was living on Catherine's money and in a manner of speaking this could even from time to time be regarded as true. It was she who suggested they rent the beach house for the summer instead of paying for it by the day and thus running the risk of finding it already taken. It was she who gave him money to pay for a month of meals at a time at the trattoria, on the grounds that she often ate there alone while he worked on his stack of sketches. It was she who rented a car to take them there and back, and that was what did it.

He could never drive that car, even though he could overlook all the rest, without feeling like a kept man. The fact that the relationship was not a sexual one (and this Irene, outsmarted for once, had never once imagined) seemed, perversely enough, to make his independence even more of a pressing matter; a cicisbeo was worse than a hired lover. So he got the car, and it went immediately to his head.

He had not ever in his life owned a car, though he had once begun to save for one—having felt exactly the same way then as he did now—that he couldn't drive around in cars owned by the family of Linell McIntosh. He recalled that former time, and seeing how much better off now he was than he was then, he could begin to burst into hoarse and rasping song while wrestling through Roman traffic, something few people, it can be safely said, have ever been capable of. His songs were mainly those of a decade before, or even wartime, and he could not, Catherine told him gently, pulling down her skirt, carry a tune. But he went on just the same: "I'd rather have a paper doll to call my own. Then have a fickle-minded real life girl. . . ." A Lambretta skidded to a pulsing stop before him. He almost had ten accidents a day; to Catherine's mild dismay he seemed not to notice these minor things. It occurred to her, though she did not say it, that he was a sort of comical counterpart of Mario, the Italian he spoke of so often. That he would any day now enter his ten-year-old Austin in the mille miglia, like a man in Texas who had been so proud of his ploughing mare which could also do, all day long, a shambling gait he thought of as a plantation walk, that he entered her in a swanky horseshow in Fort Worth and literally expected her to win every prize.

She did not like Barry to know that he amused her. His art, she saw, was serious, almost too serious to him, and she thought he might even be good. Besides, they were giving each other health, that precious thing so few people will ever think they will ever need. Until they get sick. Your mind can get sick before you know it, thought Catherine, and soon you do not see any more, you do not hear any more, you walk but do not know where you are going, you forget to eat. "What, Barry? What did you say?" "What comes after 'Send me one dozen roses . . .'?" "'Put my heart in beside them . . .'" "Good girl!" At a stop light on the Barberini he smacked her on the cheek.

Linell McIntosh eluded, Irene pushed indefinitely aside, himself not dead in Siracusa after all, himself at least to all appearances the lover of a rich American signora molto simpatica, and besides the owner of his own car—at this point, grinding gears, he laughed at himself. But the truth was, in spite of all this foolishness, his heart, perhaps foolish also, was genuinely high. For success had begun to glimmer before him again, that swamp light, that foxfire, that delicate resplendent butterfly dipping from flower to flower over a wide meadow, sailing easily over the ditch too wide to jump and gone by the time he had plunged down and scrambled muddy and spent up the farther side. He felt success rise indefinable in his throat when he dragged up out of the Mediterranean one fair morning at nine that curious wide shell, open almost to flatness at the front, scrolled mysteriously into its own secrecy toward the rear, sensed its deep sexual suggestion of openness and mystery, its colors too a deceptive contrast, dull brown without, the interior obscurely flesh-colored and filmy with the elusive iridescence of the sea. He began at once to remember Bernini; the moulded stone his triton sat upon in a public square in Rome was a shell supported on a pedestal of dolphins, while the figure drank his fill from a great conch, drenching his neck and shoulders with a lavish gush of water. A step further and he would consider doing colored sculpture, as the Greeks had done. He always wondered why this was practiced no more. And so stood transfixed in the sunlight until Catherine, perched on a rock with some post cards on her knees, thought he looked somewhat like a statue himself, just by thinking of them, his skinny tough body poised about the shell on which he gazed as though all creation would burst from it at any minute. She remembered Latham with a captured chipmunk held tenderly in his hand while his finger stroked the tiny frightened head. "Look, Mother, just look. See the stripes? He's perfect, and scared to death. Don't shake, don't tremble." Did she feel nothing of what Barry wanted her to feel for him because he always brought Latham to her mind? Barry claimed to be older than he looked, but she could never really believe him. She imagined that he took easily to girls like the rattle-brained Arkansas girl he had at one time, haphazardly, it seemed, even married. They were all limited in their pretty little heads, Catherine imagined, and he quickly ran out the other side of these relationships. She only hoped he didn't get hung up on her. She was too fond of him for that to happen.

Once at night, staying with him at Sperlonga after a day of swimming in a sea freshly running after a rain, he had picked her up as she lay half-asleep in a ratty old beach chair after supper and wine, and carried her to his side of the shack and laid her down beside him. But though she put her arms around him, she presently fell asleep, as softly quiescent as a child. The next day he hardly spoke to her. "Maybe you think something is wrong with me?" she ventured at lunch. If he looked hurt and was hurt, it was something, she saw, that in his charity he had not given a name to. "Why you instead of me?" he asked irritably. That broke it up, and presently they were laughing.

In the afternoon he polished the car with the remains of their drinking water, whistling tunelessly. They might have been in a back yard in Texas, Catherine thought, after Sunday dinner. That night at a crossroads returning to Rome, a car clipped in from behind, failed to stop and raked across their fender. The only odd thing about it was that Barry, so often wrong, was completely in the right. The other driver, a portly Roman returning from the country with his daughter, a rather sullen girl whose mind was obviously elsewhere, had been entirely at fault. Barry, inspired by his own righteousness and by the car madness (his identity now so close to the fenders and doors and bumpers it seemed his own body had been run down), exploded in a volley of Italian. "Cretino!" he finally shouted. It seemed to him later that anyone should have known better than that. Insurance cards were exchanged like dueling notes. The Roman said nothing, but bowed, held the door for his daughter, if daughter she was, and allowed Barry to drive on ahead. "I should call him," Barry said, two days later, "and tell him I'm sorry." He had just received word from the States that a minor fellowship he had applied for had been granted. The shells had already led him somewhere. He had sent sketches of them in by the ream. His heart was mellow. "I'd just forget the accident," Catherine said. She added, offhandedly, as a wealthy Texas girl always did, "The insurance people will take care of it."

Barry, who knew only too well how things taken for granted, like medical care and insurance, value received for value given, meant nothing in Italy, heard this with a touch of apprehension. He saw himself groveling in agony before the public telephone in Siracusa with none to help and no assurance he would be able to get back into the room he had quitted because whether he was dying or not the padrona wanted no long-distance supplementario on her bill. God, what people! Then he forgot it all. He had a secret little plan for making even more money than the fellowship would bring him. He had been told by a Cockney spiv he knew who worked around the Italian tourist offices in the Piazza Esedra that some people who ran cars up to the border to renew their permits made the practice pay handsomely by smuggling contraband French and Swiss merchandise over into Italy. "They keep a lookout for certain names only. By the time you could even get suspected, you could have made a million or so lire. These chaps are well informed. They know exactly what they're doing. They even warn you that now's the time to stop it. You stop, take the profit and never do anything like it again. It happens all the time, why shouldn't you?" Barry dismissed the idea, but it had come back to him more than once. Catherine would never know it;

the thing that amused him to consider was Irene's self-righteous tirade if she ever found out. Irene, who had cheated Charles all over Siracusa, and for all he knew was at it still, tearing off to find Mario on every provocation. He wondered what had been left out of his make-up that he could never see the latent morality in money. In this sense he was like an Italian. Money always stood in the way of everything he wanted and kept trying to color all his deeper satisfactions. He wanted to slap it aside, like so much cobweb. Linell McIntosh's family had thought it was all right to dismiss everything in the world which had to do with art (they even expected him to see the light and dismiss it too), but the minute he touched their money, you could hear them squalling all the way to New York. If this was right, he hoped he'd never see it.

While he was still pondering all this, he and Catherine stopped by his rooms on returning from the sea on a late July afternoon and found a down-at-the-heels quiet stooped man waiting at the door. He was doing a routine check on foreign cars in Rome, he explained, and would like to see Barry's documents. The upshot was that Barry owed the Italian government twenty million lire. From that moment on, Barry had not a moment's peace. The fine hung above him like the blade of the guillotine, suspended night and day with unmoving accuracy, every time he looked up into those velvet summer skies. They were like the eyes of Linell McIntosh, he thought, and hastened off to his next appointment, a white hope for escape, reprieve, or even justice. Like a hound subject to fits and owned by no one, he ran daily through Rome, going to see semi-amused lawyers who thought all Americans were either rich or had access to money, customs officials who said one thing one day and another the next, confidence men who took his bribes to win the ear of personal friends in high administrative positions whom, it turned out, they had never even met, going next on side trips on buses to Milan and Bologna to locate the Australian who had sold him a car with fake documents and had by now mysteriously disappeared, to long conferences with a Lloyd's insurance man who was a member of the exiled Polish aristocracy, and all, all, he finally had to face, dragging himself to yet another fruitless appointment with an English tourist he had bribed to hide the car in a haystack outside Rome, because he had been an idiot in the first place and having paid for the car and insured it and got his driving license, had never once suspected that it could have been in Italy for eight years without ever having had the slightest right to be there. Once stirred up, tribe after tribe of Italian bureaucrats began to join the torture circle, drumming and dancing about him, occasionally hurling a flaming brand. Once he inquired, he found himself charged with the accumulated fines of ten other people who had previously owned the car, all now vanished and not to be found. Like the contraband which he had planned to traffic in himself, the car had, with the help of postwar confusion, been smuggled into Italy. Barry lost weight until he was skin and bones, rushed around so much he had no time even to shave, and was plagued by a nervous stomach. Why did this happen to me? At long last, he remembered the crossroads at twilight, the exchange of insurance cards and the one word "Cretino!" splitting the soft air. Thoughtlessly in his pride before Catherine, he had hurled this word at a quiet signorile Roman, in the presence of his daughter or mistress. Now all of Italy had turned on him. His work was at a standstill, he was ashamed to go to Charles Waddell, in anguish lest Irene should know of his humiliation.

Only Catherine was privy to his misery. She sympathized and offered to write a check. He could pay her later, she said. Money was not important, she told him. He rejected the very idea.

He could not understand, he said, why, since so many people had been far more at fault than himself and had shrewdly and deliberately violated the law, he had through ignorance to take all the blame. This was a legal matter, Catherine suggested. She had not been married to a lawyer for nothing. No, said Barry; things always went wrong for him, always. Catherine did not agree or disagree. A sense of anxiety had begun to pervade her. Why was he so easily brought down? Wasn't it simply because he had no money? No, it had been his effort to appear well before her which had led him into the whole purchase of the car. A desire to protect him awoke, yet she saw plainly that he was destined to get in over his head before he knew what was happening. Arkansas (he had been lied to, driven beyond endurance), Siracusa (fleeing his estranged wife, he had had a plausible collision with a boulder out from Agrigento and had landed beneath the façade of a Greek temple with his knee gashed open), now Rome. He should have known, she thought. It was exactly what he was afraid of her thinking. I should have known, he admitted, but it was too late. His only excuse: he had been thinking of seashells. It was not enough.

I do not wish to protect any man, thought Catherine, in matter-of-fact Texas terms, though her manners prevented her saying so. "I'm worrying you, Barry," she said. She added, with the sincerity of wanting to think she was telling the truth, "In a way, you see, it's really all my fault."

She gave everything on a silver platter, as was her habit, and then, gathering up the exquisite bag she had bought when coming by to keep a dinner date with him, she walked out of his studio and away, lonely again, with the country she had almost discovered, just as Barry had almost discovered the taste of success, dissolving in her every step into unreality.

Desperately lonely, after a few days, she sought out Irene, who asked her to lunch, as Charles was away.

Catherine industriously kept her promise to Barry and said nothing to Irene about his imbroglio. They lunched on the terrace with Charles' pots of roses withdrawn to sentinel distances.

"What happened to your marriage, Catherine?" Irene came right out and asked. Nobody on two continents had ever asked her that simple question. Not even phalanxes of psychiatrists had once come up with anything so plain.

"It was anxiety," Catherine answered at once. "Jerry had to be great and he almost made it. It was the almost that did it. He had to prove something. He could prove it absolutely"—she gave a game little shrug—"only in bed. And he had to keep on proving it, in every bed there was."

She felt suddenly better. She had astonished herself. But was this true? How neat it all looked, how easy it all was to say. If he were there, if the door were to burst open as it had so many times—? She turned her head sharply aside, drawn by the sense that this very thing was about to happen. Irene had not said anything, but her face had taken on the obscure meditative look of a cat. Catherine had a sudden feeling. "Do you know Jerry?"

Irene looked surprised. "Know Jerry? Of course not."

"I became rather crazy at times," Catherine confessed. "I could not tell what was going on. There was a shot fired, for instance—" She stopped, and Irene did not urge her on.

"Very few people *can* tell what's going on," Irene said. "The world is too complicated. My theory is that even the ones running it don't always know what is going on. I personally think for instance that all last winter Charles did not know what was going on."

"In his job, you mean?" Catherine innocently inquired, thus giving it away to Irene that Barry had talked about her affair with Mario.

Irene nodded. "He always said he couldn't explain it because it was secret." She giggled. "I thought he couldn't explain it because he couldn't explain it."

They both fell to laughing, and the hour being three o'clock, Catherine took her leave.

Irene was left with the essence of this woman's very self lingering about in corners and on chairs. She did not know if she liked it. She perceived a clear spirit groping out of the dark, and terms like this, quite foreign to the Waddell household, must have been brought in from outside. Irene adjusted the strap of her sandal, and wondered if Catherine would make it. She can't leave the dark because Jerry Sasser's back there in it; that's the whole thing.

So she thought and went to let the twins in. They had just come back from visiting Hadrian's Villa at Tivoli, were burnished with sun, and voluble with information, their pockets stuffed with shards of mosaics picked up in the ruins and bits of colored marbles. They knew about it all, even to Antinous, and wanted to tell her everything.

FOUR

Barry finally had to leave Rome. He still owed the Italian customs twenty million lire and the harder he tried to pull himself out of this trap the more deeply he got drawn in. The affair became like a giant squid, sucking him down into the depths and squirting ink in his face. He got out from Naples on a Greek freighter sailing to New York. It looked to be the same as the one they had seen in the harbor at Siracusa when he fainted near the Fonte D'Aretusa. He had to leave all his sculptures. He had a dreadful half-dream, half-fantasy on the boat, which was very poorly ventilated, that Linell McIntosh had come back to Rome and found the studio, had announced herself as his wife and was believed, so using her authority to pack up everything there and have it stored somewhere in Rome where no one could be counted on to respect it and where the crates would doubtless after several months be broken into and the contents sold off as junk in the open-air market, the space being needed for opera scenery. His work, his life! He drove himself through layers of anguish and shame, felt defeated by that country which had seemed so fair and free when he had come to it, thinking himself, at that time, defeated by America. Had his years abroad been utterly wasted? They had.

Yet so persistent was his curious soul that on the fourth day out he stood on the top deck, doing nothing for hours on end but admiring the sea. Whatever else it did, he reflected, defeat could wash you whiter than snow, as the old hymn of his childhood went. He experienced great peace at the thought of his native land.

It was Catherine who salvaged the work. Irene and Charles left in the early fall, for good. Their European years were done, they said to everyone, a phrase, as applied to them, to grip the heart; it was elegaic and superb. The return of yet another Republican administration, the Hungarian suppression—all had let Charles know that his finest hour was done. He took the pulse of things and foresaw a long dreary bureaucratic struggle with not much by way of new surfaces to leave his mark on. In September when everyone came back to the city, Irene gave a grand party, renting the grounds of the palazzo where they had had their apartment for years, placing a small orchestra on the paved entrance near the stone lions. Lights glowed, candles flickered, couples danced in the hallway and on a raised platform outside. A long table was spread, spumante gushed, and stronger potions also were passed about by white-jacketed waiters and little maids. There were movie stars and writers and diplomats and business executives and counts and countesses, and even the nurse who had delivered the twins, just back from Germany where she had seen the Passion Play and visited Anastasia. She was about to sail for home. Catherine came back from the Lakes where she was visiting somebody wealthy who had a villa, and Mario came, at Irene's suggestion, as Catherine's escort.

Catherine liked Mario and would always remember dancing

with him. She always liked to dance back in Texas and doing it here again after so long, she felt like a young girl. His face was witty and nice. Why aren't more men like this? she wondered when he laughed. He wore a white dinner jacket and taught her Italian phrases. But mostly he lived within his own silence, keeping to what he knew. When he danced, he was courteous, but he danced his own dream. Irene passed in a haze of green chiffon, her sandals golden on the fine gravel. Once only she danced with Mario. Some people looked and others looked away. It could be thought, so exquisite they seemed in the motions of parting, that they had both wanted it this way because this was so exactly the way it had to be. They were both shaped up for perfection of some sort and so they got the full of it, even the dregs, out of having some great internal demand for the whole of nature and nothing short of it. Mario was a champion, after all, and once rode down the Veneto in a white open-topped car while hundreds cheered and tore at him. He had taken a race for Italy. So that night, nobody upset anything; nobody had once, in all of Rome, felt compelled to speak to Charles, nor would they now. Nothing broke except their hearts.

Tall, preoccupied, noticing everything and nothing, Charles passed here and there among the guests as he might have walked among rose trees. "Do you hate to leave?" a hundred people asked him. "No party can go on forever," was what he said, one of his sincerer comments. The cheers of V-E day were ringing in his ears; he could close his eyes and see the great tanks in slow triumph on the Champs Elysées.

The next morning Irene herself went down the Veneto, walking alone on yellow leaves beneath the plane trees. This, too, was herself, in full step with her every notion. Who on leaving Europe, on parting from a lover forever, appreciated quite so much the damp yellow leaves fallen on the pavement along the Veneto? Even Charles thought this about her, and knowing full well where she was likely to be going, his heart filled up with tender anguish.

Charles himself was busy sorting papers, waiting for the packers to arrive. He was personally moved by their departure in the light of its historical perspective. Europe had been his theatre since he had been attached to the Office of War Information in London early in the war. He had fought in Italy, had arrived in France in time to see the Liberation of Paris. Irene had come out to him in Nuremberg, having left the twins with his parents in Ohio. She had come with her eyes wide open, ready to discover everything. Maybe some people would say it was herself she discovered. (Charles got restless when conversation like this was thrown at him.) Anyway she picked up momentum from every new experience, and since Europe was in a plundered condition she set about clearing it up to suit herself. He could only guess now that hundreds of American women, in those times so up for grabs, had had at least a go at doing something along these lines. A little money went so very far and there was all the gilt and fine things and bric-a-brac. So she was up and running and he thought it would soon play out and begin to bore her, and that was when, instead, she shifted into top gear and began to scare him. Charles had always taken a Middle-Western view of society; a dinner jacket was something he struggled into with reluctance; receptions, weddings, funerals and every human ritual he took as a necessary evil, to be got through as painlessly as possible. He generally thought of something else the whole time. But here was Irene, always running in with news of somewhere they could go, of something to be seen and heard, of who was new to meet. Before his eyes he discovered her, first as the center of their growing acquaintance, then of an enlarging swirl which dragged in group after group, and gradually seemed to be taking in all of Europe. A good deal of it trailed with them from Germany to Paris, where new circles formed about them. At the time Rome was mentioned as his next post she already had visited there and laid a social groundwork more formidable than most foreigners on the spot achieved in several seasons.

The first thing all this did, in Charles' view, was knock hell out of his private notions of economy. He had believed in savings, investments, insurance policies, and the planned life. He could now see at one glance the way things were shaping up, that if illness or bad luck ever left him without a job there would be nothing to do but go home to Ohio and pitch hay. When he said this to Irene she thought he was being funny. They had a quarrel which lasted for a week. But he was not too obtuse either to see that she was benefiting him, however indirectly, far more than she was injuring his bank account. Everybody either knew the Waddells, or wanted to know them. Their name was mentioned everywhere. In one respect at least, she never failed him: she was discreet. She never gave away, by a single glance, anything that might work to his disadvantage. He could safely leave her in charge of a roomful of enemies, and return hours later to find them chewing over existentialism, or the Salzburg Festival. The greatest trial in his career, the goof in Cairo, had missed her completely because of Mario. He could suppose with a rueful smile, as he let the packers in, that this had been the great trial in her career as well. She must be gone to meet him now. Her lover. The word, so familiar by now as to be as commonplace as dog and cat—who was sleeping with whom was a big question in the Waddell world—still was not a home word for Charles and never would be. He felt embarrassed to have to think it.

Charles had his appetites but was not primarily a sensual man. He must have known for years, now that he thought of it, that Irene had depths he might awaken, discover to her, but never exhaustively explore. Now this knowledge, though to him only a fragment of his totality, like a tiny pointed sliver, drove deeply into him where it hurt the most. He put it aside; in many ways, not the least of which was physical age, he felt at times to be her father. A father suffered at his daughter's defection, but in his suffering, if civilized at all, he hoped for the best, was moved with pity, took nothing too personally. Here Charles failed and floundered. He could see the jump and make himself run toward it, but he could not go over it. At the point of refusal, chaotic questions swarmed in his mind. Was Mario the only one? If she was discreet about Charles' affairs, had she learned, all this time, also to be discreet about her own? He thought of all the long periods he had had to be away from her, and shuddered. Nevertheless, he believed that Mario was the only one because he believed in her taste. Some would have said Irene had an eye for brass as well as gold, but if so, she did not know it. She would have saved herself, instinctively, not purposefully, for something like this, maybe even (here he reached a great romantic conclusion, so unlike him that it made his head spin) just precisely for Mario and none other. He shook his head to clear it: he would never risk thinking anything like that again. It was dangerous. Later on, his doubts returning, having fed on God knew what and grown accordingly, he came to wonder if Mario was the last. He grew suspicious of Barry, something which in the past he would have hooted at. Why did he hang around if he didn't care for Irene? When were people moved exclusively, blindly, by sexual drives and when weren't they? Before these questions he stood dull and helpless, and there was none to take his hand.

Deeply concerned with duty as a young man, with education, with a grasp of foreign affairs and public policy, he had refused or scanted what opportunities there had been for the big emotions to grow in, and now this green time was gone forever; it was too late. He had grown, through the years, terse with people, short, for he had painfully learned that warmth and affection were generally misunderstood, all too often taken advantage of, and were the American mannerism Europeans were quickest to view with contempt. Germany had taught him his longest lessons here, and France had given him a postgraduate course. By now his sharp manner was proverbial; he no longer wished to be liked, nor was he.

So where was the heart at all? he wondered (as he guided the packers on, mainly by opening the doors from one room to the next), that it should now wake up with this tiny splinter in it? He would not think of it. Let it fester as it would. He went out on the terrace.

Will and Tom were sitting in a couple of canvas lawn chairs, reading Gibbon. One had volume two and the other volume three. He wondered how they had got even this much out of step. He had often wanted to say, "My son, my son." It seemed a joke on this desire that he had to say instead, "My sons, my sons," this not being at all the same thing.

"Have you finished packing?" he inquired.

"All done," said Tom.

"Can we help?" Will asked.

"No, but thank you." His eyes became clouded. "Thank you, son."

The boy smiled at him. The world was there.

◆

On October 12, 1957, Irene and Charles sailed from Naples on the *Leonardo da Vinci*. They and the twins were photographed on the first-class deck, and their picture appeared in the Paris *Herald Tribune*, the Rome *Daily American* and one of the Italian papers, along with a brief summary of Charles' career abroad.

◆

Catherine went through one of her happiest periods when she rescued Barry's sculptures. She wondered why Irene and Charles had done nothing along these lines, and was somewhat shocked when she called on them about the matter. She understood that people got severely tried and lost a good deal of their "niceness" in Europe, but she was not prepared for them to dismiss her so firmly. Charles said frankly he thought it would be no great loss to the art world if Barry's things got thrown in the Tiber; maybe, he said, people would discover them ten centuries later and put them in the Vatican museum, but he doubted it. Irene said she considered this to be unnecessarily harsh but thought that Barry had enough connections in Rome to have the matter seen to. "I nursed him when he was really sick," she pointed out. "Why did he leave like that? People say he was in some mess about a hot car. He should have had better sense."

Catherine still thought that it would have been very easy, no matter what they thought of Barry's business sense, to have the sculptures shipped to their boat. She herself wished to fly back. There were, though she did not say so, certain doctors she had to see after so many months. "I'll pay for them," she said. The Waddells exchanged glances. "I know we sound hard, to you," Charles muttered. He got up to pour himself a Scotch. "Did anybody see my skis go out?" he inquired. "The boys' are still here." "That's because they wanted all their gear together," Irene said, "so as not to get mixed up with ours. Yours went yesterday." She turned to Catherine with a sigh. "I know you think we're awful," she said, "but sometimes you just can't do any more."

"Why doesn't she do it herself?" Charles asked after Catherine left. Irene hung a cigarette in the corner of her mouth. "It is difficult. I guess I wouldn't like to go through with it." She laughed. "I guess, too, she thought we cared."

This singular pair did not at that moment pause to mention even to each other that they had not only met Jerry Sasser in Rome, but had had a meal with him. He had come out to look into the interests of an oil company he now worked for, which had branch offices in Rome. He had looked up the Waddells because they knew Catherine. He had learned this from some people in Washington.

The three of them dined at a small outdoor restaurant on Via Lombardia, and they told him everything they could. Charles decided he was not so bad, but Irene drew something of a blank on him. She had heard it blazed abroad at one time that he was marvelously attractive, but she couldn't see it. He looks like Phil Harris, she thought, only he's not got curly hair. He's even from Texas, too. One thing she did see, however, that Charles missed completely. Charles told Jerry that Catherine had developed a platonic attachment for a young sculptor, and he thought this was a good thing as the boy was a cheerful sort, though always half-starved. Jerry wanted to know if he was also a queer. Charles said that Barry looked exactly like a bantamweight prizefighter. "Except that *they're* all queer," said Jerry, as Irene, who knew that was coming, chuckled. The Waddells seriously concurred that Barry was if anything too much drawn to pretty young girls. It then flashed through Irene's mind that Jerry Sasser did not quite believe them and that furthermore his interest in bringing the subject up at all had to do with his own vanity, rather than anything that might confront Catherine. She was touched by the smallest imaginable chill, the kind that results from hearing a fingernail scrape against slate. That too went away quickly because she knew too many people and had to say goodbye to all of them. She could not keep up, not possibly, with everything about everybody. The next day, Jerry Sasser flew to Paris.

After the Waddells' departure, Catherine spent days getting the sculptures packed by Bolliger and clearing the lot through customs. She changed her plans and took a boat back, and thus gradually, stage by stage, in her frail but patient way, like a pioneer woman plodding West, she restored Barry's work to him. He was by then in New York, had got a job as a garment packer to see him through and worked at night. When he saw what she had done, the whole earth seemed renewed. His joy, his gratitude flowed quickly into love. He heaped her with praise and tenderness; he all but left the earth altogether behind, rushing in on her before lunch one day at the Plaza to beg her to marry him. When he came to earth with a crash, like a homemade airplane in a cotton patch, he limped for a long time, licked sores, lost his job and drank too much. But through it all he was returning in spirit to his own personal defeat, which was always there waiting for him, like a plain but faithful wife whom through the years, since he couldn't get rid of her, he had to learn to love.

Catherine ultimately reappeared to him and they met for the first time as lovers. Her necessity, he ruefully realized, had been brought on by her having to see her husband again, and for the first time he saw the extent of her much-talked-about darkness, which he had been inclined to dismiss. She only needed "understanding," he had boldly said, as if he didn't know better than that, as if any "understanding" in the world could have been brought to bear on Linell McIntosh, for better, for worse, for any purpose at all. He saw at last, at close range, Catherine's madness and could describe it only as a heavy eclipsing shadow which she was powerless to lift. Just the same, his tenderness for her, expressed even for one single time, wrote his own anxiety off into fulfillment. He loved her but still she passed afloat in his world, as diaphanous as a treasured ghost. Beside her, Irene seemed to him coarse and at times almost evil, and the whole Waddell world a sort of underscoring of a lurking corruption that he could sense everywhere. As in Perry Mason, the gun was there and the man looked dead. You could figure it out any way you wanted to. The bomb threat came and went, but the other, nameless thing was worse, subtler, more profound and powerful, and it did not show any sign at all of going. He longed for the angel, but when he risked saying this to Irene, she treated his confidence summarily. Angels never crossed the ocean. Well, this was true; how could he answer it? Therein lay her extraordinary power.

Where Paths Divide

Catherine's house was a quiet one; it was in a small Massachusetts town strong enough and old enough to envelop her. The house was in no way artistic or impressive, and things of Latham's lay about it in the pleasant disorder it was her nature to like. She had finally come back to herself by means of Latham, who had been there all the time because he studied animals who had been there all the time. At least Catherine put his nature down to animals; she did not see how two Texans could ever have produced him, and she rather thought too that his close brush with death as a young boy had been like the permanent touch of a sacrament. The flamboyant sweep of the times, that had torn his parents apart and driven their lives in opposite directions, he completely eschewed. One leg permanently smaller and shorter than the other, he read with his sneakers or loafers propped disparately on footstool, fire fender or porch railing. He collected colored slides of wild life, most of which he had lain in the woods for long hours to photograph; he mounted shells and butterflies and wild flowers in glass frames, each labeled with its particular Latin name a yard long. Specimen pheasant, quail, duck, goose, eagle, hawk and gull looked down from shelves pegged with iron supports like the dark-varnished pine walls of the wing he lived in.

Latham had not shot or trapped any of these creatures, nor would he; the only thing like this he could do without qualms was to fish. He had even felt a bit bad about buying stuffed creatures, for somebody had had to kill them someway. Catherine said absent-mindedly that that would go on anyway; she was not about to shed tears over two or three birds more or less in the world. Latham, however, succeeded in getting her worked up over the extinction of certain species and she found herself writing checks to various game preserves which still depended on private finance. Though the family in Texas believed that Latham would never amount to much because he was a cripple, he had a stiff enough job with the Massachusetts Game and Fisheries Commission as well as certain research rights gained through a foundation grant in cooperation with the state university. The research had to do with fish propagation as related to the relative purity of streams and lakes and to this end Latham had a whole basement area of the biology building to operate in; it was filled with tanks of water, some clear and some not, in which the fish either swam or did not swim. To Catherine, each time she went in to find Latham and looked at the fish, they seemed to be thinking about something, the same thing, over and over. She wondered what it was.

Catherine saw her son with a sense of reserve. She saw him as a boy who would never have to go and fight in a war, who would always live in a quiet house with some quiet girl, whose children would look a little like something startled in a wood. Already he showed a tendency to take up with girls he felt a bit sorry for, and almost, his senior year at the small college he had chosen to attend, married a girl who was part Negro. Catherine said it was okay if he really loved her. After this he and the girl decided to become just good friends. He took the friendship seriously still and wrote long letters to her, spinning out all his thoughts. About his father he did not speak very much, and Catherine wondered why this had come about. It seemed that in Latham's terms there was nothing much to say.

It was as if he didn't have a father, only a sire who had no more stuck around after he was safely on his feet than a male moose would have done. If he had ever suffered over this, spent twisted nights of summer anguish, had dreams of the return of a man who would regard him with love and interest and blessing, all this in turn now must have come to seem like a dream. He once said to Catherine apropos of nothing but his own train of thought (they had been driving back from the Cape where they sometimes used to meet when Catherine went to New York in the summer to shop or visit), "It seems in a way he was always a myth. You can't blame a myth for anything, so I don't blame him." "You don't ever see him?" she inquired. To which to her amazement, he replied, "Oh, yes, sometimes." At that moment, on the highway at twilight, as they curved around the side of a low hill along a climbing road, a rust-red doe came up out of a cut in the woods along the slope to their right. She loped slowly with a fluid motion, her small back hooves hardly seeming to touch the pavement, crossing the road a good fifty yards ahead of them, and having made the opposite side in her long somewhat awkward stride, though awkward with the fresh quality of that which had not been before observed by human eyes, she in one upward bound, which seemed almost perpendicular but which flowed quickly toward the easy moment of descent, cleared the wire fence they had not even noticed was there, and vanished among the trees. Catherine had slowed the car until she passed, but whether she ever knew they were present or not neither of them could tell.

"You see him," she repeated.

"He stops by the college sometime."

"Why didn't you tell me?"

"You aren't supposed to see him. He drove you crazy or something."

"But now," she said. "Now all that part is over—in the past."

Latham did not reply.

Jerry, she knew because Priscilla had found out and told her, was living in Washington with a woman called Bunny Tutweiler, who had had two husbands and one divorce. "I guess she's his common-law wife," Priscilla had said with distaste. "He's the only person I know still common enough to have such a thing." She never spared Catherine anything about Jerry. "They have a daughter," she said. "Dear Lord," said Catherine, "the poor little thing. Have you got a picture of it, Priscilla?" Anything was possible. "Of course not," said Priscilla. "Maybe he calls her his mistress," said Catherine; "that would make it better, wouldn't it?" "Why do you always take up for him?" Priscilla asked. She was not angry now; she would never be angry with Jerry Sasser again, having seen him crumble. "Well, he was my whole life for nearly forever," said Catherine; "why shouldn't I?" "Why don't you marry Barry?" Priscilla asked. "Marry Barry?" She laughed. "Maybe because it rhymes."

Nevertheless, she had a devotion to Barry and wrote notes to him from time to time. Thus she found out that Irene had put goldfish in one wall of her apartment in New York; they seemed to be immersed in green water because the glass was green. Priscilla had picked up the notion from Irene also and was thinking of doing the same but could not get Millard interested. He said people in Merrill thought they were crazy enough as it was. Catherine made a mental notation that wherever she went fish were apt to be observed at eye or elbow level. Thinking their one thought she did not know.

◆

Charles Waddell, though Irene was too coarse fully to comprehend it, kept on being gnawed by jealousy. It was the one feeling he could never quite escape even when asleep. It did not rise to passion; he did not hate Mario, loathe his wife, want to slaughter anyone. How could he confront her and thus perhaps rid himself of it? Did he want to confront her? Was it, in any terms she would recognize, even possible to do so? He knew there were many harbors she could set sail to on her own; for him there was only her.

His jealousy, once it took its firm and secret hold, made him even more unpleasant than was his habit, made him a failure after his return from Rome, almost drove him into alcoholism. Who understood?

Well, as it turned out, the twins had more than a little comprehension of it all. They did not believe their mother's version of the Florida trip, that Daddy was worried because he did not have any money and so had stayed in the Keys. Money, they could already see, was not hard to come by. With the unexcited gravity so many war and postwar children have, probably because they have spent so much time with their grandparents, Will and Tom held long discussions, the identical dark blond duck tails on the napes of their necks moving slightly from side to side as the long muscular tendons rose and shifted in time to their thought and talk.

They had got longer-legged since Florida and sat about the lounges at the Virginia academy they attended (they were not, by their parents' request, allowed to room together), talking over things they had noticed, with the gravity of a United Nations committee meeting. Occasionally they laughed.

When their father descended on them from Florida, he found one of them right away—Will: he was in the library. Tom was in the pool. The twins got to go into the town for dinner and that was when Charles began to discover them in their great, complex totality for the first time. He became a listener, an observer at the chance and casual unfolding of their habits, lives and thoughts. A phrase here and a joke there struck him with the freshness of light, night-long rain falling on land as dessicated as a two-year-old corn shuck in the corner of a barn loft. He had spent so much time worrying.

Realizations came across to him now with the rapidity of summer lightning. How to make his face remote, how to withdraw his elation from them, lest in their infinite discrimination they became embarrassed at him. Oh, this took great skill, sharp moment-to-moment control of tension within, smooth relaxation without. Summit conferences were a snap, playing Hamlet at the Old Vic was nothing, compared to what was now crucial for Charles Waddell to get through without goofing. All the while, his spirit, a child itself, it now seemed, splashed about with overgrown baby gurgles, the awakening to his children like the primal contact with water in a tub. Careful! He had to make it seem that he was the recipient, that it was to him they were coming with their interest in space capsules, atom-splitting cyclotrons, ballistic missiles, something called the new math. An infinitude of wonders. The earth alive with it, space, too.

To himself when alone, Charles gave full rein, not wanting alcohol for the first time since the war started—before that he had been abstemious. His spirit burbled. He remembered whole blocks of conversation word for word. "We've decided Mother is our little sister," Will had said. "Oh, no, we decided she was younger than me but older than Will," said Tom, who in some way or other did seem the older of the pair. A whole log jam in Charles' spirit had broken up. If he had only asked them before! She was a venturesome child, seductible, overweight, easily impressed, comical. He almost howled with laughter. Far into the night, he lay on the tousled bed of his motel room and beat his fists into the pillow with sheer delight. When you conquered Irene, the world was yours. He began from this point to put the twins' wisdom far beyond what was even human—they had seen his dilemma, he believed, the secret gnawing at his heart, and had liberated him on purpose, like a pair of small Oriental sages disguised in chino trousers and brown leather loafers. It occurred to him later that they were able to do this because sex was less of a real terrain to them than deepest space a trillion light-years away; but some residue of his belief in their wisdom remained and would always remain. They had known instinctively, the way straight young savages might track game without ever being told exactly how, the trouble in his breast.

That night he slept the sleep of peace, completion and a new beginning—all, all. Life had opened before him a great and joyous future. To be a father. But he had been a father for years. He hadn't really noticed. What then had he noticed? His duty, service, information, programs, current history, personnel, Irene. The twins had been, after all, so very much her ornament.

Before the school principal the next day, his hat off in the office lit by spring sunlight, with redbud springing into bright tenuous life against the greening haze in the big campus oaks, he tried to hide his pride behind a sober frown. "So are they doing well?" The principal frowned. His heart sank. "I don't think you realize, Mr. Waddell, how exceptional your sons are." He nearly exploded with joy. The rest of the conversation was a blur. Leaving the school was the hardest moment of his life. But then he could hardly wait either to get home to Irene. He had forgotten all her foolishness. Perhaps he had driven her to it by never noticing how wonderful those kids really were. (This was sheer fantasy; even he knew that.) Perhaps, he darkly thought, she herself had never truly seen them. The turnpikes fled away beneath his homing speed. The city hampered him; it was molasses to a fly.

Now he burst into the apartment and was enfolding her with strong delight. A letter promising a job did not amaze him, though everything could touch him now. He took her thoroughly to bed, slept the great sleep, awoke to one of her excellent dinners, and over coffee broke the news to her. "Do you know? Do you realize?" "Realize what?" "Those boys!"

From then on that was all there was. For the whole weekend they talked of nothing else. They forgot about liquor and did not answer the phone. Irene dragged down old snapshot books, resurrected letters. He stared at her in wonder. "You kept all these? All this time!" He called up his parents, back in Ohio. They would all come for a family visit soon, he assured them. If they aren't dead of heart failure before midnight, Irene thought. Charles went for months—sometimes, she suspected, for years—without writing them a line. He heaped affection on her. "Do you remember the day I met you, how you had on that big cream-colored hat? Why don't women wear wide-brimmed hats any more? Can you tell me that?" "I had borrowed it," she said, "just for graduation. It was a costume. I had to give out programs." "Get another one," he pleaded and stroked her in a rapture of content. "The boys will go into science. It's absolutely certain." "They'll be space twins," said Irene, drowsily, in her uncanny accuracy about the world, predicting what had not yet occurred to anybody. "Masters of the air," he said, and that halted him. "I'm turning into a fatuous old fool," he said. "Poor darling," said Irene. "They were there all the time." "All this time! I know it. I say it to myself."

He did not reckon on it, but the twins were far from perfect. They had already, together, drowned animals, mutilated insects, read salacious books and pamphlets and scrutinized filthy pictures, though they did not keep any. They were sometimes cruel to stupid boys, in a way that could be caught on to only later, if at all, and had both had separately rudimentary homosexual experiments. Irene rather imagined without being told that all this was true; Charles could have got it down with difficulty and come up somewhat sobered, a good while later, with the obvious truth: that these things were all phases and would soon be forgotten by everyone, including Will and Tom. But at the moment no one broke in upon him with any fact. The boys stood in his mind's eye, their very phrases, laughter, eyes, ears and lashes he found printed on his brain to read and reread. Will had a slight cast in one eye; for years he had known this but for long periods could not have remembered, if asked, which one it was true of. Now in Greek perfection, their boyish shapes, mature manhood just around the corner, grew into his own identity and gave him youth to sport in once again. "Hey, I see why Barry has to sculpt people," he said. He padded about half-naked and barefoot, going from window to window. "Hey, let's go to a movie. You know, something old-timey . . . isn't there an old one on? Clark Gable, Myrna Loy, Claudette Colbert?"

He was drunker than he had ever been.

◆

"Why don't you tell her?" said Jerry Sasser to Bunny Tutweiler.

"Tell her she's illegitimate? You must be crazy," she said.

"Somebody's going to tell her, sooner or later. It might as well be you. In the long run she'll respect you for it. What is it when a girl is a bastard? What's the feminine of bastard? Didn't you used to teach school?"

"I never taught school in my life," she said. "Where'd you get that? You're making me sick anyway." She had a strong way of coming out with things. She had rust-red hair, freckles, crow's feet, an ill-defined nose, good practical figure, not very good taste.

He was sprawled out on the couch in the less than elegant apartment they had in Washington. His job—still with a legal firm retained by a Texas oil complex in which the Latham interests also figured—was in a slow period. He sat up too late and drank too much. For a time after the Texas debacle he had got to travel; where people never heard of him he was naturally more effective. But he never liked anywhere but America, really, and by now most people had forgotten his troubles anyway. Bunny would sit up half the night with him, or as late as he lasted, drinking with him, even though she had to keep strict office hours and get up early. She had a good sound tough nature and if anybody hurt her, she came right up and at them, hitting back. She thought he was a little bit strange at times, but knew he had had problems in the past.

She had probed around in these, rather more from curiosity than any other motive, and was satisfied that her already half-formed notion, namely that all Texans were apt to be crazy, was correct. She thought that Catherine must have been a weak, oversensitive woman who was not with it. On the other hand, maybe Jerry had played around a lot. She felt a twinge of jealousy to have missed this glamorous, handsomely got-up, fast-paced period of his life. She would have known how to have made it all work, would have got some fun out of it. It never occurred to her that without Catherine's money and backing, it would never have been possible in the first place.

Bunny Tutweiler would have married Jerry Sasser, but he never asked her to. He was not divorced, nor was she. Having been through one divorce which had got mixed up legally and dragged on for a year and a half, she did not want to go through another unless Jerry would do it first. For some reason not clear to her, he did not want a divorce. She thought it had to do with money, what he stood to gain if still married to his wife. There had been things about psychiatrists, too, unpleasant to consider, let alone stir up again. Bunny decided with her feminine intuition that more than anything else all this embarrassed Jerry. When she got pregnant she left it up to him whether she would have it or get rid of it. To her surprise, he wanted it. A girl. Was he disappointed? His one son had been a cripple. No, he was pleased and named her himself: Diane. Where did he get it? Didn't know. Always liked the name. He wondered nervously if she would be pretty or not. "At that age you can't tell a thing," Bunny told him. Bunny was always correct. After six months exactly, she had a sitter come in and went back to work. She couldn't stand staying at home all day. She was always up early, hair freshly done, nails perfect. All the things she had were ordinary—Revlon make-up, pink hair curlers, nylons drying on plastic coathangers fitted with clothespin hooks in various colors. To the crisp clacking of her Middle-Western accent, which always reminded him of a typewriter run by a very good but not extraordinary typist, his drawl found ways and means of returning to his speech: it was easy to be a mean Southern boy again. He tried to teach her chess once at one A.M., but by three she had learned nothing whatsoever. "Nice to find your limitations," he said and put the set up for good. After that they played gin rummy; she usually beat him except when he took a spell of caring. "Tell her," he prodded her, opening out his hand after the deal, glancing at it, furling it and setting it face down on the board to pick up his drink. "Go on in there and say, 'Diane, honey, you're a natural child.'" She gave him a funny look. "You must be drunk," she said, and played the nine of spades. "If you won't tell her, I will. Sure. I'll tell her some day." He took the trick. The rest of the evening they did not say anything. The apartment was still in every unremarkable inch of it. One day he disappeared.

There was no way for her to look for him; he was not really her husband. What right do you have to inquire, would be the first thing they would ask. His office called but she said she just didn't know. She looked for something in the papers for several days, considering writing a personal, or getting a private detective, then did nothing at all. She opened the mental file of all she had had to discover about men, and thought how all of them were different and each one had taken a lot of getting used to. A generation before she would have run a little house in a small Middle-Western town, been active in societies and had three or four children and a plot of sunflowers. If a sunflower with a monstrous face had come up, she would have gone out and cut it down. Two centuries before she might have gone out of a frontier fort to get some dry firewood and been captured by Indians and been very glad when they let her go. "If you're going to order anything from the delicatessen," she told Jerry, early in their relationship, "get the largest size they have." "Why is that?" he inquired. "Because they do a standard mark-up over the regular supermarket price on all the items, and so with the biggest size you're bound to get the best buy."

When Jerry came back from his disappearance, he said he had gone away because there hadn't been much doing at the office. He took an apartment to himself. He came by every night for dinner, paid half her bills and everything for the child. They sat up at night and drank and played gin rummy. He's just got a wild streak, she thought. All men are different. Everything was just about the same.

On fine Sundays he took the little girl out alone with him for drives along the Potomac, over into Chevy Chase, out in Maryland farmland, once all the way down to Delaware. That was when Bunny started getting mad. Why didn't he want her to go too? If I leave him, I'll take her with me, she secretly thought. She's mine, after all.

"Daddy says I'm a natural child," said Diane. "What's that mean?" "It means you're pretty and smart," said Bunny Tutweiler, "but don't tell Miss Parsons; it's a secret."

But with that she really determined to leave him, for something deep inside went fierce and strong-jawed enough to bite an iron nail in two. Then, for the first time, she got scared. She was riding the bus to work, holding on to a strap, on a brilliant Washington day still warm, though it was late October. Maybe he was just wild and crazy. The day blurred; her head felt as though she had forgotten her coffee. Did she love him maybe?

Sentiment to her was as bad as quicksand. She sank into a vacant seat, feeling stunned and trapped. It was like being caught by Indians. Oh, Lord!

◆

Barry Day met a nice girl, fell in love, and married her.

He had to pay off what he owed in Arkansas, get a divorce, legally change his name from Bernard Desportes. It all took a lot of doing but he went through it happily and patiently, like a brave little boat which had got out too far and had turned back toward shore at last. He had met the girl when he had a job at Macy's; she had worked near him in the cataloging department and had got into a snarl that was clearly her own fault. He supposed it was the wrong time of the month or maybe she hadn't had enough breakfast. She shook when they descended on her to stand over her and ask a lot of questions. She cried and nearly fainted. Barry took all the blame and got fired, but he was ready to quit anyway. He had never seen anyone so grateful, and able to do something for a woman for the first time in his entire life, it went right to his head. He fell in love, she fell in love. It was absolute. She adored him.

Irene could never get her name right; was it Ellen or Helen or Eleanor, or Ellene? When Barry mentioned her he could never quite say it, a sure sign of love. None of them ever got to know her well, doubtless because there was really nothing to know. She was young but not girlish, good to look at, but not beautiful or even pretty, well-dressed but not elegant, and as far as anyone could tell she was as good as nature itself. She had no peculiarities except a deep anxiety to do well. It was this that had made her cry over her mistake at Macy's, not her period or lack of money or want of food. This one little weakness had landed her all of Barry Day.

Now her quiet look assured everybody, including him, that he was a great artist. They had a child before anyone could stop to think about it. Catherine never got to know her well either, though she had her and Barry, and the baby too when it arrived, up to her house in Massachusetts several times.

"The reason you feel that way," said Irene, on one of the rare occasions when she and Catherine met in New York (Priscilla, who had been introduced to Irene on one of her trips East, now saw the Waddells more than Catherine did; she could enter with Irene on long meditative sessions about modern living, together they could gain a speechless nirvana of decision about clothes, people, food and decor, a special exalted area of transfiguration which comes to women who have dealt through a lifetime with products, styles, and who is who and what you can get where) . . . "the reason you feel that way is that there is nothing to know. She loves him; that's all there is to know."

Catherine drew back from accepting anything as flat as this. "He's complex," she argued. She remembered her feeling for him, the extent of it, entering into the smallest detail—his tuneless singing as he sponged the car at Sperlonga, his rock-bottom despair over the car, his eagerness to please, hold, stabilize, satisfy her that one time they had stayed together in New York—God, how she had needed to trust him—his forgiveness of her madness, of himself, of them both. I won't just summarize him, she thought, I won't do it. "Will she just never, never know him?"

"If it doesn't matter to him, why should we worry?" Irene said.

"I don't know, but I—"

"There are too many people now," said Irene. "What good does it do to be complicated? Nobody has time to know all about us, follow us, remember us, feel for us. Love is something else now. It's just a kind of sinking into something, a sort of vanishing."

She wore a linen suit, pink and dark blue, and was resisting sweets. Catherine had sunburnt forearms and had scratched her hands up doing yard work in the country. "If that's really true, we might as well not live," she said.

"Oh, we can live, all right," said Irene. "Not once but a dozen times. Three dozen lives." She laughed. "Assorted pastries."

Was this happiness Irene was carelessly describing? I'd rather be unhappy, Catherine thought. "I've only one," she asserted. With Irene, to give her credit, Catherine could always state things, and perceiving at once the truth, more or less surprised out of her, of this one statement about herself, she came to rest in it, as though it had been chiseled out on a stone. She wasn't sure she was unhappy, though. She had taken unhappiness for granted for ages, but had not really thought about it in a long time. How long a time? She didn't know. Life had taken on an aspect of timelessness. She had to think to make out what year it was, or her own age.

On these matters, Irene was right up to date. She knew that she and Catherine had both slipped the forty mark and that she had never expected this to happen to her. To everybody else maybe but not to her. They had really got together over Barry, Irene recognized. They both had a strong sensual tie to him, had held him tight in the throes of what might have been death or might have been love, had been held by him. Nothing but spiritual poison can dissolve a tie of the flesh, and spiritual poison had been left out of it when Barry was fabricated.

"But maybe she does," said Catherine, with one of her sudden inspirations.

"Does what?" asked Irene.

"Maybe his wife does appreciate him, feel for him, see everything we did, know him better than we did."

Irene closed her eyes. This was one of Catherine's innocent cruelties. Maybe it was true. "Catherine," said Irene, "doesn't it occur to you that we would do better not to think so? Can we find another Barry now?"

"I couldn't, but maybe you could," said Catherine, waking up and finishing a chocolate eclair. "You just said we had a dozen lives."

"I loved Barry," said Irene.

"I still love him," said Catherine. "I think his work will succeed now," she added.

Irene burst out laughing. It was a final twist of the knife.

"What about Priscilla's girls?" Irene asked. "She says she's bringing them to New York this fall for the theatre."

"They're selfish and mean," said Catherine. "They have a lot of boy friends. They're racing toward the altar like a pair of fillies. Millard will be glad. He'll get his house back, all his books and records. Maybe some day Merrill will blow away in a tornado. If it did I might see Jerry again, the way he really is. If that town had never existed, we could have existed."

"That's one of those things you can't prove," said Irene, to shake her out of it. She had to go and shop for a dinner party; Charles had business visitors from Denver.

"I was in Denver once," said Catherine.

"I guess we've all been just about everywhere," said Irene. "Except Mexico. Charles and I are going in January. They say it's mystical."

◆

Irene got ready for her party sooner and more easily than usual. She had help now, for Charles was in the swim again, had landed a high executive position in a firm that published the best nonfiction, in paperback: political science, science, sociology, business research, public documents, both historic and current. It was the newest field. Even the goldfish knew it.

She knelt on the sofa in her long crepe hostess skirts and stared out at East River. It was dark already. The traffic was forever. Catherine, she thought. She must be home now. A Southern woman in that little town in Massachusetts. Cold blue evenings. Knowing the druggist, knowing the postman, knowing the neighbors, raking leaves. And not unhappy. Not crazy any more. Just out of it.

Practically everybody in the world is out of it, thought Irene. I guess they do all right. I will always be in it, she thought. I created it. It is me. If it hadn't been for me Mario would still be grubbing around in libraries, lecturing on Hegel. Now he's a retired national hero and has his picture in magazines.

Charles was coming in, a load of fresh red chrysanthemums under one arm.

"I saw Catherine today," said Irene.

"Catherine Sasser? How is she?" On his way to shave, he did not stop for an answer. "Letter from the boys," he shouted from the bathroom. "Came to the office. Oh, Irene! When Parker's wife gets too much she goes on the prowl. Apt to be scenes. Got to watch it." He came into the living room, buttoning a clean shirt. "Is something the matter?"

"Why?"

"I never saw you look that way in my life. Are you sick? Worried?"

"No, just thinking."

But what about? She couldn't say exactly, that was the trouble. The great anonymous thing that Catherine had let in on her at long last had been trying to get at her, she now realized, all her life. The wild daisy, pure in sunlight, that we see by the roadside from the car window is gone only slightly less quickly than we can pass it, only slightly more quickly than we, in our little lifetime. Where was the cat she had had as a pet for a little while as a child? Her own mother, aging, unable for fifteen years even to go uptown, sat all afternoon daily on a narrow porch in Maryland. She had sat there this afternoon. What did she think about, every day that way? Did it matter what she thought about? Catherine has stopped by the grocery for a loaf of bread, she thought. Latham may call; Latham may not call. There are still lakes in the woods which no one sees. Somewhere within five minutes of her maybe the police were knocking at a door to catch an old man who had forged a check. And all over the city, swarming, the unknown, the voiceless, the quiet, the good, the evil, the loud, the corrupt, the sick, the dying, millions on millions, reached out to one another, caught and held or failed to catch and hold. To be good, not to be mad, to accept, live, perceive, with steadfastness and grace . . . was that all? To love, to love, to love, constantly, the very rhythm of it like a beating heart? What about it chilled her, touched her with dread? She lit a cigarette and stubbed it out.

"Not there," she said to the maid. "You can't put red chrysanthemums next to goldfish. Put them on the other side of the room."

The doorbell rang. Its positive note broke up the surface of her mind, drew all her instincts together, quivering inward toward the moment. The challenge of movement, new people, the always possible future. Talk of the New Frontier was in the air. On and on. Did it never stop? she sometimes asked herself, now with wonder, now with weariness, occasionally with something like horror. But the next question always was right there, waiting for her: what if it did?

Rising, she touched her hair at the mirror, readjusted a single scarlet flower. If Barry did make a great success, it would be she, not Catherine, he would come round to. Who but she would know or even help to create its significance? She turned, settling her face, her smile, toward whatever face should appear.

◆

When Catherine drove in late from New York, shadowy in the night, Latham rose from the doorstep where he had been sitting, like a quiet animal. He limped toward her across the lawn, giving every flagstone, every flower and tree he passed its total and infinite value.

Barry Day ran up a cheap stairway and opened a golden door.

Jerry Sasser played all afternoon with his little girl, throwing a big orange ball on a beach in Delaware. It was past dark before they turned to go inside.

Bunny Tutweiler had an accident at a Washington traffic circle when coming home from work. She was rushed to the hospital in an ambulance, but did not recover.

The Grey World

Dark and impassive as a savage, a carved, great-featured face lived constant in his mind among the ruins of his own lost glory. Jerry Sasser himself still went daily about something that at least resembled life. The carved face was no longer his own, but neither was it anyone else's. It was beneath these lofty ceilings, echoing passages, still arches, that he was lonely, because, no matter how many people he saw or dealt with, none of them came here. He would not bring his daughter here, and though he had twice in foolish illusion, which mainly came out of a bottle, kept Bunny Tutweiler up all night telling her about it, she had not at any point registered the awesome truth which even the existence of the ruin conveyed. Everything was alike to Bunny. She could deal with anything. Only Catherine had seen and had known; she had not been able to stand it, though perhaps to say why was beyond her. What it all meant, what had scared her, was power.

In the vast carved language of power, every particular thing—every reason, every decision, every individual—had no word to match it; nothing could in itself be felt as permanent and inviolate, nothing could quite merit life. The balance was all; the world was a forest with a fire in it. He had long ago accepted this; on an admiral's staff during the war he had slipped by default of a public relations officer into doing a p.r. hitch himself; before he knew it he was supplying a conveyer belt with words. He found out what was being done, and more than that, he found out what could be done by him. The words went out through machines which relayed facts which could be proved, and which, all added up, came out to make a grand total which was always the same: Americans were superior to all others, acquitted themselves well, had right on their side, and some were braver than others. He discovered what everybody had been doing all the time, not just in war or over the machines, but all their lives, only they did not know it. They had been shifting words around to suit themselves. It was enough to make you laugh out loud. Once you got the key to life every door was apt to open. The sea was vast and blue, the ships beautiful, the combat a blur of blank tension and mindless trial, the islands green as paradise. He cared for no one and went up quickly.

The words which opened doors were by no means final, and once a door opened and you got inside there were other doors beyond that and more words necessary to open those and others beyond those, a labyrinth, with life getting better, every step of the way. You had to remember the facts: these could be juggled and arranged, but never altered. If people got hurt it was because they did not keep the facts in mind or had never learned them, or because they had used the wrong words. If he himself damaged anybody then he could always remember that everybody got hurt sometime and would get hurt again. Let them learn. Only the impulse of power could stop and start things. A vantage point had to be chosen, a point of observation, high as you could get, not apt to be noticed, with an unobstructed view of the main current, its swirls and eddies, rise and fall. A fascination began that kept him going long past the war, year after year, kept him alert, attractive, busy, offensively negligent to the point of contempt of individual moments in whose essence, where Catherine was concerned, life's beauty and passion lived, or could live.

Then one day somebody did to him what he had learned to do to others. He pitched into the current and was swept aside. He was buried at Sandy Gulch like the boy beneath the wagon. Nothing could unite him to his past, yet he felt oddly alive, an escapee from a life sentence. If he saw Catherine again, everything would wake up; chains would grow from his wrists and ankles, turmoil and passion would churn up, longing, ambition, the long proofs and trials of commitment to her, to the Lathams, to his son, to Merrill, to the sovereign state of Texas, to the United States of America. In her quiet person, she united everything. She would literally go mad rather than give up her unity. He wanted her to stay his wife forever just so long as he never had to go back. The only trouble was that he loved her. His glory had failed, that was all. There was no going back. He knew now he had never been good, even back in those days when he cottoned up to the Lathams and taught a Sunday school class, progressing by rhythmic, unconsciously calculated degrees to being a civic leader and favorite Kiwanis speaker. He now recognized he had been that worst of all human things, a pretender at goodness for where it could get him. It was far better to pretend at nothing in order to move toward glory.

Now, look what happened. His goodness was false face; his long trajectory of glory had fizzled out in the sand; if he went back to start again, back to Merrill where he would have at least to touch ground, the Lathams would inevitable gang up on him. They would do it as simply as thinking about it: by seeing that he confronted that remembered face out of which his soul had awakened, his father.

Perhaps the one good thing he had ever done, he now considered, was to try to love his father. In trying to love, he did love—to try is to succeed—and then there was the horror which he couldn't even call horror because of his love. There was the hot fall night of his seventh birthday when his father lit not the electric light in the little dusty sunken one-story house under a mulberry tree, but a lamp with a glass chimney, globed at the base, and heating the small blade of a pocket knife over this to sterilize it, pierced his own flesh and drew blood from his wrist and let drops fall into a glass of water. The glass had once contained cheese spread. "This is your power," his father had said. "And it is mine." He had been startled up out of bed and led into the kitchen half-asleep, his father carrying the lamp down the hall before them. He stood barefoot on the linoleum and drank a couple of swallows, very small ones. The water was not even discolored; it didn't taste like anything much except water. Then his father drank. "You're old enough to begin because you can remember now. To remember is everything. Time adds to time. Each time you will remember the others. You are never to speak of it. There are only the two of us here. Later you will find others. It is a bondage and cannot be broken. We are spreading. Everywhere."

Still dazed, he blundered back to bed in the dark, his heart beating strangely. The next day it seemed like a dream. His father did not mention it. He had already been wakened once before like that and told that his mother had died. He remembered her well, from way over in the city, in Dallas, and how they had all lived as one family in a little house on a street with a lot of little houses, regularly spaced out, and every much alike. He remembered laughter from those days, and late conversation from other rooms. Then one early morning he was standing in the hall dressed in a new suit, which they had bought for him without telling him about it and told him to put on. It made a wool smell in the chill winter house, that peculiar stretched-out, dry, uniform chill of a Texas winter. His mother's tears were smeared on his face, and now his sisters bent close to him, those two sharp girl-faces, grey ever after in his memory. They hugged and pulled at him. He was smothered in woman smell, the dim pervasive odor of their clothes hung in closets, damp things left lying in the bathroom. He walked away with his father. It had all been explained by then. His father would be a teacher in a town. He would live with his father. His mother would come soon. "Soon, soon," his mother said. She came, but seemed a visitor. His father scarcely spoke to her except with the removed tones of a careful householder, a pastor perhaps receiving a parishioner. She did not stay long, but went away. "Hush," his father said when he asked why. One day his father explained. He said she had never acknowledged the truth. He said he had pondered it: was the truth for women or not? The Bible seemed to be in doubt also on this point. If she had listened to him, she might have been with them still. But she could not listen; something prevented her. It was a mystery. He decided to try her by taking a job away, at some distance. He could leave the girls but not his son. A son was the true line, the thread of life, the truth-bearer.

All these things came in the form of strange quaking night-confidences, when, his brain confused with sleep, he would be called out to the sitting room, not to the strange ritual but to the stranger divulgences, things he had to know, fed to him out of his father's mind like secret spiritual food. Why couldn't he be told something at an ordinary hour? He didn't know. Perhaps his father had no control in this way, but the information in all its precise quality emerged at odd hours and quickly sank back, as if a fish had surfaced for a moment, out of the stream of sleep. All of it ran the risk of seeming a dream. But what is closer than a dream, or in the long run more real? It was his daylight father he learned to love, a meditative, friendly, conversant man, lonely and observant, like all self-styled thinkers in odd little towns, content to be thought learned and peculiar, reposing himself in charity, modesty, regularity, never going into debt.

Years passed without any strange summons, the whole blood-smeared legend put away in a locked closet, like a Halloween costume or an old lion's skin, motheaten and torn in places, wanting the dignity of flesh. One day he learned that his father had himself written the books he was always reading, especially on Sunday afternoons.

There were several copies of each, and in one, yellowed clippings contained words of praise for them, one written by a U.S. Senator, another by a multi-millionaire.

In time he was given the books. He could never read them. He promised to and he said that he had, but he could not. Sometimes, after dark on Saturdays, strange cars pulled up and parked at their trailed-out end of the street, and men got out who would talk to his father until a late hour. The next day they were all to be found, the owners of those voices, at a small brown-painted house on a side street down behind the business section, where, tightly closed in with cloth-covered windows, they would hold a service, light the lamp, pass the cup about.

He preferred never to think about it between times. He was always the youngest one present. They would all shake his hand solemnly, acknowledging his privileged place. One day they asked him to pray. He had been sitting thinking of something else, and when it got through to him what they wanted, he knew they had asked him not once but several times. He got up slowly and slowly too the odd revelation once more suffused his spirit, a thing that came out of closets, out of midnights; he felt he was falling helplessly. He woke up on the main street of Merrill, to which he had fled. For a long time that day he wandered around and did not dare go home. When he did return his father did not underestimate what he had done. He did not speak to his son. "I didn't mean it," Jerry said, clinging to the door, leaning in the threshold. "Next time I'll try. I'll really try." "You never will," said his father, continuing to read. "I have failed."

Professor Sasser made one last try in behalf of the faith, when he gave his books to Catherine. He talked rapidly that day, imposing on the girl's young manners, her pliancy, her awakening love. He told her too much at once, talking desperately, stumbling over his words. For this was his last chance on earth, and his son, watching him in something like agony, knew it. What had he done? He had startled and sickened her, that was all. *Blood Bondage of Messiah's Brotherhood.* The sacred cup. The Holy Grail was an old cheese glass. Oh, Father, Father! How can you be like that?

"What did you do in that funny church, Jerry?" Catherine asked him. It was a bright spring Sunday morning, sometime around Easter in Dallas when he was in law school and they hadn't gone to church for the best of all possible reasons. Their freshly spent love clung around them, fragrant and dense, undispersed, and out of this bright cloud he was laughing. He could not stop laughing. "We drank blood," he said. She began laughing too. They could not stop. "What did you do?" he asked her. "We drank grape juice," she said. "It was a substitute." Later in the day, he caught her observing him, out of the depths of a chair where she was supposed to be reading the Sunday papers. "We shouldn't have laughed like that," she said. "It's all sacred," she added. "And anyway, I always liked feeling you were different from ordinary people, that there was something about you nobody could know about." He did not answer. His father was aging, poor, deferential to his son's wife's wealthy family, kind to all alike. But the thing that had taken him from his mother and isolated him with this man's passion and tried out of the night to find a voice to reach him, tugging at him like a black tide, that was forever shut away. It occurred to him that a religion is valid or not valid only by the numbers of people who can be persuaded to believe in it. His father had in every fiber of his spirit believed. He could not reach his son. Nothing in the length and breadth of Texas, that unenlightening land, could come forward to say that this was not a tragedy, if a tragedy is an impasse and a man's life swept into it. He groped, wanting to drop it all, the whole subject, wanting her to drop it too. Yet it had attracted her. It accounted for the small veil of difference, of wonder and mystery, that lay in her mind about him. It was the promise of manhood not yet, on that Sunday morning in Dallas, entirely his own. So he held on, not wishing to sever utterly the thread of the past, for it might be leading him to his own fulfillment. "I never meant to laugh at him," he told her, withdrawing. She nodded. When he said a thing like that, she understood him. If life were made up one percent of decencies, one percent of decent attitudes and right answers and good generous things to know, Catherine would never fail to understand it. It was when even that one percent was gone and not to be found that she went crazy—or crazy was what the psychiatrists were trying to say by calling it a lot of other names. According to Jerry, she wasn't crazy at all. It was all the swing of the same identical pendulum, side to side. She could not give up what she was. And a big part of what she was, was her knowledge of him. There was no way to make her lose it.

He went to Bunny Tutweiler's funeral. It was in a funeral home in Washington and he got there too late because he couldn't get a taxi in the rain. Her husband, Bentley Tutweiler, was there, sitting alone in the parlor which was the living room of an old-fashioned house with white Corinthian columns out front. They had put in a linoleum floor which was highly waxed. He had once seen a convention of undertakers and morticians lobbying against some bill they thought unfair to them; they looked to be having as good a time as anybody, but he hadn't been able to push through the crowd without a chill down his spine; they seemed to represent death out of life instead of in life, as though the moment of death were a melting into their arms and into coffins and graves just as one might get upon a stage by disappearing into a dressing room and getting covered with a wig and masked in make-up. Once back of the footlights you confronted the human race in new terms. Poor old Bunny! Do I applaud now? he wondered.

He shook hands solemnly with Bentley Tutweiler, to whom he wished to present himself as a friend whom Bunny had for reasons best known to herself asked to look after her daughter in case anything happened to her. This was only an opener. He, in truth, intended to fight for Diane if he had to forge a marriage certificate. But Tutweiler got up, removed a handkerchief from his breast pocket, blew his nose and shook hands. "You must be Jerry Sasser," he said. "She wrote me about you. It's all right about the little girl." That finished that. Jerry almost laughed. Maybe if he could have laughed the little chill would go away. Oh, stop it, Bunny, he wanted to say, Come on out, the game's over. But once you got that going, he might have to see it apply to everything. Stop, Catherine, stop running off, stop going crazy; it was all a joke, we'll go to the drugstore and laugh about it. But at the moment of upheaval, the moment of certainty, the moment of focus and flesh, everything would be real again—Merrill would wake up and be there, same as ever.

There was a huge green plant with oblong shiny green leaves in the corner. Muzak was playing, and one at a time the funeral home functionaries came out in frock coats with white carnations in their buttonholes and mumbled appropriate words, inquiring whether they wished to have the coffin open or closed. Jerry deferred to Bentley Tutweiler, who said he didn't know. "Closed," said Jerry desperately. If they left it open she might jump out of it. The door opened and three more people came in. One was Bunny's girl friend, Jeannie MacFarland, with whom she had once, between men, shared an apartment. The other two were from the law office. They were late because they couldn't find the address. More flowers came in, in baskets, like a school recital in Merrill, and other chairs were brought. The morticians' footsteps did not make any sound at all. Some of the flowers were wet from the rain; when Jerry saw that he thought of Catherine. Maybe things would work out somehow so that Catherine would eventually take Diane. That would be a long time off. Right now, in the discreet apartment he was about to rent out near Arlington, he was going to hire a quiet ample mulatto woman to look after the child, and weekends he would be with her. She could continue to climb around all over him, sit on his shoulders, explore his ears, pull his eyebrows, and crawl up under his coat. She would put her hand in his and walk along the Potomac. They had been there last weekend, and a fish came up and looked at them. He would have long serious talks with the mulatto woman, who would believe him to be a fine, sincere man whose wife had tragically passed away. The closed grey coffin rolled in. They were asked to bow their heads in prayer.

Why had the morticians been lobbying in Washington? Right now he forgot. They were in danger of having some law passed which was prejudicial to their profession, but what were they doing to make a law necessary? Were they usurping the rights of ministers of various faiths by interring the dead, returning the body to the earth, consigning the soul to God? Were they taking advantage of the family's grief and guilt to put up prices on coffins and embalming, counseling fraudulent methods for preserving the flesh, as if anyone was going out with a spade in fifty years to see if the guarantee had been fulfilled. After fifty months even, who cared? Were they presenting bills too large or selling cemetery space which didn't exist? Were they cremating on the sly to save space? But cemeteries were municipal property. Were undertakers go-betweens for municipality? Was there a little city hall system involving rake-offs? Bunny, who always thought of everything, had had burial insurance. He didn't have to look into anything very much, only put them on to getting in touch with her estranged husband, whereabouts unknown. He was easy to find and had appeared as quick as anything. He was not a bad-looking man, though a little bit skinny. Perhaps he had even been a good lover; maybe she had luck that way, though why he couldn't say. She was pliant and satisfying and the heart could rest, not being required.

It grew on him out of the quietly bowed heads of the five of them that nobody was going to blame him with anything. If she had been worried increasingly about him and what was going to happen next during the last six months, she had not complained to anybody. That was something. Solid value received. (Thanks, love. Jolly good girl. Some talk for a Texan. Shouldn't confuse her now, poor old Bunny.) Let her rest; she had disappeared perhaps through wanting to. Catherine had disappeared but they had found her in a Fort Worth hospital, suffering from exhaustion. "I found your mother, Jerry." "Mother! I haven't got a mother. She died." "Yes, you have. Your father told me. Forgive me for not telling you before." What did anybody say to that? "That's okay." Mustn't upset her. "I can give you her address. I have to give it to you because I can't—" "Can't what?" "She could be a place for you, don't you see? I can't any more. I just can't. It's run out. There isn't any more." "We'll talk it over when you feel better." "It all fell through, didn't it? The scheme about the magazine and all." "How did you know? Look, I'll pay your family back. Someday, somehow." "It isn't paying back, Jerry. That's not the point." "I don't want a mother, Catherine, can't you see that? You put her on to me— Look, I'll pay your family back. Someday, somehow. I promise." "I know but even if you do, I still can't stand it. I can't be the world you live in. Let's drop out of it . . . run a filling station, anything." "It's still just the world, always the same." "Don't quarrel, hold on to me. Just hold on to me. Please. And forever. Please." He held her. She had a few tears left, fresh as rain. "Jerry, I can't go another step." "What happened after you left, before you found my mother?" "I can't remember." "I think you dreamed it all; she's dead." "I didn't. No. But she didn't believe me. She had seen your picture in an article once about Washington politics and thought you must be some other Sasser." "That's funny, even though it said from Merrill." "I think that one said from Dallas." "Should I go say here is your long-lost son $100,000 in debt? I have to go now, or jump out the window when the family comes." His hand, lingering on her arm, suddenly tightened. "They'll try to make you leave me." "Leave you!" Her laugh was quick, girl-like; it came out of nowhere, starlight in hell. Her face was worn down to nothing. His heart plunged into a broad river of pain. Footsteps sounded in the corridor, trooping along: the Lathams. If not now, then later. His kiss almost pulled her up by the roots, in which case he would have certainly had to leave her to wither and die in the sun, for he wasn't going to stick around and face them. He got out and in the corridor and around the corner, out and gone, just in time. They didn't see him, but would they have, anyway? He was invisible already in a grey world. Things had broken. His clean working order was destroyed. Sludge was pouring in from everywhere. He would take it and keep on. A grey life in a grey world. Not for Catherine. Impossible. As though he were still present before her, he could see her eyes grow vacant, blue and vacant, the woman quality receding to nothing. Eyes of a little boy. Color of fair Texas spring day. Hardly perceptible pale eyebrows, outlining the bone above the socket. He had to move fast to keep a jump ahead of thoughts like that. Thoughts like that would kill you.

"What are you doing now?" asked Bentley Tutweiler. They had repaired to the Mayflower for a drink.

"Juggling figures for the oil companies. Now they've settled depletion allowances, gas allotments are all the rage."

"Oh, that's right. Your wife's family was in oil."

"Not working directly for them. Indirectly, I would say. It's all done by companies now. No private ownership direct. Wildcatting is subsidized. Do you know the industry?"

"Can't say I do. Insurance is my game. Adjustor."

"Interesting life."

"Yes, it is. There wasn't anything really wrong with Bunny and me. We just couldn't get along. I guess that's all there is, ninety percent of the time."

"Yeah, guess that about says it."

A more amiable man could never, in any crisis, Jerry Sasser judged, be hoped for; and to think he had simply fallen out of nowhere. A treasure indeed was Bentley Tutweiler. Perhaps all Tutweilers were treasures. Hadn't he once known a jeweler named Tutweiler? Are you a Jew? he wanted to ask. He didn't look it, but might be half or a quarter Jewish. Bunny was not Jewish; her name had once been Sanders or Saunders, something like that. He had got that straight before Diane was born. What difference did blood make? He didn't know and didn't want to know.

"Tutweiler, boy, you're a great guy," he said. His second drink was taking hold. He was running the verge of laughing, but had to fight it off. He slapped Bentley Tutweiler on his thin shoulder. He was overdoing it now, concentrating on looking straight at the color of the whiskey, far too solemn and after-funeral-looking. They had stood around together in the cemetery in the rain, which had brought on the practical rightness of going to a bar.

"Hey, I'd like to bring the kid by sometime."

Just calling her "kid" meant he wouldn't ever do it; she wasn't a kid at all. But it was the signal for a lot of sentimentality. They wallowed in it up to the neck through a third and a fourth and maybe—God alone knew by then—even a fifth drink. At the end Bentley was weeping. He had a soul, after all. Jerry Sasser was weeping because he didn't have one. When he finally got bored, at the end of what the bourbon could do for that day at least, he said he just couldn't talk about it any more, and left. He said it hurt too much. In a way, it did hurt. What was it that hurt? he wondered. Another phase gone; time passing. He did feel for Bunny, some way or other. He wondered if she ever knew what had happened, or had she lost consciousness at once. He had not been inclined to ask.

The next week he found the mulatto he was looking for. He realized when he found her, this comfortable, somewhat aristocratic, certainly gentle and practical housekeeper and nurse, that no power on earth would persuade Priscilla that he was not also living with her, a woman Catherine would instantly have realized he would behave more like a gentleman with than anyone he had ever known, a woman he would never touch, whose sense of what was appropriate to hear he would never violate or even ruffle. He saw her with immeasurable satisfaction the day he brought her to the new apartment he had rented way across town, shaking the dust of the Bunny Tutweiler area off his mentality forever—all that pink soap. He was out near Arlington now and had done some choosing, grey curtains for the living room and the rudiments of some solid new furniture. He had got her dressed in plain gingham and she had a sharp little dark animal face, broad at the top with dark eyes slightly scared since her mother's disappearance. He was saying to the new woman, "As I told you, she is a natural child." The woman did not change expression. "I remember," she said. She reached down to Diane, not to shake hands but to take her hand. Diane had to lift her own up a little way, and placed it, white in the dark one. "We're going to see about your room," said the woman. "I'll open an account for you at Garfinkle's. I'll pay the bills. She has to have a good room, her own." The woman's eyes widened slightly; it was a leap of trust, of confidence, she had not expected. He shoved his hands in his pockets, turning away. He was acting, slightly. It startled him. Once he had begun this way in a situation he would be expected to keep it up. If he was acting at all, didn't it mean that he didn't really care? Did he care? He had certainly meant to care. For the first time in a long time, his glory spent, the proud ships gone into history, the dazzling white uniforms never to be put on again, the language of the innermost inside to spring to his tongue no more (but Bunny Tutweiler, at least, in his life no longer); he had meant to care. What astonished him now was his deep travail, his own will to seriousness. Whether other people knew it or not he was always retaining his right to swerve off—when he ran out of his father's church that day, that had set up a pattern, practical and even wise. But the tableau of three—child, nurse and father—would bear the closest scrutiny. For one thing, it required him to remain. It demanded that he should never laugh. He had, in other words, not to wonder why he was acting once, but to become an actor. Tableau would follow tableau. He would discuss Diane daily, weekly, monthly, yearly, with this woman who was already doing grave honor to them both. It would be an endless program. He could not have asked for better. In times away alone with the child, they would instantly, with perfect consent, pick up their life together, walk along the shore, look at the sea, walk in the park, look at the Potomac, climb up and sit on Lincoln's knee, count the miles on the speedometer in the car, eat through all the different ice cream flavors at Howard Johnson's. Time would pass; she would grow, go away, school life, some boy's clumsy forcing of her lips, the world's deep waters. He idled through the conversation, feeling handsome again for the first time in years; his squint relaxing, his drink-roughened skin freshening. He stood straighter. The woman by her correct speech, the very occasional use of Sir, was creating him, perhaps almost consciously, to suit herself, what she thought he should be as regards this child. Holding the child's hand; the child consenting to this, grown calm. Calmly himself he remembered women, remembered them all, that army, those feminine phalanxes which hovered in memory back of Bunny Tutweiler, who had been a sort of Great Divide, and which had started after Catherine, who had been a sort of Jumping-off Place. How pretty, how perfect they had all had the gift to seem, at least for their little moment, and that was something. It was quite a lot. Perfect little girls, Catherine used to say, thin, mad, faithful, accurate, brushing her cornsilk hair, the hotel mirrors giving him three of her at once. Those perfect little girls who ran America. Stewardesses, perfume clerks, restaurant hostesses, nurses, secretaries, receptionists, on back to WAVES and WAC officers and Red Cross girls. Carefully packaged, expertly wrapped, opening at a touch—Jesus! His vision blurred, encompassing the child in gingham. He had to get out. May she be nothing special, he thought, addressing nobody special; just measure up completely when the time comes, have her moments when some good man will think a fresh perfection has come alive out of the world's most glowing ad for the country's most admirable product. In the meantime: "Will you read to her? She likes that." The small face came into focus, brightened, looking up. She adores me, he thought: adores me. "Sure, we'll read. We shall certainly read,

Diane." What to read? What to get her? Catherine would tell him. He would ask Latham to ask Catherine. He went out.

His father had never gotten in that final plea, the plea to Latham. You have to leave something undone. It had been in his mind, certainly: Latham, the blood descendant, though crippled. The final chance. Catherine had known it, sensed it, too. It was one reason she had never had Latham in Texas much. Professor Sasser had seen him, but only at the Latham house. She would not permit this terrible exposure—the books brought out, talk of "the truth, the one truth." She was too polite to mention it, but not too gentle utterly to defeat any move to get Latham up at that end of the street. Jerry had rejected Latham. He went to see him now, truncated impatient visits. The boy's goodness irritated him. He felt himself observed and even loved, but loved in observation only, like an animal, his habits recorded with open-minded curiosity, no criticism. Latham learned everything, an astonishing heap of knowledge, by quietly and accurately observing the great big world. Diane! She did not say much. He folded her up into a small dark object and set her next to his heart, a temporary warmth. He had to go see Latham from time to time to see if Catherine—

He walked in the fresh crisp city. Trees spring-touched and warm along the handsome street, a florist's shop on the corner near the traffic circle, sprays trickling like a gush of spring rain down the glass, clever idea. A blur of irises behind the glass, tall and sentinel. Kennedy-looking flowers. New administration. New glory for new heads.

He walked with sharply slashing heels, long accurate Texas walking, shoulders inclined to hunch and slope now. He straightened, long profile leveling, young woman in the corner of his eye. Rounded shoulders, short skirt, blazer, rounded calves, short stiletto heels, pretending she hadn't noticed him and maybe she hadn't. Maybe they didn't notice any more. He doubted it. They were angling toward each other, about to cross paths before the florist's window. He slackened sail to let her pass, but turned it on her, catching her attention, saw himself taken quickly in, the long line of his cheek and jaw still good, eyes grown dark as tar the more they drew her into true focus, straight brows, harsh, motionless forehead. For a minute he had her and she knew it. The moment broke off in the sort of jazz they were both able to give it by simply spinning past each other and not looking back, both forgetting instantly, letting the day, which had become slightly different, take up what had happened, whatever it was.

With Diane one day he had seen the President go by, wife beside him and someone else. In the old days he would have known who it was. "It's the President," he had said. "Remember that." The motorcycle escort slowed at a stop light, sputtered, turned; the car moved soundlessly, uncurtained, the occupants clearly visible. A few people turned and waved. He did not. "Look," he said to Diane. "Remember." Those beautiful people. "Daddy held me up once to see them. He said, 'Look, baby, it's the President.'" Already he spoke out of shadows.

But the shadows were at least great big ones and moved leaping on distant walls, where people still did not know what to think of him, namely in Texas.

"What's he doing?" Priscilla begged Millard to tell her. For Millard saw him, from time to time. Millard had some weird kind of sympathy for him. For Millard had a theory of action, the necessity of its not even being disguised as anything either good or bad, of the command to motion being as primal with humanity as gravity was to objects; he believed that very few people could recognize this but he thought that Jerry Sasser could. He saw Jerry lost to the family without trying to prevent it because he knew the family would never face the truth Jerry was a walking illustration of, namely that there was no such thing as a moral or an immoral action. Only reflection, meditation, ascribes motives, divides sheep from goats, approves or condemns, refuses to note from what foul or idiot source even the pure love flower has sprung. He never discussed all this directly with Jerry. The family by default had landed in Millard's hands, just as Edward's defection and flight had placed it in Jerry's once. It was only that Millard had the good grace to keep in touch with the dethroned and exiled. He even visited him.

Donning togas of contemplation, they strolled through ruined gardens. Millard pondered aloud on Texas becoming bone-dry, stripped of oil. Without new discoveries, in twenty years, at the present rate, it might be possible. What about natural gas? How much could you get out and why could you be allowed to get out more than somebody else, like the Hickmans? He thus got Jerry action-directed, like giving an all but insoluble puzzle to a bed-ridden person with a fetish for order. It was pure carrot and stick. Suppose Jerry found a way to ruin them all? Suppose he found a way to make millions? He would do either one, Millard mused, maybe depending on what he'd had for breakfast. He did not think of Catherine because it seemed to him that about Catherine there was no longer anything to think.

Millard himself was a sort of white hunter in darkest Africa, going to Washington, getting on the phone, lunching the brother-in-law, setting baits and traps, smearing the blood of rabbits and kids all around on the foliage. Jerry mentioned something in passing, only a phrase, as Millard, after a short argument, took the lunch check: "the grey world." This stuck with Millard as he got a taxi to the airport. So Jerry knew it; the phrase made a deep sigh rise within Millard, restoring his own humanity. Jerry knew what he lived in, had chosen it. At one time which Millard remembered clearly, Jerry Sasser had been clear as glass, and the girls he had chosen, picked like flowers from border to border and coast to coast, had all been clear-eyed and white-toothed; you could spin them around like sculpture on a pedestal and there it all was, every jot, toenail, eyelash, flat wafer of temple, blunt bone of sacroiliac, etc., etc., etc., all fulfilled. Now Jerry lived with some woman with a messy name and somebody had got drunk and careless, not only conceived a child but in another misguided mood decided why not keep it. Jerry didn't know that Millard knew this. Perhaps Jerry loved the child, Millard thought. He found that thought, as regards Jerry, almost disgusting. It spoiled the clarity of Millard's vision of him. Like a termite eating patiently into an oaken timber, one microscopic love insect would finally get to the heart, and there would be Catherine, immovable. He didn't like it.

The plane took off. It was misty. The grey city, touched out in white monuments, mainly to the dead, dropped away below.

It was somewhere along during that winter of Millard Warner's first visit to him, early 'sixties, that Jerry became aware that Charles and Irene Waddell were around Washington. Every time he saw them he experienced rage that almost amounted to fury. Once Irene was in a Japanese restaurant in make-up that looked strongly Oriental, though he knew she was the sort of woman who if you asked her about this it would turn out she not only had not done it on purpose but had not really thought about it, the whole way through the lunch. Once at a crush at the British embassy where Jerry had been asked along to escort the divorced wife of a Congressman he used to know, she came up to him with immense aplomb, to reveal that she had been aware of his being in Washington all these years—he took it that all this had its genesis in Catherine and that artist he had never liked the sound of. She went on to say that she and Charles were giving something next week and could he come. He accepted and then did not appear. What did she want? To talk about what she knew and he knew and then maybe they would both know something new. Common knowledge of knowing Catherine, unspoken, but giving an added *je ne sais quoi*. Charles was on a publications committee for the White House, something cooked up between the culture-conscious administration and the New York publishing houses. Of course, he would be there, once his party got back in power. He had acquired a quiet, heavily polished air, like something in the furniture department of the best department store. His wife had picked the new manner out for him, no doubt, and got him to wear it without his knowing he had it on. It was necessary, Jerry saw, grudgingly admiring her good sense, for the simple reason that the Waddells were older now than the New Frontier image allowed one to be. He had once himself had this sort of feeling about things. One day somebody from one of the big welfare bureaus approached him with a feeler; a job was in the air. He made a connection—as tenuous, gossamer as a spider web that could only float invisible in air and appear as something unprovable across his eye—to Irene. He turned the job down. He would not welsh on what he was. Nobody need show up to tell him that neither Charles Waddell nor any other man was giving that woman all she wanted.

And now he was in Nassau on a yacht, consulting with some British and Canadian oil men about rights in the North Sea and East Anglia. One lazy night in February, moored off the pier before the Harbor Club, water burning under moonlight deep black as oil, he happened to bring up Jasmin, which was the company that owned Millard Warner's Oklahoma distribution and development rights, and someone had heard of Warner. Jerry stirred in the depths of a Barcelona chair, resting its steel frame legs on the wall-to-wall deep blue carpet of the yacht's little salon, and said yes, that Warner was his brother-in-law, and that he had once suggested to him as a joke that with a government contract to process crude oil he could use byproducts for marginal income. Warner had actually investigated to see if Jasmin could do this. The way Jerry laughed you couldn't tell but what the affair had actually succeeded and from the way the Britisher looked he knew the reference would not escape cataloguing. Millard Warner a crook. Millard was one of the few good men Jerry knew, and having read somewhere that nothing could hurt a good man, he did not feel too bad about having, in the course of making up a good story, tried. One of the Canadian wives, pink-gowned with pink sandals, platinumed hair, was looking him over. She was not subtle. He encountered her later in the ship's corridor and bowed past her. Her daughter, tanned black and wearing silver, was a bell-ringer. She shimmered when she went up the steep narrow stairs. Later he stood at the rail and heard somebody scream, a girl-scream. Fallen overboard, was what he instantly thought. Had she committed suicide, that lovely thing, had a nightmare, or been awakened by a drunken guest who had blundered into the wrong cabin by mistake, been awakened by a drunken guest who had blundered into the wrong cabin on purpose, had agreed to go ahead and try it, might as well, and so been broken into in terrifying advent for the first time. First time? Incredible. But that could be a falling overboard too. He guessed they screamed sometime. The girl had not seemed unhappy or happy either, at cocktails—just closed, confined. So many people are that way now, he thought; she had not responded very much to his conversation. She was so black she must have spent untold hours in the sun, blackened eyebrows winging straight up, eyelids brushed with silver. Now her scream was silver, too. He watched the moon shimmering on the water and did not stir. If she had hurtled past his nose, going from upper deck straight down to her doom, would he have jumped in to save her? Nice of you, so nice of you, Mr. Sasser, I'll always be in your debt, you saved my life, Daddy will make you a vice-president for life. He would never do anything to be nice. Had he ever? Now that he thought of it, he didn't think so. He always had a motive: a two-birds-with-one-stone killer. "Did you hear her scream?" "I thought I heard something but it barely woke me. I was drunk." So it might come to saying that; so what? If it was only that original falling overboard, the hot assault on the virgin gates where blood out of season would spill to scare her, blood of midnight, she would be glad if no alarm were sounded at all. And then it would be nice of him not to have said anything. He guessed if she were drowning it was all over by now. The moon beat plunging against the wise old water. He could have had the hostess, unwrapped her pink article at a time; he hated pink. Catherine had never worn it. Could he have had the silver girl? Felt the scream coming on, eased her past it, clever as the skillful maneuver of a racing driver, the sharpest corner taken without a screech. Diane might give a small squirrel cry one day. Drowned at midnight. Oil-black water. He had been powerful to say nothing, not even to turn his head. A visiting Roman, walking the early-to-bed streets of the provincial town, having praised the local wine, genuinely admired the governor's daughter, rejected the not-quite offer of the governor's wife, thrashed his business out, thrown them quite gratuitously, just for the hell of it (but necessary, as necessary for him as for them), the raw, dripping meat of somebody's corruption and greed, either wished for or actually carried out. It was a joke, making conversation, never meant it. Everything fair in the family. Families all crucify one another all the time. Shimmer of foreign moonlight. Death of foreign girl would make the New York papers no more prominently than loss of her virginity. She could send out cards perhaps. He had got a sympathy card from Catherine when Bunny Tutweiler died. It was the one time he almost went and looked her up. She had done it in her own personal humor, being funny as hell, and he almost went and said What the hell do you mean? The trouble was he could never stop being a crook.

The scream resonated through the empty ruin of his glory, bounded from arch to dome to cornice, ricocheted in abruptly turning passages, disturbed the spider webs over the low portcullises of waste courtyards, knifed between the upright stalks of unpruned self-seeding plants, crashed like a tiny flimsy but expensive foreign-made car against the walls where weeds grew up in crevices. The dog lifted his head and growled. Diane got out of bed and came running to him and sat in his lap. "You oughtn't to be up barefoot. You'll catch cold, sugar." Southern talk of his off-and-on accent. He had turned it on in Nassau, slurring soft and easy into the warm air, uplift and bite in the middle, drop and drag at the ends of phrases. You called them "sugar."

By maneuvering certain interstate contracts on the grounds that the Latham estate now included Oklahoma holdings, just as the Warner estate included Texas holdings, and hence both were not strictly speaking exclusively a Texas concern, he more than doubled for the family the amount of natural gas they were allowed to export. Families like the Hickmans could get themselves somebody in Washington, he guessed, or arrange for a daughter to marry into a Louisiana, Arkansas, Mississippi, or Oklahoma oil family. About the only clever business trick Priscilla ever pulled. In the long run he was going to pay back his $100,000 debt six times over, as long as nobody decided to challenge the legal set-up. There were still enough leftover political connections to make sure nobody did. It was up to Millard Warner now to ring up certain names in Washington, but what names? They had been supplied to him by Jerry Sasser. Jerry Sasser reflected, filling in the loops of letters on the telephone directory, letting his mind idle in his office, that he had never had anything at all against the Hickmans and neither did anybody else any more. So if things were still working against them through the Lathams, it was totally without animosity. Local history did not keep on repeating itself. Those two families would hardly bother to stop making money long enough to remember anything unpleasant about each other. Someday there would be intermarriage, no doubt.

"I'm making a lot of money for you," Jerry told Millard, having come down all the way to Merrill to explain it to him.

"You could also ruin us," Millard said, "by using the same system in reverse. You could get it all thrown out of court right now."

"I could if I wanted to."

That was if you could call not making another million ruin—they would always be wallowing in wealth to their eyebrows and could, if they wanted to, buy His and Her airplanes from Neiman-Marcus to give each other for Christmas, one on either side of the swimming pool at midnight when Santa wriggled in through the air conditioning. But even though ruin was a myth and the necessity of further increase from natural gas was a myth in the myth land that money is to the rich, Millard still liked to meditate on it all.

He put on his rough English tweed jacket, worn-out elbows

with leather patches, and went up to get the mail, and Jerry was left with Priscilla coming in from the grocery with a brown paper sack.

"I guess you'll stay and eat," she said.

"No, I guess not," he said. Then he said, "I just came back to say what I'd done for you, that's all." Then he said, "You know I always wanted to fuck you, Priscilla. You wanted it too, back then."

She looked up with sea-green eyes. Millard must have got hold of the reins somehow. She used to be a nut. Her hair, loose and expensively waved, had gone gray. She looked good, not like Catherine at all any more, but good, he guessed. She looked spoiled rotten with wealth, faintly like Elizabeth Taylor. "I got crazy about Millard as a result of you going bust right in front of us. I wouldn't do anything for you now."

"I never asked you." He wondered if she still was a bit of a nut. "Don't tell Millard," he said. "I like him."

"He wouldn't do anything, even if we went through with it."

"I didn't know you knew that."

She had gone in the kitchen with the groceries and he was raising his voice to her and she to him. It seemed they had been conversing for centuries whether present to each other or not. "Isn't that like saying he's not a man?"

"Well, no, he's just not a violent man. He thinks it all out. Maybe he's got a notion you're already dead." When this happy thought occurred to her, she came out of the kitchen beaming with satisfaction.

The elder Lathams being away on one of their interminable forays to Dallas to see doctors who had to remove and run biopsies on every mole and wart old age had scattered upon their flesh, Jerry went up the street to the house with the turret and by searching through it for three hours, basement to attic, finally found the books his father had given to Catherine.

The funny thing was that the nurse he had got for Diane, that fastidious and aristocratic mulatto image of all that was correct and right-smelling, had recently got converted to something that sounded suspiciously like what he had heard all the time as a child. He was going to her, he thought, straightening up with sweat pouring off him—it was Millard who had given him the key, unbeknownst to Priscilla—and give her the books: "Is this what you mean? It all came from my own father, what a coincidence. But how did you get hold of it? No matter, now we can have it proved that color doesn't matter, blood being always the same, or so it says here. Chapter and verse." Of course, he would get right out of his own carefully built-up character, it would kick hell right out of his home situation to say that, be a traumatic experience for his daughter to see him flying his true colors, watching him blast apart the carefully built-up, smoothly running menage, her own security shot out of a tree like an old deserted bird's nest. He was capable of doing it, that's what scared him. He sat down on an old locked-up trunk and smiled at himself; the spectacle he could create was extraordinary. He was capable of doing it because he knew that however awful he might get, life itself could always go him one better. It was always something you couldn't believe. From the first call out of the night, which was his father, to the last one, which was death, it was not anything that made an occasion for reverence. The Lathams, if they came in right now, would temper their feelings about what he was doing there with tender consideration for all the money he knew how to bring in, and it might turn out they were glad to see him after all. (It was Catherine they thought a little peculiar: she preferred Massachusetts to Texas.) No, in spite of all the shaking and worrying he had taken care to give it, life was not even a story. It all pranced away like a mad chorus line, with pairs and trios coming on from time to time to sing their little heavily costumed parts. Catherine with weeping willow in hand, Irene Waddell the lady of fashion, Priscilla and Millard doing some sort of jive, other parts for comic tangos off and on, and himself a restless has-been warrior, occasionally dropping his helmet which whammed like a tin washpan. His laugh echoed in the empty rooms wherein had lived and hoped and shuddered and cried and laughed and thrilled and been bored and grown up, sulked, lay sick, vomited, dreamed and giggled, Catherine, and Edward and Priscilla. Edward was a ghost in the turret—was he actually there? Had Millard said something about it? If so, the laughter would bring him out. But he wasn't. Had he perhaps died? Had someone told or written him, or had he seen it in the paper, Edward Latham is dead. Shoe manufacturer in St. Louis. Living in old-fashioned suburb, taking drugstore-purchased medicines for ailments of veins: Iron Aid, Hadacol, Nature's Spelled Backwards, verging on witch doctors. All that stuff had done was dissolve him, if he was dead. This house had once seemed so large, so imposing, so comfortable. Good smell, clean sheets, freshly washed and shining hair of the rich little Latham girls who turned their snooty little noses up in air and trudged home without a backward glance, all the way down the long street, their heels going snipsnipsnip. But she watched him sometimes from the corner of the classroom, from the other side of the playground when the north wind hit, too fierce to play in, dull, depressing. Streams of cold dust. He was already smart. Now the house seemed small, Victorian-stuffy with overpriced things in old-fashioned taste, poor tacked-on passes at renovation, the TV room, the glassed-in porch with sentimental ugly articles held onto with death grip. Also a smell of age. Now it was the last place he wanted to be, instead of the first. There had been all the world-wide comedy in between. The sculptor who might as well have been making coathangers all his life. Had had three names, none memorable. The Warners who had discovered it was fun, all this and a million dollars too. Charles Waddell who had peddled Americanism all over the globe, once having been assaulted by a monkey on the streets of Cairo, while his wife spread for some Italian all over Sicily. But now Diane's heels went ahead of him from time to time and that was not funny. And there had been the glory, the ranked fleet in the Pacific, far as the eye could see, and that was not funny. And loneliness and bleared out interest and lagging powers, and that was not funny. In the Dallas airport he rented a locker for twenty-five cents and put the two books inside and much later on he dropped the key in the first river he passed. Perhaps a fish got it, like Jonah and the whale. His father had thought this story symbolic and it was so explained to be, he had noticed, when he tried to read the books, but the fact was perhaps it was in a way literal, too, and now his father himself reposed in the belly of a catfish, who might one day spew him up to whoever cut the fish open, saying Locker No. 241, Dallas Airport. Could anyone with a shred of imagination resist not going there? The dead would rise, resurrection was certain.

The laugh had resounded far past the turreted house of the leading family of Merrill, had troubled, as the silver scream had done, his own lofty ruin which stood about that actual house, like an enveloping shadow of something five times grander. Now it died. The dog had stirred, but his daughter was still asleep. Maybe when Catherine was mad she was only laughing in the turret. She used to laugh for no reason, from time to time.

He went back to Catherine and confronted her for the first time in a thousand years. She was lying in a glider in late summer on the side porch of her New England house, sun on her face, hair catching the sun, freckles, no make-up, broken nails from gardening, reading in a grey wool skirt and white blouse. She did not get up. "Hello, Jerry."

A canyon roared out silence between them. They held to their ears a conch shell as big as Pennsylvania Station.

"Catherine," he said. "What have I done?"

"I don't know," she said. "I guess I just don't know anything you haven't done."

"Does it matter?" he said.

"I don't know."

"Can't you just let it go?" he asked.

"Oh, but I did! A long time ago. The question is, can you?'"

"You mean disown, deny, throw away . . . not say I'm sorry, not repent or anything . . . but just shed it . . .?"

"Well, if you aren't sorry, I just thought I'd mention it."

"I'm not either one. I'm not sorry, and I won't disown. It was me, Catherine. It was me."

He had a sense that the phone was going to ring, that Latham was going to limp up the walk unexpectedly home because of a half-holiday, that the mailman would come or a committee on something. He had a feeling that a thousand threads of interest and mutual sympathy, generosity, even emotion, united her to this unlikely town, to this whole snow-cursed, summer benevolent area. He would have liked to sweep it out of her head, her life, her heart, at one blow, coldly, like spaying a cat. He would drive her crazy again, and tear open every old wound. She would let him; it had never mattered personally to her as long as some character in himself could resist, define, hold itself detached from the world of lie, main-chance and smear, the well-acted tableau. The grey world. The nothing that was always threatening everybody. He accepted corruption. It was the only way to meet the terror within. If there wasn't enough of it, he invented more.

She saw her one chance and took it. "Latham told me you had a daughter. Don't you have a picture of her? I'd love to see."

He had one in his pocket. A little dark girl in a field full of flowers, blue and yellow and red. The picture was in color. The flowers were all those girls he used to know. If he gave Catherine this, it would be all over. He would be melted down forever, his ruins gone in a flash fire like cardboard gothic, not even asbestos, let alone stone. She had known right where to stand and strike the match.

"I have a right not to let you see it," he said. "You know I have."

She smiled. "I know." She started to read again, then glanced up. "I might love her."

He saw her through a red boiling passionate haze of all his times and doings. A car was pulling up at the front steps and people were getting out; Latham was limping in from the drive; the mailman was just leaving; and the telephone had started to ring.

"You would," he said. "Oh, Catherine, you would!"

She leaped up to embrace him before everyone arrived. He just got out in time. The moment, melting, clung to him present as a dream, for a long time after he left.

◆

"Go back to Catherine?" he said to Irene Waddell, to whom he inevitably drifted at a dinner in Washington where a lot of Texans were being entertained, though how she had got there he didn't know. "Go back? It's a killing thought. Like oil and water. Something is wrong with it."

"Still," said Irene, wisely, "you both must have suffered a great deal."

ABOUT THE AUTHOR

ELIZABETH SPENCER was born in Carrollton, Mississippi, in 1921. She graduated from Belhaven College in 1942 and received an MA in English from Vanderbilt University the following year. For two years she taught in schools in Mississippi and Tennessee, and for a year was a reporter on the *Nashville Tennesseen*.

Spencer's first novel, *Fire in the Morning*, was published in 1948, and was declared by the *New York Times Book Review* one of the best first novels of the year. It was followed in 1952 by her second novel, *This Crooked Way*, while she was teaching creative writing at the University of Mississippi. In 1953, she received a Guggenheim Fellowship and was able to go to Italy, where she lived principally in Florence and Rome. Her third novel, *The Voice at the Back Door*, won several awards, including the Rosenthal Award and the Kenyon Review Fiction Fellowship. In Italy, she met and married John Rusher from Cornwall, and was able to extend her Italian stay until 1956.

The Light in the Piazza, first published in *The New Yorker* in 1960, was brought out also as a novel and was the basis for a movie of that name in 1962. Most recently it has become a musical drama, premiering on Broadway in 2005. It won five Tony Awards and is still being performed in theaters throughout the United States.

Five other novels have followed, including *No Place for an Angel*, *The Salt Line*, and *The Snare*.

Spencer's stories have appeared often in *The New Yorker* and various magazines. *The Southern Woman* (1998) is a selection of the best known. *Starting Over*, containing nine recent stories (Norton/Liveright), appeared in 2014. It was named by *Booklist* as one of the best books of the year.

Elizabeth Spencer now lives in Chapel Hill, North Carolina.